GW00858951

RAINBOW WARRIORS

1

By Shirley Bear Fedorak

RAINBOW WARRIORS SERIES

The Caretaker's Quest, prequel

Rainbow Warriors, Book I

ACADEMIC BOOKS

Anthropology Matters

Global Issues. A Cross-Cultural Perspective

Pop Culture. An Anthropological Perspective

Cultural Anthropology

Windows on the World. Case Studies in Anthropology

Human Evolution and Prehistory

Canadian Perspectives in Biological Anthropology and Archaeology

SHIRLEY BEAR FEDORAK

RAINBOW
WARRIORS

1

Copyright © 2021 Shirley Bear Fedorak

All rights reserved. No part of this book may be stored or reproduced in any form or by any electronic or mechanical means except in the case of brief quotations embodied in articles or reviews without written permission from the publisher or author.

The characters and events in this book are fictitious. Any similarity to real persons, living or dead, is coincidental and not intended by the author.

YuJu Publishing Penang, Malaysia

To comment or ask questions:
shirley.fedorak5@gmail.com

Be sure to subscribe to my newsletter at:
https://www.shirleybearfedorak.com

Cover designed by Miblart.com

Dedication

To my children, Lisa, Simon, Kris, Rachel, and Cory,
and to my grandchildren, Yuna and Julia.
May you always enjoy lives of health, peace, and safety.

When the earth is ravaged and the animals are dying, a new tribe of people shall come unto the earth from many colors, classes, creeds, and who by their actions and deeds shall make the earth green again. They will be known as the warriors of the Rainbow.

Ancient Hopi Prophecy[1]

CONTENTS

FOREWORD

This book was a long time in the making, but it has always been there, waiting. I began writing the outline for *Rainbow Warriors* and the six other books in the series when I was teaching anthropology courses at the University of Saskatchewan. I often encountered students and peers who considered people who were different from them as somehow lesser or strange, and indeed, the other.

The concept of 'other' has always bothered me. All people, no matter where they come from, what they look like, or who or what they believe in, have the same needs—to be loved, to feel safe, and to live good lives. The young people in this series all share these needs even though they have been placed in unconscionable situations through no fault of their own. I wrapped their lives in the environmental collapse of earth's ecosystems that we are about to face in order to show how their struggles will be our struggles.

Over the years, and through countless hours of research, I have embraced and appreciated the strength and wisdom I found in each of the four cultural groups featured in this series, but make no mistake, this is a futuristic, fictionalized account of these cultures and the unique ways they might react to Turmoil. I do not claim to know or understand all there is to know about the Siksiká Blackfoot, Malikun,

Ju/'hoansi, and Yanomami as they are today. Nevertheless, I hope you enjoy these stories and come away with an understanding of how humans are so alike in all the ways that matter.

Shirley Bear Fedorak
2021

Chapter One

THE SILVER TOWER

Elk Ridge Siksiká Blackfoot Refuge
2129

I blamed the silver tower for everything that had gone wrong. It even smelled evil, a metallic stench that puckered my nose and burned my eyes.

Storyteller sang of Southerners building the tower before my People moved north, but why would anyone build a tower in the middle of nowhere? Chief Roy fancied the tower linked all the ancient satellites orbiting in space, but what was the sense in that? Most everyone was dead or long gone from Mother Earth.

"Come on, Honey, let's do this."

Honey pranced her way up an abandoned animal trail and stopped near the chain-link fence surrounding the tower.

I looked up, hundreds of feet up. Blue and yellow light imps streaked up and down the tripod legs, and a disk the shape of a flying saucer circled the tower's peak.

I slipped off Honey's back and wiped down her golden coat. "Bet you're dreaming of a swim in the creek, aren't you, girl?"

She nickered and her soft nose nudged me. Then she snorted and her ears flattened. She shook her mane and pranced on the spot.

"Easy girl, what's wrong?"

An invisible force slithered up my legs. Hopping from one foot to the other did not stop the needle-like stings. I took a deep breath. Big mistake. Tiny sparks slid down my throat, burning and choking me. Soon my People would need breathers even on a good day.

A red light shot up the tall spike jutting out of the revolving disk. The beam pierced the swirls of pink and green poison floating across the sky and disappeared. Was it heading to one of the space stations where rich people hid from Turmoil?

A pulsating siren blared and tore at my ears. I dropped to the ground and cowered behind a boulder. "Great Apistotoke, protect me."

Honey shrieked and galloped away.

A flying machine flickered in and out of my vision, then settled on the revolving disk, and the siren faded. Four strangers dressed in black hazmat suits climbed out of the flyer and disappeared into the tower.

I staggered to my feet and rubbed my burning ears. The stinging shocks ran up my legs and tingled the tips of my fingers.

But enough. None of it mattered, not the sirens, nor the flying machines, and not the nasty, stinging ground. I was going in. I wrapped my sweat-soaked hair in a messy twist and fetched wire cutters from my backpack. "Okay, let's see what secrets you'll give up."

"Hali! What're you doing?"

I dropped the cutters, and my heart skipped a beat.

Atian limped toward me, a scowl on his handsome face. His black braid was dripping down his bare back, and water droplets glistened on his broad chest. He had been swimming in the creek again.

Faded blue jeans hugged his buff body, and here I was, wicked in raggedy cut-offs and a dingy white t-shirt two sizes too small. I tucked stray hair behind my ears. "Why don't you go home, Atian? This is none of your business."

He snorted. "Oh really, so telling Nootah and Ida I found your fried carcass draped over the fence is none of my business?"

Always the same with him, he knew it all. "What are you babbling about?"

He flipped his wet bathing suit onto a metal pole holding up the fence. Sparks and flashes of fire shot into the hot air. His bathing suit sizzled and shriveled into a ball of melted syntho.

I jumped back and landed in his arms. "What! That fence has been dead as darkness forever."

He wrapped his arms around my waist and nuzzled my neck. "Started up a couple months ago, my pa said."

My skin tingled where his smooth hands touched me, and his breath smelled of cinnamon. I leaned into him for a brief moment, then slipped out of his grasp. "But where are they pulling the power?"

His piercing black eyes gazed at me, and an unreadable expression flitted across his face. "Hali, we don't even know who *they* are." He nodded at the tower. "That thing has power, why not the fence?"

"Well, *they* are inside the tower, didn't you see them land?"

He backed away, like I knew he would.

"Outsiders are here? Let's go before they spot us."

I stamped my foot and an extra strong shock travelled up my leg. "I'm not leaving. I've had enough of secrets and archaic taboos. I need to know what this tower is for and if it's a danger to us. Maybe those suits will give me some answers."

The famous Atian frown appeared right on schedule. "Kind of risky, don't you think?"

Shocks rippled up and down my legs, and my inner spirit screamed warnings. We should be moving, not quibbling. "Aren't you tired of not knowing? We're stuck up here in the North while the rest of the world is going to hell, and I'm pretty sure that tower holds some answers."

"Yeah, but—"

I headed for the fence. "No buts, come with me or leave."

He wrung the water out of his braid and pulled on his black t-shirt. "What choice do I have, you'll get yourself killed if I leave you alone."

I sneaked a peek at him from beneath my lashes. A trick I learned in middle school. A frown creased his perfect brow, his usual expression around me. We were childhood besties, but lately he acted all weird and bossy around me. At first his behavior confused and hurt me, then it ticked me off, but now I mostly ignored him. If only he wasn't so good-looking.

He brushed past me and took the lead. "How do you plan on sneaking inside, mighty trailblazer?"

A good question. "We'll keep looking until we find a way in." Lame, but Mr. Know-it-all was not getting the last word.

We followed the fence, slipping behind scrubby thorn bushes and long-dead tree trunks, and searched for a break in the links. Sweat trickled into my eyes and blurred my vision, but I kept going.

Atian broke the awkward silence. "Are you going to the gathering tomorrow night?"

A snort slipped out before I could stop it. "What choice do I have? The tribal council commands and we obey."

"Well, it sounds important."

His words sent a chill up my back. Important meant bad news, like low water levels, herd disease, or more poisons in the air.

Atian stopped suddenly. I ran into his backside and hit the ground hard. He grinned down at me, and my stomach flip-flopped. The same grin from middle school when he liked me.

"Next time watch where you're going, but you might as well stay down there. I've found a way in." He pointed to a small hole dug under the fence, behind a stunted willow bush.

I measured the opening with my hands. A skinny person would fit. "I wonder who made this hole."

"Who cares? It'll get us in, and if we're lucky and nobody shoots us, it'll get us out."

My hair crackled as I slid through the hole, and my teeth ached from the fence's hum, but on the other side the stingy shocks stopped. I ducked behind a dying ninebark bush and studied the tower. "It seems bigger from up here."

Atian crouched behind me. His breath tickled my neck and distracted me from my scouting.

"What's next, Sherlock?"

How should I know? Besides, when did exploring become a planned event? Trust Atian to ruin my fun.

I peeked around the lone snowball flower hanging from the bush. Glacial boulders, some the size of a woodshed, lay scattered across the field, and a door I never noticed before flickered in the tripod leg closest to us. "We'll use those rocks for cover and head for that door."

Atian pointed up the tower. "See those drone-cams?"

Four whirly-birds floated fifty meters in the air. They swiveled back and forth, their shifty red eyes searching the perimeter around the tower. "Yeah, so what?"

"No way are we gonna sneak into that tower without being spotted."

"So what if they see us. We're just nosy kids. Why would they hurt us?"

I kept my head down and dashed for the first boulder. Atian gasped for breath behind me. Scared or was his mangled leg hurting when he ran?

He touched my arm. "Let me go first."

When he was halfway to the next boulder, I ran after him. We did this two more times without the drones reacting. Maybe we could pull off this caper afterall.

Hiss.

A searing red gash ran the length of my right arm. Yellow blister bubbles popped up along the welt, and my arm burned as bad as when I tripped and fell against our wood stove. Tears streamed down my cheeks, and I bit my trembling lip. "Oh crap."

"Hali! Get down! They're AI lasers, not cams!"

No kidding. I flattened against the dead grass. A beam of sizzling heat swept past my ear and scorched the ground beside me. I rolled behind the nearest boulder. First one, then another beam hit the rock, sending heat pulses and shocks through my body.

"Hey, over here!"

The drones swiveled their sensors, and a flurry of laser fire erupted on the other side of the clearing.

A tall, thin man dressed in green camouflage zigzagged across the clearing and ran around the boulders in crazy-wild circles. His tactics worked and two of the AIs collided, but the other two hovered above us.

The man waved at me.

"Hey, that's Matwau."

Atian grunted. "What's that pain in the butt up to?"

I grinned. "Showing more balls than you."

I ran after Matwau, and we reached the entrance to the tower at the same time. But Atian chose a different route. Almost there, a laser beam caught him on his good leg. He fell and rolled the last few meters to the door. The drones zoomed around the tower.

A smirk crossed Matwau's gaunt face. "Nice finish, hero."

Blood seeped through Atian's jeans. I knelt and stretched the scorched hole. His thigh resembled a semi-cooked elk steak.

His golden skin paled at the sight of his seared leg, but he pushed me away. "It barely nicked me."

Okay, be that way. "Fine. Your sizzled hide, not mine."

Matwau fiddled with the door's touch screen. "Those bugs will be on us any second."

"Did you see the flyer land on this thing?" I said.

He nodded. "A neo-glider, it's the only aircraft flying in this soup, but I'm surprised we spotted it, they're stealth most of the time."

He tapped codes on the screen but nothing happened. "Okay, enough playing nice." He kicked the door, and the frame shattered from the force of his boot. He winked at me and offered his hand. "Care for a look-see, my lady?"

A warm flush crept up my neck, despite my best efforts. Atian could learn a few manners from this guy.

I took his hand and stepped into a twenty-first century shrine. "Oh! The air's so cool, and I taste clean." Good, maybe my blush would go away.

The hexagonal room resembled photos of first class airport lounges in my father's Beforetimes magazines. Silver columns supported the high ceiling, and pearly white walls gave off a soft sheen. Most amazing of all, hundreds of books lined wooden bookshelves on either side of a gold and black fireplace. My father would love all the books.

I rubbed my feet on the plush, white carpet. "Oh yes, I could live here."

Matwau surveyed the room. "Somebody's living the good life in this lounge."

I had to agree. "No dust bunnies or cobwebs. This isn't some Beforetimes relic, this baby's in use."

Atian hobbled into the tower and fell onto one of a dozen blue lounge chairs. He did not say a word, but the scowl on his face told me loads.

Matwau leaned against the broken door frame. "I don't suppose you two cray cray's thought about how you're getting out of this fix."

Atian clenched his teeth against the pain and lifted his wounded leg onto the lounger. "We'll figure it out."

The AIs zoomed around the tower and opened fire. "Mat!"

Matwau dived into the room a second before a beam scorched the door frame. The AIs flitted away.

I ran my hands along a gleaming cherry wood bar on the far side of the room. Sparkling wine glasses hung behind the bar, and an assortment of dark bottles with strange names like Jack Daniels and Smirnoff sat in a neat row on the counter.

Matwau joined me and opened a bottle labeled Dalmore single malt. He sniffed the bottle. "These guys enjoy the good stuff."

I touched his shoulder and whispered, "Mat, please don't."

His lips tightened into a thin line, but he set the bottle down. "Sure, no problem."

Yeah right. How long before he gave in?

Matwau plopped down on a lounger and waved his hand in front of the monitor. "Update."

The monitor lit up, and the lounger swiveled to face a platform in the middle of the room.

"How'd you do that?"

"We had comps linked to the Net at Duck Mountain Refuge when I was a kid. Lost it by the time I turned thirteen."

Holographic images paraded across the platform. Grim-faced men in gray military uniforms stared into the distance, then tigers, elephants, and polar bears snarled at an invisible audience.

"I thought they were extinct."

"Who? Pompous military-types or wild animals?"

"Both."

The holo transformed into vast fields of vegetables and flowering fruit trees inside a warehouse so large I could not wrap my mind around its size. Little children were planting seeds in raised rows of dirt, while an overseer waved a laser at them. "Where is that place, and who are those kids?"

Matwau coded the console. "My guess is trafficked kids doing somebody's dirty work."

A blue-eyed woman sparkled and took form on the raised platform. Her blond hair was pulled back in a flawless bun, and she wore a tight-fitting gray uniform that showed off her perfect figure. String music played in the background when she began to speak.

The Ark will provide worthy humans with shelter for hundreds of years while Earth restores its ecosystems. Then man shall rise again.

"Man shall rise again?" Matwau's dark eyes narrowed. "By all the spirits above, hasn't man done enough to this poor old earth?"

"How about, women shall inherit the earth?" I said.

Matwau shot me a mischievous grin, and my cheeks flamed. Again.

The avatar settled on the holo platform. *A hostess will be with you shortly.*

"They know we're here."

"Relax sweetheart, it's a sensor recording."

"Actually, the young lady is correct."

We turned. A middle-aged man dressed in a gray uniform stepped through a flickering door and aimed his laser at us. He appeared well fed, even paunchy, something not common among my People. He had the same blond hair and blue eyes as the avatar.

"Who are you?" I said.

The man you are referring to is General Cardiff, Commander of the New World Ark.

Matwau scowled. "Arkers, like in the holo? You're commander of that slave pit?"

General Cardiff's brows knitted together. "Thank you, Alice, that will be all."

The avatar sparkled and disappeared.

The general glared at us. "You delinquents have broken into a top security installation."

I glared back. "This is Siksiká land, you're trespassing."

General Cardiff rocked back and forth on his polished shoes and chuckled. "You know little girl, you've got spunk. Too bad your breed will be of no value in our new world order."

My breed? New world order?

Matwau pushed the monitor away and stood up, his body posture keyed for flight or fight.

I touched his arm. "No Mat, don't do anything."

"So what kind of sick game are you playing, Cardiff?"

The general focused his glare on Matwau and sniffed. "Young man, are you aware that break and enter is an offence punishable with life in prison? And you destroyed two of our drones."

Matwau folded his arms and adopted a stance similar to Chief Roy when he was annoyed. "And what government would that be? And this prison is where? Come on Cardiff, what gives?"

A smug look crossed the general's fleshy face. "The Ark will save the best of mankind, and we will repopulate the Earth."

What mankind was he referring to? Not First Peoples, I'd wager, nor women. "What about the rest of us?"

His steely eyes shifted and took on a glazed sheen. "Survival of the fittest, what a bunch of humbug. Survival of the richest, I say. We'll rule the world without riffraff like you tagging along, begging for crumbs."

Atian limped over to us.

The general noticed his twisted foot and grimaced. "Enough silly questions, none of this applies to your kind anyway." He waved his weapon. "Let's go, upstairs with the lot of you."

I followed the boys into an angular shaft with shiny golden walls. A whoosh of air lifted us high into the tower. I took a moment to collect my stomach when we stopped. We followed the general into a cold, round room jam-packed with whining machines. The metallic odor was back. No one was working at the crowded workstations. "Where is everybody?"

General Cardiff's expression darkened. "They were no longer needed."

I swallowed. Okay, this wasn't funny anymore.

Cardiff waved to chairs. "Cool your heels in here while I take care of some business, then we'll decide your fate."

The general stepped out of the room and waved his hand. A sparkly barrier shimmered in place. We were trapped.

Photos of grim-faced men dressed in military uniforms lined two of the dull gray walls. The general's cousins? Red dots flashed across a holo map covering the far wall. The largest dot hovered over the Amazon forest in Beforetimes Venezuela. I poked the dot and the holo jiggled. "I wonder what these dots mean."

Matwau stopped pacing the room like a caged tiger long enough to study the map. "Arker sites." He traced his finger along a route from the eastern woodlands. "Passed a few towers on my trek north."

He ran his hands through his brown and golden braids. "Is it hot in here?"

I poked the dot over our refuge. It jiggled and a name came up: Elk Tower. "The chief's right, the towers are for communications. And the slave kids, what's with that?"

Beads of sweat dotted Matwau's high forehead and his body vibrated. "They've been sneaking into the tower for a couple months. Sometimes in gliders, other times in skimmers. I'm guessing whatever scheme they've hatched, it's going down real soon."

Maybe there was more to this snotty Cree than I had given him credit for. He was braver than pole-up-the-butt Atian, that much was certain. "You've been spying on them?"

Matwau ignored my question. "We need an escape plan and fast. I won't last much longer in this tin can."

Atian snickered. "Don't be so melodramatic, Cree. Besides, the general left a guard on the door."

"Do you honestly think they'll hurt us?" I said.

A wet line was forming on the back of Matwau's green shirt. "Don't be naïve, Hali. When they're finished whatever they're doing up there, they'll get rid of us."

How had a little exploring gone so wrong? "But why? We're just snoopy kids."

"These guys are evil dudes, they're not gonna leave any witnesses. Besides, you heard him. The Arkers don't plan on leaving anyone alive besides their elite group."

Matwau's eyes took on a haunted look. Why?

"They kill the innocent as easy as the guilty."

"So what's the plan, hotshot?" Atian said.

Matwau gave Atian a bemused look, then turned back to me. "Hali, you stand in front of the door. When I activate it, the guard will rush in and we'll deck him."

"I'm the decoy?" My voice squeaked.

Matwau winked and talked out of the side of his mouth like a gangster in Benji's comic books. "Sweetheart, I'm betting your winsome beauty will addle his brains long enough for me to punch him out."

I blushed. Why did I keep doing that?

"Ready?"

"No, I'm not ready, this is insane."

"Ready?"

I struck a pose and nodded. What else could I do?

Matwau waved his hand, and the door sparkled and disappeared. Right on cue, the guard charged in. "Hey, what the—?"

Matwau decked him but not hard enough. The guard rolled to the side, jumped to his feet, and reached for his holster, all in a split second.

"Look out, he's got a gun!"

"Oh no, that's not gonna happen." Atian karate-chopped the guard's arm, and he dropped the gun.

The burly man whirled on Atian and pushed him against the wall. "Think you're a tough guy, do you, well lights out for you." The guard pulled back his fist.

"No!"

Matwau stopped the guard's fist and jumped on his back. The guard danced around trying to dump him.

I dived for the gun and pointed it at the guard. "Stop or I'll shoot."

The guard grimaced, but stopped in his tracks when I cocked the gun. Now where did I learn to do that?

Atian grabbed a console and hit the guard over the head. His eyes rolled back in his head, and he sank to the floor.

"Hali, find us something to tie him up."

I snatched silver packing tape from one of the cluttered work stations.

Matwau wrapped tape around the guard's wrists and ankles and taped his mouth shut. "Okay, let's go, they'll be on us any minute."

Atian held back. "What about the drones?"

"We'll spread out, take different routes. At least they won't catch us all."

"Oh, that's comforting."

The shaft did not respond to Matwau's commands. "Blasted door."

Heavy footsteps thudded down the corridor. "Mat, we're out of time."

"Then we go down the fun way."

He jumped into the abyss. I laughed and jumped behind him. We slipped and slid around and around the tower and landed in a heap at the bottom.

"Get off me, Matwau."

"Ouch, my jaw. Hali, get your boney elbow out of my face."

Matwau helped Atian to his feet. "Can you make it?"

Atian brushed him off. "I'll make it."

We scurried back to the gap in the fence, dodging laser beams buzzing over us until my head spun. Ten meters from the gap in the fence, Matwau cried out and dropped to the ground.

"Atian, Mat's been hit!"

He doubled back. "Stay put, I don't need you down, too."

I hurried after him and helped pull Matwau behind a boulder.

"Hali, why can't you ever listen?"

"You're not the boss of me." I shook Matwau. "Wake up, Mat."

He groaned and sat up. "Gawd, that thing packs a wallop."

"Can you move?"

Matwau grinned. "Just watch me." He waited for a break in the lasers, then sprinted for the fence and dived through the hole. I tucked in behind him.

"Will those drones follow us?"

Matwau pulled singed fabric away from his skin. "They've never come after me on this side. I don't think they're programmed beyond securing their borders, or I would have been a goner long ago."

My heart pounded and not from the shocks running up my leg. "Wow, what a rush. That was too fun."

Atian scowled at me as he crawled through the hole. "Next time you want some fun, don't call me."

Okay, enough. "I didn't call you this time."

I loosened the wooden clip holding my twist in place, and a tangled mass of purple and blue hair tumbled down my back. I shook my head to loosen the waves.

Atian caught his breath behind me, and Matwau stared at me, an inscrutable expression on his gaping mouth.

Really?

Lightning struck on the other side of the valley, near our eco-dome, and the air crackled with deadly energy. A second later thunder rumbled in the black and green clouds spinning overhead. We had minutes before another storm broke.

I whistled and Honey came running. "Atian, take Honey and we'll meet you at the dome."

Atian's face darkened. "I'll get back on my own, thanks." He turned and fast-limped down the slope.

Matwau shrugged and followed Atian down the hill. "See you at the gathering tomorrow."

In one easy leap, I landed on Honey's back. "Let's beat the storm home, girl."

I leaned into Honey's smooth gallop, and we left the tower in the swirling dust.

The screen door whipped back and forth on its rusty hinges, harder and harder, until it snapped and blew away. Wind rushed into the cabin and upended the old cupboard. Dishes crashed to the floor and shattered into a thousand pieces.

Papi clapped his hands. "Benji, Leyla, under the table, hurry."

The wooden floor buckled and a heavy soapstone sculpture slid across the room, narrowly missing Scruffy. "Meow!" She dived under the sofa.

The banshee howl of the wind raised the hairs on the back of my neck. I covered my ears and crouched under the table, afraid to open my eyes, afraid our little cabin would fly away like poor Dorothy in *The Wizard of Oz*.

Wolf huddled on his special blanket behind the wood stove. He whimpered and hid his eyes behind his giant paws.

"Come here Wolf, come here, boy."

He dashed across the room, slid under the table, and pushed his cold nose into my armpit.

I scratched the great oaf behind his ears. "What a wimp."

Papi had found the silver wolf cub shivering beside his mother's corpse a year ago and brought him home to me. The little fur ball wormed his way into my heart, and now I couldn't imagine life without him.

The wind picked up speed and a deep rumble, like a train roaring down the tracks, grew louder and louder. Our log cabin shuddered and creaked.

Benji crouched under the table, his butt up in the air, and his head under his arms. "Evil spirits are coming to get us! They're coming to get us!"

Mama cradled little Danny in her arms, but his lungs whistled as he gasped for air, and his eyes were closed. "Hush Benji, we're safe inside the cabin."

Was my mother right? Were we safe? The Siksiká had inherited a patched dome from a bankrupt developer, but two years ago fierce winds moved north and tore a hole in the dome. Now it barely slowed the storms.

Leyla clung to our mother and coughed until she cried. "I can't breathe, mama, it's so hot."

Mama brushed wispy black curls away from Leyla's damp forehead and kissed her. "I know, baby girl. Lightning's set off another fire in the woods."

Wolf licked Leyla's face. She pushed him away. "Ugh, Wolf get away, you stink."

Papi reached for our breathers. "Afraid it's time, kids."

Ten years ago, Chief Roy and three of the Elders trekked south and brought back enough breathers for everyone in the village. Where they got the breathers remained a mystery, but to this day rumors the chief had pulled off a major heist persisted.

Leyla cried and pushed the breather away. "No, I don't wanna, it smells worse than Wolf."

"Hush child."

Mama set the filters and seals on the rubber mask and pulled it over Leyla's face, then slipped one on Danny. He did not notice.

"Deep breaths, come on you two, deep breaths."

Papi handed breathers to Benji and me. "Listen kids, we'll make it, Mother Earth is shouting her anger, that's all."

Benji puckered his chubby cheeks. "Why's she so angry? I ain't never done nothing to her."

Chapter Two

THE RAINBOW WARRIORS

Chief Roy lifted the smoldering sweet grass and offered the braid to the four corners of Mother Earth. "Gitche Manitou, cleanse our hearts and minds, and fill our souls with love."

He lit a clump of dried sage in an ancient clay bowl. "Purify this gathering and remove all anger and ill-will."

The wispy vapors thickened and took shape in the roof rafters. I blinked, but no, they were up there all right. I poked Benji. "The Sky Beings are here."

"Shh."

"Don't shush me, Benjamin Kitchi, the Sky Beings are circling us and that means trouble."

Benji tipped his head and squinted. "Nope, can't see nothing but a bunch of old cobwebs."

A Sky Being shaped like a woman wagged her finger at me. Her long black hair hung down her back like garter snakes weaving in the wind, and her orange eyes shot red sparks into the smoky air. She swooped down and hovered in front of an unsuspecting elder, then flitted back to the ceiling.

Angry Sky Beings in the village? But they were supposed to protect us. A knot of fear churned in the pit of my stomach. This was not good.

Twelve elderly councilors shuffled into the lodge. The women wore soft deerskin dresses and blue and pink earrings carved from seashells my People traded with coastal First Nations long before Turmoil. Fluttering eagle feather headdresses covered the men's heads and quillwork decorated their leather leggings.

Village drummers beating hide-covered drums and humming a sacred song followed close behind the elders.

Storyteller came last.

He wrapped his red and black story robe around his thin body and settled on his telling stool. In a soothing sing-song voice, he began his legend. "Long ago Mother Earth was fresh and new, but sad and lonely. Old Man and Old Woman said, "We must fill this world with plants and animals and make Mother Earth smile again.""

"And so Old Man and Old Woman created the forests and streams and covered the land with green grass and food plants. They filled the streams with Fish and Otter, the forests with Bear and Deer, and the blue sky with Hawk and Raven.

"Then Old Man and Old Woman shaped People out of clay to enjoy the riches of Mother Earth and to fill the land with children's laughter. Old Woman showed the women how to pick berries and dig for roots, and Old Man showed the men how to hunt for Bison running free on the prairie.

"The First Peoples spread across Mother Earth. Some of the People roamed the land and hunted bountiful herds. Others dug in the dirt and grew food for their families. Still others caught fish in the friendly lakes and rivers. The

People prospered and their future seemed bright. The time had come for Old Man and Old Woman to leave, but they promised to return if ever needed."

Storyteller's voice grew solemn.

"Then one day strangers came to our shores and told us this land was no longer ours. They pushed us aside, and we watched as they wounded Mother Earth and stole her riches. We mourned as her waters and skies turned foul, and the creatures who fed the First Peoples disappeared.

"At last Mother Earth could stand no more, and she turned against the people, even the First Peoples. Her winds grew angry, her waters poured over the land, and she turned away when the merciless sun bleached our bones and burned our forests. The dark days of Turmoil were upon us."

I fidgeted on my hard wooden chair and scratched my laser welt. Why was I here? I had heard this legend many times before, beginning when I was so small my chin barely reached Storyteller's knee. What good did rehashing the past do? Nothing could save the First Peoples from Turmoil.

"Those nations still standing moved to save some of their people. They called the project Noah's Ark. They sent the best of their young ones to space stations circling Mother Earth, for how long, no one knew."

My ears perked up. Noah's Ark? Did the space stations have any connection to General Cardiff and the Arkers?

"Others, hardier folks, began the long voyage to distant planets in glorious spaceships. But that left billions to die as the storms raged on, and one by one the great cities fell dark."

Storyteller glanced at the ceiling. Did he see the Sky Beings?

"The First Peoples waited, their hearts broken, but they remained steadfast. They would not abandon Mother Earth. Three years ago, the World Council of First Peoples reclaimed the land, sea, and sky." Storyteller bent his head and sighed. "No one noticed."

The thick smoke turned the listeners into shadowy figures, and an eerie silence filled the lodge as we waited for Storyteller's saga to continue. My hollow stomach chose that moment to rumble. Loudly.

Benji giggled, and I elbowed him.

The shriveled carrots and turnips I had eaten for supper did not fill my long, lean frame, but our elk meat ration was not due for another five days. I was hungry. Nor could I remember a time when I wasn't hungry.

But hunger was not first on my mind. Why were some from my village missing from the gathering? Benji and Leyla were there, but not Danny. My best friend, Sinopa, wasn't sitting beside me and whispering about a boy she fancied, nor was loudmouthed Chogan disrupting the meeting. But Atian sat in the front row, and stony-faced Matwau paced the back of the hall. Why us and not them? The fear knot in my stomach tightened.

Storyteller began again, his head still bent.

"In my dreamtime, Gitche Manitou came to me and said: My son, Mother Earth no longer protects her People. We must save some of our children so that First Peoples live on. The Wise Ones have prepared a great city beneath the sea that is safe from the ravages on the land. Send your hopes for the future to this city."

Murmurs spread through the lodge, and the People glanced at each other, worry and confusion reflected on their faces.

"First Peoples do not hide in the sea," a man at the back of the room said.

"And what of those who cannot make their way to this city—the old, the weak, and the sick?" said another.

Chief Roy raised his hand for silence and strode into the center of the room. A black patch covered his bad eye, and his gray hair was tied back in a fuzzy ponytail. He resembled an aging pirate.

He hitched up his baggy pants. "The First Peoples of Earth must survive. Three years ago, the World Council began building an underwater city on a secret site. The city is called Maniton."

"Old Man and Old Woman appeared in my dream," Storyteller said, his head still bent and his words soft. They said: We have sent messengers across all the lands of Mother Earth calling for young ones to journey to Maniton. They will fulfill an ancient prophecy and become the Rainbow Warriors."

Storyteller lifted his head and gazed at us with red-rimmed eyes. "You are our Rainbow Warriors, my children."

Pandemonium erupted in the gathering lodge.

I froze in my seat. This could not be happening. It must be a Sky Being dream.

My father rose to his feet. "Hundreds of years ago strangers swooped onto this land and told us our children must attend their schools and learn new ways to survive. Is this another such tale?"

Some people clapped, others murmured.

Chief Roy bowed to my father. "Nootah's words are wise, but those who claimed to know best are no more. Our children will live with other First Peoples and learn the old ways, and someday, when Mother Earth has forgiven us, they will reclaim this land."

"Then this is good."

Papi sat down and reached for my mother, and though sadness shone in his brown eyes, he smiled and squeezed her hand.

Mama returned his smile through her tears. "My children will live, that is all I ask."

Well, I wasn't smiling. I stood and faced the chief and Storyteller, my hands on my hips. I took a deep breath and willed my heart to slow. "I won't leave without my parents and my brother."

Chief Roy gazed at me with a kind, but firm face. "You must. This is your destiny."

I stamped my foot. "I won't go." They couldn't make me—could they?

"Halerine Ananda, Gitche Manitou has bestowed a special gift on you, a gift First Peoples will need in Maniton."

I felt for the leather medicine pouch attached to my hip pocket. My healing powers. Barely two and wobbly on my feet, Grandmother hitched me to her shoulders and took me on her treks into the woods searching for herbs. I learned the secrets of healing on my grandmother's back.

Chief Roy's good eye crinkled. "Besides, given your recent exploits, I assumed you and your partners in crime would jump at the chance for more exploring."

I peered at the chief from beneath my lashes and eased my sleeve over the laser welt. How did he know I had broken our unspoken taboo? Did blabbermouth Atian tell him?

One little girl buried her head in her mother's lap and sobbed. "I don't wanna go."

Ten-year-old Willow reached for her. "Be brave, Etta, we are the Rainbow Warriors."

Rainbow Warriors? I shuddered. Doomed warriors was more like it.

Atian caught my eye and held my gaze for a long moment. I looked away first, shaken by the question and the promise in his eyes.

"When do we leave, sir?"

The spell was broken. There he went, taking over again. "Seven days hence."

I gasped and clutched my aching sides. A week? I had to say good-bye to my family and the only home I'd ever known in a week? And Honey and Wolf? Agonizing pain cut through me, and I turned away. No one, especially not Atian, would see me cry.

A Sky Being swooped down and hovered in front of me. What treachery were the Sky Beings planning? Was this their fault? I hissed. "Go away."

The imp fluttered her silver wings and zipped back to the ceiling.

Storyteller's words weighed heavily on my People, and they argued late into the evening. At last, my father put an end to the discussion. "People of the Siksiká, what choice do we have? Our fate was sealed when the dome cracked. If we want our children to live, this is the path we must follow."

My heart sank and a dull ache tore at me. Papi was right. Another family had lost their home thanks to last night's storm. And even if the worst of the storms held off, which they wouldn't, our food was running low. My People would die. The young and old first, then everyone.

Chief Roy nodded. "Nootah speaks words of wisdom. We have no choice. Go home little ones, say your farewells, and ready your hearts and minds for the long and difficult journey ahead."

The Sky Beings whisked away. Mission accomplished?

Ten-year-old Tomko stood and flounced zis spiky hair, pink for the day. "So who will take us to Maniton?"

Chief Roy smiled a sad smile. "Gitche Manitou named me your guardian. For my last duty as chief of the Siksiká Blackfoot First Nations, I will lead you to the gathering site in Vancouver."

"Vancouver?" a woman said. "But the coastal cities are gone."

"Some parts of the city are still above water. The children's guides from Maniton will await them at one such site."

"How long do we have, chief?" Matwau said.

He consulted his bio-comm. "The pick-up date is in fifty-seven days."

"Just a minute, chief." A man at the back of the room stood. "I demand a place on this quest."

I held back a groan. Wouldn't you know, sour-faced Samoset would be the one to cause trouble. Matwau and his father had somehow crossed the scorched badlands after a superstorm tore up the Cree homeland in Duck Mountain Refuge. They begged entrance to our village a year ago, and Chief Roy welcomed them for Matwau's sake. Bet he was sorry now.

"Councilors Ore and Sereida are accompanying the children, Samoset."

Samoset strode to the front of the lodge and glared at the chief. "Why them? They're ancient, their time is over. So is yours. We should have some say in who gets to live."

Chief Roy held up his hand and shook his head. "The councilors and I are escorting the children to the pick-up site in Vancouver and only that far. This is not a gift of life for anyone but the children."

Samoset's sneaky eyes gleamed. "We shall see about that." He stalked out of the gathering lodge.

Five-year-old Etta sniffed and rubbed her eyes. "But who's gonna look after me in Maniton? I'm just a little girl."

Chief Roy's knees creaked when he crouched beside her. "Nice people are waiting for you, Etta m'girl. They'll help you grow into a strong and fearless woman."

Etta popped her thumb in her mouth and stared at the chief, her sweet eyes wide and brimming with tears.

Chief Roy stood and faced his People. "We have been given a chance to save our children, the rest is of little consequence."

The chief's unspoken message hung in the air. He and the councilors would not be returning to the land of the Siksiká First Nations.

"Faster girl, go faster."

Honey's golden coat shone with sweat and her sides heaved, but she surged ahead, and I leaned into her. The scorching wind wiped away my tears, but nothing could wipe away the pain cutting into my heart.

We raced across the desolate valley. In the days before Turmoil, yellow and purple flowers covered the valley floor in a magic carpet, and juicy blueberries dripped from thick bushes. A meandering creek brought fresh water to the Siksiká and attracted flocks of plump ducks and geese for our hunters. Even timid woodland bison crept out of the boreal forest at dusk and grazed on the sweet grass. But the world of my grandfathers was long gone, and in its place a sky covered in pink and green poison clouds hung over a dying meadow and a dry creek bed.

I ducked under a puff of poison floating in the air. If more smog from the South drifted north and settled to the ground, my People were doomed.

A neo-glider swept over the valley, invisible if not for the murky air. My heart filled with rage, and I shook my fist at the glider. The Arkers used stealth technology and lived in fancy towers while the rest of the world sank into the dark ages, and I had to hide in a bubble under water for the rest of my life. How was that fair?

Honey slowed to a trot.

"Keep going Honey, we don't have to go back, we don't have to say good-bye."

Who said I had to obey Gitche Manitou? What stopped us from running away? I sighed as Honey ignored my command and came to a halt. Honor, duty, and fear, that's what. Chief Roy's words as the gathering broke up haunted me: "No one ever claimed life was fair, Halerine Ananda.

All any of us can do is our best. You have been given a chance at life. Don't squander it."

I picked shriveled chokecherries from a scraggly tree and ate them, but I should have taken the berries home to Danny-boy.

Tears blurred my vision as I dismounted, and I tripped over a rotten log. Honey nudged me, I threw my arms around her neck and wept. I wasn't a warrior, rainbow or any other color. I was a young girl with a home and a life, but tomorrow we were leaving. Forever. "Oh Honey, how can I say good-bye?"

Honey whinnied and nipped my shoulder. Her soft nose tickled my neck.

I wiped away my tears and smoothed my windblown hair. "I know girl, it's show time." I mounted and urged her on. Honor, duty, and bloody fear won out.

The gentle slope surrounding the ceremonial bowl teemed with Siksiká waiting for the ceremony to begin.

On the crest, Honey reared up and neighed loud enough to wake our ancestors. I patted her neck. "Show off."

I slipped off Honey and strolled down the slope and through the gathering. My moccasins glided over the dead grass without making a sound.

People stepped aside and allowed me to pass. "That dress ..." someone murmured, but most of the crowd had gone quiet.

When my grandmother gave me the white antelope dress and moccasins three years ago, she said, "Guard these treasures well, Halerine Ananda, and pass them on to your descendants. They are a symbol of our People and of better times to come."

I searched for my mother in the crowd. She was wiping away tears. I swallowed the lump rising in my throat and marched up to the podium. I would not cry, not in front of my People. I was Halerine Ananda of the Siksiká Blackfoot First Nations. I would not cry.

"Halerine Ananda, good of you to join us."

I bowed my head. "I am sorry, Chief Roy. My heart needed time."

The chief turned to the People. "We are gathered here to bid farewell to our beloved children and wish them safe journey. Let us begin."

Drummers beat a slow rhythm, and the twelve Siksiká elders entered the clearing and took their seats. An elderly grandmother poured sweet grass tea in sacred wooden cups. The sharp, aromatic scent floated through the gathering. I accepted my cup with shaking hands.

Chief Roy studied us, his eyes lingering on me a touch longer than the others. "Each of you will carry our name and our history with you into a new world. In this leaving ceremony, we take the opportunity to thank you for your sacrifice and wish you good fortune."

Councilor Ore joined the chief. She was holding a woven basket.

"To safeguard your journey and ensure your success in Maniton, we offer each of you a sacred totem," Chief Roy said.

A totem? But some of the children had not undergone a vision quest. How could they receive a totem? Memories of my own vision quest came back. I had fasted and prayed for two days, and on the evening of the second day a gray boat the shape of chief's sacred pipe rose above me, and then I was floating inside a huge water bubble. I couldn't see the sky or land. My vision made sense now, but the knowledge did not fill me with peace. What kind of future would I have living underwater?

Chief Roy reached into the basket. "Halerine Ananda, I present you with a prized dreamcatcher, one made by my many-times-removed ancestor, Nadie Nijlon, and blessed by the moon goddess, Komorkis. May it guide and protect you all of your days."

He handed me a blue and silver dreamcatcher, more beautiful than any I had ever seen. I accepted the gift and held the Red Willow hoop to my heart. The dreamcatcher's spirit whispered in my mind, *Hali...*

"Thank you, chief. I shall cherish the dreamcatcher all of my days."

"Never give up dreaming, Halerine Ananda. Your dreams shall sustain the Siksiká children through their long journey and guide them as they grow into adults."

He knew about my visions?

Benji stepped forward.

Chief Roy placed a wooden carving of a prairie tipi in Benji's hands. "A builder you shall be, Benjamin Kitchi. Build fine homes in Maniton, but never forget your role in rebuilding the Siksiká nation."

A grin crossed Benji's face. He puffed out his chest and held the tipi up to the pale sun. "That's me, a mighty builder."

Leyla stepped forward, but kept her head down.

"Young Leyla Apikuni, I charge you with writing epic poems recounting our Peoples' great deeds and our hope for the future. You will be our storyteller and our knowledge keeper in Maniton."

Leyla peeked at Chief Roy from beneath her thick lashes, and her eyes danced as she accepted a porcupine quill and inkpot totem. "I promise to write a really good story, all about us rainbow heroes."

Etta sucked her thumb and shuffled closer to the chief.

"Miss Etta Alsoomse, Gitche Manitou has a special gift for you." He handed her a miniature beaver totem. "For

your kindness and gentleness, a trait the children will need on this journey."

Etta popped her thumb out of her mouth and smiled. "I'm being nice to everyone, I promise."

Tomko approached the chief, a mischievous grin on zis cherubic face. Zis spiky lime green and fuchsia hair brought a warm smile to many faces.

The chief handed zim a war shield with a bison, a pipe, and a tomahawk painted on it. "For your bravery and good deeds, Tomko Shanahwane of the Siksiká Blackfoot, I offer you this gift."

Tomko's chest swelled and they preened. Behind Chief Roy's back, zie stuck out zis pierced tongue at Benji.

Benji scowled. "Ah, zie ain't never been brave."

Chief Roy cocked his head to the side. "A Two-Spirit must be brave above all others, young Benjamin Kitchi."

A slight smile touched Benji's lips, and he touched elbows with Tomko.

Matwau and Atian stepped forward at the same time.

Atian shouldered Matwau. "It's my turn, get back Cree."

"Who says? Step away, little man."

"Enough!" Chief Roy glowered at them, his bushy eyebrows nearly touching. "You boys represent our hope for a peaceful, unified future for all First Nations. Act like it."

He handed Matwau a totem. "Matwau Meewatin of the Cree First Nations, I give you a Morning Star for the courage and wisdom you will need when you choose your path in life. May your destiny bring hope and light."

Strange words. Since when did Matwau have a choice in his path? None of us had any choice.

Chief Roy opened a leather sack. "Atian Sokanon of the Siksiká Blackfoot First Nations, I present you with this split-horn headdress as a symbol of your strength and leadership. Lead your People wisely as you move into the future."

Murmurs drifted through the gathering. The bison horn was prized among Blackfoot warriors, and only a great leader ever earned its magic. The horn had been split and polished, then attached to a rimmed felt hat. Weasel, skunk, and possum furs were hooked to the horn. My People had owned this headdress for many generations. What were the elders telling Atian and the rest of us with this gift? And what about that cryptic message to Matwau?

Chief Roy glared at the boys, and his lone eye sparked a warning. "See that you serve as role models for your People, and never let down these virtues."

The boys backed away from the podium, no longer poking or jostling each other, but I doubted détente would last long.

The ceremony continued until all the Rainbow Warriors had received their new totems.

A white-haired Sky Being flickered in front of my face. She smiled and nodded her head. I smiled back. Her face distorted and the smile swelled into a dark void, and her teeth morphed into fangs. Small people writhed in agony inside the void, and Sky Beings flew around the body of a little girl. My heart lurched. Was the little girl Leyla or Etta, or one of the other children? What was the Sky Being trying to tell me?

A banshee howl echoed across the valley. No one heard the cry except me. I clutched the dreamcatcher to my hammering heart.

Storyteller and First Elder climbed the hillock and gave short speeches, and a few parents offered well-meaning advice and solace. I tried not to squirm, but I was tired of standing. Benji had already flopped down on the prickly grass.

At last, food was shared.

Benji stuffed a raw turnip in his mouth. "About time, I was starving."

I nibbled on toasted bannock and smiled at his antics, but my vision from the Sky Beings had cast a dark shadow over the ceremony and ruined my appetite.

Honey was grazing on the hilltop. Would anyone notice if I went for one last ride?

Matwau sidled over to me. "Some ceremony, huh?"

I shrugged.

A smirk warmed his chiseled features. "You know, Halerine Ananda, your entrance reeked of contrivance. You should be ashamed of yourself."

"Shameful, I agree."

"Oh, I'm not complaining. That was the most impressive moment in this long, boring day."

Too bad the Sky Beings didn't scare the living daylights out of him. He would not be so bored then. I wiped crumbs off my dress and scowled at him. "Don't be rude, Mat. Our People are grieving. They needed to say good bye."

"They're your people, Hali, not mine."

"But you're coming with us tomorrow."

Matwau shrugged. "Better than hanging out here until the end, but don't think I'm one of you. I'm Cree and I'm all alone."

"What about your father?"

He pursed his lips and his gaze turned to Samoset, sitting away from the other guests and gorging on a platter of food meant for several. "Yes, there is Samoset."

"And the chief honored you with a Morning Star."

Matwau nodded at Atian limping toward us. "Nothing compared to what your boyfriend-wanna-be picked up." He winked and left as Atian joined me.

"What was that all about?"

"Just making conversation. Why?"

He kicked at a clump of dirt. "He's no good, Hali, stay away from him."

"Good grief, now you're telling me who to hang with? Get over yourself, you're not the boss of me."

I headed for Honey and one last ride.

Chapter Three

THE BADLANDS

The eerie calls sent shivers up and down my spine. I couldn't see him, but he was up there all right, flying high above the foul air. On the day after Storyteller delivered the Wise One's message, Raven flew into our village. My People believed Raven was a messenger sent from Gitche Manitou to guide us on our journey. I was not so sure. Raven was a trickster, and what were the odds of Raven and the Sky Beings showing up at the same time without some mischief brewing?

Benji plopped down beside me and munched on his second synthed apple. "Well, here we are, stuck in a giant yellow grub, heading into nowhere."

That pretty much summed it up. Seven days ago I had a life. A difficult one, but a life I loved. Now, because of Storyteller's vision, I was trapped on an ancient biopod with two dozen Siksiká children and one cynical Cree, searching for a city that might not even exist.

The biopod's groans and creaks grew louder. I stroked its luminous inner shell. "Poor old thing, you're not any happier than the rest of us, are you?"

Heyho no no

Councilor Ore laughed. "I feel its pain. My kinks are acting up, too."

Fifty years ago a wealthy collector donated the sentient transport to my village. The elders placed the biopod in sleep mode and parked it in the bush. Papi took me to see the biopod when I was six. "We're saving it for a rainy day," he'd said.

Well, that rainy day was here.

I stood and stretched. "Come on, Wolf, let's explore this old tug."

I'd begged Chief Roy to let Wolf come with us. He relented when I showed him the canine breather I had fashioned.

I passed Councilor Sereida, and she patted my arm. "Would you mind checking on the wee ones, dear, they're much too quiet for my liking."

"Yes auntie."

Atian was sprawled on a lounger and flipping through a dog-eared mechanics magazine. He ignored me. Well, two could play that game.

The kids were huddled in their stuffy sleeper pod, misery and fear etched on their pale little faces.

I boosted the air freshener. "Hey kids, why don't you play a game or something?"

No one moved.

Benji pushed past me and flopped down on his sleeper. Wolf crawled in beside him and hung his huge nose over the edge of the bed. "Hali, are we ever gonna go home again?"

What could I say? "I'm sorry, Benji, but Papi explained this to you, remember? The North won't protect us for much longer. Maniton is our only hope."

Benji kicked the back of the seat in front of him. "Chogan said we won't make it to Maniton."

That troublemaker. "Chogan isn't a Rainbow Warrior, and he's scared of what might happen in the village."

"But what about mama and papi, and Danny-boy?"

He knew, his eyes said as much, but I guess he hoped I had a better answer. "They'll do the best they can for as long as they can."

"But—"

No, no more questions, I couldn't bear it. "I have to go."

Matwau was sitting in the back of the sleeper pod, away from the other children, but next to the one real window in the pod. He stared outside, his face closed and distant. Sweat dripped down the side of his face, and an untouched ham and tomato sandwich wilted in his shaking hand.

I sighed. As if our situation wasn't miserable enough, we had Matwau. "Everything okay, Mat?"

He looked through me. "In this new and ugly world, life can change in an instant."

Quote of the day? I pushed past his stony expression and sat down. "Tell me."

"If you haven't figured it out yet, I'm claustrophobic."

"Uh huh, and?"

He leaned back in his lounger, a scowl plastered across his interesting but not-quite-handsome face. "Life isn't going according to my plan."

I half-laughed, half-sobbed. "Oh really? I didn't know."

He bristled. "I wanted to study archaeology, and I thought ... never mind."

"Archaeology? Really?"

"I'm not Samoset, Hali. I had dreams."

"I know Mat, but you strike me as more of a, well I don't know what, but archaeology?"

He shrugged. "Sounded intriguing to me. I like old stuff, history."

"Far as I know, all the universities shut down long before we were born. Maybe in Maniton—"

He scowled at me. "Maybe in Maniton, what Hali? We'll be trapped in an underwater prison. No artifacts to dig up down there." He sighed. "And books, well books don't interest me much."

How could I counter his resentment? I felt the same way. Maybe even more. "You'll find your place, Mat, we all will." So lame.

"Better be a really big place with high ceilings and lots of lights."

Haunting strains of *Trail of Tears* drifted through the pod. I swallowed and squeezed my eyes shut to hold back the tears.

"Tell Atian to play something cheerful on that clarinet, or we'll all turn into quivering jelly," Matwau said. His voice cracked.

I peeked into Atian's sleeper. The glum look on his face told it all. I took a tentative step closer. "Matwau says play something cheerful or we're all goners."

He nodded and let loose with *Tatanka*.

On the way back to my seat, Chief Roy stopped me. "Halerine Ananda, I'll be counting on your help with the younger children."

"Yes chief." I agreed without thinking, but by the time I reached my cushion, I was ticked. What did I know about taking care of little kids? I was a kid, too. Who would take care of me? Besides, why couldn't Atian and Matwau babysit the kids? They were almost eighteen, more than a year older than me.

I flopped down on my cushion seat.

The seat grunted.

"Sorry."

Leyla tapped me on the shoulder. "Hali, I miss mama and papi."

I pulled her into my arms, and she popped a well-worn thumb into her mouth. "I do, too, baby girl." Benji joined us, and I reached for his hand. For a change he didn't protest. Even Wolf sidled closer and curled around my feet.

The parting had been hard on us all. We had huddled together on our last evening and talked.

"What will you do, my father?"

Nootah wiped his red-rimmed eyes and took a ragged breath. "Our People moved North hoping life would be easier, but when the permafrost melted and filled the lakes and streams with silt, we lost the lake trout. Then the caribou drifted northward before dying out." He sighed. "With each passing year, we've worked harder for less. If you children have a chance for a better life, then we're willing to sacrifice everything."

"But—"

"No buts, Halerine. You can't imagine how we scoured the region for feedstock to activate that old biopod's synthesizer. Cost us half the elk and bison herd to get what we needed." His voice broke. "They made us beg, called us no good Indians."

"Oh papi."

Nootah shuddered. "It's done. As for us, the water up here should last our lifetime if we're careful. This old eco-dome still offers some protection. And the herds, well, we'll hope for the best."

"But the poison air?"

"Might not drop down."

He stroked my cheek, like he did when I was a little girl. "My beautiful daughter, our legends will speak of your bravery. Carry our name into the future and save our People."

"Yes, my father."

He touched the feathers on my dreamcatcher. "Guide her well, sacred spider."

I swallowed a lump in my throat and reached for my mother.

She opened her arms and held me one last time. "I love you with all of my heart, dear daughter." Tears streamed down her beautiful face. "And I will miss you for all of my days." She kissed my forehead and straightened my wayward braids. "May Apistotoke and Gitche Manitou guide you and protect you."

"But I don't want to leave." My voice quivered, but I couldn't help it.

"No, sweet girl, don't say that. I can't bear my children dying before they have ever lived." She clasped Leyla and Benji to her side. "Please Halerine, they need you."

I gazed at my parents and tried to hold their faces in my forever memory. I brushed limp hair away from little Danny's face. He would not live out the winter. And Honey? How it hurt to leave her.

I shuddered and pushed away the sad memories, but the dreary scene outside the biopod did little to cheer me up. Dead bushes and tree stumps poked through the clay banks on both sides of the highway. In Beforetimes, the land we travelled through was a maze of small lakes and rivers, and the green hillsides teemed with bears and deer. But not anymore. The lakes and rivers had dried up, and the animals slipped away.

When we crossed over the boreal tree line and moved onto the bald prairie, the world we knew disappeared. The wind never let up, not even at night, and the dry heat cooked the life out of everything but the weeds growing in the cracked soil alongside the crumbling highway. Villages and sprawling towns along the highway sat empty and worn out, the people long gone or starved in their beds.

Even the sky looked different. Dark, angry clouds circled above us, and pink and green swirls of poison floated closer to the ground than in the North. The biopod's purifier howled day and night sucking up toxins slipping through its seals.

I leaned back and closed my eyes. What a dreary, dangerous world we were plunging into without any idea of what awaited us.

"Nothing much to see out there," Benji said.

I glanced at the screen again. "No, not much."

A skinny gopher sat on its hind legs and watched our biopod circle around a burned-out Volkswagen. The biopod hissed, and the gopher skittered under a rusting trailer stuck in a dry bog.

"Poor little guy must be having a tough time surviving out there."

Leyla pressed her nose against the screen and licked the steam from her breath. "Where are all the fluffy trees and mushy ponds?"

"I don't know, sweetie."

A whirlwind sucked loose soil and tumbleweeds into the hot air and kept pace with the biopod. How long before the North turned into this nightmare? "Chief calls this place the flatlands."

Benji leaned over and whispered in my ear, "I'm calling it the badlands."

I ruffled his spiky brown hair. "Badlands, it is."

Six thousand years ago, the Canadian prairies turned into a scorching desert. Scientists called that era the altithermal, and it lasted three thousand years. This altithermal might last forever.

A wave of dizziness washed over me, and the dismal prairie disappeared. In its place, fields of ripe wheat swayed in the soft breeze. A farmer waved from his combine on the edge of the field, and a grain truck bounced over the ruts to join him. A pretty village with neat rows of white houses and manicured lawns nestled in the nearby valley. Children played ball in the schoolyard, and young mothers walked their baby carriages along paved streets lined with quaint stores full of good things to eat.

"How did it get so bad?"

The wheat fields melted away, and I shook my head to clear the vision.

Atian leaned over my seat and stared at the gloomy countryside whizzing across the screen. A frown creased his handsome face.

So now he was talking to me?

I searched for something witty or sensible to say, but he was standing too close. "We haven't received any real news for a long time." One by one the cities and towns had gone silent, and for three years now only an occasional traveler brought us scraps of news. "I've said it before, we were hiding in the North while all this happened around us."

"We were the lucky ones then, that's a war zone out there, after the battle's been lost."

I had to agree, a war-torn wasteland. Tales of half-crazed bandits beheading anyone they ran into, flash floods sweeping away entire towns, and raging fires burning even the air, had trickled into our village. If half those stories were true, we were in for big trouble.

Dread filled my heart, and my dreamcatcher buzzed against my chest. I opened my mouth to beg Chief Roy to turn back, but Benji interrupted me.

He pointed up the skylight. "Look it."

I moved aside a leather dreamcatcher hanging from the ceiling and craned my neck. The biopod was cruising under rusty pipes suspended a hundred meters above the highway. Beforetimes Canada fought a water war in 2044. Canada lost. Powerful water corps moved into the North and built the unsightly pipelines, for all the good it did them. They drained Lake Athabasca and Great Slave Lake in less than a decade, and then the Southerners perished from thirst.

My plea died on my lips. We couldn't go home. The water was almost gone, and the villagers needed what little was left.

Atian shook his head, and the crease between his eyes deepened. "I've had enough of this crazy land already." He headed back to the sleeper pod.

I followed his lead and slipped into my sleeper. Flopidoo the bunny waited on my bed. I flicked its long ears and curled up with him. If only I could sleep and forget. Even for a short while.

Banshee screams woke me in the night. I staggered into the lounge pod and revived the wall screen.

A green glow lit up the viewer and swirls of sand, and something else danced in and out of my line of sight. "What on earth?"

"*Aa*, 'tis a strange weather phenomenon."

Chief Roy slipped into the control pod. "And I've a bad feeling. We'd best be moving on." He swiped his hand across the biopod's sensors, and the console lit up.

Roswell, our driver, ducked into the pod, still in his sleeper pants. "Take us out of this soup, bio."

The biopod hissed and rose on her jets, but her bulk barely moved. Roswell repeated his command. Still no movement.

Ooh-ee ooh-ee

Chief Roy scratched his head. "Something's holding the pod back."

I pointed to the screen. "Maybe that?"

A thick green swirl, resembling an ethereal shape, pushed against the biopod's flank. Was that a face floating in the midst of the green? Did the others see it?

Ooh ooh

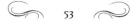

Maybe the biopod saw it.

Chief Roy activated the external sensors. The eerie howl intensified.

"Almost words," I murmured.

Hali, listen ...

What was my dreamcatcher trying to tell me?

Matwau frowned at me. "It's a weather pattern, Hali, nothing more."

Beads of sweat peppered his forehead, and the pupils of his eyes had gone pinpoint. I reached for his hand. "Mat ..."

He pushed away my hand. Okay then.

Atian joined us. "What's up?"

"Something out there is keeping the pod from moving on," Roswell said.

The biopod shuddered and slid backward, dangerously close to the bank of a dried up ravine. Were we being pushed?

"Right, this isn't funny anymore." Roswell punched codes into the console. "Bio, shields up, anchors down."

The biopod's armor descended over her membrane, and she pushed heavy spikes into the ground. The shaking stopped but not the howls.

Benji waddled into the lounge. "Hali? I can't sleep, something's making creepy noises."

I wrapped my arms around him. "It's an angry wind." But the wind was more than angry. It was haunted. Poison chemicals, bone dust, microbes, and bacteria had all meshed together and become life—or death—or whatever, and now it had us trapped.

"We'll wait it out," Chief Roy said. "Angry or not, it's bound to move on."

The hours crawled by, and the howling winds rattled my nerves. I keyed my cushion for silent sleep mode and settled down for a long night. Benji and Leyla crawled in with me.

A pulsating thump on the biopod's rooftop woke me from a light doze.

Aihee

"Something's walking on top of us, and the biopod doesn't like it," Matwau said.

I rounded on him. "Something? I thought you said this was just wind."

He shrugged. "Okay, how do you explain the thumps, then?

How indeed.

A feeble light filtered through the dust, enough for me to see Sky Beings dancing in the wind. Were they making the noise?

We waited, and eventually we lost our view of outside.

Roswell grunted. "We're being buried in dag-blasted sand."

I gulped. Buried alive.

The air grew stale and shallow. Leyla's fingertips and lips slowly turned blue, and she heaved with each breath.

Chief Roy gazed at Leyla and frowned. "We can't wait much longer. The bio's filters are no longer bringing in fresh air."

"I'm sick of this unhappy wind," Leyla said. "How can a person concentrate on important stuff when it's being so noisy and grumpy."

Unhappy wind. Trust a poet to sum it up better than the rest of us. "Chief, what if we talk to the wind? Tell it we're travelers moving through its land and that we won't hurt it?"

Chief Roy and Matwau stared at me as if I had lost my mind. Maybe I had.

Atian snorted. "You've got to be kidding."

I jumped out of my cushion seat and stared the three of them down. "Have you guys got any better ideas? Well, do you?"

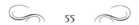

Chief Roy grinned and threw up his hands. "Let's give it a try, then. Nothing to lose. Roswell, open the comm." He pointed to me. "You're up, dreamcatcher."

Stepped in it, I did, but the chief was right. What did we have to lose?

Oh mighty wind, we mean you no harm. Guide us through your land, and we shall be on our way. Grant us passage and our gratefulness will last for all time.

Nothing.

Oh mighty wind, allow us free passage. We beseech you in Great Manitou's name.

The wind slowly died down.

Atian whistled. "Well, I'm impressed."

He sidled over and his hand touched mine. Goosebumps rose on my arm. His dark eyes gazed at me with an expression I hadn't seen in a long time. I had to tame a supernatural wind before he liked me again?

"Biopod, release your spikes, but maintain your armor," the chief said.

The biopod wiggled and shimmied out of our sandy tomb. Back on the surface, the pod shook like a wet dog and shed the sand. Calm, though still greenish, landscape greeted us.

Oh mighty wind, we thank you for your kindness. The Rainbow Warriors take your message with us.

Chief Roy glanced at me, a question and a twinkle in his eye. "A dreamer you shall be, Halerine Ananda. Thank you for your wisdom."

Roswell woke up the console. "Move out bio, before the wind changes its mind."

The Sky Beings flittered away. Good. I'd had enough of their games.

I curled up in my cushion, but my mind refused to sleep. What other dangers would we face if even the wind wanted to stop us?

Chapter Four

THE DARK TOWER

I had my answer soon enough. A half-finished tower, black as midnight, loomed over the weed-infested highway. A bevy of transports and neo-gliders flew equipment and beams up to gigantic cranes parked on the upper sections of the tower.

"Well, I'll be darned. Never thought I'd see another one of those behemoths," Chief Roy said.

I swallowed, but my mouth tasted like sand. Time to fess up. "Uh chief, I need to tell you something. We met a guy named General Cardiff in the tower back home."

Chief Roy frowned, his bushy eyebrows nearly touching. That was never a good sign.

"Perhaps we should have a little chat, Halerine Ananda."

In fits and starts, and with Matwau and Atian's help, I recounted our run-in with the general. "So that's the whole, creepy story."

"You say hundreds of towers are located all over the world?"

"According to the map in the Elk tower, yes."

He conferred with his bio-comm. "Nothing on record. They must have waited until civilization pretty much collapsed before they started on the towers. But I'm still thinking they're nothing more than communications links and depots. The real Ark, the one you viewed on the holo, is waiting for those villains to go a ground."

Roswell opened his comm. "We're getting close, chief. Should I look for a detour?"

Yes! My heart squeezed in my chest, and my dreamcatcher weighed heavily around my neck. "Please chief, find another route before it's too late."

"No, we'll keep going for a spell, see what happens."

A chill ran up my back, and I shivered. "See what happens? Chief, they're genocidal maniacs. They tried to kill us. The Arkers want us all dead. Cardiff said so himself. They're planning to make sure no one survives Turmoil except for them. Rich people always had plans to save themselves. The rest of us be damned."

"Hey now, Halerine Ananda, I'm betting nobody will notice our passing by."

I shivered again. Find another way, find another way, I beg you, kept repeating in my head.

"Chief, we had a run-in with tower creeps on our way to Elk Ridge. They're slavers. They use people for fodder, and they don't care what happens to the likes of us."

Matwau's voice cracked and a tortured expression flitted across his face before he had time to rearrange his features in their usual sardonic pose. Something very bad had gone down on their journey to Elk Ridge. Something that hurt him deeply.

The tower loomed over the highway. Lights flashed up and down one of the tripods. The other two stayed dark. But my skin crawled. Eyes were on us, red bulbous eyes.

Leyla sidled over and took my hand. "Hali, I'm not liking this one bit."

"Me neither."

The biopod jerked to a stop, and I flew off my seat and landed on Tomko. Matwau landed beside us, his sandwich squished against his chest.

"Oomph, get off us Hali, you're heavy."

I picked myself up and dusted off crumbs from Matwau's sandwich.

Chief Roy called the control pod. "What happened, Roswell?"

"Nothing. The road's clear but the biopod's stuck, and she ain't budging."

"Open the airlock."

Chief Roy donned his biosuit and breather, then stepped through the airlock and walked a short way up the road.

Atian came to stand by me and rested his warm hand on my shoulder. "So far so good."

Suddenly, the chief jumped back and clutched his chest.

Atian opened his comm. "Chief, are you okay?"

The chief staggered back to the biopod, still holding his chest, and crawled through the airlock. A faint burning odor surrounded him, and black singe marks crisscrossed his suit. "Some sort of barrier darn near ripped out my innards."

I set his cushion to monitoring mode. "Let me check you over."

The cushion enveloped him in a sheen. A monitor beeped and an alarm rang. The chief's heart was out of rhythm. I pulled an oxy-mask out of the cushion and strapped it to his face. "Lie back and try to relax. Take slow, deep breaths."

He closed his eyes and breathed slowly. His heart rate steadied, and the cushion eased off.

Atian checked the screen. "Turn around, Roswell, we'll find another way. This barrier, whatever it is, can't go on forever."

Roswell coded the biopod, but Matwau pointed to the screen. "Too late."

A neo-glider landed on the road behind us and blocked our retreat. Militia men jumped out of the glider and surrounded the biopod. A drone swooped in, its beady red eye whirling. In a mechanical monotone, the drone said, "You are under arrest for trespassing on federation land. Follow our commands and you will not be harmed."

"So what do we do now, chief?" Atian said.

Chief Roy pushed away the cushion monitor. "Can't see that we have much choice, lad. We'll play along."

I leaned back in my cushion and held my cramping stomach. Visions of General Cardiff's cold eyes haunted me.

The leader of the militia motioned the biopod forward, and this time the invisible barrier did not hold us back.

The chief aimed his bio-comm at the militiaman. "He's using some kind of blocker that's holding back the barrier long enough for us to get through."

We parked in the shadow of the tower. The humming from the tripod reverberated through the air and sent chills running up and down my spine.

Leyla and Etta clung to each other. "H-Hali?"

I hugged them both. "Breathe easy, kids, they won't hurt us." A little lie. General Cardiff had no qualms about sending the AIs after us back home.

The drone zoomed into the viewer's range and beeped. "Step out of the pod with your hands up."

Chief Roy glanced at me. "I'm sorry, Halerine Ananda." He led the way, and we trudged behind him.

The militiamen stirred and talked among themselves when we stepped out of the biopod.

One of the men hawked and spit. "Fresh meat."

The hair on Wolf's back stood up. He crouched and growled at the militiamen.

The same man raised his laser and took aim at Wolf.

What kind of a monster would shoot a dog? I stepped in front of Wolf. "Run Wolf, and don't come back!"

The laser beam grazed his tail, but Wolf dashed around a slider and disappeared.

The leader of the militia approached us. He had a guy-next-door face. How could he do this?

"My name is Corporal Haskins. You are trespassing on federation land, and that's a capital offense."

Matwau snorted. "Corporal? Federal land? Come on, chief, these guys are opportunists. There's no federation anything, and there's no military."

I pulled on Matwau's sleeve. "Be quiet, do you want to get us killed?"

Corporal Haskins stared at Matwau, a question in his eyes, then motioned with his laser. "Let's go."

We followed the corporal into the tower. The plush interior smelled antiseptic clean, but banging and grinding from the construction above shattered the calm.

Benji's mouth dropped open. "Whoa, a computer what still works."

A slight smile touched the corporal's lips. "Much more than a computer, kid." He waved his hand over the screen, and a holo-game floated above the boys.

They stared up, mouths gaping.

"You kids can use the holo while we grown-ups have a little chat. Sergeant, scrounge up some juice and snacks for the kiddies."

The sergeant frowned "But sir?"

"Just do it. They deserve that much."

The hairs on the back of my neck stood up at the corporal's words. We deserved that much, why? What were they going to do to us? The story of Hanzel and Gretel reared its ugly head in my buzzing mind.

The corporal spoke into his comm. "We've got them, general."

I stiffened. I knew it, the general was behind this.

"About two dozen kids and six grown-ups." He glanced at me. "Yes sir."

He covered the comm. "Are you the girl who broke into the Ark on the Siksiká refugium?"

No use lying. I nodded.

"Yes, general she's here, along with her cohorts and three old-timers." He paused and his face darkened. "Yes sir, I understand."

Oh, this was so not good.

He closed the comm, and a frown creased his forehead. "I'm sorry, but I'm under orders to confiscate your biopod. It's military property now and so are the kiddies."

Chief Roy crossed his arms and scowled. "We are on a mission to take these children to safety, and it doesn't involve interference from the likes of you."

A strange light flickered in the corporal's eyes. Was a Sky Being hiding inside him?

"Safety? There's no such thing anymore."

"These children are nobody's property, they're children, and you bloody well know it."

The corporal jabbed his finger in Chief Roy's chest. "Listen chief, I've got the fire and the power. If General Cardiff says these kids are his, then these kids are his, regardless of what you or I think."

"What does this general want with the children?"

Matwau hissed. "New slaves."

Haskins waved his laser at us. "Take a seat while we figure out how this is going down."

The boys barely looked up when we entered the lounge. They were half way through a hundred levels of a Terminator game. Fake lasers flew through the air, and vibrations from explosions and air sirens shook the room.

Benji stuffed potato chips in his mouth and waved his laser at robots threatening civilization, all at the same time.

"This is way cool. I want to spend the rest of my life eating potato chips and playing holos."

Councilor Sereida covered her ears. "How do they know what to do? They've never played these games."

Chief Roy helped himself to some of the chips and sprawled on a blue massage lounger. Etta crawled onto his lap and sucked her thumb. "I'm of the opinion kids are born with computing chips in their brains, just never got to use them until the computer age." He groaned as the massager swept over his back. "Oh, that feels so good."

I touched my fingertip to a screen, and it sprang to life. Images of online magazines floated across the viewer. I chose a Teen Pop magazine dated 2042, just before the water wars. Before everything went to hell. I ignored the tiny voice in my head scolding me for falling prey to stereotypical girlie stuff. So what, I told that voice, I could be dead in an hour.

Corporal Haskins startled me out of a fashion daze.

He and half a dozen men with lasers surrounded us. "Fun's over, kiddies, time for your shift."

That strange look was back in the corporal's eyes.

Just as I feared, we were being fattened before the feast.

Chief Roy faced Haskins. "Corporal, you're condemning these innocent children to slavery."

The corporal scowled. "Just following orders."

"That pathetic excuse has been used in defense of inexcusable atrocities for centuries."

Corporal Haskins frowned. "Hold tight, chief."

We stepped out of the tower and a blast of hot air hit us. The militiamen herded us toward a quarry.

Atian glanced at me, a sick look on his face.

Corporal Haskins put out his hand and stopped me. "The general has requested your presence, miss. I'll collect you later."

Chief Roy stepped in front of me. "Corporal, Halerine Ananda is part of our family. She's not going anywhere with you."

Atian joined him. He put his arm around my shoulders and for a brief moment, I leaned into him.

The corporal whistled and his militiamen surrounded us. "Get this through your thick skull, chief. We're under the general's command."

"And what are your plans for the councilors and me?"

Haskins shrugged. "For now, you and the old ladies can wait in the biopod."

He mustn't know about Roswell. How could we use that to our advantage?

Haskins led us to a cramped pen beside the quarry. Dozens of emaciated children, some as young as Etta, huddled on the shady side of the pen. A few of the children sobbed, but none of them glanced up.

Haskins opened the cage and pushed us in. "Acquaint yourself with all the trappings in your new home. I'll be back in ten minutes for your first shift."

The cage held little of comfort, just bare ground and a reeking shed in the far corner for an obvious purpose.

We sat apart from the other children. Etta snuggled in between Leyla and Willow. She sniffled and sucked on her thumb. "I want my mama."

Benji's lower lip trembled, and he hiccupped. "Hali, I don't want to be a slave." He clutched a packet of pretzels to his chest.

I folded him in my arms and kissed the top of his head. "We'll get out of this mess. Don't give up." Would we? My doubts were building with each passing minute. I wanted out of this world, away from towers, creepy generals, and dead things. Maybe Maniton was not such a bad idea.

Atian scuffed his worn shoes on the gravel-covered ground. "We're breaking out of this joint."

Matwau frowned. "Oh yeah, and how are we gonna do that, genius?"

"Remember what Storyteller said. We're the Rainbow Warriors, not the general's slaves. We'll wait until dark then make our move."

Corporal Haskins reappeared and banged his baton against the cage bars. "Shift change."

The slave children groaned and crawled to their feet. Except for one child who did not move. The corporal signaled his men, and they dragged away the tiny body.

We followed the other children through the winding construction site, past bottomless pits without protective barriers and steel beams whizzing overhead on questionable pulleys. We dodged heavy equipment dumping loads of cement into casings and welders' sparks flying through the air. Leyla bent over in a coughing fit when a truck belched diesel fumes. The place was a veritable death trap.

The slave children staggered toward the quarry, their feet wide apart to keep from falling. My heart ached for them. How could their worn-out little bodies work for hours in this soul-sucking heat?

We entered the dusty quarry loaded with rock rubble and boulders piled beneath a cliff. My vision blurred for a second, and I watched the cliff collapse on slave children. I shuddered. Please Apistotoke, let it not be a future-dream.

A bald-headed overseer with massive shoulders and arms covered in tattoos waved a laser whip at us. "Get to your stations!"

The slave-children shuffled away, their backs hunched against the overseer's ready lash. He studied us, an evil grin plastered across his bloated face. "New recruits, I see." He flashed his laser. "Listen up newbies. From now on, you do as I say. No back talk, no slagging. Understand?"

No one moved.

A laser beam sliced the ground and narrowly missed Tomko's pink sneakers. Zie danced away.

"Understand?"

"Y-yes sir," we said in unison.

"Good, now pair up with a slave and learn your work."

The laser whip slashed the air and seared the cuff on Benji's jean shorts. "Move it!"

The overseer turned to the boys and I. "You big ones?" He pointed to a rock crusher lurking on the other side of the quarry. "Feed that hungry beast, and don't be slow about it, or you'll be its next meal."

Corporal Haskins stopped me. "The general's ready for you."

I glanced at Atian and Matwau, certain my face reflected the fear on their faces.

Haskins led me into the tower. We climbed eight flights of stairs, and by the time we reached the zenith, I was huffing.

Haskins took a deep breath. "Sorry, the lift won't be functional this high for a spell."

What a strange man. One minute he was herding slave children to their certain death, the next he was apologizing for the lack of an elevator.

He waved a flicker door open and led me inside.

I gaped at the luxurious apartment. Muted lights cast shadows on the mauve walls, and soft music hummed in the background. Whiffs of lilac wafted through the room. A bed the size of my room back home took up one corner of the room. Its golden satin comforter gleamed in the dim light. I gulped.

The general was standing in the shadows near a well-stocked bar. "Well, Miss Blackfoot, so nice to see you again."

The corporal backed out of the room, but not before a flash of pity crossed his face.

I clenched my jaw and faced the general. "What do you want?"

Cardiff's brows knitted. "My, my, that's no way to greet your savior."

"Savior? Don't you mean kidnapper?"

He grinned. "You sure are spunky. An interesting quality in this day and age. I'm tired of pathetic weaklings groveling at my feet."

I crossed my arms. "Well, you'll be relieved to hear I don't grovel."

"I never doubted it."

He handed me a wine glass half full of yellowish liquid. I sniffed it.

He clinked his glass with mine. "It's wine, chardonnay reserve 2036. We saved some of the finest wine left on this godforsaken continent before the wineries burned to a crisp."

"What do you want?"

"Why your sweet company, of course."

I laughed.

He frowned. "You do realize you won't last a month in the quarry. Up here you'll live in the lap of luxury."

"Not interested."

He moved closer and pulled out a short dagger. I flinched, but with a flick of his wrist he slit the band holding my hair up and it cascaded down my back. Great, my last hair band.

"Magnificent."

He pulled me into his arms and ran his pudgy finger down my cheek. I turned away from his fetid breath.

"This is your last chance for salvation."

Okay enough. I pushed him away. "Until you tire of me and then you'll toss me into the quarry. I'll take my chances with my friends."

His grip tightened on my arms. "I could insist, you know."

Could I talk my way out of this jam? "General, I didn't take you for a man who would force a young girl. Surely there are many women who would be happy to share your bed, you being such an attractive, powerful man." The words tasted bitter in my mouth, but they worked.

Cardiff studied me for a long moment, then tipped his wine glass at me. "Very well, I won't bestow my favors on an unwilling participant."

Well, that was a relief. At least he wasn't a rapist.

He chugged his wine and opened the door. "Corporal Haskins, you may take this ungrateful creature back to her friends, and make sure she works a full shift."

Halfway down the stairs, Corporal Haskins stopped and squeezed my arm. "Good for you."

We loaded rocks on the deafening conveyor belt for six hours, and we would have worked longer if not for a vicious windstorm sweeping over the prairie. The wind picked up loose stones, and the swirling sand turned the air brown and sucked out the oxygen.

I tasted grit in my teeth and pulled my breather over my nose and mouth. "Atian, Matwau, where are you, I can't see you!"

The conveyor belt ground to a halt, and thick oil oozed out of the grisly machine.

Matwau grabbed me by the scruff of the neck and pulled me close. "Sand got into the bearings and seized the machine."

"Where's Atian?"

Atian reached for my hand. "I'm here, Hali." He shouted in my ear. "We have to find shelter, this is gonna get really bad!"

We clung to each other in the fierce wind, and like old people. we bent over and pushed against the knife-like sand.

We made our way across the quarry and joined the other children huddled against a pile of rocks.

Metal screeched and a piece of yellow siding tore off a nearby shed. It flew straight for the overseer. He ducked but not before a sharp edge shaved off his right ear. He howled and danced around as blood spurted across the dusty ground.

A boy, no more than ten, snickered at the show. The overseer whirled on him and shot the child in the forehead. The little boy fell to the ground, a beatific smile on his face.

I checked for a pulse. None.

Matwau sighed and turned away. "No more worries for that poor kid."

The wounded overseer staggered toward a shack with a red and white cross painted on the side. He waved at one of the guards. "Get the slaves back to their pens! They'll work double shifts tomorrow."

The guards herded us back to the pen.

"Protect the kids, this sand can rip off their skin!" Matwau said above the howling wind.

We formed a tent over the children with our bodies. The sand pelted us, like tiny knives cutting into our body. Before long we were covered in bloody pricks that grew larger as the sand beat on us. I bit my tongue to keep from crying out with each skin prick.

The storm raged until the sun dropped below the horizon. Then the fierce winds disappeared into the clouds.

I bathed our wounds with fetid water from a pail near the latrine. If we ever got out of this mess we would need polymers to stave off infection.

"Thank you," one of the little girls said. Her sunken eyes gazed at me, and she reached out to touch my arm. "My mama." She sighed and closed her eyes for the last time.

I brushed away my tears.

Matwau handed me a semi-clean handkerchief. "I'm sorry, Hali. These kids don't deserve this."

That night, a guard shoved bread and water through a small opening in the pen. The starving kids dashed for the food, but we were too tired to move.

Atian hunkered down for a nap. "When everyone is asleep, it's over the fence we go."

A crack and sizzle pulled me out of an exhausted stupor. The bars on the cage sparkled and hissed, and an ominous hum encircled us. The kids scrambled away from the sides of the cage. Shocks slithered up my legs, and I moved closer to Atian.

Matwau pulled on his boots. "We need another plan. They've charged the cage."

My mind retreated to some dim place in the past, a place where slavers and poisonous air did not exist.

"Psst, psst."

A weak light danced in the night air. "Who's there?"

A disembodied voice said, "Come with me if you want to live."

We crawled through the dark to the far side of the pen. Corporal Haskins flashed his white teeth in a weak grin. "Always wanted to say that."

One of his men tapped a gizmo against the gate and it opened. I counted Siksiká children as they scurried out of the pen.

"Hide in the pod. We'll take you out tomorrow at dawn."

"But what about the other children?" I said.

He clenched his jaw. "If we free them, Cardiff will catch more kids to take their place. I'm trying to save the ones who have a chance. Those kids are goners in a week at best."

Goners. How could innocent children be goners? But my choice was clear. Save my own or risk everything, but their hopeless faces would haunt me forever. I paused outside the biopod. "Wolf, where are you?"

Wolf tore around the other side of the biopod and wagged his tail. "Woof!"

I tussled with him. "Good dog, in you go. You must be starving."

Chief Roy's weathered face broke into a smile when we slipped through the airlock. "I'm mighty relieved to see you rascals."

"Corporal Haskins set us free. He's taking us out tomorrow morning."

"Hmm, interesting man."

Without a murmur, the weary children headed for the showers and bed. Even Benji staggered past me, muttering something about bugs in his hair.

Dawn could not come fast enough.

The pinkish sun peeked over the murky horizon as we followed a military skimmer down the broken highway. Another skimmer trailed behind us, and a neo-glider hovered overhead.

Chief Roy studied the monitor. "We're almost home free, kids."

No sooner were the words out of his mouth, and we took fire. A gray skimmer zoomed into view, firing at the biopod and our escorts. Cardiff!

No no ooh-ee

"Biopod, shields up and into the ditch."

The pod slipped into a deep irrigation ditch beside the road. She raised her armor and cowered under loose brush as the battle raged over us.

The military skimmer behind us opened fire on the rogue skimmer, while the neo-glider whizzed in and out of its path. They outmaneuvered the enemy skimmer, and a final volley of laser fire burst it into flames. It spiraled out of control and crashed in a field.

The boys cheered and clapped their hands. "Yay!"

The skimmer behind us and the neo-glider zipped away, and the lead skimmer detoured down an overgrown side road.

"Follow the skimmer, biopod," Roswell said.

Inside an abandoned village, the skimmer stopped and Corporal Haskins stepped out.

"Roswell, be ready to shield this tug if things turn bad," Chief Roy said.

My stomach churned. Why would Corporal Haskins let us go, only to wipe us out?

Leyla slipped into my arms. "Are we gonna be slaves again?"

"No sweetie, you're safe now." Lying to the kids was becoming a bad habit.

Corporal Haskins approached the biopod. Sky Beings fluttered around him, but he appeared not to notice.

The chief opened the comm. "Corporal?"

"Chief Roy, take the next left, and you'll find a gap in the barrier. I can't hold it open for long so don't dawdle. Ten klicks up, turn back on the highway and be on your way."

The chief heaved a sigh. "Thank you, Corporal Haskins. We owe you our lives."

The corporal gazed into the distance, and a haunted look crossed his face. "Can't stand any more death, especially not young ones. Lost my own two years back. No more."

"What about you? Won't the general be after your hide?"

The corporal managed a feeble grin. "My men and I are heading west, away from this madness. We're smart enough to know the general isn't planning on inviting us on his little adventure."

"I wish you good luck, sir." Chief Roy hesitated. "The general?"

"Don't worry about him, we'll keep an eye on his comings and goings and do our best to hold him off."

The chief closed the comm and set the camouflage. "Roswell, take us out."

Chief Roy's words should have made me feel better. We were free again, but take us out where? I wasn't naïve enough to believe Cardiff would let us go peacefully. And who or what else was waiting in the wilderness?

I pushed down my fears and snuggled Leyla into the cushion. "Let's take a little nap, sweet girl."

A yellow sheen enveloped us. The seat checked our vital signs, then lowered our body temps to sleep mode. The Beatles' *All You Need is Love* hummed inside the seat, and a sweet mist oozed out of the seat.

Leyla snuggled close. "Hali, I smell mama."

"Me too." Sometimes a bit of tech wasn't such a bad idea. I fell asleep dreaming of home and my mother's rose water.

Chapter Five

BADLAND BANDITS

I woke to a loud bang, and the biopod slid to a stop. Now what? Why did every sleep end in a crisis?

Ooh ah, ooh ah ah

Roswell threw up his hands. "That's it folks, the jets on sphere six are done for. She won't budge another inch." He checked the sat-maps. "I'll head into Westlock for parts." He frowned. "If'n they gots any."

Chief Roy's good eye turned inward, and he consulted his bio-comm. "Appears there's a transport depot in Westlock, you stand a good chance, old friend."

"I'll go with you, Roswell, you might need my help carrying stuff," Atian said.

He climbed into a blue biosuit resembling an old-fashioned diver's suit. The suit's internal life support swung into action and sent clean oxygen flowing through it. He took a deep breath. "Ah, that feels so good."

The farther south we traveled, the thicker the goop. As of yesterday, no one was allowed out of the biopod without a suit. I sealed Atian's breather and snapped the fittings in place. "Don't take it off."

His eyes twinkled. "I wasn't planning to."

Chief Roy scanned the horizon and handed Atian a water kit. "Temp's rising, but the wind's steady. Be vigilant, lad."

Needles of unease prickled the back of my mind. This was so not good. "Take Wolf along, in case of trouble."

I slipped Wolf's mask over his head and waited for a snarky comment from Atian, but he only sent me an inscrutable look, then he followed Roswell through the airlock. The three of them boarded the bio's glider and zoomed away.

Tomko pulled on Chief Roy's sleeve and smiled sweetly. "Can we explore or something? Our tush is sore from sitting so long."

The chief shook his head. "Sorry lad, much as I'd enjoy you scallywags out of my hair for a spell, you're staying put." At their disappointed groans, he grinned. "How about a game of chance? I'll spot you ten cookies."

Benji jumped up and down. "Yeah, Mexican train!"

Leyla's lower lip morphed into a major pout. "I wanna play Mex-train, too. How come boys get all the fun?"

I tucked in her lip. "You can play, sweetie, Mexican train isn't a boy's game." I fixed the boys with the evil eye, and they gave in without a whimper.

Leyla ran for the board. Back in a minute, she set up the game. "Okay, each of you gets seven dom-noes and no cheating."

"Ah, she's gonna boss us," Benji said. "I don't like playing games with goils."

Chief Roy grunted. "That'll change."

I wandered through the biopod and picked up scattered clothing in the boys' sleeper. The air in their sleeper reminded me of the gym in our old school. "Bio, air fresh, please. Double dose." I chased a wayward roll of toilet paper into their bathroom and tossed their grimy bath towels in the refresher. I patted the appliance. "Good luck."

The generator in the storage pod was humming along and keeping the cache cool so at least that wasn't a problem. I pushed a feedstock box over the hatch, turned, and bumped into Matwau.

"What are you doing, Hali?"

My heart thumped in my chest. "Gosh, you scared me. I'm straightening up, why?"

He shrugged. "No reason."

How much had he seen? He was studying me, a deadpan expression on his face.

"Your kiddies are raising a ruckus."

What now? "They're not my kiddies."

"Well, the old ladies are asleep, and the chief's nowhere to be found, so you're up."

"And you couldn't do anything?" I pushed him aside and hurried into the lounge pod.

"Hey you putz, quit farting!" Tomko said.

"Wasn't me," Keme said. "Benji did it."

Leyla tossed down her last domino. "I'm out."

Benji slapped his forehead. "A goil beat us, we're pathetic."

Leyla grinned and bit into a chocolate chip cookie.

"Sweetie, wouldn't it be nice if you shared your cookies with the boys?" I said.

She took another dainty bite. "Nope."

Etta pulled on my tunic and pointed to the screen. "Hali, I'm seeing Atian and he looks messed up. Chief Roy's helpin' him."

Atian was leaning against the chief. Blood oozed out of a tear in the right side of his biosuit, and he was limping more than usual. Scrambling into my suit, I hurried outside. Wolf was jumping up and down and barking through his mask, and Raven screeched overhead. "Quiet Wolf! What happened?"

"Thugs jumped us when we left the depot. They stabbed Roswell and stole the glider."

"Is Roswell dead?"

Atian shrugged, then winced. "Maybe, I don't know."

"How'd you get away?"

"I fought off a goon the size of a bear, and Wolf crunched his leg, otherwise I'd be a goner." He held up two yellow jet packs. "But I saved the packs."

"Roswell might be dead or badly hurt and you're prattling on about a jet pack?"

Chief Roy held up his hand. "Hey now, Halerine Ananda, we need these packs. Atian might have saved our bacon."

Behind the chief's back, I stuck out my tongue. Childish, but the look on Atian's face was worth it. Then his eyes flickered, and he sank to his knees and sprawled on the ground.

"Atian!"

I unzipped his biosuit and lifted his torn t-shirt away from the wound. "Oh no."

"How bad is it?" Chief Roy said.

A deep gash ran along his right side. "Bad enough."

A cloud of black flies honed in on his blood. I swatted them away, but they swarmed him. "Let's move him inside before flies infect the wound."

Councilor Ore lowered a table from its perch on the ceiling, and we placed Atian on it.

"Benji, fetch my pack and the medi-kit. Tomko, I need hot water."

The boys scrambled to do my bidding. No sass for a change.

"Leyla, you and Willow bring me hand towels, lots of them, and not from the boys' bathroom."

Chief Roy and Matwau tugged the biosuit off Atian, and I doused his wound with disinfectant. That woke him up.

"Hey! What're you trying to do? Kill me?"

"I'm saving your ungrateful hide." I hid my shaking hands. "Seems you'll do anything to win an argument."

Atian scowled and tried sitting up.

I pushed him down. "Oh no, you're not moving." I dug a long, thin needle out of the kit and made a show of threading it. What I wouldn't do for a surgical stapler.

Atian's eyes widened. "Get that needle away from me, Hali. Nobody's sticking me."

"Don't be such a baby. You've got a hole the size of Etta's fist in your side. You need stitching up."

Etta slipped her fingers into Atian's hand. "It'll only hurt a little bit, Atian. Be brave, Hali's fixing you."

Councilor Ore grasped his shoulders.

"Keep him still, auntie. I wouldn't want to stitch the wrong hole."

"Very funny." He gritted his teeth. "Get it over with, then."

He blanched when I pulled the first stitch through. I kept up a running litany, all the while pulling stitches through his soft, warm skin. "You're one lucky puppy, you know. A couple inches higher and we'd be burying you right now."

Beads of sweat peppered his forehead by the time I finished. I dug moss and herbs out of my pack, mulched them, and slapped the green goop on his wound, then wrapped gauze around his side. Atian gazed at me as I worked, and my stomach tightened. What was he thinking?

He reached out and almost touched my hair, then pulled back. "You don't give anything away, do you Hali?"

Could he hear my heart beating? Did he feel what I felt? "I—"

Chief Roy put a hand on my quivering shoulder. "If you're finished doctoring Atian, let's make camp, then we'll be needing a little pow wow."

"Biopod, make camp," Councilor Sereida said.

The bulky pod slowly curled into a circle and lowered its carcass to the ground.

Ooh-ee, uh uh, ooh-ee.

An air-tight canopy slid over the center opening. The biopod's filters sucked out the poisons from the air and blue, pink, and yellow lights shimmered on its skin.

Chief Roy held open the airlock. "Okay troops, out you go."

The children burst through the airlock and ran around the cozy enclosure. "Yay!"

Tomko brandished a stick and skipped across the clearing. "We're Princess Leia, ready to slew you!"

Benji pulled his lips apart in a grotesque grimace. He chased Leyla. "I'm Horned Snake, and I'm gonna eat you."

Leyla covered her face with her hands. "Eeek, somebody save me!"

Etta hid behind Willow. "Me too! Save me from the monsters."

Willow grabbed Leyla and Etta's arms. "Those silly boys don't scare me none, let's get them."

The girls turned and chased the boys around the circle. "We're helamonsters!"

Leyla roared like she imagined a helamonster roared.

"Let them wear off all that energy, maybe we'll enjoy some peace tonight," Councilor Ore said.

Councilor Sereida grinned. "First time all day they've shown any spunk, poor little tykes."

Chief Roy helped Atian into a lounger and wrapped him in a Plains blanket depicting Sky Beings. We all owned Plains blankets. My grandmother began weaving my red and black Horse blanket the day I was born. The blanket was my only memento of Honey. Chief Roy guarded his Circle of Life Elder blanket and wouldn't let any of us near it with our grubby fingers.

"So what do we do now, chief?" Atian said.

The chief raised an eyebrow. "We? You're staying put, young man."

Atian's face darkened. "You can't rescue Roswell without me."

I blinked and put on an innocent face. "Why not? We've got Matwau, and the chief, the councilors, and me—oh and Wolf."

Atian guffawed. "Two light weights and three geriatrics. Wolf is Roswell's only hope."

Chief Roy grinned. "Hey, who you calling a light weight?"

"Yeah, I changed your pants and taught you how to fish, young man," Councilor Ore said. "And I recall whopping you at just about everything, and I can do it again if I set my mind to it."

"What? Change his pants?" Matwau said.

We laughed.

Atian sent murderous looks our way. "You know what I mean."

"I stitched you up using old-fashioned thread. If you move around, the stitches will rip and your guts will fall out."

"Don't be such a drama queen."

"Care to find out?"

Chief Roy bit into a strip of synthesized elk jerky. "Enough you two. We'll manage without you, lad. Besides we need a semi-adult caring for the kiddies."

"So I'm reduced to babysitting?"

I grinned. "They'll probably end up taking care of you."

Chief Roy rubbed his hands together and hitched up his baggy pants. "Right, now down to business, do you know where they took Roswell?"

Atian shrugged, then winced. "They dragged him behind the depot. I didn't see him again."

"Was his suit intact? Was he alive?"

"Far as I know."

"I'm thinking we can't wait for dark, let's be off," Chief Roy said.

Matwau ran his hands through his blue hair rolls. "But we don't have any weapons or a real plan."

The chief grinned. "We'll improvise."

Matwau rolled his eyes and headed for the storage pod. When he returned with our suits his breath reeked of liquor. Now wasn't the time to chew him out, but just wait.

We donned our biosuits and slipped out of the pod's side door without the children noticing.

Walking across the flat prairie at ground level was different from riding high in the biopod. Layers of pollution floated close to the surface, at times so thick we waved our arms to part it, and with little to stop it, the wind swirled around us and mixed with the pollutants. Leyla was right. The wind was unhappy. Hell, the whole land was unhappy.

Matwau pulled out his hand drum and tapped it softly. He glanced my way. "It might help, the land needs it."

Councilor Ore upped her suit filtrator. "Bless me, it's filthy out here,"

Chief Roy batted away a puff of guck. "*Aa*. Sulphur and ammonia."

I crouched beside Wolf. "Show us the way, boy."

Wolf barked and set off at a brisk pace down the cracked and weed-infested highway. Matwau and I kept up, but the geriatrics soon lagged behind.

Chief Roy leaned over his legs and gasped for air. "Keep going, we'll catch up."

We jogged across a barren field. Matwau kept glancing at the sky. "What are you looking for?"

"Neo-gliders."

"Why?"

He remained silent for a long minute then shrugged. "An old habit. Back at Duck Mountain I took out a lot of heavy equipment. They tracked me for quite a while. Open spaces like this still make me nervous."

"But Cardiff has had you in his clutches twice now, and he didn't go after you."

He grinned. "He never saw me do the deed. None of those guys did."

I hesitated then plunged on. "What happened on the trek to Elk Ridge, Mat? And don't say nothing. I see it in your eyes, hear it in your voice."

"I'll tell you when I'm ready."

The strain in his voice tore at me. "I'll wait."

Half an hour later, we crouched behind a burned-out truck on the outskirts of the deserted town.

"Badlands ghost town," Matwau muttered. "Saw enough of those on our way to Elk Ridge."

We jumped at a shrill cry. Raven landed on the truck's cab and fluttered his feathers. My throat tightened. A warning from the Sky Beings?

Matwau waved his arms. "Shoo. You'll give us away."

Raven screeched and flew away, his powerful wings beating a path through the thick smog. How did he breathe in all that guck?

"See anybody?"

"Yeah, one waster. He's patrolling the street."

I peeked over the truck box. A man with stringy black hair and over-sized work boots shambled down the street. A bandana covered his nose and mouth, and he held an old hunting rifle over his right shoulder.

"When he gets to this end of the street, we'll take him out."

"I suppose you want me to play decoy again."

He grinned and my heart lurched. Matwau? Get real. Not with his issues. He wasn't even that good looking.

"Hadn't occurred to me, but now that you mention it."

The guard sauntered over to the truck, and I prepared to do my sexy thing, but stopped at the sound of water falling into a puddle. I covered my mouth to hold back a giggle. The guy was peeing against the truck tire.

His last pee, it turned out. Matwau grabbed him in a chokehold, and the guy went down.

I peered at the prone body. "Is he dead?"

"Hope so."

"How can you say that so easily? You just killed a man."

He grinned and reached for the rifle. "Must be my nasty Cree blood."

I stopped his arm. "No, Mat. Chief Roy said no guns, remember?

He frowned, but left the rifle on the ground. "Means we're sitting ducks. Guess I'll have to use my razor-sharp wits."

We ran across the yard, dodging scrap metal, chunks of broken cement, and a shattered street light. A rusty tractor squatted at the end of the street, the tires long since pilfered, but the wreck made for good cover.

Matwau pointed to a drab gray quonset. Scorch lines from a fire marred one side of the depot, and it leaned to the left at a precarious angle. Any day now the whole thing would tumble to the ground.

"That's where they took Roswell, I'm betting." He peeked around the corner. "Coast's clear."

We slid along the wall until we found a door. The rusty hinges screeched when Matwau pushed the door open. All but the dead heard that one.

The light inside the shop came from feeble sunrays slipping through the holes in the roof. Birds in the rafters flapped their wings and searched for a way out of the dingy building. Or were they Sky Beings, here for a show?

Matwau scowled. "Wish I had chief's comm light."

Boxes with crude labels lay scattered around the hollow depot, some overflowing with electronics and appliances, others held rolls of credits and stacks of old-fashioned cash.

A malnourished rat scurried under one of the boxes, and I shuddered. "Compu-coms, toasters, synthesizers, what would they need with any of this stuff? Power grid's long gone. And money, how crazy is that?"

Matwau shrugged. "Doesn't seem to matter to them. They're looters, and this is their stash."

Chief Roy had warned us about gangs of men roaming the badlands and stealing whatever they found even if it was useless. Hoarder mentality.

"I see our glider," Matwau said.

Sure enough the flying skateboard leaned against a wall, the yellow ready light beeping.

"Roswell, are you in here?" Matwau whispered.

"Oh-h-h."

"Roswell?"

"Over here."

We followed the groans and nearly tripped over Roswell's feet in the dim light.

Matwau crouched beside him. "Easy fella. We'll have you out of here in no time."

"Might be a bit harder than you think, Indian."

I whirled around. "Who said that?"

An evil cackle echoed through the depot. Someone struck a match and lit a kerosene lamp.

A gang of gaunt men covered in grime and dressed in shabby orange jumpsuits surrounded us. None of them wore breathers.

A tall, slovenly man sporting a crooked nose and a jagged scar running across his cheek and over his right eye, stepped into the light. "Well, well, what do we have here? A young buck."

The tall man sauntered over and yanked on my braid. "And a girlie-squaw."

I jumped away.

The men laughed.

"Touchy, ain't you girlie-squaw?"

The tall man's mouth turned nasty, and his right eye twitched. He grabbed me by the neck and squeezed. "Get this straight, squaw, you be my property now, like these here boxes of loot, and you'll do what I say, understood?"

I said nothing, but that only infuriated him. His greasy thumb dug into my throat, and I couldn't breathe. Matwau was shouting, and Wolf was barking. No Wolf, don't do anything, he'll kill you. Darkness spread around the edge of my eyes.

"Let her go."

The tall man turned at the sound of a gun cocking.

There stood the chief and our two old councilors, looking brave and determined, and so out of place.

Chief Roy aimed the dead guard's rifle at the tall man's chest. "Don't think I won't use this, young fella. I'm a skilled marksman."

Never in my life had I known the chief to touch a gun. Siksiká men and women hunted with bows and arrows.

The tall man removed his hands from my neck. I dropped to the ground, wheezing and coughing.

A twitch danced across the tall man's cheek. "Take it easy, Indian, I wouldn't a hurt her much."

"Back away, now. All we want is our man Roswell, and we'll be on our way."

"Oh, is that's all?"

Chief Roy nodded at the glider beside Matwau. "And our transport."

Claude scratched his head with an oversized hunting knife. "Well, that might be a problem. See we don't have one of those things. Kind a looking forward to trying out that contraption."

"You wouldn't know how."

The twitch intensified. "You calling me stupid? Cuz I got no patience with anyone calling me stupid."

I opened my mouth to warn the chief, but no words came out.

Matwau turned in time to see a bandit sneaking up on the chief. He decked the guy and stood ready to take on the other bandits moving in. They thought better of it and stepped back.

A young man with buck teeth and crossed eyes patted the tall man on the back. "Let them go, Claude, we don't need this right now. A storm's brewing."

Claude considered his bandit pal, his body stiff and ready for combat. Then he relaxed and nodded. "Be gone, then."

But the sly look on his face worried me, and Raven's warning rang in my ears.

The chief and Matwau picked up Roswell, and I grabbed the glider. We hurried out of the depot and into the purple and orange dusk. The bandit was right. A storm was coming.

"Take Roswell back on the glider, Matwau. The rest of us will hoof it."

Wolf led the way through the darkening prairie. Hisses and swishing surrounded us. I gulped. Snakes. Hundreds of them. I clutched Chief Roy's arm. "C-chief, I can't."

He waved his bio-comm at the ground. "Only one or two, Halerine Ananda. Be brave and follow in my footsteps."

Yeah, sure, be brave. My heart in my mouth, I followed behind the chief, but every swish and hiss sent me into paroxysms of fear.

The wind picked up and tossed tumbleweeds and silt at us. I shielded my eyes and pushed ahead. If I stopped, I would lose sight of the chief. Halfway back to camp, we caught up to Matwau.

He put his hand on Chief Roy's shoulder. "Roswell is waiting for you."

Roswell coughed. "Chief?"

Chief Roy knelt beside him. "What is it, old friend?"

"I'm done for, chief."

Chief Roy opened his mouth to protest, but then he sighed. "I am much aggrieved."

"Get these kids to safety, old man." Roswell closed his eyes.

The chief checked Roswell's pulse with his bio-comm and sighed again. "He's gone."

Matwau cursed and walked away. I followed. He took my hand and I let him, but I had no words.

Chief Roy joined us. "We'll take him back to the biopod and bury him. I'll not leave this good man to the scavengers."

Benji flopped down on a bench. "I'm pooped, let's tell ghost stories."

"After dinner," Chief Roy said. "Councilor Sereida, these ruffians can set up the tables and stools if'n they're so frisky."

"Ah chief, I said I'se pooped."

"Pretend you're Luke Skywalker."

I programmed the synthor for a spaghetti dinner with shaking hands, and I bit my lip to keep it from trembling. A litany of horrors ran through my head. Five days into this fool's journey and already we'd been slaves, a ghost wind buried us alive, and bandits killed Roswell and injured Atian. When we headed out in the morning, we would leave behind our first grave. What was next? Who was next?

"Should take about ten minutes, I'll be back before then." I hurried into the pod, slammed the bathroom door, and slid to the floor, sobbing into my hands. "I can't do this, I want to go home."

No Hali...

I squeezed my dreamcatcher. "No, you can't make me. I want to go home."

A knock jolted me out of my misery.

"Hali, are you all right?"

I splashed cold water on my face. "I'll be out in a minute. You should be lying down."

"Well, the synthor's making gurgling noises, and Chief Roy's threatening to open the lid."

"Oh no, he can't." I dashed out of the bathroom and caught the first tray as it shot out of the cantankerous synthor. "I guess supper's ready."

The kids lined up for their trays, the girls in a neat row, the boys pushing and shoving.

"Storm's nearly here, don't dawdle over your food," Chief Roy said. He dug into his spaghetti, then sat back and made a face. "Halerine Ananda, with all due respect, how about some grown-up food tomorrow night? I've a hankering for venison steak and mashed potatoes."

Councilor Sereida grunted her agreement.

Benji wiped sauce off his chin. "Why? I loves spisghetti."

"You would."

People in our village might not eat tonight, and here we were arguing over our next meal. "I'll see what I can do." I avoided looking at Atian, but he was watching me. Was my face puffy and red?

Leyla sighed and shoved her plate away.

"What's wrong, sweetie?"

She crossed her arms and frowned. "Well, I for one feel sorry for this old pod. She's our friend, and she don't gots a name."

Atian smirked. "She?"

Chief Roy took up the game. "What's her name, then?"

"Running Eagle! Ahura! Elsa!" the girls said.

Benji scowled and slammed down his fork. "Hey, those are dumb goil names from olden days."

The boys countered. "Wakanda, Katoyis, Thor!"

"Voyageur."

I turned around. Matwau was gazing at me, a cocky expression on his face. I clapped my hands for silence. "Hey, how about voyageur? We're heading into the unknown searching for a new life, like early explorers in Beforetimes Canada. Some of our own people became voyageurs."

The kids glanced at each other.

Tomko shrugged. "Seems okay, but we like Elsa better."

Leyla's nose twitched. "Hey biopod, *Voyageur* is your new name."

Yippee

"Yeah, we're voyageurs and Rainbow Warriors," Benji said.

"You should thank Matwau, voyageur was his idea."

Matwau's lips parted in the shadow of a smile, and I caught a glimpse of a different young man, one I might like. I returned his smile.

"*Voyageur* it is, then," Chief Roy said. "Good job, Matwau Meewatin, now what's for dessert?"

"Vitamin-enhanced chocolate zucchini cake."

Etta clapped her hands. "Oh goodie, my favorite."

Chief Roy rolled his eye. "More kid food, but not bad."

The wind shook the canopy and thunder and lightning crackled in the air. I brought up *Voyageur's* security screen. A funnel cloud danced along the edge of dark storm clouds, and a row of plow winds was headed straight for us. We were camped out in the open with not a tree nor a valley in sight.

Wolf flattened his ears and growled low in his throat.

"Right kids, tell your ghost stories and eat your cake in the sleeper pods," Chief Roy said. "Councilor Ore, hunker this old girl down."

Voyageur straightened out and pulled back her canopy. She pushed her spikes deep into the ground and lowered her armor.

Uh-uh ooh-ee

We were enveloped in silence, an oasis in the midst of the raging storm.

"Eerie, isn't it?" I murmured.

Matwau patted *Voyageur's* membrane. "Not half as eerie as what's going on outside." He nodded at the screen.

A rusty tractor, suspiciously similar to the one in Westlock, flew through the air and sent up a cloud of dust when it landed in the field across from *Voyageur*. Pieces of gray metal whipped back and forth in mid-air, not quite making landfall. Had the depot given up the ghost, and what about all the loot inside? I got my answer moments later. A parade of blenders, toasters, and monitors floated along a vicious wind current, and thousands of cash bills and credits turned the sky snow white.

Chief Roy chuckled. "That junk will make Vancouver before we do."

I shuddered and turned away from the frightful sight. "Time for a bath, Benji. You smell like a wet dog."

"Ah Hali."

Leyla gathered up her dolls and headed for her bed. "First thing tomorrow, I'm gonna teach *Voyageur* how to talk real words."

Chapter Six

THE DEPOT GANG

I jumped over a rock outcropping and ran through the thick jungle, darting this way and that, but the scarfaced man kept gaining on me. Any moment he'd take me down. "Atian, where are you, I need your help!" But Atian was gone, and I never told him.

A Sky Being, half old woman, half green lizard, loomed over me. I screamed and ran the other way.

"Halerine, you will not escape. Join with us."

"No!"

I kept running, but my lungs burned and my legs ached. A deep rumble spread through the earth, and the ground dropped away from me. I grabbed a tree branch and hung over the angry water swirling below. A Sky Being swooped down. Stringy black hair hid her crazed eyes. She reached for me with bony claws.

"No! Leave me alone!"

The branch cracked, and I plunged headlong into the raging water.

"Ouch!"

I rubbed my head where I had banged it on the dreamcatcher hanging over my sleeper. I waited until my

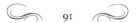

breathing slowed and my heartbeat returned to normal, then I climbed out of bed and staggered to the bathroom for a drink of water. The vision had been blurry, full of hidden meanings, and perhaps warnings. A shiver ran through me.

I searched the discarded clothing scattered across my sleeper for a clean tunic and headed for the canteen.

Leyla giggled. "Morning, sleepy head."

After all my scolding, I was the last one up." Sorry, a bad dream messed me up."

Our merry band of castaways was congregated around the central view screen. "What's up?"

"Take a look outside," Chief Roy said.

A curl of black smoke rose from a burning ranch house and mixed with pink clouds hovering overhead. One side of the house had collapsed, maybe from last night's storm, and a frilly white curtain waved through the gap. A man holding a rifle stood outside the house. He wasn't wearing a biosuit or a breather.

"How can he breathe?" Willow said.

Councilor Ore peered through the view screen at the puffs of green and yellow smog floating in the air. "He can't, not for long."

The man fired his gun into the air when *Voyageur* slowed down. "Be gone, ain't wanting no strangers around here."

A small body lay on the ground beside him.

"I spy somebody dead," Benji said.

"Benji!"

But all the heartbreak and death around us had hardened our hearts. How could we feel sorry for strangers, even a child, when our own People were dying?

Chief Roy shook his head. "We'll be moving on then, nothing we can do anyhow."

I headed to the canteen. "Who wants breakfast?"

A chorus erupted. "I do, I do."

"Bacon and eggs, grilled tomatoes, and blueberry bannock."
I tapped codes into the synthor. "You've got twenty minutes
to wash up."

"Ah Hali, I'm clean enough."

"Benji, you haven't taken a shower in two days, now
march."

He dragged his feet and followed the other kids to the
showers. "Wish you'd stayed asleep."

Twenty minutes later the synthor discharged trays of
food at lightning speed. I caught them with a practiced arm
and lined them up on the tables.

Chief Roy helped himself to the sizzling bacon. "I'll have
to fix that thing one of these days."

"Chief, you know what grandmother said about salt and
fat."

He glowered at me. "Halerine Ananda, when I need
a nursemaid, I'll let you know." He pretend-scowled.
"Besides, if my days are numbered, I'm sure as hell gonna
enjoy some elk bacon."

What could I say to that reasoning? "Food's ready, kids."

Benji dashed into the canteen and grabbed a tray. "About
time."

His hair looked suspiciously dry, but I held my tongue.
I would get him later when he least expected it.

"Hey Tomko, you gonna eat that ketchup?"

Tomko batted zis curly eyelashes. "What's it worth to
you, Benjamin?"

"Not beating you at checkers."

Tomko slid the ketchup across the table. "You've never
beaten us, you jerk-off."

Chief Roy popped a strip of bacon in his mouth. "Enough,
or I'm getting all the bacon."

The kids gobbled their food.

"Umm, I ain't never tasted anything so good," Benji said.

"Haven't ever."

"Okay troops, when you're finished, put your dishes in the washer."

"Ah chief," Benji said.

Chief Roy raised an eyebrow. "Listen you whelp, in the olden days you'd be washing those dishes by hand on the riverbank. Now move it." He headed for the control pod. "We're moving in ten."

Leyla plopped down on her favorite cushion seat. "*Voyageur*, are you ready?"

Uh huh

"Okay, first word is Leyla."

Layee

"Leyla."

Leyee

"Good enough. Next word, love."

Luv

"Now say, I love you, Leyla."

Luv luv leyee

I settled in my cushion seat and pulled out my Beforetimes book. On his last trip South, a dozen years ago, papi filled his pack with books from an abandoned library. "We'll not sink into ignorance and savagery if we have books," he'd said. He gave me *The Life and Times* on my sixth birthday. "Guard it well, Halerine, this book is a record of how life used to be."

I opened the heavy red book to *Prom Night*, one of my favorite stories about teenagers who lived before Turmoil. I sank into a magical world of golden ball gowns, fancy up-dos, and sparkling jewelry. My handsome boyfriend whisked me around the candlelit ballroom, our feet light as fairy dust. I was Cinderella, Pocahontas, and Tindayl Merde all in one. Not Halerine Ananda, the homeless dreamcatcher.

Chief Roy's grumbling pulled me away from the book. "Trouble?"

"Road block," Atian said.

The chief maneuvered *Voyageur* around an overturned fuel tanker.

When the energy grid collapsed most nations returned to old-fashioned fuel oil. What they could get, anyway. The tanker must have been a late delivery that never made it.

"Do you think there's any gas left?" Councilor Sereida said. "We could use more fuel for the freezer's generator."

Chief Roy waved his hand over the console and *Voyageur* slowed, but a gaping hole in the side of the silver tanker answered Sereida's question.

"Too bad."

Wolf's ears perked up, and he barked a warning. Too late, a dozen men swooped over the truck and jumped on *Voyageur*.

Matwau hissed. "The depot gang."

The hair on the back of my neck stood up. "Take cover!"

Rocks pelted the biopod.

No-way no-way ah-no

Voyageur lowered her shields, but not before a heavy stone crashed through the front screen. Chief Roy ducked and his hand brushed the control pad. The biopod slid to a stop, giving the bandits all the time they needed to pounce.

I grabbed Leyla and Benji and pushed them under the galley counter. "Stay there. Hide everyone!"

The children scrambled for bathrooms and closets.

Chief Roy unclipped his braid and loosened his long silver hair to cover his ear chip, then rolled the sleeve of his leather tunic over his wrist implant.

My heart pounded in my chest, and I signaled Atian. "Follow me."

For once he listened.

We slid along the floor and crawled between chairs and tables and slipped into the storage pod. "Take whatever you can carry. We'll sort it out later."

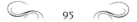

Atian touched my cheek. "Hali, if—"

Banging on the airlock stopped him.

I dragged a heavy box back to the lounge pod and ripped it open. "Oh no." Sereida's maple syrup toffee. Well, no help for it. I stuffed packets of candy in my pockets and down the front of my shorts.

Benji peeked out of the galley, and his frightened face broke into a grin. "Candy."

I tossed bags into the hideaway. "Shh, Benji, fill your pockets and no sneaking bites. Leyla, you, too."

Atian squirreled away small packets of blueberry and venison pemmican. At least pemmican contained some nutrition and would fill our bellies. "I'll be right back."

Atian held out his hand to stop me. "Hali, they're boarding any second."

I squeezed his fingers. "I just need one second." I reached for the bio's touchpad and coded the synthor, then crawled back into my hiding place.

"I'm hoping they take the food and leave us alone," Councilor Sereida said. "Great Manitou, protect us."

The bandits forced the airlock open using a crow bar and rushed in. So did the foul air.

Leyla coughed, and I slipped her a breather.

Claude strode into the pod wearing a dilapidated biosuit and holding a makeshift mask in his hands. "Well, well, what do we have here?" He tripped over Wolf. "Outta the way, ya mangy dog." He kicked Wolf in the butt.

Wolf crouched and bared his fangs.

Wolf could tear open the looter's throat in a second, but then another thug would shoot him. "Wolf stay."

He sent me a bewildered look, but obeyed.

Claude pushed his way into the storage pod and whistled. "Hey lads, we found us a real haul, I'm thinking."

The thugs tramped through *Voyageur* and plundered the food and water.

"Well, well, methinks we got ourselves a low-life stowaway."

I peeked around the corner. Claude reached into one of the larger cabinets and pulled out a bedraggled man with a gaunt face and shaggy black hair. Empty containers and scraps of food spilled out of the cabinet.

Claude waved his hand. "Phew-ee."

"Samoset!" Chief Roy said. "What in tarnation are you doing here?"

Samoset's mouth twisted into an ugly snarl, and he pointed at Matwau. "Staking my claim, that's what. Where my boy goes, I go. We only got each other."

Matwau slid lower in his seat, and the haunted look on his face tore at me. Would he ever be free of Samoset?

"All right, all right, we ain't got no time for family feuds," Claude said. He shoved Samoset into the lounge pod. "Sit down and shut up."

Benji held his nose as Samoset walked by his hiding place. "Ew, what's that awful smell?"

"Sami never washed," Leyla said. "You'll smell that bad if you don't shower for real."

Claude clapped his hands. "The rest of you snots, show yourselves or I'll shoot up the place."

The children crept out of their hiding places and clung to each other. Even Willow was trembling.

"Sit here, so I can keep an eye on you." Claude scratched his greasy hair with the barrel of his gun and bared his brown-stained, rotting teeth. "So what to do with you papooses?"

"We are of no risk to you, sir," Chief Roy said. "We're moving on, bound for Vancouver City."

"Not making that, you ain't, not without water and air. Should put you out a your misery."

The worry on Chief Roy's weathered face terrified me more than the thug's words.

"Surely you wouldn't kill innocent children."

Claude scowled. "Maybe not, but I've got no trouble shooting a mouthy old buck, 'specially one that killed my man."

"I killed him," Matwau said.

Claude pointed his gun at Matwau. "You might be next."

Etta started crying. "Mama, mama!"

"Stop your caterwauling, kid!"

She cried harder.

"All right, out you go! The lot of you! Get going!"

"But you can't leave us on this desolate road," Chief Roy said. "The children will die!"

"I'm still thinking of putting you out of your misery. Take your pick. A long walk or I'll shoot you where you stand."

Chief Roy blanched. "At least give them their biosuits and breathers, they won't fit you anyway."

Leyla tugged on Claude's sleeve. "Please sir."

Claude looked into Leyla's sweet face and something shifted in his miserable expression. He shrugged. "Take them, then, and be gone."

Chief Roy and the councilors gathered up our gear. Atian tucked his clarinet inside his suit.

"Take your packs," I whispered to the children.

Tears rolled down Leyla's cheeks. "Good-bye *Voyageur*, I love you."

Voyageur wheezed.

Samoset shoved the kids out of the way and scrambled off the pod. He grabbed a breather from the pile, then tossed it and swiped Matwau's.

Claude hopped off the biopod and ripped the breather out of Samoset's hands. "Here, wear mine if you're so picky."

"But it's torn."

"Good enough for the likes of you." He put Matwau's breather on and took a deep breath. "Much better."

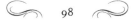

"Serves you right Sami, being so pushy," Leyla said.

Samoset snarled.

I slung my leather backpack over my shoulder and hurried past Claude.

"Whatcha got there, girlie-squaw?"

"Oh nothing." Nothing except ten water-filled canteens that stood between us and dying of thirst.

"Come on, what's in the pack?"

"Girl stuff. You know, sanitary napkins, underwear, and such." I offered the pack and held my breath. "Wanna see?"

Claude pushed the bag out of his face and leered at me. "Sure you don't want to come along?"

My stomach tightened. "Certain."

"Suit yourself." He turned and climbed into *Voyageur*.

Matwau hoisted his backpack and the mysterious leather bag that never left his sight and grabbed a breather. "Wait! Take me with you."

Claude chuckled. "Now why would I do that?"

"I don't belong here, these guys are not my people. I can shoot, and I'm betting none of your boys know much about controlling a biopod."

Samoset sidled closer. "Hey boy."

Matwau snarled and pushed Samoset away. "Get lost."

I held my breath.

Claude stared at Matwau for a long moment, then nodded. "Well, come along then, but try anything funny and you'll be out on your butt, a bullet between your eyes."

I stood rooted to the spot, my mouth open like a guppy sucking in air. How could Matwau do this? How could I be so wrong about someone?

An ugly sneer on his face, Claude closed the access hatch on me.

Voyageur, now a rusty gray color, jumped to life, and away the bandit gang went, leaving us choking on the swirling dust.

"Get into your suits, quick like," Councilor Ore said.

Raven screeched overhead. With my luck, the Sky Beings were circling above us, ready to swoop down and taunt me.

"So, what do we do now, chief?" Atian said.

Chapter Seven

HERE COMES SANTA

eat waves shimmered across the badlands, reminding me of the old spaghetti Westerns my father watched when we were still on the grid. At any moment a steely-eyed cowboy might ride over the horizon and rescue me. I waited. Nope, not a hint of a cowboy.

We ate the gooey candy on the first day and suffered stomach aches that night. The next morning we happened upon a spindly blueberry bush, one the birds hadn't found. We gorged on the shriveled fruit. That night Wolf caught a scrawny prairie chicken. Chief Roy roasted the bird over a spit, and we made a festive meal out of it, despite scarcely a mouthful for each one of the children. Atian's stash of pemmican might last us another day or two. Then what?

My heat-dazed mind kept thinking of my family back home. What were they doing right now? Was Danny getting better or had he died? Did my gentle mother miss combing my hair until it shone? Or remember how she clucked her tongue when I came home with purple and blue streaks in my hair and a rose tattoo on my ankle?

"Chief, we need to talk."

I sighed. We were hungry, thirsty, and our feet ached, but whiny Samoset was our worst misery. Without Matwau to hold him in check, he had become incorrigible. Matwau. How could I read someone so wrong?

"If you weren't such a wimp, we'd have guns and we could a fought off that gang, killed the lot of them. Why, I bet we'd be half way through the mountains by now, and my boy would be where he belongs, with me."

"People with guns are the ones who get shot, Samoset, not the crooks."

Samoset snorted. "Nonsense."

"I'm thirsty."

"I know, Benji, but we haven't much water left." Two half-empty canteens. "Can you wait a bit longer?"

"Okay, I'll try.

The brittle goose grass beside the broken pavement moved.

Benji squinted. "Hey, what's in the grass?"

"Not sure, but don't get too close, it might bite."

I clutched the back of his shirt, but he fought me off. "Ah Hali, don't be such a scaredy-cat." He stuck his hand into the grass and held up a green lizard with a pointed nose and bulging eyes. "It's a baby gecko, see? Can I keep him, huh, can I?"

The gecko lifted its nose and chirped at me. The lizard from my dream? I stepped back. "I'm not an expert on lizards, but that little guy looks half-dead and he smells of skunk. I don't—"

"Ah come on, Hali, lizards don't bite."

"Chief, a little help here?"

Chief Roy shrugged. "Fine with me, but you'd better be taking care of it, and that lizard doesn't get any water until we do."

Benji grinned and tucked the gecko inside his biosuit. "I'll give you food and water soon as I can, Gecki."

We climbed a hillock on the outskirts of Beforetimes Edmonton. A dingy brown haze hung over the city, though an occasional highrise spire peeked through the guck.

Chief Roy checked his bio-comm. "Thick as gumbo. Will be another century before this smog clears." He raised his arm and the comm recorded the scene below.

I side-stepped the bleached bones of a child clutching a black and white terrier and gazed at the desolate landscape. "Why did they do this? Were shiny new cars and all their toys worth ruining everything good? No wonder Mother Earth turned her back on us." I tossed dead grass seeds into the air. "I am sorry for the selfishness of humankind. Forgive us, I beseech you."

Atian wrapped his arm around my shoulder. "No use getting worked up, Hali, it's too late."

His arms around me felt so good. I stepped away. "I can't help it. How could they?"

Tomko pointed to steel skeletons, their siding reduced to heaps of rubble. "What happened to the skyscrapers?"

"Tornados." Chief Roy looked east. "There's one now."

A dark blue funnel cloud loomed over the city, then dipped down and touched the ground. The wind howled and screeched, and raised the hairs on the back of my neck.

The chief kept his bio-comm humming. "Let's wait and see where that monster heads before we plot a course."

The tornado destroyed everything in its path, like a jackhammer ripping up a sidewalk. It sent debris swirling hundreds of meters into the air, then as suddenly as it popped up, it vanished into the circling clouds.

Atian balanced on one foot and rested his maimed leg. Lines of pain marred his tired face. "So what's the story with this Edmonton?"

Chief Roy grunted. "Held out longer than its cousins in the South, despite all the storms."

"How?"

The chief merged with his bio-comm. "Temps stayed cooler so farmers grew food for longer than most other places."

"But it's all gone now."

Chief Roy sighed. "Aa. Heat waves rolled in and farmers had to abandon the land. The store shelves emptied, and people grew angry, then terrified. They couldn't survive without flour, eggs, and toilet paper. Many couldn't figure out why the government wasn't taking care of them." He cleared his throat. "The water and power grid shut down, and that's when people got it through their thick noggins the government was gone. Civilization pretty much ended at that point."

"Sounds horrible," I said. But then, what wasn't horrible about this new world?

"Aa."

The chief's bio-comm kept feeding him data.

"People panicked. They swarmed towns and suburbs and snatched up anything they found. Decent folks turned on each other, killing over a bag of sugar. Gangs roamed the streets. Without clean water and sanitation, typhoid broke out. Millions died."

Etta gasped. "They all died? Even the little kids?"

"Afraid so, Etta m'girl. Some families stayed in their homes and waited for the end, others ran away or tried to reach family, but vigilantes shot dead scores of refugees before they reached the next town. T'was the Wild West all over again."

I gazed at the tragic city. "Do I want to head in there?"

Chief Roy shrugged. "We can't walk around it. Too far for the kids." He looked to the sky. "Sides which, we don't know who might be following us so it's best if we keep moving."

I wiggled my blistered toes. Leyla was limping like an old woman with corns, and some of the other kids were not much better off, but the chief was right. We had to keep moving.

Chief Roy swung his wooden cane and headed into the megacity. "Right, follow me troops and step lively."

Halfway down the hill he stopped and squinted at a dirty rag hanging from a dead poplar tree. "Is that what I think it is?"

Atian snagged the cloth with a broken branch and flipped it onto the ground. "It's an old shirt, so what?"

"Not just any shirt, this is Matwau's shirt. The lad's leaving us a trail of breadcrumbs."

Samoset cackled. "That's my boy, a chip off the old block."

Atian huffed. "Yeah right."

Chief Roy studied the ground, then bent and brushed away a pile of dead leaves. He held up a water canteen and a hefty bag of trail mix. "He's giving us a chance at life, he is."

My heart sang. Matwau hadn't betrayed us. "Line up, kids, we've got water and food."

Benji downed his handful of fruit and nuts in one swallow and offered a piece of dried banana to his gecko. "Never tasted anything so good, hey Gecki?" He poured a little water into his hand. Gecki chirped and crawled down Benji's arm to slurp the water. His belly full, he sprawled across Benji's shoulder for a nap.

Benji tucked the gecko inside his biosuit. "Sorry Gecki, in you go, the air's bad out here."

"Cheep, cheep!"

Leyla limped around a garbage bag wrapped in a spider web and headed down the hill. "Enough dilly-dallying, let's rescue *Voyageur*."

We walked up a wide street lined with boarded-up storefronts and side-stepped mustard and goose grass pushing through the buckled sidewalks. The stillness sucked at my soul, but making any noise seemed wrong. The streets of Edmonton had become a shrine to the passing of humankind and its civilization.

Councilor Sereida shook her head and in a low voice said, "It's an urban war zone."

"No, it's a ghost town," Leyla said. "Spirits are everywhere."

Benji snort-laughed.

"Don't you hear them? They're whispering, the ghosts of all the people who used to live here." Tears rolled down her cheeks. "And they're crying." She turned her big eyes to me. "Hali, why?"

My heart broke, and I hugged my little poet. "Let's go, sweetie. It's too late for them, but not for us."

Chief Roy stopped in his tracks. "Bless me, am I seeing things?"

Our illustrious leader forgot his age and climbed through the shattered storefront window of a Starbucks coffee shop.

Atian shook his head and chuckled. "He won't find any coffee, you know."

"Let him enjoy his fantasy for a little while."

The chief popped his head out and crawled through the window. His back creaked when he straightened up. "Need to start acting my age."

"Find any coffee, chief?"

"Nope. Should a known, I guess."

"Maybe I'll be more lucky." Atian pointed to a dangling shoe sign and held up his foot. "Could use a new pair, don't you think?"

The soles on his replicated Air Jordan sneakers were worn thin, and his big toe peeked through the right shoe.

Alas, only a lonely pair of silver stiletto heels sat on the uppermost shelf.

"You'd look good in silver, Atian," Tomko said.

I laughed along with the rest of them, but worry nagged at me. How would we manage without *Voyageur's* synth? We all needed new shoes, and we always coded the synth to build special shoes for Atian's disfigured foot.

Tomko picked up a baseball rolling down the street and tossed it to Benji, then on to Keme. Willow jumped up and caught the ball meant for Tomko, and the game was on.

"Good," Chief Roy said. "Might keep them from noticing the carnage."

I dodged a slider, its windshield splattered with dried blood, and tried to shield Leyla, but she caught sight.

"Hey, they gots kids in that car, and their mommy is kilt with a bullet." She looked at Samoset. "See, Sami, that's what guns do."

Samoset scowled and ducked his head under Leyla's glare.

Atian limped toward a camouflaged vehicle parked at an intersection. "The army must have tried to keep order for a time. This personnel carrier is a real beaut. Say, I wonder ..." He jumped on the vehicle and disappeared down the hatch.

We waited.

"Think he can start it?"

Chief Roy grunted. "Doubtful. These old carriers are made out of twenty-first century metal alloys. Controls will be rusted out."

The carrier growled and hissed, and jerked to life.

"Well, I'll be."

Atian's head popped out of the hole. Black soot covered his face, but he grinned from ear to ear. "Care for a ride, anyone?"

"Yay!"

The kids piled on the machine and clung to every knob and rail. Samoset jumped on the back end.

Atian waved to me. "Come on Hali, I dare you."

Oh, was that a dare? I hopped up beside Benji.

Chief Roy helped the councilors, then joined them. "All right, lad, move this buggy out."

Atian punched the control panel, and the monstrous transport rumbled down the road, the pavement cracking in its wake. The carrier crawled over a derelict slider in the middle of the street without pausing. The slider crumpled like tin foil.

Benji and Tomko cheered. "Whoopie!"

The carrier snaked its way through piles of rubble, abandoned vehicles, and even a body or two, but ten klicks later, it gave its last gasp.

The kids groaned.

"Fuel cells died," Chief Roy said.

Atian patted the old machine on the rump. "Fun while it lasted. Thanks for the lift."

Back on our own two feet, Atian scanned the desolate street.

I wiped the sweat dripping down the side of my face. Was it getting hotter? "What are you looking for? Another carrier?"

He shot me a cheeky grin, and my heart fluttered.

"Some place cool before we fry our brains."

"Aa, I be thinking along the same lines." Chief Roy glanced at the sky. "And a storm's a brewing."

The words no sooner left the chief's mouth, and the wind picked up. Dust and loose garbage swirled in the air.

Etta batted away a carton dripping with green goo. "Yuck."

Lightning flashed across the sky, followed by an ear-splitting clap of thunder, and hail the size of golf balls rained down on us.

"We need cover!" Chief Roy said.

He yanked the boards off a greeting card shop and we dashed inside. Rats squeaked and scurried out of our way. Angry purple clouds dipped low and touched the ground.

Atian pointed. "Here comes that blasted twister again."

The tornado tossed sliders into the air as if they were Lego blocks, then danced to the side and sheared off the corner of a glass skyscraper. A shower of blue glass floated to the ground in slow motion, and the hundred-story building leaned to the left. Corroded steel groaned and snapped.

"Breathers tight!" Councilor Sereida said.

The structure crumbled in slow motion. A cloud of dust blanketed us when it smashed into the ground and disintegrated.

"Well, now we know what happened to all them skyscrapers," Tomko said.

"Those skyscrapers."

We headed down the dusty street. Rumbling thunderheads rolled over us, and lightning flashes lit up the sky.

"I'm not liking the looks of those clouds," Chief Roy said.

A fat raindrop fell on my cheek, then another.

Etta pulled her blue t-shirt away from her skin. "My shirt's getting dirty."

Sure enough, mud drops splattered my once-white shirt and plastered the thin fabric against my skin. I crossed my arms and made a mental note not to wear white again if I ever found new clothes.

Leyla held her nose. "Stinks."

She was right. The air smelled of wet dirt and dust, of rusting metal, and wet, decaying flesh.

Chief Roy watched the turbulent sky. "We need safe cover." He pointed his cane at a concrete box the size of a hobbit house. "Let's try in there."

Atian held his wounded side and grabbed my hand. "Come on."

My fingers tingled from his touch, but I didn't have time to enjoy the sensation. The twister had changed course and was bearing down on us. A red stop sign whipped past my head and wedged into the side of a storefront. "That was too close."

We reached the squat shed. "What is this building?"

"Don't know, but I'm hoping there's a basement."

Atian kicked the door open using his good foot and led the way into a slip tube. "Slide!"

The children laughed and squealed all the way to the bottom. Wolf covered his nose with his paws and whimpered. Atian gave him a shove and down he went.

I patted his head when he reached the bottom. "Good boy."

Wolf curled his lips and bared his fangs at Atian.

Tomko stood up and slapped the dust off zis pink short shorts. "That was some awesome."

We stepped into an underground cavern. Our shoes crunched on the dusty granite floor, and our voices echoed in the vast emptiness. We passed through a rickety turnstile and multi-colored lights flickered and came on.

"Must have a hidden power source," Atian said.

Chief Roy took off his breather and breathed deeply. "Air's good enough."

Etta ripped off her breather and tossed it across the room. The children laughed and clapped their hands.

"No Etta, we'll need them again," I said.

She grinned. "I know, but that sure felt good. We better not need breathers in Maniton, or I'm not staying."

Willow pointed to the ceiling. "It's so pretty."

Crystal and golden chandeliers with light bulbs in the shape of candles hung from the marble ceiling. Strings of cobwebs wove their way through the lights and hung down to the floor all wispy and ghostly-like.

Tomko wiped at the spikes in zis florescent pink hair. "Wonder where that spider's hiding."

Benji laughed and nudged Tomko. "Wouldn't worry about it, that color will scare away any spider."

"What is this place?" Willow said.

"It's a t-tube station," Atian said. "Wavers float on magnetic waves running through this cavern. In Beforetimes these underground tubes connected all the cities, and wavers whisked people from one city to another. They took the place of planes when the air got so bad hardly anything could fly."

I stared at him.

His face reddened, and he shrugged. "What? I would have been a transport engineer if the world hadn't gone to hell."

Leyla tugged on my sleeve. "Look, Hali, Beforetimes magic."

A fake spruce tree sat in the corner. Leyla hobbled over and gently touched the red and green glass balls and tiny figurines hanging from the branches. "What's this for?"

Chief Roy checked his bio-comm. "Must be a Christmas tree."

"Christmas?"

"Aa, a holiday celebrated by some folks in Beforetimes. Something about a baby born centuries ago, parents giving their children presents, and everyone eating too much food and chocolate."

Benji rubbed his stomach. "Sounds yummy."

Tomko pointed to a holo on the wall. "Whoa! Wouldja look at that?"

Cartoon images of a fat man in a red and white suit and a deer with a red nose flashed on the wall. Tomko tapped the red nose and music started up. *Rudolf the red-nosed reindeer had a very shiny nose, and if you ever saw it, you would say it even glows.*

"Is that Christmas music?" Leyla said.

My heart broke at the wistful look on her face. "I guess it is, sweetie."

"Nice." Her voice shook a little. She touched the tree one more time, then turned her back and limped away. Tears glistened in her eyes.

The fat, jolly man dressed in a red and white suit winked at me. Another vision? But no, I was still in the station surrounded by my worn-out kids. The sign above the fat man read, Here Comes Santa Claus.

Chief Roy straightened from inspecting a water dispenser. "Okay troops, I've found drinkable water."

We lined up for our turn at the fountain.

Etta jumped back. "Ew, Benji's lizard is taking a bath in the water."

"Benji!"

"What? He's as clean as me."

"That's nothing to brag about." I cupped my hand and gave Wolf a long drink.

Tomko skipped over to a cactus-shaped orange and green neon sign. The sign read, *Amigo's*. Zis posed.

"That orange clashes with your pink hair, Tomi," Benji said.

"What would you know about fashion, boy-o? Besides, we're thinking of green when we find *Voyageur*."

Benji rolled his eyes. "Hey, I bet they gots food in this place."

The children followed Benji into the restaurant. They sat down at funky wooden tables covered in red and white checkered tablecloths and played with the lime green Mexican plates on the tables. Photos of movie stars and rockers from the twenty-first century covered the bright yellow walls.

The spaghetti western actor hung in a place of honor. Papi would have been thrilled.

Benji pointed to the purple ceiling. "Look at those flying machines."

Sure enough, models of ancient airplanes hung from thick cords. Hundreds of them.

Atian poked a blue and yellow plane with a broom handle. The plane whirled around a short flight path and set off a chain reaction. Soon all the planes were flying in dizzying circles.

"Dig-o," Benji said.

The planes took on a life of their own, whirling around as children clapped, and their parents raised their glasses in praise. The restaurant overflowed with happy, laughing families. Christmas music played on the loudspeaker, and Santa Claus handed out white- and red-striped candy. My heart soared.

One little girl stopped in front of me. She wrinkled her brow, then ran back to her mother. She pointed, but her mother did not see me.

"The planes are slowing down," Benji said.

My vision evaporated, and I was back in the t-tube station. We watched until the planes stopped.

"Wonder why this place was left alone at the end," Atian said.

A hole in my heart ached for Beforetimes, when families were happy and safe. When my People were rebuilding their lives. "Maybe they couldn't bear destroying something so perfect. Or maybe dishes and toy airplanes no longer mattered." I sniffed.

"What's wrong, Hali?" Atian said.

"I'm sad and hurt and furious. All this fun stuff and we'll never get to enjoy any of it. I hate them, they wrecked everything." I wiped away my tears. How silly, crying over toy airplanes and a Santa Claus that wasn't even part of Blackfoot culture. Seemed all I did was cry. "We're supposed to be the Rainbow Warriors, but we gave up everything, even the little we had, and for what?"

Atian wrapped his arms around me and kissed my forehead. "Maybe we'll celebrate Christmas in Maniton, or we'll make up our own holidays and traditions. How about Landing Day or Safe Haven Day? And we'll celebrate all the Blackfoot ceremonies. We'll be all right, Hali, I promise."

"Will we?" I shrugged out of his arms though they felt so good, or maybe because they felt so good. "Come on kids, there isn't any food in here."

Chief Roy was plugging coins into an upright metal box and grumbling. "I can't convince this ornery machine to hand over its loot."

Benji peered through the grimy glass. "Chips! This thing's got chips, and drinks, and everything I ever dreamed of!" He shook the box. "Come on, open up, I'm dying out here."

"Step aside, little man." Atian swung a metal bar into the glass and it shattered.

The children surged forward, but the chief stood in front of the dispenser and held up his hands. "This is not a free-for all, you scallywags. One package each, now line up, nice and orderly."

Benji accepted his bag of barbecue chips and held out his hand for another one. "For Gecki, chief, he's starving.

"Scat, and don't be lining up again."

A twinkle in his eye, Chief Roy waved a bag in front of my face. "Care for some Skittles, Miss Halerine Ananda?"

I popped a candy in my mouth and hugged my sides. To borrow a line from Benji, nothing ever tasted so good. I tucked the bag into my backpack. Could I stretch the candy until we reached Maniton? Would they have Skittles in Maniton?

Willow's long legs were sticking out of a garbage disposal built into the wall. "Hey, I found something."

"Digging through old garbage is dangerous, young lady," Chief Roy said. "Might be rats or sharp edges."

She kicked her legs and backed out of the chute holding a square box covered in pearly flecks and redwood blocks. "This isn't garbage, chief."

Tomko pushed Benji out of the way. "Let us see, your fat butt is blocking our view."

Willow pulled three dog-eared books out of the box.

Chief Roy thumbed through one of them. "A graphic novel, I'm thinking. Something called *The Zone*." He picked up the other two. "*Guardians of the Galaxy VII* and *Superman XX*."

"Superman! I heard about that guy. Can I read it?"

Benji reached for the book, but the chief held it high. "Not with those grubby hands, young man. This book is a fragile antique."

"Does that mean I have to take another bath?"

Tomko giggled and slapped Benji on the back. "Another one? You never took the first one, but you're safe 'til we find *Voyageur*."

Willow held up a rectangular plastic pad the same color as Tomko's hair. "What's this?"

Chief Roy waved his bio-comm over the artifact. "I believe it's what they called a cell phone. Never used one myself, but if I recall my history, teenagers of the early twenty-first century couldn't live without one. Bio-comms replaced those contraptions by the time I was mobile."

Willow pressed a button and the phone beeped. "Wow, it's awake." She tapped the pad and tinkling music played. "What's a Candy Crush?"

"That's odd, it must be a hundred years old and it's working," Atian said.

Chief Roy shrugged. "Satellite connections are still operational. Must have some kind of sleeping battery or a self-charger."

Willow tucked the cell in her back pocket and grinned. "Finders-keepers."

Tomko pulled out a black t-shirt with a giant red tongue on the front.

Chief Roy shook his head. "Don't ask, I haven't the foggiest."

Tomko tossed zis worn and filthy pink t-shirt into the garbage chute and pulled the new one over zis head. The tongue leered at us. "Perfect."

"Yeah, for a girlie boy," Samoset said.

Tomko stuck out zis pierced tongue at Samoset. Leyla giggled and Benji patted his back. "Ignore him, Tomi."

I pulled out a snuggly gray jacket with a hood and a package of ancient chocolate called Lindor's. We shared the crumbling chocolate and the jacket fit Atian, not that he needed one in this heat.

"Appears these are artifacts from Beforetimes," Chief Roy said.

"Then how come nothing from First Peoples?" Tomko said.

I did not have an answer.

The chief clapped his hands. "Okay troops, time for a rest."

The children found corners and niches. Etta was asleep in minutes, curled up beside Leyla, her thumb in her mouth.

Atian took my hand, and led me to the back of Amigo's. I stopped. "Oh!"

A flickering candle lit up a table set for two. Atian pulled out a chair and I sat.

"Would you care for some wine?" He poured water into two crystal wine glasses. "I hear this was a good year."

I laughed and clapped my hands.

With a flair, he opened two bags of Kettle barbecue chips and poured them onto plates advertising Amigo's. "Compliments of Chief Roy." He placed Coffee Crisp and Kit Kat bars beside our plates. "For dessert."

Soft Mexican music played in the background as we ate our treat. "When did you have time to do all this?"

He grinned, and my heart flipped. "While you were popping Skittles." He took my hands in his. "Hali, I've been wanting to talk to you."

Oh oh. I took a sip of water. "About what?"

"About us."

Too many years of snarking and ignoring me. I couldn't let him off easy. "Us?"

Atian wiped his brow. "Look, I'm sorry, okay. It was too hard to see you every day and then you'd push me away."

I gasped. "I pushed you away? What about all the times you sneered at me, or made fun of me in front of my friends? Huh? What about all those times." A sob escaped my lips. "I thought you hated me."

He held up his hands. "Hey, I said I'm sorry. I was a jerk. I know it, but I want to make things right between us before ..."

I swallowed. "Before what?"

"Before anything happens. I couldn't bear it."

I stayed quiet, thinking. What should I say? He was giving me an opening, but I couldn't get the words out. Not here, not now.

He stood and held out his hand. A warm smile curled his lips. "Care to dance?"

Really? But his warm eyes mesmerized me, and I took his hand. He pulled me close to his chest and nuzzled me ear. My body melded against his. His heart was hammering as hard as mine. How many times had I dreamed of this? Even if it never happened again, I'd have this one moment.

I wrapped my arms around him, and we swayed to the unfamiliar music. His lips against my neck sent shivers up and down my spine, and I breathed in the rich cinnamon smell I loved so much. Did he feel what I was feeling, the ache that tore at my very being?

He pulled back and looked into my eyes. Kiss me, Atian. Hurry up before something happens.

A shrill whistle pierced the quiet station. Too late.

T-train 236 arriving on schedule.

We broke apart and Atian's face closed up. "Guess we better see what's going on."

"Whoa! Wouldja look at that?"

Tomko leaned over the edge of the wave. Chief Roy grabbed zim by the britches before zie fell in.

The waver coasted to a stop. A series of spider web cracks crisscrossed the black membrane and green mold grew in the cracks.

"Hey, it's full of people," Willow said.

Tomko whistled. "Dead people."

Rows of skeletons dressed in dark business clothes sat on the waver. Some stared straight ahead with empty eye sockets, others had fallen over. The skull of a woman with long blond hair leaned against one window. Was she gazing at the passing scenery when she died?

"Hey chief, can we ride the waver?"

"A good idea, Benji. Atian, see if one's heading to Vancouver."

Atian studied an electronic map with flashing lights. "Nope, they circle around Edmonton. All the waves outside the city are broken. Red lights are blinking on every line."

Stand back, t-train 236 about to depart. Stand back.

Chief Roy sighed. "On a trip to nowhere."

"Will the wavers ever stop?" Benji said.

The chief shrugged. "If the power cells wear down, or the membranes rot."

Samoset wiped nacho crumbs off his grimy checkered shirt. "Playing trains might be nice and all, but don't we have a pod to rescue?"

Sweat trickled down my neck from the stifling hot air, even this deep underground. I wrapped my damp hair around the top of my head and held it up. I hadn't found a new hair clip since Cardiff cut my old one and *Voyageur* never figured out how to make one. Maybe I should chop off my hair. An image of my mother's disapproving eyes rose in my mind. She would know. "Where do you think the bandits have gone, chief?"

"No telling, but now they've got food and supplies to barter for ammo and liquor."

T-train 437 bound for St. Albert arriving on schedule.

St. Albert? "A traveler told my father about survivalists hiding in St. Albert. Maybe this is a crazy idea, but what if the bandits took *Voyageur* there?"

Chief Roy shrugged. "Best clue we've got, Halerine Ananda." He clapped his hands. "Everyone on board, this is our ride."

Tomko gaped at the chief. "You want us to do what?"

"Never mind, get on the waver."

The children climbed on the waver, but they hovered in the doorway, far away from the skeletons. Wolf whimpered and refused to board the train.

Chief Roy picked up Wolf, with Atian's help, and deposited him in the rail car. The poor wolf covered his nose with his paws and closed his eyes.

"Move in, kids, they won't bite."

Leyla held her nose. "But they stinks."

Etta copied her. "Don't touch the dead people."

"Breathe through your mouth and seal your breather. We'll get out soon." I took my own advice, but the odor clung to me.

Chapter Eight

SEA OF GARBAGE

We rode the ghoulish waver across the battered city. At one station, plumes of smoke from a burning apartment building swirled through the waver car and choked us.

"Breathers tight," Sereida said.

A woman and three children screamed and waved a white cloth from the penthouse balcony.

Chief Roy sighed and shook his head. "Look away troops, nothing we can do for them."

The cries for help echoed through the waver long after we moved on. I pushed down my own anger at this dreadful world and lifted Etta's breather to wipe away her tears. "We couldn't help them, sweetie."

At another stop, cement pile-ons, sandbags, and burned out vehicles blocked the pockmarked street. The tops of men's heads peeked over the barricades.

"A range war is about to go down," Atian said.

Gunfire let loose.

"Aa, we best move on real quick-like."

The waver pulled out, but not before a bullet whizzed through a window and narrowly missed Samoset's ear.

Leyla pressed her nose against the grimy window. "Look, a sea of garbage."

A garbage dump strewn with old clothing, plastic bottles, and garbage bags went on to the horizon. Roof peaks and street signs peeked out of the trash. An over-powering stench seeped through the waver's broken windows and not even our breathers filtered out the stink.

I blinked. Was the sea of garbage rippling in the wind?

Leyla gasped. "The sea is moving!"

Councilor Ore peered over Etta's head. "No Leyla, that's people moving."

Small bands, maybe families, were foraging in the garbage. They hardly glanced our way when the waver slowed to a stop.

"Where'd all the trash come from?" Benji said.

Chief Roy shrugged. "The wind, maybe, or people stopped caring where they dumped refuse. I'm betting garbage pick-up lost out early on."

"A park," Leyla said. "I see a kids' park. Can we stop and play?"

Tomko snorted. "Yeah, a dead park in the middle of a garbage dump. You really want to play in that?"

Leyla wrinkled her nose. "You're no fun, Tomi. That park gots swings and merry-go-rounds waiting for us little kids."

"Yeah, but—"

"And that red and yellow teeter-totter is way bigger'n the one back home. Bet I could whop you on it."

"Bet not."

"Kids ..."

Swan boats, their white paint peeling, rested against the dock in a dried-up pond, and empty ball diamonds waited for ball players who would never return.

Benji sighed and his shoulders drooped. "Could a been fun."

A park without kids, a lake without water, and a waver full of dead people. I hated this new world. Maybe the spacers had the right idea to get as far away as they could. "I'm going for a walk."

I entered the next to last dead-people car and sat down in a vacant seat. What if we didn't find *Voyageur*? Or Matwau. It all seemed so hopeless.

Paper rattled.

Dead people didn't make noises. I studied the skeletons dressed in business clothes. One passenger wasn't dead. "I see you, please come out."

A middle-aged woman, dressed in a navy suit much too heavy for the scorching temps, stood up. "I'm sorry, dear, I didn't mean to startle you."

I closed my gaping mouth and swallowed. "Y-you're alive?"

The woman smiled and patted her coiffed blond hair. "Yes, for a time."

I licked my parched lips. How long since I'd worn lipstick or any kind of make-up? Maybe never, but this woman, stuck in the middle of hell, was fully made up, right down to a light shade of pink lipstick and soft blue eye shadow. Dainty pearl earrings hung from her ears, and she wore white gloves. My blue feather earrings seemed out of place beside this fancy lady.

The woman carried a mask of sorts, but she wasn't wearing a biosuit. How did she survive in this smog slew? I searched for words. "But where are you going, ma'am?"

She fluttered an embroidered handkerchief, frayed at the edges and yellowed with age. "Why, to work, dear."

A hint of perfume wafted through the car and mixed with the dead smell. "Work?"

She picked up her brown leather briefcase. "Why yes, I'm a bank manager in St. Albert."

"A bank's still open?"

She blinked. "Oh yes, I open the bank every day. I have a responsibility to my customers, you know."

Okay, this was getting weird. "But the people are all gone."

"Oh, they'll come back, I'm certain of it, and they'll need money to buy houses and cars and-and everything." She smiled again, but her cheek twitched.

"I see."

"What about you, dear? Where are you going?"

"Vancouver."

She covered her mouth with her handkerchief and tittered. "Vancouver? Oh my goodness, that's such a long way for a young girl to travel all alone."

"Oh, I'm not alone."

She perked up. "There are more of you?" She clasped her hands together. "Oh, I should dearly love to meet them." She held out her hand. "My name is Juliette."

I wiped my grubby hand on my pants and shook her gloved hand. "Pleased to meet you. My name's Halerine Ananda. If you'd like to meet my family, follow me."

I strolled into the next car, Juliette in tow. The kids stared open-mouthed as she followed me down the aisle. "Everybody, this is Juliette. She's riding the waver to work in St. Albert." I sent a silent message to the chief.

He winked and gave me a slight nod.

Tomko opened zis mouth, but Chief Roy raised his hand and stopped zim. "Good afternoon, Miss Juliette. I'm pleased to meet you. My name is Chief Roy Danforth."

Juliette offered her gloved hand. "Why thank-you, chief, I'm so happy to meet all of you. And children, what a blessing."

Leyla pulled on Juliette's skirt. "Excuse me, ma'am, but we're looking for our biopod. Have you seen it?"

Juliette blinked. "Well now, I'm not so sure, but a couple days ago a vehicle resembling a fat, gray grub paced the waver for a spell. A considerable size, it was. Is that what you're looking for, little girl?"

I held my breath.

"Which direction did the vehicle take?" Chief Roy said.

"Why, I believe it turned off at the St. Albert exchange."

Chief Roy bowed. "Thank you, Miss Juliette, you've been a big help in our quest."

Juliette's attention drifted off, and she stared out the window.

St. Albert, next stop.

Chief Roy whistled. "That's our cue, kiddos."

Juliette patted her hair and straightened her slim skirt. "Mine, too."

"But we're still in the garbage sea," Benji said.

"Doesn't matter, this is our stop."

Benji edged in front of Tomko at the exit.

"Hey!"

The boys pushed and shoved their way off the putrid waver. I jumped down and separated them. A familiar odor of hot, poison air greeted me. "Breathers sealed."

Chief Roy offered his hand, and Juliette stepped off the waver like a princess. She hadn't put on her mask.

He bowed again. "Been a real pleasure meeting you, Miss Juliette. I wish you well."

Juliette's face crumbled. Tears and black mascara rolled down her pale cheeks. "Take me with you, Chief Roy. Please, I beg you. I can't stand it any longer!"

"I'm sorry, but we can't help you. You see, the councilors and I are escorting these children to a pick-up point in Vancouver City. After that, we'll be on our own, left to the vagaries of this desolate land, same as you.

Juliette trembled and her voice shook. "Take me with you, take me with you."

The chief wrapped Juliette in his arms and patted her back. "I've nowhere to take you."

Juliette sniffed and nodded. "I understand, just let me find my compact, I must look an awful fright." She dug in her briefcase and pulled out a pearl-handled pistol.

Chief Roy backed away.

Juliette pointed the handgun at him. "Take me with you, or I'll shoot you where you stand."

Chief Roy sighed. "You don't mean that, Miss Juliette. Believe me, if I knew of a safe haven, I would take you there, but I don't. You're much better off in familiar surroundings."

Juliette shrieked. "I can't live like this!" She turned the gun on her head.

"No!"

She fired and dropped to the ground.

Leyla and Etta screamed.

The screams drew the foragers from the garbage dump. They flooded the station.

Chief Roy clapped his hands. "Girls, stop screaming. Loneliness and despair drove her out of her mind. We couldn't help her."

Leyla hiccupped. "B-but all the blood." She took another peek and gasped. "I see brains!" She screamed again and Etta joined her.

The chief threw up his hands.

"Uh, chief, I hate to interrupt the girls' scream fest, but we'd better move on," Atian said. "Those folks from the garbage dump are moving in, and they don't look friendly."

"Atian's right. They'll cut off our escape route, if we don't hurry," I said.

Atian picked up Etta and I grabbed Leyla, but we were too slow. The foragers surrounded us on three sides. Trapped, we backed up against the waver.

"Tarnation."

They shambled toward us, in no particular hurry, but covering a lot of ground in a short time.

"Talk about a zombie apocalypse," Atian said.

Not quite zombies, but close enough to raise my hackles. Their vacant eyes stared through us, and they moved in a stiff-legged, jerky manner. Ragged clothes hung loose on their emaciated bodies.

"What's that creepy noise?" Benji said.

"They're humming."

Atian grabbed Benji by the scruff of the neck. "We need to scram."

Chief Roy pried open the waver's doors. "Right troops, back in and out the other side, real quick, before this contraption moves on."

On the other side of the waver, we hurried off the platform and ran down a narrow path through the sea of garbage. The deeper we ran, the higher the garbage rose above us. Rats squeaked and scurried out of our way, and we tripped over clumps of garbage. The mob behind us pushed through the garbage, widening the path with their clumsy bodies. The garbage mounds shuddered and shifted under their onslaught.

"I can't see," Leyla said.

Benji huffed beside her. "That's cuz there ain't no sun."

He was right. The mountain of garbage was leaning inward and blocking our view of the sky.

I dodged a plastic trash bag rolling down the garbage hill. Then another. "If those piles lean in any farther, they'll come down on us!"

"Aa, pick up the pace and don't touch the garbage!"

I opened my breather to scratch my nose. Big mistake. I sucked in putrid air and choked on fumes from decaying food and waste. Tears laced with methane and ammonia burned my eyes.

Leyla wheezed. "Hali, I can't breathe." She stopped and bent over, coughing.

"No Leyla! Don't stop!"

Atian scooped her up and kept running. We twisted and turned through the garbage tunnel. Faster, we needed to go faster. At last, we lost the mob and stopped for a water break.

I checked all the kids' breathers. "No one take off your breather, the air in here is toxic."

"Okay, let's go," Atian said.

A whimper stopped me. "Who's there?" I took a closer look at the bizarre garbage mountains. Tunnels, dozens of them, were burrowed into the sides. Some tunnels were large and low to the ground, while others perched high on the walls. A tunnel city? "Hello?"

Wolf barked at the tunnel.

A little boy peeked out of one of the tunnels. His face was covered in angry welts, and his breath came in labored jerks.

"Little boy, what are you doing in there? This whole place is coming down."

He wiped his dirty sleeve across his face and sniffed.

"Leave us be," a disembodied voice said.

"No, you've got to get out."

A baby cried deeper in the tunnel.

Men poked their heads out of other tunnels. Most looked in worse shape than the little boy. Dirty brown rags hung off their withered shoulders, and what little hair they had hung in straggly clumps from skulls covered in festering sores.

"We been livin' here plenty a time. The hill's solid," a man in an upper tunnel said in a weak hiss.

"No, it's not, and the air in here is full of poisonous gases."

A man covered in weeping sores peered out of a tunnel close to me. He tossed a clump of oozing cardboard at me. "Leave us be."

"Hali! Come on! We can't help them. The mob's closing in and the mounds are moving!" Atian said.

"Please, won't you come with us?"

"Be gone!"

A rumble warned me before the ground shook. "The mountain is coming down!"

"Hali!"

Wolf took my hand in his mouth and tried to pull me away. "Okay, Wolf, I'm coming."

With one last look at the little boy, I ran after Atian. A dull roar behind warned me not to stop. I kept running until I reached a rise above the garbage, and turned to watch as the sea of garbage slowly collapsed and buried the tunnels. Muted screams and cries reached us.

I covered my ears. That poor little boy. They'd never burrow their way out of the slide.

Atian huffed beside me. "That was too close."

I blinked away burning tears and kept running.

Chapter Nine

THE SURVIVALISTS

We stumbled out of the sea of garbage and stepped into an urban nightmare. Derelict vehicles, many with skeletons inside, clogged the streets in a never-ending parade of death. Rats and feral dogs scurried out of our way, their muzzles caked in dried blood from their latest feast.

"This is St. Albert?" Tomko said. "It's nasty."

Leyla sighed. "Oh, I'm so depressed."

Benji snickered. "You're such a drama queen."

"Am not."

"Am too."

Choking smoke and chemical fumes from burning buildings swirled around us.

"Make sure your breathers are sealed. This air is foul," Chief Roy said.

Etta huffed and crossed her arms. "Look at this place, people lived here, and now they're all deaded."

Chief Roy took her hand and led her along. "Aa, 'tis a terrible sight."

A pair of suede shoes covered in ash sat at the edge of the road. Atian checked the size. "Nope, won't fit any of us."

I laughed. "*Voyageur* will fit you with bionic shoes, you don't need somebody's cast-offs."

"Yeah, well *Voyageur* isn't here right now, is she? And we might never find her." He held up his shoe. His big toe peeked out of a hole. "I'm running out of options."

Willow stepped around a pile of human bones, some with flesh and hair still attached. "Yuck."

"Double yuck." Tomko said and pointed.

Three mangy dogs were playing with a human skull, tossing it in the air and catching it in their jaws.

Benji swallowed and made a retching noise. "Where's the rest of the body?"

Chief Roy shook his head. "You don't want to know."

Wolf's ears perked up, and he barked a friendly greeting. The stray dogs stopped chewing long enough to snarl, then went back to their game.

"Easy Wolf, they don't want to play."

I batted away a plastic bag, but clouds of bags floated in the air.

"Long after humans disappear from Mother Earth, there will be plastic bags," Chief Roy said. "An eternal testament to our excesses."

Some of the bags caught in swaths of snakeroot covering the crumbling ruins of apartment buildings. Chunks of cement, worked free by the insidious plants, littered the sidewalk.

Leyla headed over to white flowers hanging down the side of a building and reached for one.

"Don't touch them, they're poisonous," the chief said.

Her lower lip pouted. "Nothing but danger around every corner. Well, I'm sick of it."

Poor little tyke. I hugged her. "We'll be safe soon, sweetie."

"No, we won't. This horror will last until the end of my days."

Tomko snickered. "Sounds like the title for a poem."

Lasers whizzed through the air. "Take cover!"

Leyla scowled at Tomko. "See!"

Chief Roy peeked around the corner. "The owner of a grocery store is shooting at a pack of looters." He backed away. "We'll be taking a little detour here, don't need more trouble."

"Wouldn't mind getting my hands on them lasers," Samoset said.

"You'd shoot yourself in the foot, no doubting that," Leyla said.

Samoset snarled and we laughed, a hysterical, exhausted laugh.

A lone truck passed by, and we ducked into an alley clogged with debris.

Etta pulled on the chief's leather tunic. "See chief, some people still gots vehicles what's work."

The older kids snickered, but Chief Roy nodded. "Aa, that they do, Etta m'girl. Old combustions, something we be needing."

"Right now we need sleep more than a car," I said.

We cut through a cul de sac that seemed less decrepit, like the fancy houses were lived in. Stray cats and dogs fled when they spotted us, but the hair on the back of my neck tingled. We were being watched. I clutched my dreamcatcher, and it hummed in my hands. What did that mean? "Maybe we should keep moving chief, seems kind of creepy here."

"No, I think this is the right place." He picked up a blue backpack leaning against a twisted lamp post. "Matwau's pack."

I gasped. "He's here?"

Atian grumbled. "Oh great, the smasher is back."

Chief Roy flipped the latch on a gate to the backyard of a two-story brown house. "First, let's find us some shelter."

Benji kicked a square basin on the back deck of the house. Dried green slime caked the sides of the basin. "What's that?"

Chief Roy shook his head. "Don't rightly know, reminds me of a mini swimming pool."

We slipped through the shattered patio doors, and a swathe of must and mold hit us. The chief set his bio-comm to air purifier, but I kept my breather on. The children flopped down on overstuffed green sofas. The dry leather crackled and burst under their weight.

A wooden bookcase full of delicate crystal glasses and useless knickknacks hugged each side of a stone fireplace. I picked up a tarnished picture frame. A dark-haired man and a woman with bright eyes smiled at me. They cuddled two little kids, a boy with mischief dancing in his eyes, and the girl, a miniature of her mother. "A family used to live here."

Councilor Sereida picked up other photos. "I wonder who they were. They had two kids and three grandchildren."

"Then no more."

"People stopped having kids when things got bad, Halerine. Even in the North."

I nodded. Danny-boy was the youngest child in our village, and he was three.

A red ceramic bowl filled with mummified apples and oranges sat on the cracked kitchen counter. Atian ran his fingers along the marble counter, leaving a finger trail. "If not for all the dust, we could pretend the family just stepped out for the day."

I turned and gazed at him. "They're long gone and never coming back."

He grasped my hands and pulled me into the next room. "I know, and we can't let this happen again. We'll teach our children to respect Mother Earth."

Our children?

His lips touched mine, gently at first, then he pulled me close. His strong arms ran the length of my body, and a deep ache stirred inside me. "Atian—"

"Holos!"

Atian winked and backed away. "Later."

I took a shaky breath.

The boys made a beeline for a wall-sized holo screen. Benji and Tomko played with the touch pad controls, but no matter what they tried, the screen would not wake up.

Benji clutched a handful of holotabs to his chest. "Hali, wouldja look at all these holos and VRs, and we can't play any of them."

"How about some supper then?"

Benji's face lit up at the mention of food.

I scrounged in the messy pantry and found vacuum-packed beans and pork sausages hidden behind a dusty rice cooker. We heated the food on a propane camping stove Atian dug out of the basement storage room.

Benji shoveled brown beans. "Umm, I'm so hungry."

Samoset hovered on the edge of the kitchen. He might be a cretin, but I couldn't let him starve. "Here Samoset, have some beans."

He grasped a plate with shaking hands, but nary a thank you.

Benji gulped down a glass of water, letting some drip off his chin. "Ah, that feels so good."

Gecki poked his head out of Benji's suit. "Eeek?" He crawled into the glass and made noisy, slurping sounds.

"Benji! Who knows what diseases that creature is carrying."

Tomko licked zis dry lips and tickled Gecki's chin when he came up for air.

"Have some water, Tomko."

"We're waiting to see if Benji dies before we try it."

Chief Roy chuckled. "Bio says the water is old and stale but safe."

Tomko watched Benji for another minute, then gave in. Zie chugged water and poured some over zis head. "So good."

"How about sleeping in a big bed? That'll feel good, too. Come on, the lot of you."

I picked up Leyla. Her cheeks were flushed, and her little chest heaved. I felt her forehead, and my heart sank. "Chief, Leyla has a fever."

Chief Roy frowned. "Maybe she's just tired. We'll see how she's doing in the morning."

I ground dried willow leaves and mixed them with water. "Here sweetie, drink this, it'll bring down your fever."

Tomko dashed out of a bedroom. "Hey, these kids got real books!"

A loud bang and sounds of shouting and laughter woke me from a vivid dream, a nice one for a change. I was riding Honey across a lush, green meadow at breakneck speed. Her golden coat shone with sweat, and her sides heaved as she flew over the ground. I urged her to run faster and faster until her legs left the ground, and we flew into the bright blue sky.

I crept down the stairs and peered through the grimy front window.

"We've got company," Chief Roy said.

I wiped away some grime and took a closer look. "Voyageur!"

"Aa. We picked the right place, thanks to you and Matwau."

The biopod was parked on the far side of the cul de sac, her beautiful membrane a dull gray and badly dented. "Why does *Voyageur* look so beat up?"

"I suspect the old girl is keeping the extent of her abilities under wraps. She's not even complaining."

"I coded the synthor to my command only."

Chief Roy raised an eyebrow. "Sneaky, I'm impressed."

Men staggered around the biopod, clutching bottles, and talking and laughing. One of them looked like Claude. Torches and a bonfire lit their way.

I squinted in the dim light. Where was Matwau?

Wolf growled low in his throat and pawed the worn carpet. "Easy Wolf, don't make any noise."

Atian came up behind me and slipped his arms around my waist. I leaned into him. Could he feel my heart hammering against his chest?

"So what do we do now, chief?"

His breath tickled the back of my neck. "Isn't it obvious, we'll steal her back."

"A diversion then, that's what we be needing," Chief Roy said.

The councilors joined us at the window.

"Look, they're carrying stuff into that house," Councilor Ore said. "If we slip around back and start a fire in there, they'll come a running."

"Then the chief and I can hijack *Voyageur*," Atian said.

"What about the kids?"

Councilor Sereida stared at me over her antiquated bifocals. "Can't have them slowing things down, now can we?"

I sighed. "All right, I'll take them."

"We need a rendezvous point," Chief Roy said. "How about that hospital parking lot we passed down the hill?"

I gulped. Our plan was iffy. What if some of the men stayed with *Voyageur*? What if her power was gone? What if they couldn't get away? I shuddered and pushed down the what if's.

The chief placed his hand on my shoulder. "We'll be fine. Go now, Halerine Ananda."

I hurried upstairs and tiptoed through a jumble of arms and legs sprawled on the carpet. "Kids, wake up."

Benji yawned. "Why, what's wrong?" He removed Keme's foot from his chest.

"We're leaving. Put on your breathers and follow me. Hurry."

"I don't feel so good, Hali," Leyla said. "My feet hurt."

I pulled off Leyla's blanket. Her feet were red and swollen and covered in inflamed blisters, and she was burning up. My herbs couldn't deal with this. She needed polymers. "You have a little infection, sweetie. I'll get you some medicine at the hospital."

Atian met me at the bottom of the stairs. "Be careful with the kids, Hali."

I bristled and said the first thing that popped into my head. "You're not the only one who can protect these kids."

He dropped my arm and backed away. "Suit yourself."

I was tempted to bite off my tongue.

One by one the sleepy children toddled out the back door and into the hot night air. The moon's ghostly sheen lit our way. "Not a sound Wolf, understand?"

"Psst, Hali."

I searched for the voice in the dark shadows. "Mat? Is that you?"

He stepped into the light and took Leyla from me without being asked. "You got my messages?"

I resisted the urge to wrap my arms around him and hold on tight. "We did. I'm glad you're not a traitor."

Matwau chuckled and his face gleamed in the moonlight. "You never know. But I remembered your story about St.

Albert, so I suggested this might make a good hiding place for their haul. They bought it, not too swift, those guys. I crossed my fingers you'd figure out where we were headed."

"Chief followed your breadcrumbs."

Strong whiskey fumes surrounded him, and he was staggering a little. My heart sank. He had been doing so well. "Mat, what happened?"

He scowled. "Nothing, I'm fine, just had to play the part."

I gazed at him. Was he okay?

I jumped at a loud bang and Leyla stirred. "We'd better move on."

We circled around the cul de sac, keeping to the shadows, and disappeared into the night.

"Chief Roy!"

The children crowded around him, but I followed more slowly. If only I had paid more attention to our surroundings when we reached the hospital, then I might have noticed the survivalists before it was too late. We were trapped because of me.

Chief Roy read my mind. "This is no one's fault, Halerine Ananda."

He turned to the tall, thin man who was holding an old hunting rifle. The man's dirty blond hair was hacked off at the neck, and his haunted eyes reflected despicable things he had seen and done. He was dressed in green hospital scrubs and farmer's socks peeked out of his worn sandals.

"Do you have a name, sir?" Chief Roy said.

"Michael's the name. When the city collapsed a few of us hospital staff formed this little survival group and holed up here."

"But how do you survive?"

Michael shrugged. "Been living off the land, bartering for what we can't steal. Air's good enough to breath in here most days, so we're not complaining."

"We'll leave you in peace, then," Chief Roy said. "I'll collect my charges, and we'll head on to our destination."

Michael stared at the chief, his face a mask of cynical resignation. "And where might that be?"

"Vancouver City."

Michael gave a snort-laugh, only his eyes weren't laughing. "Vancouver? You'll never make it through the mountains. Millions died on that route." He stopped. "Say, how'd you get this far? Luke, check outside, see what this old buck used for wheels."

I held my breath, but Luke found nothing.

Michael scratched his dirty hair with the rifle barrel. "So what to do with you folks? You can't stay here, feeding too many mouths as it is. Can't let you go either, you might tell others about our little hidey-hole."

Chief Roy drew himself up to his full height, all five foot six inches, and hitched up his baggy pants. He glared at Michael with his good eye. "I assure you, my good doctor, we have no interest in your stake. As I said, we're headed to Vancouver. Don't you think there's been enough killing in these parts? Let these kids go."

"Wait—you're a doctor?" I said.

Michael wiped his bleary eyes. "Used to be. Dr. Benson before Turmoil."

"Please, can you help my little sister, her foot's infected. Do you have any medicine?"

Michael knelt beside Leyla and examined her foot. "Yep, that foot's infected all right."

Leyla coughed and Michael squinted at her. "She's asthmatic?"

I crouched down. "I-I don't know. She coughs a lot, but that's cuz of all the pollution."

Dr. Michael pressed a stethoscope to her chest and shook his head. "More than that. She's got asthmatic shadows under her eyes, and her chest is tight." He stood. "Hold on, I'll find the kid some meds."

Dr. Michael left, and I whispered, "Where's Atian? Is he all right?"

"He was behind me when these guys nabbed me. I closed the door, hoping they wouldn't see him."

Chief Roy spotted Matwau hunched in a corner. "Young man, we owe you a debt of gratitude. Welcome back to the flock."

For a moment I glimpsed last night's Matwau. He smiled and nodded. "Glad I could help, chief."

Samoset snorted. Matwau's face closed up, and he lapsed into gloomy withdrawal.

Chief Roy glanced around the dreary children's ward. "Where's Wolf?"

I swallowed a lump in my throat. "He attacked and one of the survivalists pistol-whipped him. I-I think he's dead, chief."

"I'm sorry, Halerine Ananda. He was a warrior true and blue."

I couldn't dwell. "So tell me."

"We watched and waited while the bandits drank themselves silly. When the torches burned low, I gave the word, thinking they might be unfit to react if I waited much longer. The councilors snuck into the backyard next door and lit a fire on the deck, then they slipped away." Chief Roy chuckled. "The flames raced across those dry wood shingles and spread through the house in minutes."

"What did the bandits do?"

"One of the drunken sops spotted the flames. He shouted and staggered toward the burning house. The rest followed and we ran for *Voyageur*."

Samoset hawked and spit on the worn carpet. "If we had guns, we could a rid ourselves of them looters right there."

The chief pulled Etta onto his lap. She cuddled into his arms and sucked her thumb. "Funny how vermin show up when all the work is done. Samoset was first into the pod."

"Hey, you ain't got no call talking about me in that tone."

"*Voyageur's* okay?" I said.

"*Aa.* For a heart stopping moment she wouldn't respond to my signal, but then she curled into a circle and raised her shields. She gave me enough time to recharge the power cells, but my heart was in my mouth the whole time."

I shuddered. "I can't imagine."

"The grand old dame uncurled and tore down the street shouting *Leyee! Leyee!* The bandits tried heading us off, but she out-maneuvered them."

Leyla clapped her hands. "Yay for *Vogy!*"

Vogy?

"We reached the hospital in ten minutes, but we waited until dawn broke before we eased into the parking lot at the rear. We knew something was amiss when you didn't show, so Atian parked *Voyageur* behind an abandoned semi-truck."

"How'd they catch you?"

"I opened a back door into the hospital, but the click of a rifle stopped me in my tracks. The good doctor bid me step inside. I pulled Samoset in and closed the door."

"Would a stayed in the pod, but that boy kicked me out," Samoset said.

Matwau cleared his throat. "Michael's coming, chief."

Chief Roy stopped talking.

Michael squatted beside Leyla. "Okay buckaroo, bed down here for the night. We'll figure things out tomorrow." He sprayed creamy white foam on Leyla's feet and handed me two containers. "Do this three times a day, and give her these polys twice a day." He handed Leyla a pink pipe and a soft rubber mask. "This is your inhaler, young lady. Use it in the morning and at night and anytime you can't breathe easily."

Leyla groaned. "Not another stinky mask."

I held out my hand. "Thank you, Dr. Benson."

Michael looked pensive as he took my hand. "You're welcome. First real patient I've had in a long while."

The children played with plastic toys and puzzles in the playroom, but they kept glancing from me to Chief Roy.

Etta tugged on the chief's sleeve. "What is it, Etta m'girl?"

"Chief, I'm seriously worried about Atian."

He kept a straight face. "The lad will show up when it's safe, and then we'll be on our way."

Michael escorted Councilors Ore and Sereida into the children's ward, a resigned expression on his face. "Tell me, old buck, are there any more of you we should expect?"

"That's the lot of them."

Michael left, muttering to himself.

"We'll sleep on the floor," I said. The shag carpet was more inviting than the moldy beds, and keeping everyone together seemed like a good idea.

I snuck into the nurse's station and filled my bag with meds and bandages to last until Maniton, and joined the kids on the floor.

Leyla snuggled close. I brushed damp curls away from her flushed cheeks. My sweet baby sister, nothing must happen to her.

"Tell me a story, Hali, about mama and a magic kingdom."

"Once upon a time, in a land far, far away there lived a princess named Leyla."

"Psst, psst."

What was that annoying sound? I rolled over for a more comfortable position.

"Psst."

I opened one eye and caught sight of a shadow at the window. Atian! I swept the cobwebs away and opened the dusty window. I wrapped my arms around his neck and pulled him close. He lifted his breather and kissed me, and I kissed him back. Then I kissed him again. "How'd you find us?" I said against his warm lips.

"I'll tell you everything later. *Voyageur* is waiting. Can you skip out?"

"We'll meet you at the service door in five minutes."

Atian kissed me again and disappeared into the night.

I shook Chief Roy. "Atian's here."

Matwau picked up Leyla, and we followed the sleepy children down the deserted hallway and out a side door. *Voyageur* was parked behind a giant mound of garbage.

Raven settled on the rear of the biopod and cleaned his blue-black feathers. "Caw, caw!"

I waved my arms. "Some help you were. Scat."

"Woof!"

Wolf hung his head out of the pod's airlock.

"Wolf! You're alive!"

Atian grinned. "Found him on the garbage dump. Quite a bump on his noggin, but otherwise he's all right."

Leyla clapped her hands. "Oh Vogy, I'm so happy you're safe!"

Voyageur reverted to a luminescent yellow. *Leyee, Leyee. Whoopee! Peeps back. Whup, bang!*

"You taught her all those words?"

Leyla shook her head. "Nope, she's picking them up on her own."

"Well, everybody better watch their language, then." I glared at Tomko and Benji. "Right?"

Chief Roy patted *Voyageur's* rump. "Nice to see you, old girl."

Hiya ol' man

Atian nodded to Matwau. "Thought you were gone for good."

"Sorry to disappoint you."

"Boys, play nice."

"Anyway, thanks for the breadcrumbs."

I glanced back. A lone figure stared out of a hospital window on the upper floor. I waved and he waved back.

"I wish you well, Dr. Benson," I said softly.

"*Voyageur*, head for Jasper City," Chief Roy said. "Time to make some serious tracks."

Leyla plopped down on her cushion seat. "Time for another lesson, Vogy. Say I love you, Leyla."

I l-l-luva you, Leyee.

Chapter Ten

SWEET REVENGE

Even at dawn, the heat was suffocating. I was so tired of being hot and sweaty. Maybe the air would be cooler up in the craggy mountains at the far end of this desolate plain. Maybe we'd find a river or a deep, cold lake and take a swim.

Ooh ooh hot Leyee hot hot

"Atian, hover this tug or her jets will melt like ice cream."

"Aye, chief, but she can't do it for long."

Sweat soaked through Atian's white muscle shirt, and his tanned arms and shoulders glistened. I touched my lips, the memory of our kisses still fresh.

We'd made good time for a few hours after leaving Edmonton, but now abandoned cars and trucks clogged the crumbling highway into Jasper City.

Chief Roy muttered under his breath. "If this gets any worse, especially in those mountains, we're in deep trouble."

I scanned the valley. A gray tower stood on the highest peak. Its dark, brooding presence chilled me. As I stared, the tower's massive tripods broke free from its rocky prison. It strode across the valley, crushing everything in its path.

Voyageur raced for the mountains, but the tower was gaining on us. "Full speed!"

Leyla sat up. "What's wrong, Hali?"

A shudder ran through my body, and the vision passed. I kissed the top of Leyla's head. "Nothing sweetie, go back to sleep."

She spotted the tower and cringed. "Oh no, not again."

I hugged her. "Don't be scared, baby girl, that old tower is all built and done for. They don't need slave-kids." I smiled in what I hoped was a convincing manner.

"Well, maybe." She snuggled into her cushion seat and fell back to sleep.

I coded the seat to monitor her body temp and gently rock her.

Chief Roy awakened his bio-comm and recorded the tower. "Been expecting more of those behemoths to show up."

White and red lights shot up and down the tripods, and streams of electricity sparked on the spiral top. One of the tripods was scorched half way up. Wonder what that was all about?

The air around the disk shimmered. Was a glider landing?

The highway took us to within a klick of the tower. I shivered again and turned away. "We'll never be free of them, will we?"

"In Maniton, Halerine Ananda, they can't touch you in Maniton." Chief Roy sighed. "They're not good for Mother Earth, I'm knowing that. Once I drop you youngsters off, I'll do a little scouting, see what I can find out about them." He grinned. "Maybe a little sabotage, here and there."

I needed to know the chief would be safe after we left him. "But you'll get into trouble."

"We've got trouble right now," Atian said.

A neo-glider zoomed into view, and I tensed. Matwau sat down beside me and clasped my hand.

Chief Roy grunted and peered through the skylight. "It's hovering above us. Keep going, lad."

At any moment the glider might drop a sat-bomb and vaporize us. Where was Corporal Haskins? He promised to keep Cardiff away. I squeezed Matwau's hand and waited. On the outskirts of Jasper City, the glider veered off and headed for the tower. We breathed a collective sigh.

I let go of Matwau's hand, and he shook out his squished fingers.

"Not sure if that was a good sign or not," Chief Roy said.

"What is this place?" Tomko said. "Everything's a boring white color."

He was right. The sleepy resort town of the twenty-first century had morphed into a sprawling megalopolis. Row upon row of condo ghettos surrounded the historic inner core, only they weren't so white anymore. Sooty scorch marks tinged the walls and the dead grass beside them.

"How come so many people lived here?" Leyla said.

"Same as Edmonton. The temps rose in the South, and refugees flocked to the mountains—cooler, more food, and cleaner water. That's when the town grew into this sprawling city."

Tomko checked zis hair in the monitor glare. Bright blue today. "At least we're in the trees again."

Benji huffed. "Yeah, but they're shrimpy trees, and they don't stop the wind. I hate wind, it creeps me out."

A spindly moose wandered through the condo suburb and nibbled on a patch of sickly yellow grass peeking through the broken pavement.

Etta took her thumb out of her mouth. "Poor old moose, all alone."

"Chief, *Voyageur* is running hot."

"Aa. Her a/c is done for. We'll spend the night here, let the old girl rest."

Atian parked the biopod between two blackened apartment buildings.

Leyla woke up and patted the pod's membrane. "You're out of the hot sun, Vogy."

Um goodie

"Let's take a little look-see, haven't been in this town since I was a boy. The land is drenched in rich history. The countless people who built it—"

"Destroyed it, you mean."

"*Aa*, they did that, too. But not out of malice, Halerine Ananda, more from ignorance and greed." He checked his bio-comm and tossed his breather aside. "Air's clean enough for a short walk."

Benji whooped and dropped his breather. "I'm counting the days until I ain't never wearing that stinky thing again."

"I'll stay and guard *Voyageur*," Samoset said.

We ignored the lazy bum.

We strolled down a street wallowing in mounds of garbage, some still in the ripe, rotting stage. The putrid odor oozed down my throat and my insides gagged. "Should have kept our breathers on."

Rats feasting on the rotting refuse skittered out of our way as we passed.

Tomko held zis nose. "That garbage smells like the toilet after Benji's been in there for a while."

Benji swatted at swarms of flies drawn to the garbage and punched Tomko in the shoulder all in one smooth motion. "Why does it smell so bad?"

Chief Roy grunted. "Not that far gone. I'm thinking some still live around here, or they left not long ago, so lots of fresh garbage and such."

Two bodies sprawled beside a pockmarked slider. "Lots of flesh left on those bones. Carrion birds and insects haven't done their job yet. Yep, still people around."

Willow gagged and hurried Leyla and Etta away.

I rubbed my shoe against the road surface. Gooey black tar stuck to my skidders. "Street's melting."

Atian dashed across the pavement and stood on a patch of dead grass. "Not ruining my new bionics."

We all wore new shoes and new clothes, thanks to the replicator. And the synthor was pumping out good food. Funny how simple pleasures most people took for granted in Beforetimes, like food and clothes, meant so much in this new world.

We passed a cowboy boot store with a fake hitching post out front, and a shop covered in bright pink siding promising costumes for little girls' Barbie dolls.

Leyla sighed. "Always wishing I had a Barbie."

Most of the stores had scorch marks. "Who would try to burn down these buildings?"

"Not sure it was a who, maybe a what," the chief said.

"Look at the twins." Etta pointed to a pair of buildings leaning against each other. If one toppled so would the other.

"They're bestest friends."

Thick green vines dipped and curled around the buildings and grew out of the concrete walls. In another decade the high-rises would resemble twin mountains covered in a green carpet. If they were still standing.

"Well, would you look at this," Chief Roy said. "Smack dab in the center of all these bland high rises, here's a little real history."

A two-story stone house with pointy roof peaks and scads of gables sat in the middle of the concrete jungle. Grassy meadows and tall trees, dead now, surrounded the building.

"It's like a fairytale house," Leyla said.

"I remember this building from when I was a boy," Chief Roy said. "Was a tourist information center back then."

"Can we go in and rest awhile?" Benji said. "My feets hurt from these new shoes."

The chief peered inside a gaping hole in the stone wall. "Seems safe enough."

He and Matwau pried open the front door. A pigeon flew out of the door, its wings battling against the wind. "Inside troops."

The back side of the house was gone. Hungry rodents had chewed wooden furniture beyond recognition while brown leather chairs were layered in pigeon poo. Chips of wood covered the floor. My feet crunched on the messy litter as I walked over it.

"Termites slowly eating up the floor," Chief Roy said. "Right, you scallywags, get some rest any way you can. We're heading out in a couple hours."

A volley of bullets peppered the entrance.

"Everybody down!"

Atian pushed Tomko to the ground. "The depot bandits!"

Etta stood in the middle of the room, her terrified gaze fixed on me.

"Hide Etta!"

"I-I can't."

Chief Roy dashed across the room and scooped her up, but a bullet grazed his shoulder. He tossed Etta to me and crawled back to kids trapped behind an old couch.

"Etta, where's Leyla and Benji?"

"I d-don't know, I done lost them."

I craned my neck and caught a glimpse of Leyla's pink and yellow ponytail peeking over a couch. "Leyla, over here."

She crawled along the edge of the room and wrapped her arms around me. "Those bad men are getting on my nerves."

Etta hiccupped. "Me too."

"Where's Benji?"

"He went outside, said he needed a pee," Leyla said.

149

Etta pointed through the door. "Look it, the biggest bad man gots him."

Those creeps had Benji? "You two stay with Willow." I headed for the entrance.

"Halerine Ananda, come back here."

I ignored the chief. Claude had my brother. I peeked around the door. "Benji, where are you?"

Claude dragged Benji into view. The poor little guy's pants were suspiciously wet, and he sported a swollen red eye. I stepped out of the entrance. "Let him go."

Claude snickered. "You sure are gutsy, girlie-squaw. I could shoot you where you stand." He swatted Benji on the head. "Stop squirming."

"What do you want?"

"Well now, got myself real used to the comforts in that there transport. I'm wanting it back. Sides which, me and my boys could get where we're going mighty fast in that thing."

They were going somewhere? "Oh, and where might that be?"

Claude smirked. "Heading to the coast. Hear tell some action going down there."

My stomach tightened. These bandits were after the sub from Maniton? Whatever the cost, I couldn't let them reach Vancouver.

The bandits crowded together, not a good tactic in conflict, but then they figured we were helpless. Matwau was circling behind the bandits, and the chief and Atian were likely waiting to make their move. I needed to stall. "I've got an idea."

"Yeah, you wanna join us?" He leered. "Could use a little warm company."

I smiled sweetly. "Maybe, but since we're heading in the same direction, why not join forces? You've got the fire power, we've got the know-how."

Claude hawked and spit into the dusty street. "Ain't needin' help."

"The biopod is programmed to my command, she won't budge for you." Not quite true.

Claude rubbed his gun barrel against Benji's temple. "Well then, I'm thinking you be joining us, lest your boy here takes a bullet."

I fought to keep the tremor out of my voice. "Let him go, and I'll come with you."

"No! Don't do it, Hali! He's a bad man!"

Claude pushed Benji to the ground and pointed his gun at my heart. "Get over here, girlie-squaw."

I gulped. This was going bad, real fast. "Benji, run into the house. Find Leyla and stay out of sight."

"I won't leave you."

"Go—I love you. Tell Leyla."

I dragged my feet. Where was my knight in shining armor when I needed him? Or maybe the spaghetti westerner on his horse?

Claude grabbed my arm. "Oki-doki, girlie-squaw, let's go find that transport."

I batted my eyelashes. "But I-I'm not sure where it's parked. I'm disoriented after all the corners we turned."

"Come on, girl, you ain't fooling me none, quit stalling."

I led the bandits away from the biopod and made a show of searching every alley. "Nope, not the right one."

We turned a corner, and I ran out of alleys.

"It's not this way, is it?" He yanked on my braid. "You've got five minutes, girlie, or I'll put a bullet in your gut and find that kid you prize. He'll die slowly, I promise."

"It must be back the way we came." This time my voice did quiver, and I bit my lip not to cry. We reached the twin buildings, and I was out of ideas. "I-I think the biopod is in between those two apartment buildings."

Claude gave me a hard look and signaled his men to fan out. "You and I be taking a little look-see."

We rounded the corner of the first building and there sat *Voyageur*. I took a deep breath. Thank goodness Atian hadn't moved her, or I would be dead about now.

"What's your name, girlie-squaw?"

Not a chance in hell I was giving this creep my real name. "Micha."

Claude hawked and spit. "A squaw name. I'll call you Sue after my dearly departed, drug-addled mother." He opened the biopod's airlock. "In you go, Susie."

A laser beam severed his right arm where he held the hatch. More lasers hit him in the legs, and he went down howling.

The bandits charged the biopod, but the kids burst out of the alleys and pelted them with stones and bricks. The thugs scattered, their shoulders hunched.

I plunged into the fray, a rock in my hand, and brought it down on Claude's head. He twitched and went still. We chased after the bandits, picking up the stones we'd used and firing them again. Matwau kept up a barrage of laser beams to move them along.

Tomko was pitching rocks from behind a concrete barricade.

"Where's Atian?" I said.

"Taking care of them bandits. He told us to hide inside *Voyageur*."

"Good idea. Come on kids, into the pod."

I kicked Claude's prone body away from the airlock and helped the children inside. I was about to seal the door when Chief Roy hobbled up, the councilors in tow. Councilor Ore had a gash across her temple, and Sereida's wrist hung at an odd angle. Both of them were grinning from ear to ear.

The chief brandished one of the lasers we'd found in an abandoned ranch house. He blew on the tip. "Getting to be a regular gunslinger, I am."

The boys loped into view. Atian's nose was bleeding, and he was dragging his left leg. An ugly welt showed through a gash in Matwau's suit.

Atian jumped into *Voyageur* and whooped. "That was some fun."

"Fun?"

"Ah Hali, revenge is sweet," Matwau said.

Benji grinned and smacked Atian's hand. "Yeah, those bandits are losers."

"Men." I shook my head. "Chief, let me see your shoulder."

He brushed my hand away. "It's just a little scratch, I've had plenty worse in my day. Leave it be."

I shook my finger. "Chief, that bullet's coming out, no arguing."

He grinned and saluted, then winced. "Yes ma'am, but let's leave the doctoring for a quieter time."

Atian climbed into the control pod and waved the console awake. "Up for a little trek, *Voyageur*?"

Whoopie

The biopod careened around the corner and skidded to a stop in front of a lone figure waving his arms.

Samoset.

"Should I?"

"Aa, we can't leave him."

"Why not?" Atian opened the airlock. "Thanks for all the backup, Samoset."

"Shut your mouth, gimp." He headed for the storage pod.

"No grub till mealtime, Sami," Leyla said.

Atian lost little time in finding the main highway and coasting through Jasper City. Matwau stood guard beside him the whole time.

My stomach churned. Next time we might not be so lucky. I surveyed our motley little group. They needed a bath and rest, but most of all they needed food. "Who's up for breakfast?"

"About time, I'm starving," Benji said.

I caught a bowl of porridge as it flew out of the synthor and set it down in front of him.

He slurped and grunted through his bowl. "Can I have some more?"

"You've had enough."

He shook his head. "I ain't never had enough."

"Time for a bath."

"Ah Hali, why spoil a perfectly good day."

Chapter Eleven

RETURN TO THE SILVER TOWER

The nightmare swept over me, and I bit my tongue to hold back a scream. How had this happened? This morning I was heading for Maniton and a new life. This afternoon I was back where it all started, locked in the silver tower on the Siksiká Blackfoot refuge.

General Cardiff was waiting for us on the outskirts of Jasper City. An ominous row of gray tanks blocked the highway, and a horde of dark skimmers and red-eyed drones bobbed in the air above us. One of the drones showered *Voyageur* in a stream of gooey mist that hardened, and we were frozen in place.

Ooh-ee no Leyee me need helpin'

Soldiers poured out of the tanks and surrounded the biopod.

Chief Roy opened the comm. "What is the meaning of this?"

General Cardiff stepped out of the lead tank. "Stand down, old buck. Surrender Halerine, and we'll let you go."

My body went cold. Not again.

Benji clutched my arm. "Don't go, Hali."

I hugged him one last time. "Hush, I won't let Cardiff hurt you."

Atian pulled me into his arms and stroked my cheek. "No, Hali, we'll find another way."

Coldness seeped into my heart. I opened my mouth to tell him I loved him, but what was the use. "There is no other way."

Cardiff's men dragged me into a skimmer and then a neo-glider. In my befuddled state of mind, I didn't notice the flight back to the silver tower, nor did I remember being led into the revolving disk. But here I was, a prisoner in General Cardiff's lavish lair.

"You do realize you won't be making your secret hideaway."

I pushed his words away. I couldn't deal, not yet. "Tell me, Cardiff, do your soldiers know how you live?"

An enormous oval bed swathed in red silk and plump pillows rested on a silver carpet. A priceless Ming dynasty tapestry hung behind the bed. Tacky, but luxurious. Mouth-watering smells wafted through the sterile air from a roast beef dinner set on a linen-covered table. My empty stomach gurgled. "They sleep in a dormitory and eat dry rations while you live like this."

Cardiff poured dark liquid from a decanter into a crystal glass. He took a sip and smacked his fleshy lips. "I'm a man of power, I deserve some comforts."

Expensive women's clothing hung in an open closet. I gulped. For me? I swallowed the bile rising in my throat. "Why don't you let us go? We're nothing to you, you've said so yourself."

He chuckled and rocked back on his heels. The brass buttons on his jacket strained against his paunch. "You're a smart girl. Of course you savages mean nothing to us, but I can't risk low-life whelps scurrying out of their hidey-hole in three hundred years and breeding like rabbits. The earth belongs to us, not the likes of you."

"Why do you care what happens in three hundred years? Your bones will be dust."

He smirked and popped a green grape into his mouth. "Oh, I don't think so. We haven't gone to all this trouble not to enjoy the fruits of our labor."

I waited.

"You see, little girl, our scientists have been working for half a century on developing a safe way for us to wait out the years, and they've done it. I'll be here, three hundred years from now, fit as a fiddle. I'll climb out of my hibernation crib and claim my rightful heritage."

I rolled my eyes.

His face reddened. "Show me some respect! You and your kin are still breathing because I say so."

I shrugged. "What do you want with me?"

Lust flashed in his cold, blue eyes. "Necessary though they may be, single-minded techies with the skinny bodies of mannequins and cold-hearted military females make poor bedfellows."

I snorted. "Afraid those women will break you down?"

Cardiff scowled. "Watch your tongue. I'm of no mind to put up with shrewish women. Good thing we're not taking any females with us into the Ark."

I raised an eyebrow. "No females? And how do you plan on repopulating the earth when you climb out of your lair?"

He grunted. "Not up on your technology, are you, girlie? We've stored enough female zygotes to grow three or four companions for every one of us." He leered. "Should be quite a feast, and they'll produce the next generation."

What a sick bastard. My stomach churned, and I'm sure my face reflected my disgust. The general was too wrapped up in his gloating to notice.

"I'm in need of some diversion until the big sleep. You'll warm my bed for the foreseeable future."

He moved closer. I stepped back. "I thought you didn't force women."

He reached out and touched my hair. "Oh, I won't force you. You'll come to my bed willingly."

"Not bloody likely."

He strolled over to a vidscreen taking up most of one wall and woke the screen to a drone hovering over *Voyageur*. "Just waiting for my orders."

I struggled to control my features. He would not break me.

He flicked the screen and the shattered dome covering the Siksiká village glimmered white and forlorn. "And of course, there's always the village." He zoomed the view. A drone circled above the dome. "Also awaiting my command."

Was that Honey grazing in the meadow? I cleared my throat and steadied my quivering voice. "For how long? Until you hibernate? Then you'll kill us all."

He shrugged. "Life is life. Even for a short time."

"Not with you."

Cardiff scowled, and his saggy jowls drooped over his bullish chin. He raised his glass to me. "I'm giving you a chance for another year. You'll live in the lap of luxury on the Ark, and your kin will not be harmed." He grunted. "Of course, I cannot allow them to reach that secret city, but they'll live for a time in a detention camp." He buzzed his comm. "Lieutenant, bring in the kit."

A young man dressed in green battle fatigues opened the door and backed in holding a cloth-covered tray.

I crouched, ready to flee. "What's that?"

Cardiff chose a syringe from the tray and skirted liquid into the air. "A little something to take the edge off."

I dashed around a marble counter. "Stay away from me."

Cardiff snapped his fingers, and the corporal jumped over the counter and grabbed my bound arms. I struggled against him. "Let me go, you pig!"

Cardiff drew near, the syringe held high. A crazed light shone in his eyes. "Relax Halerine, this won't hurt a bit."

He jabbed the needle into my neck, and my world went woozy.

Cardiff nodded at the bed. "Take a little nap, and I'll join you soon enough."

The door closed, and I collapsed in tears. All this, all we had gone through, and Cardiff swooped in and ended it. "I give up, Apistotoke. I can't go on." If Cardiff kept his word and left my family alone, I didn't care what happened to me. But Cardiff wouldn't keep his word. He'd destroy *Voyageur* and everyone in it.

I shook my head to clear it and resisted the urge to lie down on the soft bed. A weapon, I needed some kind of weapon. I staggered into the dining room and opened drawers and flung the contents. In the last drawer, tucked in a back corner, I found scissors and slid them into my back pocket. Not an easy feat with bound hands. "Come and get me, Cardiff, I'm ready for you."

My vision blurred. "Focus Hali."

I tapped the vidscreen for one last look. The translucent dome flickered on the viewer, and a vision took over. Mama was cleaning the last of the sickly carrots from our feeble garden, and papi was sharpening the axe he used to chop wood. He stopped and gazed through the crack in the dome. Was he thinking about us and wondering what we were doing? Papi, I'm up here. Help me.

I shook the vision away. Their world was no longer my world. And nobody could help me.

I passed out on the bed.

"Hali?"

Someone shook my shoulder. "Hali."

I opened my eyes. "Atian? No. Go away."

"What? Why?"

"Cuz you're not really here, are you? This is just a dream." I closed my eyes and rolled over.

Atian shook me again. "Come on, Hali, wake up and concentrate."

But concentrating was proving rather difficult. "How'd you get here, if you're so real?"

He grinned. "Oh, that's a story for another day." He untied my hands. "Let's go before Cardiff gets back."

Curious and curiouser. I tried to stand, but my legs went all rubbery. "Go where?"

He pointed up.

I gulped. Up meant the landing pad. Oh no, I wasn't falling for that game. Cardiff was tricking me into going to the Ark. "Go away, I need rest."

Atian lugged me to my feet, but I flopped down the moment he let go. "Back off, Cardiff."

"Hali, for crying out loud, it's me, Atian."

Nope.

"Move it, Halerine Ananda!"

Chief? Was he in my dream, too?

Atian half-dragged me up the stairs. "Can't risk the lift."

We climbed a hundred steps, I'm sure, and I was huffing by the time we reached the landing pad. Foul air hit me, and I bent over gasping.

The fake Atian slipped a breather over my head. "Let's go."

I took one look at the three mini skimmers parked in a row and turned back to the stairs. "Nope, not doing it."

Atian caught up to me. "Hali, Cardiff drugged you. It's me, Atian. I've come to take you back to *Voyageur*."

Back to *Voyageur*? Now I knew I was dreaming. "Yeah, right. I don't believe you. *Voyageur* is gone, done for." My knees gave way, and I flopped on the tarmac.

"Come on, Hali, wake up."

What an annoying dream. "Easy for you to say, my knight in shining armor."

Atian sighed and dropped to his knees. "I can't carry you, Hali." He took my face in his hands and kissed me. A hard, jolting kiss.

Hali.

I clutched my dreamcatcher. Maybe I would play along a little. For another kiss. I stood and tested my legs. Still rubbery, but when I concentrated, they moved the right way. Atian led me to a small skimmer, more like a rickshaw with wings. I skidded to a stop. "Wait. Who's gonna fly that thing?"

Matwau's head popped out of the cabin. "Me."

Matwau was in on this dream, too?

Atian's grin widened. "We flew one of these puppies to within a klick of the tower. Dumped it in the creek."

"We? Flew?" I headed for the stairs. "I'm out of here."

Cardiff blocked my exit, and he had brought back-up. A fearsome soldier carrying a military-type gun stood behind him.

Atian charged the general, and one of the soldiers punched him in the face. He went down.

The general smirked at me. "Nice to see you've changed your mind, Halerine."

I backed away and felt for the scissors in my back pocket. "Not about you."

He tsked tsked and advanced. My grip tightened on the scissors, and I waited for his next move. I planted my feet wide apart to keep my balance, and when he reached for my arm, I whipped out the scissors and stabbed him in the paunch.

He gasped and clutched his belly. "You bitch! Get her!"

A nearby soldier rushed me, but Matwau shot his legs out from under him.

I swallowed hard to keep from retching and dropped the scissors. I had stabbed a guy. Why didn't I feel sorry?

Cardiff moaned, then fell back.

Matwau wrapped his gorilla arms around me and held me tight. "Glad to have you back, sweetheart."

"You better not be a dream."

He grinned and helped Atian stand. "Let's go for a little ride, shall we?"

"You know how to fly a skimmer?"

He flashed a smile. "I'm a fast learner."

Great Apistotoke, help me.

Atian felt his bruised jaw. "We're out of time. Move it."

In a daze, I climbed into the back passenger seat.

Matwau waved his arm in front of the skimmer's screen, and the control panel lit up. An automated voice said, "Destination?"

"Jasper City."

"Here's your suit," Atian said.

I fell off the seat trying to put on the suit. So this was how drunk felt. I put one leg in, then the other and pulled the stinky biosuit over my traitorous body.

A soft hum oozed through the skimmer and before my foggy brain cleared, it lifted off. Just in time. A platoon of laser-toting soldiers ran across the landing site. Cardiff was lying on the ground but still issuing orders. Well, at least I hadn't killed him. Two of the soldiers knelt and took aim. The blasts struck one of our wings, and the skimmer shuddered. Soldiers scrambled into the other two skimmers, and the birds lifted off. The flap of their wings thumped the air and raised goosebumps on my arms.

"Buckle up, there's gonna be a chase!" Matwau worked the controls. "Hold on, here we go!"

I buckled my seatbelt with shaking hands. Our skimmer veered off at a sharp angle, and I clutched my stomach. "Oh, I'm gonna upchuck."

"Not in your breather," Atian said.

The skimmers matched Matwau's moves and gained on us.

"Do something or they'll team tag us," Atian said.

Matwau sent our skimmer into a steep dive, and we zoomed in and out of the northern hills covered in dried-out boreal forest. He dipped close to a swampy muskeg, then flipped the skimmer between two hills. One of the skimmers lost control and nose-dived into the muskeg. The other one hovered above us.

"That bird is heating up the fire power, we'd better scram." Matwau hit a green button, and the skimmer shed light years.

My head was beginning to clear, if not my stomach. "Will they alert the thugs guarding *Voyageur*?"

Matwau snorted. "Be kind of tough. We took them all out."

"How'd you do that?"

"Seems our Vogy has a few tricks up her sleeve. She let out an ear-piercing scream that knocked the soldiers out, and the drones dropped like stones." He winked. "We snatched a tank and headed to the tower to steal a skimmer while *Voyageur* hid in a canyon. Easy-peasy."

Why didn't *Voyageur* use her scream-shield when Claude attacked? I'd have to ask her.

We skimmed across the second coming of the altithermal, travelling in minutes what took us three weeks in the biopod.

Atian was watching the view screen. "We're almost there."

The skimmer jerked and groaned, and black fluid hissed out of the injured wing.

"I can't hold her," Matwau said. "We're going down."

We plummeted toward the barren ground. I shook my head and tried to clear the fog. We were crash landing in the middle of the badlands, and I couldn't seem to care.

The prairie leveled out, and Matwau took the skimmer in for a landing, but one of the skims caught a hidden rock at touchdown. The skimmer flipped over and rolled across some long-forgotten farmer's field. We came to rest upside down on a flat, sandy plain.

"Well, here we are. Sort of safe," Matwau said.

Hanging upside down in a crashed skimmer in the middle of nowhere. Yeah, safe.

Atian consulted his comm. "Eighteen klicks to *Voyageur*, but we can't make contact or Cardiff will track us."

"Yep, means we're hoofing it," Matwau said.

We half climbed, half fell out of the skimmer and peered into the steep gorge cutting through the plain. Tracks from extinct animals crisscrossed the gorge, and dead bushes lined a dried-up riverbed.

Atian whistled. "Good thing she stopped when she did or we'd be toast."

Matwau grabbed water canteens out of the skimmer and jogged to the edge of the gorge. "Come on, they'll be on us soon enough."

"Down there?" Atian said.

"Easier to hide. And if I'm not mistaken, this is the same gorge where *Voyageur* is hiding." He slid down an animal trail.

I adjusted my breather and followed him down the cliff side. Eighteen kliks. Might as well be eighteen hundred. We wouldn't make it, even in our suits, not without more water.

The haloed sun beat down on us and the hot wind, smelling of dust and decay, pushed us along the jagged edge of the gorge.

"This baby's left over from the last ice age," Matwau said. "Water drained off the mountain glaciers and cut deep grooves through the soft limestone."

"Too bad the river dried up," I said. "Would've saved us."

We hiked along the rough animal trail, our breathers working overtime filtering the dirty air. Matwau allowed us sips of water every twenty minutes. We trudged through the gorge, circling around piles of rocks and dead aspen trees, driven by the need to reach *Voyageur* before our strength or our suits gave out.

Sweat oozed down my back and puddled in my shoes, taking the remnants of Cardiff's drug with it. But coming down was not fun. My head pounded in time with my hammering heart, and my skin itched in places I couldn't reach.

Atian's limp grew more pronounced by the hour, and late in the day he stumbled over a jumble of dry brush and flopped down under an overhanging ledge. He gasped for air. "Need to rest for a spell."

Matwau shook his empty canteen and tossed it in his bag. "Not for long, our water won't last if we coast."

A gopher popped out of its hole and scolded us for disturbing its peace.

"And gophers shall inherit the earth," Matwau said.

A shower of small rocks trickled down the cliff and landed on the ground in front of us. Matwau put his fingers to his lips, and we sat rigid, barely daring to breathe. The boys were hand signaling a plan of attack when two emaciated goats leaped across our line of sight and dashed away.

Matwau laughed. "Wouldn't you know it?"

Atian picked up a sturdy branch for a walking stick. "Let's go, we can do this."

Could we? Our water was gone, our biosuits were drying out, and our breather filters needed changing. The race was on, would we die of thirst or poison air?

A shrill call stopped me. Raven. What now?

A low buzzing sound warned us, and we ducked under an escarpment. A drone floated overhead, its red eye whipping back and forth as it searched the terrain. Had it seen us? We waited until the shadows grew long, then ventured out of our shelter.

"If we pick up the pace, we'll reach *Voyageur* in an hour," Matwau said. "But we're goners if it takes longer."

We jogged, sprinted, and loped along the dismal terrain.

Hiss. A laser beam caught Atian square in the back, and he went down.

"Atian!"

"I'll get him, Hali," Matwau said.

"Who will get you?"

He dashed back to Atian and I followed. We pulled him into the shade of an overhang. I shook him. "Wake up, Atian."

He groaned and opened his eyes. "That was a shocker."

"Roll over, let me check your burn."

The slash across his back still smoldered. Make that a race between thirst, poison, and a laser burn seeping into his vital organs.

"Can you walk?" Matwau said.

Atian crawled to his feet and stretched. An anguished groan escaped his lips. "Yep, just give me a minute."

Laser beams sliced the air beside us. One struck the overhang and rocks pelted us.

"We don't have a minute. They'll knock the ledge down, and we'll be sitting ducks."

"They? How many are there?"

"Counted three."

Déjà vu swept over me, and I sat down on a rock.

"We did it before, we can do it again, Hali."

"How far?"

Atian checked his comm. "Three hundred meters."

I closed my eyes.

"Here's the deal. We keep running, dodging this way and that, no matter what happens. At least some of us will make it."

Atian chuckled. "Where have I heard that before?"

We hunched over, as if for a race, and it was a race. For life.

"Ready?"

I nodded.

"Go!"

We raced for *Voyageur*, dodging around bushes and jumping over rocks in our path. We almost made it, then Matwau yelled out. I looked back, still running. Mat was crawling behind a rock. Atian was limp-running behind me. I hid behind a boulder at a new barrage of beams. "Keep going, I'll go back for Mat."

"He said to keep running no matter what, Hali."

I grinned. "We don't leave our family behind, remember?"

He returned my grin and dived behind my rock as a beam crisscrossed his path. He kissed me through our breathers. "I remember. We do this together, okay?"

I shook my head. "You're wounded, and your foot is acting up. I'll be faster by myself. You head to *Voyageur*, maybe she can help protect us." I kissed him again. "Please, listen to me."

He sighed, then nodded. My words were right, and he knew it.

"Ready? Go!"

He dashed the last fifty meters to *Voyageur*, and I ran back to Matwau. The drones circled overhead, unsure of who to attack. I made it to him before their beams reached me. "Mat? Are you hurt bad?"

He groaned. "I told you to keep running."

"Yeah, well I never listen, just ask Atian."

Raven circled over head. "Fly away, you silly bird before you get your feathers singed."

A drone swiveled its red eye and zoomed in on the bird. Raven screeched and flew away moments before a beam streaked across the sky.

Matwau's left leg resembled ground meat. "Can you walk on that thing? It's plenty cooked."

"Not down to my bone. I can walk."

Voyageur was huddled in a ravine, its back end peeking out from under a ledge. A drone zoomed in on its shell, and my heart sank. But the old biopod wasn't through with her surprises. A beam shot out of her grill and fried the pesky drone. That left two.

Atian waved from the airlock. "Come on, they're resetting! Now's your chance!"

With our last burst of energy, we staggered toward the airlock.

Yippee yippee

Voyageur scooted out of her hiding place. Chief Roy opened the airlock and stood back. Beams laced the biopod, but her shields held. We fell in the airlock and lay there gasping.

"Mighty relieved to see you youngsters."

"Water." My voice croaked and I swallowed.

Benji handed me a tube. I drained it, then another.

"Hali, where were you?"

Should I tell him and break his little heart? "The silver tower on the Siksiká refuge."

His eyes widened. "You was home? Did you see mama and papi?"

"It wasn't like that, Benji. I wasn't home. *Voyageur* is our home."

Chapter Twelve

INFERNO VALLEY

Atian eased *Voyageur* to a full stop. A tanker truck with United Ballard written on the side in bold red letters was jackknifed across the road and tipped over. "That's it, we'll have to clear the road before moving on."

"Do you think it's safe, chief? Last time we ran across a tanker, we were ambushed," Matwau said.

Chief Roy sighed, and for a moment his broad shoulders sagged. "I know, lad, but we don't have much choice, the ditches are too steep for *Voyageur's* jets and too high for her hover." He straightened. "Time to pull out the artillery."

He handed lasers to me and to Councilors Ore and Sereida. "Fan out."

Looking more like geriatric commandos than dignified elders, the two old ladies exited *Voyageur* and spread out. Did they ever wonder how their lives had changed from the days when they sat around the village hearth, smoking sweet grass, and telling stories about the good old days, even if none of them remembered when the olden days were good?

I took up a position near *Voyageur's* bow, my eyes searching the sky for Cardiff's drones. They were up there, I felt their beady eyes watching us.

Samoset stepped in front of Chief Roy, hands on his hips, a scowl on his rat-face. "Hey, I want one of them babies."

The chief's eyebrows furrowed, and he folded his arms across his chest. This should be good.

"The councilors and Halerine Ananda will manage quite well without your help, but if you want to make yourself useful, Matwau and Atian are both recovering from their injuries. They could use some help connecting the towline."

Matwau's leg was healing nicely, thanks to the polymers Dr. Benson had given me, but he would bear the scars for life. Atian's back was another story. I'd stopped the burns from leaching into his organs, but he'd need reconstructive surgery when we reached Maniton.

Samoset held up his hands and backed away. "Now chief, you know my back's been acting up something fierce." He scurried into the biopod.

Voyageur spewed an electromagnetic towline, and the boys attached it to the tanker.

Atian waved. "Okay Chief, haul away."

Voyageur backed up slowly and stretched the towline taut, but the tanker would not budge.

Uh-uh, no-way.

"So much for easy." Chief Roy scratched his head. "Must be full of fuel. Okay, plan B." He boosted power and pressed *Voyageur's* front bumper against the side of the tanker. "Push hard, old girl."

Voyageur groaned and squeaked and faded to gray as the tanker slid over.

Atian and Matwau limp-ran for the biopod. "Okay, we can get by," Atian said.

"All aboard!"

The commandos crawled through the airlock and handed over their firepower. Councilor Ore pressed her lips together and huffed. "Nothing but a bunch of scrawny rattlesnakes out there."

She sounded a little disappointed.

Ooh-ee oyo-ee

Voyageur curled around the truck like a chubby caterpillar and rumbled down the road.

"Rocky Mountains, here we come."

Atian's glee proved short-lived. We caught up to a long line of vehicles blocking the road in both directions.

Samoset snarled and shoved Tomko off zis cushion. "Move your tush, girlie-boy, this is gonna take all day, and I need a nap."

Tomko dusted off zis lime green shorts and glared at Samoset. "I'm a Two-Spirit, not a girlie-boy," zie said through clenched teeth.

Benji offered zim a seat. "Never mind, Tomi, he's a creeper."

"Let's shove the sliders out of the way, chief," Atian said. "We can't waste time moving every vehicle. Cardiff could be on us any minute. *Voyageur* can fix her shell later."

Yeah no whee-oo.

I activated the screen and gazed across the valley. Something about the air hadn't felt right when I was on patrol. Raven circled above the biopod, his eerie cries ringing hollow in the morning heat, and Sky Beings flitted around him, scolding and teasing. A warning?

"Run Hali."

My disquiet intensified, and I caught at my dreamcatcher. "Chief, those sliders are full of dead people, and look at the vehicles—their paint is blistered and their runners are melted into the pavement. A-and there's no trees on those mountains, just burned out stumps. Even the grass is scorched black."

"Calm down, Halerine Ananda," Chief Roy said, but he followed my gaze.

"Halerine's right," Councilor Sereida said. "Those folks are charred. Whole families heading for the mountains, then something catastrophic happened to them all at once."

The hair on the back of my neck tingled, and I fought back waves of panic rippling through my body. "Remember the scorch marks in Jasper? And that tower is charred half way up one of its tripods."

Stunned silence.

The fear bug churned in my stomach, and I stumbled over my words. "I-I think I know what's happened. W-when the sun rises, it burns everything in its path."

"*Voyageur*, shields up!"

Yepper

The first rays of the sun peeked over the horizon and burned through a haze of green and pink clouds.

"But that doesn't make sense." Atian ran his hands through his thick hair and paced the pod. "Those people have been dead for some time. If you're right, they would have turned to dust by now and so would their cars."

I wrung my hands and shifted from one foot to the other. "I didn't say it happened every day, but it's happened at least once before."

I craned my neck and searched the sky. Raven and the Sky Beings had disappeared. Not a good sign. "M-maybe an ozone hole shifts position, or something. I don't know, but the sun did this."

Atian gazed at the murky horizon, and a worry frown creased his brow.

Chief Roy scanned the valley with his bio-comm. "Well, something wiped out this entire valley, there's no life signs except for us and a few birds in the sky."

A blanket of blistering heat, worse than the badlands, had enveloped *Voyageur* ever since we entered Jasper Valley. Her thermals strained to cool the interior and threatened to give out at any moment. I wiped my dripping forehead, and sweat oozed along my spine. "And I-I think it might be happening again, it's so hot, and it's only six in the morning."

Tomko pointed to the edge of the valley. "Look!"

The sun's rays swept over the bleak terrain, and steam and smoke rose from the ground.

Atian hissed and buckled his cushion. "Let's go, chief! Get us into those mountains before the sun reaches us!"

Chief Roy punched the touch screen. "Code red, *Voyageur*. Flight speed!"

Me yes

The rays moved closer.

Voyageur smashed through the cars like a bowling ball toppling pins and roared up the highway. Birds dropped from the sky, dead where they fell, and trees on the edge of the valley burst into flames.

Leyla gasped. "Look, the tower's melting."

The black tower overlooking the valley glowed orange and leaned into the valley. The eerie shrieks and groans of tearing metal shook the biopod. In slow motion, shrieking all the way down, the tower toppled over and landed on the valley floor. Firestorms erupted in the dead grass and swept toward Jasper City.

Leyla gave Etta a high-five. "One down."

A glider that had taken off moments before the tower collapsed zoomed through the valley and almost made it. Then it dropped like a stone.

Voyageur raced for the mountains on all jets, but the rays were moving faster. The charred caravan of vehicles behind us sizzled and some crumbled to dust.

"Great Manitou, we won't make it."

I pushed Benji and Leyla under the table and threw a wet blanket over them. Wolf squeezed in beside them. "Tomko, get the boys into the bathroom! Willow, hide the girls in the other bathroom—turn on the cold water sprays!"

Voyageur sent the last vehicle flying and tore up the side of the craggy mountain on a trucker's run-away lane. She bounced over the rough road, scraped her topside on a craggy escarpment, and slid to a stop beneath a granite outcropping. She curled into a tight ball and whimpered. *Ow-ow, ow-ee.*

Leyla kicked off the steaming blanket. "It's so hot, I can't breathe!" She sucked on her inhaler.

"Hold on, baby girl." I glanced at Benji. His eyes were squeezed shut, and he wasn't moving.

"Benji? Are you all right?"

He moaned.

Gecki popped his green head out of Benji's shirt and screeched.

"Hide Gecki."

The rays caught *Voyageur's* back end. Yellow membrane sizzled and crackled through her armor.

Aiyee

I shook my head to clear the buzzing in my ears.

Etta fell out of the bathroom, clutching her chest and sobbing.

"Hold on, everyone, it won't last long," Chief Roy said.

But it did last long, much too long, and when the deadly rays shifted, we found Sereida panting in her sleeper. Ore was patting her hands and wiping her face with a wet cloth.

I took her head in my lap. "Oh auntie, what can I do?"

She managed a feeble smile. "Nothing you can do, child. My time has come. Get these children to Maniton."

"I'll try, auntie."

Sereida reached up and stroked my cheek. "Live a long and happy life, my sweet girl." In a whisper, she added, "Atian's the one."

She slipped away.

Chief Roy covered Sereida's body with her Elder blanket. "The heat was too much for her heart, poor old soul."

I wiped away my tears. Sereida had been my grandmother's dearest friend. She was with me for every important moment in my life, and now she was gone. But I had no time to grieve. The kids were lying in a stupor, too spent to even cry.

Benji crawled from under the table. "Are we dead, cuz I feel dead?"

"We're safe, Benji."

Leyla moaned. "Hali."

Wolf whimpered and gently licked Leyla's cheek. "Ugh. Wolf, you stink."

He covered his hot snout with his paws.

I picked Leyla up and staggered off the biopod. One by one, the children followed me and collapsed in the shade of a mountain fir tree.

Atian offered them water. "Come on, Etta, you've got to drink some water."

She pushed the glass away. "No, I don't wanna."

Wolf crawled out of the airlock and flopped down on a scant patch of green grass. I poured water in my hand, and he lapped it up. "You'll be okay, Wolf. Just rest."

Smoke and fumes from melting metal choked the air. "We can't stay here long, air's too bad."

Councilor Ore handed out our breathers.

"Is Vogy all right?" Leyla murmured.

"She's fixing her skin, sweetie."

"Can you imagine Inferno Valley by now?" Atian said.

"I don't have to imagine." I walked to the edge of the outcropping and gazed over the smoldering valley. Inferno Valley. An apt name. The land was charred black, and the air was thick with smoke from fires burning along the rim. Most of the cars scattered along the highway had burst into flames, and a firestorm was engulfing Jasper. The tower lay nearby, still smoking. "I wonder if anyone was inside that thing."

"Doubt it."

"Everything's gone, Atian. What if this happens all over? The lakes and rivers will boil away. All the animal will die. Seeds won't sprout, no more trees or flowers or grass." My voice broke. "All that's beautiful will be gone forever."

His lips parted, and he smiled a sad smile. "But we'll survive, Hali. I'll make sure we do." He took my hands in his and kissed each finger. "We'll begin again in Maniton. And I don't believe this is the end of Mother Earth. She'll find a way to live on."

He stroked my cheek, and pressed his lips against mine, at first soft and gentle, then more demanding. His tongue probed my mouth, and I opened to him. Desire flowed through me, and I longed to hide in his arms, but I stiffened when his hands roamed over my body.

He moaned. "Hali, when?"

He waited for my answer, but I did not have an answer, not a good one anyway. I ached for his touch, but I couldn't, not yet.

He sighed and dropped my hands.

"Back on the pod everyone, she's cooled off and the a/c's working again." Chief Roy slapped *Voyageur* on the rump. "Time to move on old girl, before the fire finds us and ruins your pretty new skin." He turned for one final glimpse of the burning valley. "Nothing we can do," he muttered under his breath.

We found a sheltered refugium around the next mountain.

"This is a good place," Chief Roy said.

I nodded through my tears. "Sereida loved the forest." I sniffed the hot air for any hint of poison, but breathed clean and clear.

Tomko and Matwau dug the grave under a cedar tree on a small hill, and we wrapped Sereida in her precious Elder blanket. Atian played a soft melody, and Matwau tapped his hand drum as we lowered her into the ground. Willow sang the mourning song in her sweet voice.

Matwau hugged me. "I'm sorry, Hali. I know she was your friend."

"Thanks Mat." I smiled at him. Why hadn't I noticed how good-looking he was when he wasn't scowling?

He smoothed my hair and kissed my forehead. His touch sent a tremor coursing through my body, but Sereida's words echoed in my head. Atian was the one. I pulled away and looked up at the sound of flapping wings. Raven was grooming his feathers in a nearby spruce tree.

"So you're back."

Raven nodded his head.

Gentle Sky Beings danced and twittered in the air above Sereida's resting place.

"Watch over Sereida for us."

We parked for the night at a backpackers' campground hidden between tree-covered mountains. Birds chirped in the trees, and a sassy squirrel chattered at us. How long before the sun's rays seared these mountains clean and killed all the animals?

A bubbling brook ran through the campground, feeding off the remnants of a glacier high in the mountains. When the glacier disappeared, the brook would dry up like all the others.

A doe and her wobbly fawn stepped out of the forest.

"Hey chief, there goes supper," Matwau said.

"No, we'll be leaving the animals in peace, lad. That fawn will become the matriarch of a herd that one day may sustain your descendants."

I cleaned the kids' scratches and bloodied hands, and sent them for a swim. "And don't come back until you're clean."

Benji splashed water on his face and smudged the dirt. "Ooh, it's so cold. I ain't never felt cold."

His words rang true. Decades had passed since the temps dipped below freezing on the refugium, and the shallow lakes the water corps left behind never cooled down, especially after the permafrost melted. I dipped my fingers into the stream and let the cool water trickle down my neck.

Matwau cleared his throat behind me. "Hali, you're killing me."

His eyes held a question, but I didn't have an answer.

I sat Leyla down on a rock at the edge of the brook and dangled her swollen feet in the stream. "The water will bring down your fever, sweetie."

Benji splashed Leyla, and she screamed.

He smirked. "Bet you're cool now."

"Benjamin Kitchi, I'm getting you for that soon's my feet's are better."

Benji laughed and darted away. "Hey Gecki, come on in."

The little lizard squealed and jumped from one kid to another. Then he made the mistake of jumping on Wolf's head.

"Woof!"

"Eeek!"

And the chase was on.

Gecki streaked across the water, his tiny feet barely touching the surface. Wolf bounced after him, splashing the children.

Thanks to Gecki and Wolf, the kids got the bath they needed without all the griping.

The Sky Beings flitted between the children and danced away from the water. I had half a mind to splash them.

Me sleepy

Chief Roy released *Voyageur*. "Get some rest, old girl."

She curled into a ball and snored.

The chief inspected the pod's outer shell, once again a bright yellow. "New skin or not, she's looking worse for wear." He shook his head. "I replaced a jetpack in the back sphere. If any more go, we'll be walking."

Sleep came slowly that night. My mind buzzed. Conditions on the prairies had become unbearable. If the ozone hole grew any larger, the entire ecosystem would collapse. Then it hit me. We couldn't go back, even if Cardiff and his thugs left us alone. I would never spend another quiet evening with my family, or ride Honey across the meadow, or talk about boys with Sinopa. Hot tears coursed down my cheeks, but in a way, the knowledge set me free. That world was no longer my world. I was Halerine Ananda, Rainbow Warrior, and future Maniton. If we wanted to survive, that was the path forward.

Chapter Thirteen

AIN'T NO CALL

Dead tree branches, weathered boards, and crumpled sheets of tin blocked our path through Thompson Valley. Ten meter high guard towers interrupted the makeshift wall every fifty meters. We weren't going any farther until we found a new route.

"What is this place?" Willow said.

"That's what I'm aiming to find out." Chief Roy stepped out of the airlock and approached a guard at the main entrance.

The guard readied his assault rifle. "Halt!"

"Relax sergeant, we're just passing through. But what is this place?"

"Murtle River Detention Center, and there ain't no passing through."

Chief Roy frowned and set his bio-comm. "Detention center? What on earth for? They're climate refugees, not criminals."

The sergeant shrugged. "Folk's been coming here nigh onto five years looking for food and shelter." He spat on the ground. "Ain't finding much a that anymore."

"But why here?"

"Was supposed to be a relocation center for sending folks to better places in the North, excepting there ain't no better places. It's bad all over." He squinted at the chief. "But I reckon you know that."

"Aa."

We climbed out of *Voyageur* for a better look.

Atian whistled. "It's a tent city."

Mud-splattered army tents, thousands of them, stretched through the valley, many set up in the dry river bed, others under the collapsed train bridge. Rocks held down the tents against the harsh winds blowing through the mountain pass. Winds or not, the heat was stifling. Sweat oozed along my back, and I wiped my face with my damp t-shirt. This was the kind of place Cardiff planned to send everyone on *Voyageur*, to wait to die.

Chief Roy placed his bio-comm on record and kept up a running commentary. "No sign of electricity or running water in the detention camp, except for a pipe sticking out of the wall."

A little boy, not more than three, tipped his head and caught the slow drip from the pipe. Children lined up behind him. They waited only so long, then pushed him out of the way. "You got enough, Jimi, it's our turn."

Jimi slunk away, pulling up his tattered blue shorts, two sizes too big.

A young couple dodged pools of stagnant water as they trudged through ankle-deep mud in a narrow alley running between the tents. Even in this harsh environment, some were finding love.

Swarms of mosquitoes buzzed the water puddles and hovered around us. Chief Roy slapped a mosquito on his arm. "Betting there's malaria in this camp, and likely dengue."

I dug a bug zapper out of my knapsack and waved it over the kids. "Keep your breathers and suits on."

The feeble sun peeked through the green and pink sky, but dark clouds circled the camp and threatened rain.

Tomko eyed the clouds. "Wonder if they get tornados in the mountains."

"Doubt it," Atian said. "Even plough winds would've wiped out this place years ago."

A frail woman hung ragged clothes on a line snaking between and over the tents in the futile hope that rain would wash off some of the grime. An emaciated dog limped across the wretched alley and stopped to sniff a pile of excrement beside the tent. The woman threw a rock at it. "Be gone, you filthy beast."

A low growl burned in Wolf's throat.

I patted his head. "Easy Wolf."

"Atian, you and Willow stay with the kids," Chief Roy said. "We'll take a look-see and figure out how to get through this site."

Atian opened his mouth to object, but the chief held up his hand. "I'll not be risking more injury to your back if this goes bad, and I need you to have *Voyageur* ready on a moment's notice."

That seemed to mollify him.

We stepped through the gate. A row of lopsided latrines sat well back from the entrance, but the smell of urine and feces permeated the camp. I coughed and upped the filter on my breather.

Chief Roy aimed his bio-comm at a red cross painted on the side of an abandoned tent. Angry graffiti splattered the dingy white tent walls.

"NGOs were here at some point."

The sergeant lit a hand-rolled cigarette and held it between his nicotine-stained fingers. "Done up and left six months ago. Couldn't take it no more. We let them go."

I turned on him. "What do you mean, you let them go?"

The sergeant's voice was dead. "Don't you know, chickee, them walls are for keeping folks in more than keeping them out. Once in, ain't no leaving this place."

A warning tickled in the back of my mind.

Elderly men, bone thin, huddled in small groups around a makeshift fire and smoked dried cattails.

The sergeant followed my gaze. "Spend their days telling stories about the good old days." He snorted. "Not that any a these old coots remember when things were good. I sure can't."

A baby cried in a nearby tent. My heart lurched. Danny-boy's cry. Another woman bathed her child in a rusty bucket, with not more than a cup of water. The child screamed and struggled against her ministrations.

"I'm with that kid," Benji said.

Raggedy children kicked a cracked rubber ball around the alley and dodged mosquito-infested puddles. Benji and Keme joined in the game until the ball collapsed in a puddle.

"Never seen human misery on this level," Chief Roy said.

"We have to help them," I said.

Matwau frowned. "Hali, what can we do against this? Thousands live in this camp, and none of them have what they need to survive."

"But I'm a healer, Mat. I can't just walk away."

"We've a bit of time, Halerine Ananda. Do what you can while I scout around."

I fetched my medicine bag and headed for the Red Cross tent. "I need assistants. Call in the troops."

The sergeant raised his rifle. "Hey now, where's she going? She ain't been cleared. Sides which, she's an Indian."

Chief Roy scowled at the mealy-mouthed sergeant. "She's a healer, and she'll be helping these poor folks. Now step aside. We've got work to do." He stared the sergeant down. "Then we'll be leaving."

The sergeant shuffled his feet and sniffed. "Shouldn't be bothered, most of the sickos will die off once winter rains come and the malaria shows itself. Seen it happen every year."

I strode into the tent and surveyed the stark interior. A moldy wooden desk, a wobbly table, and a cupboard. That's all they left behind. "Mat, that cupboard is locked. Any ideas?"

Matwau picked up a shovel leaning against the desk and smashed the lock. The contents spilled onto the floor: vaccination kits, polymers, anti-malaria tablets, bandages, and clean water in plastic tubs. "Gawd, all these supplies hidden away."

They lined up, silent and wary at first. I cleaned festering wounds and applied antibiotic creams, washed and checked over crying, sickly babies, and gave their mothers clean water and baby food, rubbed muscle relaxants into old men's bones, and offered vitamins and advice to girls too young to be pregnant. My patients said little, but gratitude shone in their weary eyes.

Tomko assisted me. "Hali, this is sweet. We're gonna be a nurse when we get to Maniton."

I smiled. Despite the long and honored history of Two-Spirits in many First Peoples' cultures, Tomko had trouble fitting in. Narrow-minded people like Samoset made zis life even harder. Maybe zie would find a place in Maniton. "That's a great idea, Tomko. You're good with people."

Zie preened and lit up like a Christmas tree, zis face red, zis hair a florescent green for the day.

Some of the littlest children played with Wolf outside the medical tent. He licked their faces clean, and fetched the stick they threw into the street. The air filled with shrieks of laughter, and the camp was no longer quiet as a gravesite, thanks to Wolf.

Three women dressed in brown cassocks approached me. "Let us help you, kind one," one of the women said.

I wiped my sweating brow. "How can you help?"

"I have some knowledge of medical practices, and I've done what I can without supplies or medications." She nodded to her two companions. "We are Sisters from the Blessed Virgin Mary of Mount Carmel."

"Thank you, Sisters." I handed each woman a bag full of medications and supplies. "Share this with those most in need—the children first, I beg of you."

Three hours later I staggered out of the tent. Matwau caught me as I fell, and I sobbed into his shirt. "They're all going to die, Mat. Maybe not today, but soon, and I can't stop it."

He wiped my tears and hugged me. "You did all you could, Hali. Come away."

Benji and Leyla hovered nearby, worried looks on their little faces. I smiled through my tears. "It's okay kids, I'm just tired."

Leyla's lip quivered. "But you said they are gonna die."

How could I answer her? She knew the truth as well as I did, and that wasn't fair. Little kids should not suffer nor witness such suffering. Rainbow Warriors was a mistake. If we had stayed in the North maybe we would have died too soon, but at least we'd be surrounded by those we loved and who loved us. But out here? No one loved anyone.

We stood at the gate and bid farewell to the refugees. They touched us with shaky hands and smiled their thanks. Even the dead-eyed sergeant softened and slipped an old man a rolled cigarette.

Chief Roy approached the sergeant. "Try remembering these are human beings, and this misery is not of their making."

The sergeant grumbled and muttered, and avoided Chief Roy's eye. "I can't let you leave, you know." He snapped his fingers, and a half dozen guards stepped out of the shadows and pointed their firepower at us. "It's a rule. Once you enter, you stay until you die." He hawked and spit. "Even if you are Indians."

Chief Roy pulled up his baggy pants. "You don't want to cause any trouble, now do you?" he said in a quiet, but steely voice.

Matwau and Atian stepped forward, lasers pointed at the sergeant's chest.

"I'm thinking our lasers outgun your old rifles, but I don't want to find out. Open the gate wide and back away with your men."

The sergeant held up his hands. "Hey now, no trouble. No, don't want trouble."

"Then step aside and we'll be on our way."

The sergeant signaled his men, and they melted into the shadows. "Shouldn't be letting you go so easy. You're lucky the lieutenant ain't here."

Chief Roy slapped his laser against the palm of his hand. "No, I'm thinking the lieutenant is the lucky one." He turned to us. "The only route through the mountain pass is by way of this detention center."

"Can *Voyageur* make it?" Matwau said.

"Aa, we'll drive through real slow and follow the dry river bed for a spell."

Matwau gazed over the dismal site and muttered under his breath. "This won't be a ride through a park, but if it's the only way."

A tiny woman dressed in a purple shift and holding the hands of two small children tried to squeeze by us and into the camp. "Excuse me, sir."

"Halt!" The sergeant held out his battered rifle and pressed it against her chest. "Ain't no call for blackies."

Tears welled in her hazel eyes, and her worn face crumbled. "But we're starving. Please, sir, we haven't got any place else to go."

The sergeant shook his head. "Ain't no call for blackies. This here's a white folks' refuge." He waved his rifle. "Now get before I finish you off."

The woman sank to the ground. "Then kill us, for we can't go any farther."

The children cried and pulled at their mother. "Mama, mama, please get up. We got to go! Please mama, the bad man's scary."

I tugged on the chief's sleeve. "We can't leave them. Please chief, I can't bear anymore. We can't just survive, we have to help, too."

His voice choked. "*Aa.*"

He knelt beside the woman. "Come with us, dear lady. We've food for you and your youngsters."

She shook her head. "No, a little food isn't going to make any difference. We're done for, we're all done for."

I dropped to my knees beside her. "You've got kids, they need you, they need to survive." I sobbed. This was so wrong. "Please, ma'am, we'll find a safe haven for you."

Her brows knitted and she gazed at me, then she sat up and shrugged off her worn backpack. "This is all we have. If you save my twins, it's yours." A scruffy orange teddy bear peeked out of the bag.

I put the bag in her lap. "You don't have to pay us. What's your name?"

"Sophie."

Chief Roy and Matwau picked up the children, and Atian and I helped Sophie into *Voyageur*.

Samoset met us at the airlock. He hadn't left the biopod all day. Unwashed body odors swirled around him.

"*Voyageur*, bio-fresh, please."

Uh-huh

Samoset nodded at Sophie. "Who's this? You can't be picking up strays, we've got limited supplies."

Atian snorted. "Really? And what are you if not a stray, a stowaway stray, matter of fact. At least we had some say in helping this family."

Samoset snarled and pushed Tomko out of the way. "Well, they ain't gettin' any of my share." He stomped through the biopod and slammed the door to the storage pod.

Sophie followed me into *Voyageur's* cool interior and gasped. "Oh, how wonderful. You're so fortunate."

Chief Roy's eyebrows rose. "Yes, we are, aren't we children?"

"Yes ma'am, we'se real fort-nate," Etta said.

"Right troops, find your spot, we're moving out." He awakened the biopod's comm. "Open the gates, sergeant!"

A light drizzle splattered *Voyageur's* silver hull with rain-mud.

Ooo ucky

Atian eased the biopod through the wooden gates and danced her over water-filled ruts. People came out of their tents and watched our lumbering progress. Some waved, others gazed at us. The hopelessness etched on their emaciated faces tore at my heart.

A little girl, painfully thin, and wearing a colorless rag, ran out of her tent. She was crying and holding out her hands. "Food, food, please, please." She fell in a puddle, but still she held out her hands and her blue eyes pleaded.

I couldn't meet her young-old eyes, but Etta tugged on Chief Roy's sleeve. "Chief, we'se fort-nate. Why can't we share?"

He considered Etta. "Aa, indeed. Halerine, you and Matwau scrounge up all the food and milk you can carry. Atian, hold up *Voyageur* a bit."

I hurried into the canteen and tapped codes into the synthor. Matwau pulled out boxes of dried goods we'd found in the Edmonton house and lugged them to the airlock.

The synthor shot out steaming hot pizzas and chocolate milk.

Chief Roy raised an eyebrow. "Pizzas?"

I shrugged. "The food won't keep them going for long, but at least those little kids will taste something good for once in their lives."

We carried a dozen steaming pepperoni pizzas outside. Benji and Tomko helped Matwau distribute canned meat and packages of flour and sugar to the adults, while Willow, Leyla, and I handed out slices of pizza and chocolate squirts to an ever-growing throng of children. I kept searching for the little blue-eyed girl, but she never made it through the crowd.

Then we ran out. "I'm sorry, kids, that's all we have."

One little boy broke down. "But I didn't get enough."

An older girl snarled at him. "At least you got some, I ain't had nothing." She glared at me with sullen eyes.

The crowd surged forward, and we backed against *Voyageur*. "Chief, a little help."

Voyageur hissed and let out a blood-curdling scream. The children backed away.

Matwau picked up Leyla and took my arm. "Come on, Hali, we can't do any more, and a mob is brewing."

I shuddered and climbed on board. "I was trying to help them."

He shrugged. "No good deed and all that, but it wouldn't matter what we did for them, they're starving and desperate."

The mob surrounded the biopod and pounded on the hull.

"Move out easy-like, *Voyageur*," Chief Roy said. "They'll part or lose their toes."

But they didn't budge.

Samoset snarled. "This is your fault, girlie. Just gotta be a do-gooder and now look at our fix." He glared at Matwau. "You do-gooders always end up paying. Just ask the boy."

Matwau scowled and turned away but not before I caught the tortured look in his eyes.

Etta's lip quivered. "We gave them our food, now they're being nasty."

I folded her in my arms. "It's never wrong to help people." I glared at Samoset. "No matter what selfish people say."

"We need a plan and fast," Atian said.

"What if I toss some bags of food out the rear? Make a distraction?" Matwau said.

Chief Roy shrugged and nodded. "Worth a try."

Matwau opened a small access hatch and tossed half a dozen bags of oatmeal into the muddy street. The mob scrambled for it.

"Move out, Atian."

But the angry mob raced after us.

"Hurry, they're gaining."

Mud-covered rocks pelted *Voyageur*'s hull.

"They've gone crazy," Benji said.

"Aa, mob mentality. Pick up the speed, lad."

But travelling at more than a crawl was not a good idea. We rounded a curve in the road, and a boy darted in front of the biopod. *Voyageur* swerved and slid into a deep mud puddle.

Ooo ucky

Voyageur groaned and hissed as she backed her way out of the deep hole. The angry mob caught up and pushed on the hull until the jets on *Voyageur*'s right side left the ground.

Me no like

"How about a color change, Vogy?" Atian said.

She shifted from silver to a blazing red that sparkled. The mob backed away muttering.

Atian grinned. "That was easy."

Voyageur squeezed through the back gates without a whimper from the guards, and we rumbled down the dry river bed.

I leaned back in my cushion seat and closed my eyes, but the image of the little girl with blue eyes wouldn't leave me.

Sophie stared at the monitor. "I'm so glad we weren't allowed in. How can I ever thank you for saving us."

I cleared my tight throat. "How about a shower, Sophie? Then we'll have supper."

A wistful expression crossed her features. "A shower? Oh how I wish ... well, if you're sure it's all right. I mean the water and all."

When was the last time this poor woman bathed? I led her and the twins to the girls' bathroom. "Stay away from the boys' bathroom, it's scary even after *Voyageur* sanitizes it."

Ten minutes later Sophie and the twins emerged from the showers wrapped in bathrobes.

"We've replicated clothes for you." I handed Sophie a coral t-shirt and light khaki shorts, under things, and spongy leather sandals.

She reached for the clothes, then pulled back. "Oh, they're so beautiful and clean, I daren't touch them."

Tomko pressed the clothes into her hands. "We picked out the colors. Coral goes beautifully with your dark skin."

"Mika, Frannie, we have clothes for you, too."

Willow handed a batik t-shirt and green walking shorts to Frannie. The little girl gasped and rubbed the multi-colored fabric against her cheek.

Tomko tied green ribbons in her hair. "These'll keep all those gorgeous curls in order."

Mika's eyes danced. "Skidders!" He tried on his aeration shoes. "Wow, I can run a hundred klicks in these babies, easy."

"Grub's ready," Councilor Ore said.

We sat down to synthetized elk steak, baked potatoes, a bean salad, and rice pudding mixed with apples and raisins.

Sophie and her children bowed their heads. "Thank you, dear Lord, for the bounty we are about to receive, and thank you for our new friends who have saved our lives. Amen."

Amen.

Chapter Fourteen

KHAKHUA

We found a new home for Sophie and the twins in a storybook town tucked between two shallow rivers. A craggy mountain range encircled the valley, like a protective barrier against the horrors outside. Not a tower was in sight.

Identical one-story houses painted white with green trim lined the picture-perfect streets. Manicured lawns, red and pink rose bushes, and trimmed junipers surrounded each of the houses. "It's like a town out of another time."

"Aa."

Atian breathed deeply. "Air's cleaner than any I ever smelled."

A short, thin man dressed in an old-fashioned top hat and gray pin-striped suit greeted us. He tipped his hat. "Welcome to Clearton Enclave, folks. My name is Mayor Franklin Daley. You can call me Frank."

Chief Roy shook the mayor's hand. "This is a mighty nice place, Frank."

Mayor Daley nodded, a pleased look on his cadaverous face. "The mountains protect us from the worst of the pollutants, and the breeze off the rivers keeps the air cooler. We'll be all right for a spell, maybe even make it out the other end."

Wolf returned from a visit to the trees and spotted Mayor Daley. A low growl vibrated in his throat, and the hair on the back of his neck stood up. He crouched low and stalked the mayor.

I grabbed his collar. "Wolf, what's the matter with you? Calm down."

The mayor cast a baleful look at Wolf and backed away. "Is that thing trained?"

I studied the mayor. I never did like or trust people who hated dogs. "His name is Wolf, and he's my guard dog. Keeps the riffraff away."

Matwau snickered behind me. I stepped back and squished his toes.

"Hey, watch the wounds."

A bell rang and laughing, shrieking children poured out of a three-story building and skipped toward a row of yellow buses.

The mayor grinned. "School's out, I reckon."

I blinked. "Your kids go to school?" Our school had closed down when there no longer seemed to be any point. I barely reached level seven, when we were just getting to the good stuff, like astronomy and medical practices.

"You betcha. No ignoramuses in these parts anymore."

Chief Roy took Sophie by the shoulders. "We're hoping you've got room in your heart and your town for three more souls. This is Sophie and her two children, Frannie and Mika."

Mayor Daley shook Sophie's hand. "Please to meet you, Miss Sophie. Everyone's welcome in Clearton. Folks took a change for the better when civilization broke down around us. They started looking out for each other, and not judging so harshly."

"Run Hali."

A chill washed over me, and I clutched my dreamcatcher. Something was not quite right here. Frank's blue eyes were too bright, and his friendliness, too ready. I edged closer to Chief Roy. "Chief, I'm not sure—"

"They'll be fine, Halerine Ananda."

Sophie's voice cracked as she shook the mayor's hand. "Thank you for your kindness, sir."

Mayor Daley beamed. "Think nothing of it. We welcome new blood in our midst."

What did that mean?

Mayor Daley took Sophie by the arm. "I know of a little house down the street from the school all ready for a young family, and Bob over at the confect is looking for a new helper."

"Sounds wonderful, Mr. Mayor. I've always hoped my kids could get some schooling."

The mayor squinted at Sophie. "Might I ask how old you are, Miss Sophie?"

She patted her curly hair in place. "Why, I'll be thirty next month."

"Good, good, you're about the same age as me. Plenty of time for rearing your kiddies."

What did that mean?

Sophie turned to Chief Roy. "You'll be leaving soon, I suppose?"

He nodded. "You're in good hands here."

Sophie blinked back tears. "I won't ever forget the hope you Rainbow Warriors brought us, nor will my descendants for all of my days."

I hugged Sophie and whispered in her ear. "Sophie, be careful. Something's off here. Protect your children."

Sophie clasped my hands to her heart. "This is our chance to live, dear Hali. We take it or we die."

Benji tugged on my sleeve. "Wish we could stay. It's perfect here."

"Too perfect," I mumbled.

Chief Roy leaned close to me. "Aa, I feel it, too, Halerine Ananda, but the kiddies are plumb tuckered out. A few days rest might be what we need. Better here than on the wild coast, where anything can happen."

"Are you sure, chief?"

"For now." He turned to Mayor Daley. "Think we'll rest here a spell, if that's all right with you."

Mayor Daley rubbed his hands together and smiled a too cheerful smile. "Why, that's just dandy. Let's get you folks settled then."

He led us to a motel. A red six sign dangled from a pole beside the motel office and squeaked in the strong breeze.

"Don't get many visitors these days, you see, so lots of room for you folks."

My skin crawled. "Chief, can I speak to you for a moment?"

We walked a ways down the pristine street. "I think we should stay in *Voyageur*."

Councilor Ore joined us. "I agree with Halerine. We're sitting ducks in that motel if anything bad goes down. *Voyageur* is flight-ready."

"Aa."

Chief Roy rejoined the mayor and a small cluster of townspeople. "Thank you kindly for the offer, but we're comfortable in our transport."

A flash of annoyance crossed the mayor's face, but he covered with a toothy smile. "Of course, suit yourself." He held up his hand. "But if you don't mind, we'll move your transport off the street."

"Any reason?"

"As I said, we keep our streets clean and clear. This is a town of god-fearing, honest folks." He eyed Tomko's flashy mini-skirt and fluorescent green hair, a look of distaste on his gaunt face.

Townspeople out for a stroll stopped and greeted us with warm, but slightly off, smiles. They pinched Benji's cheeks and ruffled Leyla's hair. But they stared at Chief Roy and Councilor Ore and whispered behind their hands.

Not all the townspeople were as perfect as their town. Two women, not more than mid-twenties, staggered as they walked down the street and their bodies trembled, and one young man burst into wild laughter at the sight of us.

Etta jumped behind me. "What's wrong with them?"

A worry frown creased Chief Roy's brow. "Not sure, Etta m'girl."

"Notice how nobody's old as you chief," Atian said.

"Or fat," Benji said.

Atian was right. The townspeople looked no older than their thirties, and they were all thin and sickly pale, especially the trembly ones.

"Hali, I've changed my mind," Benji said. "I don't wanna stay."

Tomko fluffed zis spiky hair. "Us neither, people keep staring at us as if we're freaky."

Chief Roy put his hand on Tomko's shoulder. "We'll leave first thing in the morning, then. Heard tell there's a church picnic this evening. Wouldn't want you kids missing out on Southern fried chicken."

We rounded the corner where we had parked *Voyageur*, but she was gone.

"What in tarnation?"

A man in gray overalls approached us. "Lookin' for your vehicle?"

"Aa."

He scratched his bald head. "Tow truck done took it away."

"Where to?" Atian said.

The man shrugged. "Garage most likely."

Daley joined us. "Now, no need getting worked up none. I told you we keep the streets clear."

Chief Roy scowled, and his bushy eyebrows did their thing. "We want our transport back now, Mr. Daley, and we'll be leaving shortly."

Daley held up his hand. "Now, now the garage is all closed up for the day. The manager has the keys, and he's gone fishing."

Chief Roy's scowl deepened. "And when might he return?"

Daley shrugged. "Tomorrow, I reckon." His gaunt face brightened. "Meanwhile, you folks are invited to our church picnic, and then you can enjoy a nice rest in the motel before our celebration."

Matwau squinted at the mayor. "What sort of celebration?"

"Why *khakhua*, of course. The whole town looks forward to the monthly ritual. I think you'll find it a fascinating adventure."

"We're on a fascinating adventure, and so far I'm not thrilled," I said.

Chief Roy glanced at me. "Appears we don't have much choice at the moment."

Daley rubbed his hands together and led us into the motel. "The ladies' auxiliary took it upon themselves to outfit your rooms with everything you'll need for the ritual later tonight. We wear tribal dress, and we'd be mighty pleased if you followed our custom." He led us into the lobby.

Bright costumes hung from the backs of chairs. "Help yourself," Daley said, a wide smile on his face. "We pieced together outfits for everyone of you."

I fingered strings of purple and green beads.

Willow held up a tanned leather shift. "I could wear this."

Tomko picked up a flimsy brown breechclout. "At least you girls got a whole dress." Zie wrinkled zis nose. "Do you think we could wear one of yours instead?"

Chief Roy glared at his breechcloth. "Well, I'm sure as tarnation not wearing this get-up. Not enough here to cover my nethers."

Etta giggled.

In the lobby bathroom, the women had arranged hair adornments and pots of bright face paint. I picked up a hair clip and wrapped my hair into a twister bun. Matwau was watching me in the mirror, but a worry frown creased his forehead. "Mat, what are you thinking?"

He screwed up his face. "*Khakhua.* I've heard that word before, but I can't remember for what."

My stomach clenched. This was not good.

Chief Roy consulted his bio-comm. "Can't understand it. Nothing on *khakhua.*"

"Chief, we need to find *Voyageur,*" Atian said.

"*Aa,* you and Matwau sneak out the back way and locate that garage. Play hoodlum with my blessing and liberate our pod."

A grin matching Matwau's crossed Atian's face. "You bet."

They climbed out the back window and slipped away.

"Funny how they forget about their injuries when they're up to no good."

Chief Roy grunted. "The rest of us best play along. Get cleaned up, but wear your own clothes. We've got a picnic to attend."

At the last moment, I drew black stripes across my forehead and under my eyes. I grinned at Chief Roy. "Just a little war paint. Sending a message and all."

We climbed the hill to the white church nestled in thick spruce trees. Wooden tables laden with steaming platters of food were arranged on the lush front lawn.

Raven circled overhead, and his eerie calls added to my sense of doom.

Benji sniffed. "Oh, that smells so good."

A young woman with coiffed blond hair greeted us. She frowned at my war paint, then smiled too brightly. "Welcome to the Clearton picnic. My name is Connie."

I shook her manicured hand. She was wearing a twentieth century yellow dress, tight at her waist, the skirt poofed out with a frilly crinoline. Did people really wear such fussy clothes, even in the olden days?

"Please take your seats, one visitor to each table," Connie said.

"So you're saying we can't sit together?" I said.

Connie twirled a curl near her temple. "Well, we enjoy getting to know our new neighbors."

"We're not new neighbors, we're travelers passing through."

The woman clicked her tongue and flounced away, her crinoline bouncing in time to her strut.

We sat down. I kept Benji and Leyla beside me and dared anyone to stop me. Wolf sat at my feet. His growl kept townspeople from coming too near, and that suited me fine.

Daley stood before the townspeople. "Let us begin this picnic by welcoming our honored guests." He raised his glass to us. "Welcome and enjoy our bounty."

None of us reciprocated.

Benji broke the awkward silence. "Can we eat now?"

Daley nodded. "Dig in brothers and sisters, time's a wasting."

What did that mean?

Fried chicken, corn on the cob, and potato salad. I was near bursting when Connie strolled out of the church carrying a plump apple pie. A string of women followed her, each carrying a fruit pie.

Benji rubbed his bulging stomach. "Pies? Oh boy."

Why did this feel like fattening the sheep before the slaughter? And why were the townspeople hardly eating anything?

Daley rose and clinked his glass. "As is our custom, we will rest until sundown when we gather for *khakhua*."

I stood and headed for the motel. Had Atian and Matwau found *Voyageur*? The sooner we blew this town, the better.

We slept off the heavy meal, and far too soon a knock on my door woke me.

Daley stood in the doorway, his breechclout flapping in the soft wind. I kept my eyes on his face, much to his disappointment.

"It's time," he said.

"For what?"

He sighed. "The ritual, of course. Wake your kiddies and get dressed."

"I think we'll pass."

His eyes turned cold and an edge of steel crept into his Southern drawl. "I think you'd best accommodate us, missy, that's if you want us sheltering your three friends. They're waiting for you at the ceremony."

We trudged up the side of a tree-covered mountain and entered a deep cave. A roaring bonfire in the middle of the cave cast menacing shadows against the rough-hewn walls. The people gathered around the fire resembled Blackfoot legends of *Sta-au*.

Daley spotted me and stepped aside, a self-satisfied smirk on his face. Sophie and the twins were standing behind him. A warning?

Sky Beings flitted around the ceiling. One zipped lower and shook her finger at me. Her mouth gaped, and she held her head, then she flitted away.

Leyla wrinkled her nose. "What's that funny smell? It makes my tummy shiver."

Bleached human skulls with gaping eyes and rows of grimacing teeth lined shelves carved into the cave walls. I stopped and spread my hands to keep the kids from moving farther into the cave. Wolf hugged my legs. "What is this place?"

Daley ignored my question and faced the people gathered in the cave. "In the early days of Turmoil our people would not accept that their greedy, empty lives were coming to an end. They refused to give up their toys, even when the power shut down, and they refused to learn new ways, or help each other. This was the Starving Time."

A soft murmur, almost a hum, rolled through the stifling cave, and the people swayed in time to Daley's hypnotic cadence.

Guards moved me aside and pushed the kids into the cave. Wolf growled, but followed me. I clutched Leyla and Etta's hands and pulled them close.

"We had to change our wicked ways or face extinction. Clearton became a peaceful haven surrounded by ravage and spoil. But Clearton could not support a large and ever-expanding populace. We were forced to make some difficult choices."

He paused, then looked straight at me. "We decided to limit our lifespan. From that day onward, when our citizens reached forty years of age they offered Sacrifice. Those who became sick also Sacrificed so that others might live."

I stifled a gasp. They sacrificed people?

Daley signaled the men and woman standing along the cave walls. They removed the skulls from the shelves and stepped forward. He nodded, and they handed out skulls to each member of the gathering. "These are the remains of our dear, sacrificed citizens. They be heroes to this day."

A tall man dressed in little more than a breechclout handed me a skull. I didn't want to touch it, but I was afraid to refuse. The cold nakedness of the skull seeped into my bones, and I flinched.

Daley frowned at me.

Leyla cried and shook as she held a skull in her tiny hands. Etta sank to the ground and sobbed. She would not look up or take a skull.

Cold chills ran up and down my spine. Where were Atian and Matwau? And Chief Roy and Ore?

Daley continued his recitation. "But still we suffered. Then our great leader, who we all know went to Sacrifice with a glad heart, began the ancient ritual of *khakhua*, and our lives grew easier."

The gathered crowd raised an arm and shouted, "*Khakhua!*"

"Tonight we continue the life-giving ritual. Brothers and sisters of Clearton, I give you Brother Richard, our first Sacrifice."

Two men led a blindfolded man into the circle. His body shook, and his knees buckled. The men held him up. A well-muscled archer stepped forward, and Daley raised his hand. "In the name of our great leader, cleanse the evil spirits from this gathering. *Khakhua!*" He lowered his hand, and the archer let loose his arrow. It struck the man in his chest, and he fell onto a straw mat with a moan. Blood turned the mat red.

I turned away. How could they murder their own people?

The same men led one of the trembling young women who passed us on the street into the cave. She, too, was blindfolded.

"Sickness wracks Sister Dorothy's body, and she graces us with her Sacrifice."

He raised his hand, then dropped it. The archer loosed another arrow and hit his mark.

Etta screamed and covered her face.

Two women with machetes knelt beside the victims. The crowd hummed louder and swayed from side to side. With a thwap, the machete women chopped off the victims' heads and held them aloft. The townspeople cheered. "*Khakhua!*"

The stench of blood and death reached me. I whipped around and covered my mouth so as not to lose my dinner, but Benji dashed to the side of the cave and upchucked his meal.

He staggered back to my side. "I ain't never gonna eat fried chicken again." He gasped. "It was chicken, wasn't it?"

A woman wrapped the severed heads in corn leaves and placed them in pots on the fire.

I choked on bile rising in my throat. "You cook the heads?"

Daley scowled and came over to me. He clutched my arms in a tight grip. "Calm yourself, missy. Of course we cook the meat. We're not barbarians, we don't eat raw brains."

"Great Manitou, you eat your victims?" My voice screeched.

He shook me, and my new hairclip fell to the ground and broke.

"We cook the deceased to kill the evil inside, and we eat the flesh for sustenance. The sacrifices tonight will feed our community for nigh on to a week."

"But what about the picnic?"

"Purely for your benefit, it took all we had to feed you."

The butchers dug into the bodies and pulled out livers and hearts. One woman cut the top off the heads and pulled out the cooked brains.

Daley stuck the dripping hearts and livers on pronged sticks and roasted them over the fire. "Liver for strength of blood, brains for wisdom and everlasting knowledge, and heart for charity and kindness. May the essence of our loved ones bring inner strength and pureness to our hearts."

Hours melted away and still the ritual continued. Five more men and women were sacrificed. The same women who served us pie moved through the gathering offering pieces of cooked flesh on poplar leaves.

Sophie hesitated, then took a piece of heart. She chewed it and avoided looking at me. Her twins cried and clung to her.

Connie smiled sweetly and thrust a blackened blob on a leaf in my face. "Liver tidbits?"

Pungent fumes from the cooked liver made me gag. I shook my head.

Daley slapped my face. "Eat!"

I held my burning cheek. "You'll have to kill us, we won't eat human flesh, you disgusting cannibal!"

He snarled and strode away. "We'll see about that."

"Cannibalism as religious ritual," Matwau whispered behind me.

I did not turn around. "Mat, thank goodness. This is really bad."

"These nuts are practicing *khakhua* from the ancient tribes in Papua New Guinea," Matwau said. "They were starving, so they ate humans to survive, and they wrapped it in ritualistic beliefs to psychologically handle becoming cannibals. Explains why some of them are sick—they're infected with *kuru* disease."

"*Kuru?*" I whispered out of the side of my mouth. Daley must not see Matwau.

"A wasting disease similar to mad cow, from eating infected brains. This enclave won't last another generation."

I hissed. "Sophie."

"Warn her."

"Did you find *Voyageur?*"

Daley interrupted before Matwau answered. "We have a last Sacrifice, one that ensures continued harmony and equality in our community."

Chief Roy stumbled into the cave, his hands tied behind his back and a blindfold over his eyes. What little of his face showed was a mix of purple and red mash, and a deep gash criss-crossed his right cheek. His necklace of grizzly bear claws was missing. Close behind him, two men dragged in Councilor Ore.

Great Apistotoke! "Mat, what do we do?" But Matwau had slipped out the same way he came in.

"These new members of our community have lived long lives, far longer than necessary. They have graciously consented to be our last Sacrifices."

Chief Roy struggled against the men holding him. "We did not consent, you murdering fool!"

Councilor Ore stood stone still, not uttering a word, though tears ran down her withered cheeks. Why didn't she fight back?

Etta and Leyla cried and Wolf barked.

"Stop that racket!" Daley said. He signaled the archer to shoot Wolf.

I stepped in front of Wolf. "Chief Roy is our leader and Councilor Ore is our mother. We cannot continue our journey without their guidance. Let them go."

Daley smirked, and a few townspeople snickered behind me. "You won't be needing any guidance excepting from me, girl. This is your home from now on."

I quelled my rolling stomach. This cretin must not see my fear. "You're holding us captive?"

Daley shook his head and laughed outright. "Why of course not. We're leading you on the path to righteousness, is all."

"Righteousness be damned! Gitche Manitou commands you to release our guardians!" Matwau said.

There he stood, a mighty Cree warrior covered in war paint and wearing Chief Roy's eagle feather headdress and cast-off breechcloth. He held a laser in each hand. Atian stood beside him, the bison horn headdress on his head, and a laser and shotgun in his hands.

I dabbed at tears. My Rainbow Warriors. My heroes.

Atian pointed his laser at Daley's heart. "Release the chief and our councilor."

Daley held out his hands. "Now young fella, don't be hasty. Your chief is old, past his prime. What good is he to you?"

Matwau hissed. "Chief Roy owns more knowledge, more wisdom, and more life in his little finger than this entire group of addle-brained butchers."

You go, Mat.

Atian struck a pose and waved the laser. "I'm not a patient man. I can cut a swath through this crowd before you blink. I said release them. Now!"

Daley scowled but nodded to his men. They unbound the chief's hands and took off the blindfold. They did the same for Councilor Ore, though she did not move.

The chief joined the boy-warriors and took the shotgun from Atian. He pointed it at Daley. "We're leaving peacefully, and none of you folks are going to move a muscle, or I'll add you to the sacrifice."

Daley shifted on his feet.

The chief shot between Daley's legs. Rocks ricocheted off the walls, and people screamed and ducked. "Not a move, understand?"

"Hali, bring the kids," Atian said.

Matwau took Councilor Ore's hand and led her from the cave.

I waved for Sophie to join us. She hesitated, then followed. We hurried down the mountain trail. *Voyageur*, shining silver in the pale moonlight, waited for us at the bottom of the trail.

Yippee

Raven sat on the biopod's rear and bobbed his head up and down. "Caw! Caw!"

Sophie skidded to a stop and took her kids' hands. "No, we're not coming with you."

"Sophie, you can't stay here, they'll murder you when you turn forty."

Sophie shook her head and clenched her teeth. "My kids. They're little, they'll have many good years, God willing."

"But you'll have to eat human flesh one week out of every month."

She shrugged. "Better than not eating at all."

"You could catch *kuru*. You saw those trembling people, they're dying and anyone eating infected brains will die, too."

She sighed. "What choice do we have, Hali? My kids can't go to Maniton, they're not Firsts, and out there we'll surely die."

What could I say?

Chief Roy answered for me. "Farewell, Miss Sophie. We wish you and your kin well." He held on to Councilor Ore and stepped into *Voyageur*. "Come along troops, we have a boat to catch."

"I'm with you," Benji said. "Anything's better than this place."

"Anybody see Samoset?" Leyla said.

Atian coded *Voyageur*. "If we're lucky, the cannibals caught him."

Chapter Fifteen

A Sailing We Shall Go

The boulders and rubble towered thirty meters above *Voyageur*, burying the highway, and with it, our passage to Vancouver.

Great Apistotoke, how much more? The horror of cannibalism hadn't receded in our minds and now this? I sat down among the cow thistles and snakeroot. Enough.

"So what do we do now, chief?" Atian said.

We all knew the answer. The mountain of boulders staring us in the face was too high and jagged for *Voyageur* to climb.

Chief Roy tossed a rock into the chasm. "Abandon *Voyageur* and move on. If we're lucky, we'll find a transport along the way."

"No, we can't leave Vogy, she's family." Leyla kneeled beside me. "Please Hali, don't let them leave Vogy. She'll be all alone."

I folded her in my arms. "We don't have a choice, sweetie."

She stamped her foot. "I won't stand for it!"

"Leyla," Chief Roy said.

"No! Get away!"

"Leyla Apikuni, listen to me."

She sniffed and raised her head.

Chief Roy gazed into her heartbroken eyes. "If we stay here, we'll all die. You don't want that to happen, do you?"

"N-o-o."

"Well then?"

Leyla sniffed again and rubbed her hand over the biopod's outer skin, now a dull gray. "Bye Vogy, I'm gonna miss you. I love you, you hear?" She hiccup-sobbed.

Voyageur gurgled. *Bye bye Leyee, I l-lova ya. Vogy loves Leyee.*

Chief Roy patted the biopod on the rump. "You're a fine ship, old girl. You've taken us through thick and thin, and I hate giving you up." He sighed. "Find a way back to the Siksiká refuge if you can. They'll take good care of you."

But—

"No buts, that's an order."

Voyageur hissed and deflated.

Raven landed on her roof. He fluttered his feathers, and his beady yellow eyes stared at me. "Caw! Caw!"

Raven was telling me something, but what? I clutched my dreamcatcher. This was not good.

We left most of the water behind, along with our camping gear and extra clothing. If *Voyageur* made it back to Elk Ridge, my People could use the supplies.

Before we left, I programmed the replicator to make us new shoes. I slid my sore feet into clunky hiking boots. Once we reached Maniton, I was never wearing boots again. Maybe I wouldn't need to wear shoes at all.

Tomko tossed zis worn-out shoes over the cliff and pulled on shiny pink and green skidders. "Perfect."

Chief Roy shook his head and chuckled. "Zie's got to be color-blind."

Benji discarded the holotabs they'd pilfered from the house in St. Albert. "Gonna be real ticked if they gots poor holos in Maniton."

Leyla placed Pooh bear on the growing pile in the lounge pod. Her lower lip trembled.

"Take Pooh with you, sweetie."

She shook her head. "No, I'm doing my part. Sides which, I still gots Raggedy Ann." She wrapped her arm around Wolf's neck, and they walked away.

I stuffed Pooh bear into my backpack, and handed Atian bundles of meat and cheese sandwiches. "I'll be back in a moment."

The soft whir of cooling units in the storage pod calmed me. When would we feel cool again? I hunkered down and pulled the cache of DNA samples out of the cooler and wrapped the tubes in freezer packs.

Samoset was watching me from his corner, a speculative gleam on his face. Too bad the cannibals didn't get him. I turned away and stowed my leather dress and moccasins inside my suit. No matter what, my family heirlooms were coming with me.

Atian secured his clarinet inside his suit and opened *Voyageur's* airlock one last time. "Out you go kids, we've got a mountain to climb."

The children filed out.

"But what about Councilor Ore and the chief?" Willow said. "They're still packing."

Councilor Ore hadn't been the same since the *khakhua* ritual. Chief Roy dared not leave her alone. "They'll catch up."

We trudged up the steep slide. Tomko slipped and scraped zis knees, Etta tripped over a loose boulder and sprawled in the rubble, and Leyla's blistered feet left a trail of blood and ruined her new shoes.

We kept climbing.

Raven fluttered his ebony wings and flew away, screeching as he soared into the dingy gray sky.

Wolf whimpered and grabbed my hand in his mouth. "What is it, Wolf?"

A deep rumble pulsed through the ground and shook the earth. "Oh gawd, what now?"

"Run Hali."

A wall of rock and spruce trees cascaded down the side of the mountain. I screamed. "Run!"

I dashed over the rocks, pushing and pulling kids with me. Matwau carried two on his back and one under each arm. Atian brought up the rear, three of the youngest crushed in his arms. Tomko and Benji ran so fast their feet skimmed the boulders.

Debris whizzed over our heads and exploded around us. A rock hit Samoset on the back of the head. He staggered, but recovered, and ran faster than I'd ever seen him move. We scrambled down the other side of the slide and ran along the highway, dodging potholes and shrubs growing through the crumbling highway.

The pavement buckled in front of me. I dodged the sinkhole opening up, but lost my footing and dropped the kids. Benji tripped and landed on a patch of mountain cactus. He clutched his prickly butt and kept moving.

Boulders, some the size of houses, swept down the mountainside and landed where we stood minutes before. We kept running but at the top of a rise, I turned back at a shrill scream. *Voyageur* was sliding over the cliff. She crashed through a grove of trees and bounced down the canyon. Her screams echoed across the valley.

I collapsed in a heap and sobbed. "Chief Roy! No!"

Wolf licked my face and nudged me. "Oh Wolf, what are we going to do?"

He plopped his massive bulk on my lap and whimpered.

The avalanche careened down the slope, building on itself, and the kids writhed on the ground, but if they cried out, I did not hear them.

Atian crawled over to me and put his mouth to my ear. "We've got to move before this side of the mountain comes down on top of us."

"I can't stand, the grounds moving."

"Then crawl."

We scrambled down the quaking highway, sometimes on all fours, desperate to get away from the collapsing mountain.

"Move faster, kids!" Atian said.

At long last the slide subsided, and the dust settled to the ground. Half the mountain had come down beside the earlier slide.

Samoset slapped dust off his jeans. "Whew-ee, that was some wicked slide."

Atian unraveled his legs from two children. "Yeah, and how many kids did you carry? Hm? Give me a reason not to toss you over the side of this mountain."

Samoset scowled. "Watch your mouth, gimp."

"Is everyone here and accounted for?" I said.

Etta rubbed her skinned knees. "Everybody except the chief and Councilor Ore."

Leyla sniffed. "And Vogy."

"Anybody hurt?"

Benji hobbled over. "Me, my butt's full of cactus spikes."

Atian limped back and forth on the edge of the rock wall. "We need to find out if anyone survived."

I bit my lip and held back the tears. I wouldn't break down in front of the children. "How could they survive that slide?" I pushed Wolf off my lap and stood up. "And even if they did, *Voyageur* is buried under tons of rock."

Atian grasped my fingers and pulled me against him. I closed my eyes and let his comfort wash over me. "You don't know that. Chief Roy is strong and cagey, Hali. I'm betting he found a way."

I snuggled deeper into his safe, warm arms. He kissed the top of my head and pulled me tight. "I'm going down," he whispered in my ear.

My head popped up. "No, your back. It's barely holding together. What if you fall?"

He flashed his crooked smile. "The slide made a land bridge, I'll be all right."

"Now wait a minute," Samoset said. "Since I'm the only surviving elder on this expedition, I reckon I decide what we do next."

"Get real."

Samoset's face darkened. "Now you listen to me, boy, or I'll give you something to remember."

Atian glared at Samoset. "Touch me or any of the kids and I'll have Wolf tear you apart."

Wolf growled low in his throat and crouched in attack mode. His hind quarters quivered. Samoset blanched and backed away.

Atian turned to me. "Hali, I can't leave without knowing."

He was right, and I had to stop being such a crybaby. "What if you don't come back?"

"You'll keep going, find a way through the mountains, and get these kids to the pick-up site." He kissed my eyes, my nose, and for the briefest of moments, touched my lips. His smile promised of things to come.

Benji grimaced. "Ugh, get a room."

"Take Wolf," I whispered in his ear.

Matwau joined us. "I'll go with you, Atian."

I smiled through my tears, and Matwau rewarded me with a bashful grin. "Thanks, Mat."

Samoset reached for Matwau. "Hey boy—"

"Leave it alone, I'm going."

Atian and Matwau disappeared over the side of the mountain. Wolf bounced beside them, chasing a yellow butterfly, or was it a Sky Being?

I had to keep busy or go crazy with worry. "Come here, Benji, and bend over."

"No, not in front of them goils."

I sighed. "Girls, we need a fire. Fetch some dry branches."

"Ah Hali, we wants to watch," Etta said.

"Move it."

The kids snickered as I plucked cactus needles out of Benji's behind.

"Ow! That hurts."

"Be still, it's just a few needles."

"Easy for you to say, it's not your butt being tortured."

Tomko laughed and danced away. "You've got a big enough one, shouldn't hurt none."

Gecki popped his green head out of Benji's shirt and scolded me. "Eeek, eeek."

I rubbed the little guy's pert nose. "He's fine, Gecki, just a bit speckled."

We waited all day, huddled in a grove of fir trees away from the landslide.

Samoset sulked nearby, but as the sun sank behind the trees, he drew near. "We should be moving on, they ain't coming back."

I ignored him.

He yanked on my hair, hard enough to bring tears to my eyes. "Now look, girlie—"

"Ow, let go of me, you toad!" I twisted away from him, but a fair bit of my hair stayed in his grubby hands.

Benji and Tomko tackled Samoset to the ground, and Tomko punched him in the jaw. "That's for calling me a girlie-boy." Zie hit him again. "And that's for pulling Hali's hair."

"Enough boys, let him up." I glared at Samoset. "Get lost, or I won't stop them next time."

Samoset slunk away, his nose dripping blood, and his suit meshed with gravel and dust.

Leyla plopped down beside me. "I don't feel so good, Hali."

"Time for your medicine, sweetie."

She cried. "No, I don't wanna. That med-cine hurts my tummy."

I gave her a meat and cheese sandwich. "The food should keep the medicine from hurting your tummy." I squeezed her tight and kissed the top of her head. "Hold on a few more days, baby girl."

I rocked her to sleep while gazing at the horizon. Where were they? We had enough water for another day and food for a couple days. After that we'd be in serious trouble. At times the fear became unbearable, and I closed my mind to the possibility Atian would not come back. A picture of our life in Maniton formed in my mind: a cozy home, Atian a musician, and me a new doctor with a baby on the way. Benji and Leyla, all grown up with mates of their own. A perfect life.

A clap of thunder jerked me out of my dream. Smoke rose above the trees and mixed with the dark clouds grazing the craggy mountains. What if the storm started a forest fire? How would I get the children to safety without Atian and Matwau? Some of the kids could barely walk.

A Sky Being bobbed in front of me. "Scat, I don't want you here. How come you didn't help us in Clearton? You're supposed to be good beings, not bad."

The Sky Being smirked and darted away.

I snuggled closer to Leyla and closed my eyes to a fitful sleep full of terrifying visions. A naked man kept running after me. Then a gigantic wave towered over me, its crest full of screaming children. The air exploded, and I couldn't breathe. I pulled at something tightening around my throat, squeezing the life out of me.

"Hey-o!"

I shook the cobwebs from my brain and searched for the source of the noise. Three figures, one leaning heavily on the other two, trudged up the trail. Raven circled overhead.

Atian waved. "Hali!"

Wolf bounded ahead and plopped his gigantic paws on my shoulders. I hugged him. "Wolf, down boy." I longed to run into Atian's arms, but instead I scanned the chief. The boys were helping him walk. A bloody wound cut across the side of his head, and his arm hung at an odd angle. I held back my tears. "Chief Roy, you're safe."

"Aa." He grinned, then grimaced from a deep cut on his lip. "Pretty broken up, but it's me."

"Broken up or not, I'm so glad to see you."

"I lost my cane, dag-blasted."

"But we found the glider." Matwau held up the dented transport. "Kind of beaten up, but I can salvage it."

We helped the chief into my makeshift camp and settled him beside Leyla.

"Chief Roy," she murmured, half asleep. "You sick, too?"

I mouthed, "Ore?"

Atian shook his head.

"And you should have left me to die in peace, too. I can't walk, and we don't have a transport. I'll hold you up, and you'll miss the pick-up."

"We don't leave our people behind, remember?" But the chief was right. We were running out of time.

"Voyageur is gone?"

"Aa, poor thing. She opened her air lock, and I jumped out before we hit bottom. She saved me."

Leyla's face crumbled, and she sobbed into her hands. "No, not Vogy. I loved Vogy."

"Leyla, Vogy died a hero. Don't be mourning the old girl too much."

Atian and Matwau worked on the glider for the better part of the day.

"Okay, we've got it fixed," Atian said. "I'll scout the road up ahead, you guys wait here."

"But if we lose you."

A grin creased his handsome face. "Does that mean you'll miss me?"

My traitorous heart fluttered. I longed for him night and day. Yes, I would miss him.

He touched my cheek. "I'll be back before you know it, Hali. These mountains are dangerous, we need a little scouting." He turned to Matwau. "Look after them, will you?"

Matwau nodded.

I cleaned the chief's wounds with antiseptic and bandaged his head.

"You'll make a fine healer, Halerine Ananda."

"Wait until I've fixed your arm before you say that."

"Blasted thing's barely healed from the bullet you gouged out of me."

"Matwau, hold the chief's shoulders."

Chief Roy stiffened and glared at me. "You wouldn't be fixing to do what I think, now would you?"

I wedged my foot in the crook of his arm. "Ready?"

"No!"

I yanked hard. Chief Roy let out a scream that woke the children.

"What's wrong with the chief?" Benji said.

"Nothing, he's all better." I grinned at the chief. "Still think I'm good?"

"Oh, you're good, I'm just not liking you much." He settled down for a nap. Etta crawled into the crook of his good arm and fell asleep sucking her thumb.

Matwau and I paced the small camp, waiting for Atian. "Mat—"

"Don't say it, he's coming back."

Atian returned at sundown and flopped down beside the chief. He rubbed his maimed foot and groaned when his tortured back touched the ground.

"Let me see your back."

"It's fine, Hali. Nothing you can do right now, anyhow."

"So what did you find?" Matwau said.

"I found transportation, large enough for all of us." His eyes twinkled, and he couldn't stop grinning.

Chief Roy squinted at him. "What aren't you telling us, lad?"

"Me?" He blinked. "Why nothing. I found us a ride is all."

"And how far away is this ride?"

"Two hours brisk walk."

"So half a day for a broken down old codger."

We lined the river bank and stared at the bright yellow rafts bobbing in the shallows. The chief and I turned as one and glared at Atian.

"Is this a joke?" I said.

He blinked, all innocent-like. "What? They're transportation, aren't they? And the river is heading in the right direction, isn't it? And we don't have to worry about blocked roads."

Chief Roy grunted. "No, just rapids, waterfalls, and drowning. And we're sitting ducks for the likes of Cardiff."

"Ah, come on chief, it'll be fun. We'll sail into Vancouver like intrepid explorers."

"Oh now, don't get ahead of yourself, lad. We've no idea if this river leads to Vancouver. Rivers change course or dry up, and our old maps aren't reliable anymore."

"But—"

"But nothing, if the river deviates from our path, off we go."

"Yes sir," Atian said, but he couldn't stop grinning.

We clambered into the rubber rafts. Atian took half the children and the rest hopped into my raft along with Chief Roy and Wolf. At the last moment, Matwau climbed in beside me and picked up an oar.

Atian glared at Samoset. "I guess you're coming with me, then. Or you can walk."

Samoset climbed aboard. He grabbed a moldy orange life jacket from one of the kids and held it to his chest.

A heavy mist rolled in and enveloped the rafts.

"Reminds me of Jurassic Park," Matwau said.

At my raised eyebrow, he said, "An old movie about a land where dinosaurs roamed."

"Well, let's hope not, I've had enough nasty surprises. Dinosaurs, I don't need, but at least the mist makes us less visible to drones."

Benji danced on the edge of the raft. "Yippee! Look at me!"

Wolf barked and bounded across the raft, but his bouncing jostled the flimsy raft. Benji lost his balance and fell into the water. He surfaced and splashed water at Wolf. "Hey! That wasn't funny!"

We laughed anyway.

Matwau fished Benji out of the water and plopped him in our raft. "Serves you right for showing off to the girls."

Benji's clothes steamed in the hot air.

"You're cooking, Benji," Etta said, and she giggled.

"Rainbow Warriors, head out," Chief Roy said.

I perched on the edge of the raft, my oar ready in case we veered too close to hidden rocks, and I tried to relax. Atian might be right, this could be fun.

And it was fun, for the first few hours, but then we entered a narrow canyon. The granite cliffs closed in, close enough for my oar to touch the side, and the gentle current turned fierce. We careened down the raging river, bouncing from side to side, and hurled through whitewater rapids. Waves splashed over the raft and threatened to swamp us. My arms and back ached from steering the raft between the sharp rocks and log jams. "We can't hold it, we're going too fast!"

"There's no place to dock!"

Matwau's words were swallowed in the roar of rushing water. We hit the canyon wall and lurched around a bend going sideways and out of control.

The canyon opened up, and I scanned the shoreline, searching for a landing site before we broke apart. A quiet pool protected by massive boulders stretched along the shoreline.

"Make for shore, Hali. I think we're close to a waterfall."

I dug my oar into the rocks and pushed with all my strength, but my oar splintered. Matwau lost his balance, and his oar disappeared in the swirling water. The raft twisted and turned. I clutched the slippery side and wrapped a rope around my waist.

The water swept us through a series of foaming rapids, and without warning teetered on the brink of a waterfall. "Hold on!"

We plunged over the edge. My mouth opened in a silent scream. Halfway down, the raft hit a boulder, and I lost my hold on Leyla. A rogue wave swept her overboard, and she disappeared into a deep pool of black water. "Leyla!"

The water engulfed me, and the heavy raft pulled me deeper. I squirmed in the water and struggled to untie the rope around my waist. My breath almost gone, I fought my way to the surface and gulped in air. "Benji! Leyla!"

"Woof!"

"Wolf, where are Benji and Leyla?"

"Woof, woof!"

I waded over to Wolf. He was clutching Leyla's limp body between his teeth. We dragged her to shore, and I pumped on her chest. "No, please, Great Apistotoke, not after all this. Leyla, wake-up."

"Let me, Hali." Matwau took over pumping.

I bit my knuckles. This couldn't be happening. "Leyla! Come back!"

She whimpered, then rolled over and threw up. "Hali, I barfed."

I fought back tears and hugged her. "That's okay, honey. As long as you're all right."

Leyla curled in a fetal position and sucked her thumb. "I'm cold, I want mama."

Wolf snuggled close and licked her face. "Yuck Wolf, you smell like a wet dog." But she didn't push him away.

Soggy kids crawled onto shore, and Atian and his crew ran up.

"Benji, where are you?"

"I'm here," came a weak reply from behind a grove of dead poplar trees.

"Are you hurt?"

He crawled over to me and shivered. "No."

"Take off those wet pants."

He took off his life jacket. "I ain't taking my clothes off in front of no goils. Sides which, Gecki won't come out none."

"Is he all right?"

"Yeah, just mad at me."

Patches of driftwood lay along the shore. "We'll build a fire. Chief Roy, where are you?"

"Over here, Halerine Ananda."

"Are you all right?"

"*Aa*, but I've lost my pants."

I would have laughed under different circumstances. "Atian might have something for you, but we lost all our gear." Then reality struck and my heart sank. "Great Manitou, I lost the DNA."

Wolf barked and jumped into the water.

"Wolf! Where are you going?"

He turned back, pulling a small blue bundle.

"Oh my gawd, Etta! Help me get her ashore!"

Her tiny body was so pale and so still. Even as I started CPR, I knew in my heart we were too late.

Leyla dropped to the ground beside me and sobbed. "Etta, wake up, don't leave me. Please Etta! I needs you. You're my bestie."

I pumped and gave her my breath until my arms ached, then Atian took over, but it was no use. He finally sat back. "I'm sorry kids, she's gone."

Chief Roy hobbled over, a shredded piece of cloth wrapped around his body.

I swallowed to ease the lump in my throat, but it wouldn't budge. "We-we couldn't save her, chief."

His face crumbled and he turned away.

Leyla smoothed Etta's rumpled hair and kissed her pale cheek. "I loves you, Etta. Forever."

Benji crouched beside Leyla and wrapped his arm around her. Tears rolled down his cheeks.

Matwau sighed. "She's gone to a better place, I guess."

I rounded on him. "A better place? Who thought up such a stupid platitude? Etta's not in a better place, she's dead! And it's my fault."

I stormed off, Leyla's sobs ringing in my ears. Atian found me crouched behind a boulder, clutching Etta's broken beaver totem. He sat down beside me, not saying anything.

"Why our sweet, little Etta? She was so good."

"I don't have an answer, Hali." He sighed and wiped his tired eyes. "I know you're hurting, but we've got more trouble."

"What?"

"Willow and Keme are missing."

We buried sweet Etta on a hillside with her totem to keep her company. Atian erected a small tipi over her grave, and each of us placed a rock on the fringes to hold down the leather sides.

The life she would never have flashed before my eyes. She waved her high school diploma at me and smiled, then walked down the aisle with a handsome young man on her wedding day. Two children hung on her skirt, and in her old age, grandchildren clamored over her knees. The life she would never have, because of me.

"Poor little tyke," Chief Roy said. His voice shook and tears ran down his cheek. "I will miss you all of my days, sweet child. Safe travels to your paradise and rest in peace."

We said our farewells. All but Leyla. She stood stony-faced and dry-eyed. I crouched beside her. "Leyla, don't you want to say good-bye to Etta?"

She turned and walked away.

On the second day of searching for Keme and Willow, tinkly music drifted down the shoreline. I followed the tune.

Willow's archaic cell phone peeked out of the muddy riverbank. A game of Candy Crush was playing across the screen. I threw the pink phone into bushes lining the shore and burst into tears.

Chief Roy ran his hands through his disheveled hair, the braids long since unraveled. "I don't know where else to look, they've vanished."

Atian paced the riverbank. "We'll search farther upstream. The rapids took them along."

The chief clasped his shoulder. "Leave them be, son. Their bodies are tangled in bottom weeds. We won't find them."

"They're not dead! They're lost, is all."

"Atian, you've searched up and down the river on both sides for klicks. We would have found them by now."

He ran his hands through his hair. "But it's all my fault!"

Leyla buried her head in her hands and sobbed. "Willow, Etta."

Her first words in two days. The other children, quiet until now, broke down.

Benji sobbed. "No more Mexican train with Keme."

"Listen all of you," Chief Roy said. "We've had a terrible accident, and we'll mourn the children when the time's right, but right now we must go on."

Tomko wiped at zis runny nose. "No, I wanna go home."

Leyla stopped crying. "Yeah, we was safer at home."

Chief Roy threw up his hands and gestured to me.

I swatted away a pesky green Sky Being and sank to my knees. "Let's say a little prayer for Etta, Keme, and Willow."

The children bent their heads.

"Gitche Manitou, guide their spirits to safety." My voice broke.

"And make sure you keep them dry," Leyla said.

Chapter Sixteen

THE SPIRIT WRESTLERS

The mud-splattered school bus hiccupped and stalled. Atian pumped the gas pedal and tried again. The bus blew puffs of black smoke out the rear end and roared to life.

He grinned. "Hasn't been running for a while, is all." He ground the gears.

Chief Roy cringed. "Easy on the transmission, boy. This heap was hard to find."

We'd wandered out of the valley and into an abandoned village. Matwau found the school bus parked behind a dilapidated old house tucked into the bush. We missed Vogy, but at least Cardiff wouldn't be looking for a school bus.

The bus brought Atian back to us. After we lost the children, he had gone quiet and distant, his face dark and brooding. He blamed himself for the kids' death, and nothing I said helped him deal. I began to think he would never pull out of the funk. Chief Roy was worried, too. But slowly, day by day, the old Atian was creeping back.

He stepped on the gas pedal. "Here we go."

The children clapped. Chief Roy shook his head and muttered under his breath.

The bus careened around a corner, circled a vehicle pile-up, and ran into a bonfire blazing in the middle of the road.

"It's a trap!" Chief Roy said. "Go around anyway you can."

Atian pushed the pedal to the floor and zoomed past shadows that became men with rifles.

Tomko shook zis fists in the air. "That's showing them."

I leaned back and let the air conditioning cool me. Sweet after the sweltering sun roasted us on the rafts. My sunburn still hurt, but my heart ached more. Three precious children were gone forever. And the cache, I had lost all the DNA samples the Siksiká kept safe for generations.

We searched for the cache at the same time we searched for Keme and Willow. On the second day, I found my leather backpack on the riverbank, ripped open and empty. All those prairie species, the bison, caribou, and beaver, and all our hopes for a revival someday, were dashed. And Honey. At the last minute, I had persuaded Councilor Ahoti to include Honey's DNA for cloning. Now she was gone forever.

I curled up on a stack of old clothes in the back of the bus and willed the klicks to go by fast before something else happened.

We reached Kamloops running on fumes.

Atian shifted down. "No sweat, we're bound to find gas in a town this size."

We drove from one dry gas station to the next, until even Atian began to worry. Vacant stores lined the deserted main street. Mannequins stared at us from grimy shop windows, their naked forms a grim reminder of the looting that must have raged in the city.

Tomko sighed. "Imagine what this town used to be like, all those pretty dresses hanging in stores."

Samoset smirked. "Pretty dresses for pretty boys?"

The weasel had slipped into our camp two days after the capsizing. We ignored him, but he stuck to us like old glue.

"Do you think they gots chips or pop in any of the stores?" Benji said.

"Sorry Benji, they were ransacked years ago," Chief Roy said. "Besides, that stuff's bad for you."

Benji snorted. "Then I guess I'm good, cuz I only gots to eat it but three times in my whole life."

I hid my grin. A traveling trader had stopped at our village and treated us to our first junk food. We never forgot the taste. What I wouldn't do for a bag of Hawkins Cheezies or red Twizzlers. My mouth watered. And my precious Skittles, lost at the bottom of the waterfall.

Chief Roy tapped Atian on the shoulder. "Stop here for a spell, lad." He climbed out of the bus and disappeared into a hardware store.

I slipped my breather on and stepped out of the bus. A squeaky traffic light swung back and forth on its rusty hinges, and plastic bags slid down the deserted street. Pages from a yellowed newspaper floated by and I caught one. The headline read, "Where is the government?" June 21, 2089. How long before they realized the government was gone?

Chief Roy reappeared swinging a cane carved from dark mahogany wood, and wearing pants nearly as baggy as his old ones. He grinned. "Couldn't stand Atian's pants another minute, too tight in all the wrong places."

I admired the gargoyle on the cane's handle. "Should come in handy, fighting monsters and all."

"Aa, you never know on this trip."

Garbage was piled up against an abandoned skimmer, and swarms of flies buzzed the decaying mound. "Seems kind a eerie, what with nobody around, just their garbage," Benji said. "Where'd they all go?"

"Too hot and dry in Kamloops, even a century ago. It was one of the first inland cities to be abandoned." Chief Roy grunted. "Never did fancy the place."

We hopped back on the bus.

Matwau cleared his throat. "If we can't find people or working vehicles, how will we find fuel?"

"Good question."

"Okay, no gas in the stations, so plan B." Atian plowed through the front window of an auto repair shop and screeched to a halt beside a hulking black SUV.

Tomko and Benji cheered.

"I see our boy still has a fair bit of the hoodlum in him," Chief Roy said, a smile on his face and relief in his voice.

Atian checked the fuel gauge on the SUV. "Bingo! This one's full."

"And how do you propose we move the fuel from that monster truck into our bus?" I said.

He smirked. "It's all in the lips, my dear. All in the lips."

Twenty minutes later, I was sucking on a hose. My head was spinning, and still nothing but noxious fumes. "Ugh! This is disgusting."

Atian staggered over and shoved me out of the way. "Let me try again."

"But you're still dizzy."

Matwau was throwing up in the corner. So no help there.

"Look, Hali, we need this fuel." Atian glared at Samoset. "And it's up to you and me."

Chief Roy hobbled over. A tight grin creased his weathered face. "Let me show you how it's done, lightweights."

We both opened our mouths to protest, but the chief crossed his arms and glared at us. We closed our mouths. He hunkered down and blew into the black tubing, then sucked hard. A moment later purple gas gushed from the hose. The chief stuck the tube into one of the jerry cans. "Learned a thing or two in my misspent youth."

"Wahoo!" Atian said. "Vancouver here we come!"

"Not so fast, lad," Chief Roy said. "We've days of travel ahead of us."

"Why? We're less than three hundred klicks away."

"Have you ever been on the Sky Trail?"

"No. Why?"

"Let's wait and see what happens."

I sighed. This would not be good.

I was right, it wasn't good.

Bronze cables the size of a man's torso swooped up and joined pillars a hundred meters high. The cables hissed and groaned in the strong wind, like snakes searching for their next prey. Conveyor belts that once whipped vehicles across the interior farmlands at more than a hundred klicks an hour sat silent and unmovable, and rusty sliders and transports clogged all four lanes.

Raven circled above the gloomy scene, his plaintive calls urging us to move on. Why?

"So this is Sky Trail," Matwau said. "We never came across anything like this on our trek to Elk Ridge."

Chief Roy tapped on his bio-comm. The old comm was losing power, more each day. "Aa. Agrico built the belt in 2072 to protect farmlands and orchards from heavy traffic heading to the coast. Worked for a time."

Gale-force wind gusts shook the bus and tossed litter high into the air. A rusted car door flipped into the air and headed straight for a silver tower looming over the valley. At this distance the ominous lights running up and down the tripods were barely sparks, but that thing was alive and waiting.

A familiar chill skidded up and down my back. "Chief, there's another one."

"*Aa*, I see it, Halerine Ananda. We won't be going anywhere near."

I peered over the railing. Stumps of long-dead fruit trees kept the soil from drifting away in the never-ending wind.

"Nothing grows here anymore." Chief Roy pointed eastward. "That being one reason."

A twister crossed the valley, scouring the land and leaving a swath of bare soil wherever it touched down. The tornado veered north and headed for the Sky Trail.

"Uh chief, maybe we should skedaddle," Matwau said.

Chief Roy squinted at the oncoming twister. "Wait on it."

Clouds of dust and debris whirled around us, and we huddled in the shaking bus.

"That twister's gonna wipe us out!" Benji said.

"Chief!"

"Hold on."

I hunched my shoulders and waited for the end.

"Hali, look," Matwau said.

I peeked. The twister lunged at the Sky Trail but hit an invisible wall that held the swirling wind back. It darted south, leaving the Sky Trail intact.

Matwau whistled. "It lets the wind in, but not the twister. How did you know, chief?"

"Remembered reading how engineers were building a repeller into the Sky Trail. I figured the gizmo must still be working, otherwise this whole contraption would be in pieces by now."

"Everyone out, stretch your legs a bit," Atian said.

I swatted at swarms of flies buzzing into my nose and mouth. Would rats and flies inherit the earth once humans were gone? No, probably gophers like the one in the gorge so long ago.

I searched the sky. No Cardiff drones. Would the Sky Trail barrier keep them out?

Wolf trotted from one vehicle to the next and sniffed the tires for signs of other dogs. A timber rattlesnake snoozing under a rusty slider shook its tail and hissed.

"Woof!"

Wolf darted back to the bus, his tail between his legs. He licked the kids' faces and begged for hugs.

Matwau smirked. "What a wimp."

Chief Roy surveyed the endless line of vehicles. "Well, this explains where all the cars disappeared to."

"But what about the people?" Leyla said. "They didn't burn up or drown, did they?"

I hugged her. "They walked out, honey." Except where would they go? Conditions on the coast were worse than on the plains, had been for decades, what with hurricanes and earthquakes, and mass hysteria driving residents mad.

A high-pitched whistle vibrated the air, and a silver bullet streaked across the sky, then disappeared. Cardiff?

Atian whirled around. "What was that?"

"Relax, it's a spaceship," Chief Roy said. "Didn't know they were still launching. I used to see lots of streaks in my earlier days."

"Can we go, too?" Leyla said. "I don't like it on Earth."

"Afraid not, Leyla, spots are all taken. Sides which, you don't want to live in a tin can circling Mother Earth do you?"

"Not much different than a bubble beneath the sea," I said under my breath.

Matwau heard me. "You got that right." He tossed a stone over the edge of the belt. "Where are we, anyway?"

"In the bread basket of Beforetimes Canada, but producers shut down more than three decades ago." Chief Roy nodded at the stumps of dead trees far below us. "Not enough water for crops, and the temps rose so high herds stopped breeding."

On the other side of a barren field, a thin curl of white smoke floated into the hazy sky. "Maybe someone still lives over there, looks greener."

"Let's have a look-see."

Atian hopped into the driver's seat. "All aboard."

We scrambled in and took our seats.

Atian shifted gears. "Buckle up, we're going down, baby. Hold on everyone."

Oh boy. "What about the barrier?"

"Not meant for vehicles," Chief Roy said.

Atian swung the wheel, and the rickety bus careened down a ramp, sending abandoned cars flying over the railing. Explosions rattled the bus and puffs of blue smoke and dust shot into the air when the cars hit the ground a hundred meters below.

Chief Roy grabbed a handrail. "Mercy."

The kids screamed, half in delight, and half in terror. Down the ramp we charged, in and out of an overgrown ditch, through a break in the dead trees, and onto a stubbly field. Atian did not slow down, not even for larger tree stumps.

"If we stop, we'll never get going again," he said over the roar of the laboring engine.

We tore across the field, flew over hills, and landed in a heap of dust on the outskirts of a village straight out of a nineteenth-century movie set. Long, narrow houses with thatched roofs and whitewashed plaster walls lined either side of a clean-swept dirt street. Wooden sidewalks bordered the street, and apple trees dripping with ripe fruit swayed on the narrow meridian.

I half expected a horse and buggy to trot into view. "I wonder if this was a heritage park in Beforetimes."

"Seems fixed up, not like them other towns," Benji said.

"Those other towns."

The houses had glass in the windows, and the doors hung on their hinges. Even the thick green shrubs were manicured, and no trash or rubble cluttered the street. I pushed away memories of another on-the-surface perfect town.

"They gots trees and plants that's living," Leyla said.

A stunted pine forest surrounded the village, and an old-fashioned windmill pumped well water into a vast vegetable garden.

"Aa, this is another world."

The smoke we spotted from the Sky Trail rose from behind one of the houses.

We climbed out of the bus and stretched our stiff muscles. Samoset skulked away. Good. Maybe we could lose him.

A dog barked, raising Wolf's hackles, and a frilly green curtain fluttered on one of the houses. A draft, or was someone watching us?

"Is anyone there?" Nothing. "Hey, we could use some help out here, we've got little kids."

A door hinge squeaked, and a corpulent woman clutching a straw broom stepped onto the porch. She wore a dark blue, homespun dress reaching to her ankles and a full-length white apron. A navy polka-dotted kerchief covered her hair, except for wisps of blond curls.

Pain and fear creased her worn face. "We don't care much for strangers around here." She banged the broom on the wooden sidewalk, and nodded at me. "Best take the pretty one and skedaddle."

"We're merely passing through, good woman," Chief Roy said. "But we'd surely enjoy some friendly conversation for a spell and some running around room for the young ones."

The woman patted her apron smooth and sized up the chief. Then she nodded. "Name's Nadia."

"How do, Nadia." Chief Roy bowed. "A real pleasure to meet you. My name's Roy Danforth. Any more folks in these parts?"

Nadia stared at the chief, still suspicious. "Me and my kin is all. Safer here than outside."

Chief Roy nodded. "*Aa*, it's pretty bad out there. We've found ourselves in a few tight spots."

Nadia cupped her hand and hollered. "Come on out everyone, these folks are friendlies."

Doors opened and women and children stepped onto the porches. The women, young and old, wore drab homespun dresses like Nadia, and the same fearful expressions. The little boys were dressed in short black pants and white shirts, and homemade straw hats. Small children peeked from behind their mothers' ample skirts. Most were naked.

One little girl reminded me of Etta, except for her golden curls and blue eyes. I smiled and held out my hand. "Hello, what's your name?"

She pulled her thumb out of her mouth. "Donya. Is that a real wolf?"

I nodded. "My father found Wolf when he was a puppy. His mother was killed in a bear trap, so we used an eye dropper to feed him, and he grew into this big wolf."

Donya watched Wolf chase a mouse, his black tongue hanging out from the heat, then sidle up to Tomko and Benji for a hug. A small smile touched her lips.

"Leyla," I said. "Why don't you and Donya make friends?"

The two little girls stared at each other, then Donya broke the ice. "Wanna see my dollies?" They ran into a nearby house.

A slovenly man carrying a beat-up rifle strutted out of one of the houses. Right away, I knew the type—lazy, never amounted to much, surviving on the backs of others. Except this one showed up naked as a newborn baby. He offered his hand to Chief Roy, but not before looking me up and down.

I shifted my gaze. The guy creeped me out.

"Howdy stranger, name's Pete Verigin."

Chief Roy hesitated, then shook Pete's hand. "Pleased to meet you, Pete. Nice to be around friendly souls again."

"Oh, we're a friendly bunch all right, just don't get visitors no more."

Matwau shook Pete's hand. "Excuse me, sir, but why are you the only adult male?"

Pete ducked his head and grinned. "These women be my wives, laddie. Got thirteen of them and the kiddies, fifty-eight all told."

I gasped. "You've got thirteen wives? Isn't that illegal?"

Another look.

"Not in these parts, girlie. Lots of poly-gamist colonies living in the mountains, have been for years." He puffed out his scrawny chest. "We be Doukhobors, proud Spirit Wrestlers."

I searched my memory. Doukhobors were not polygamists. "Really?"

"We sort a meshed Doukhobor ways with poly-gamy ways around these parts. Works best for right now. Me and my wives built this here village some ten years ago."

I was betting the women did all the work.

"No authorities left to kick up a fuss, though their fussing in the mountains never amounted to much anywho. We live close to the land, knowing how to squeeze a vegetable crop out of this sickly soil, and coax eggs out of a few chickens, and milk from cows. We eat easy."

"Are you related to Peter Verigin, the Doukhobor leader from Saskatchewan, some two centuries back?" Chief Roy said.

Pete scratched his flabby backside. "Yep, he be my ancestor. Peter the lordly they called him back then. He and the rest of the spirit wrestlers left the frigid prairies for these parts in 1907. Doukhobors been here ever since." Pete frowned. "Except no more. None of my kin left in Saskabush. None here either."

"Would you sit a spell?" Nadia said. "I've a pot of borsch simmering on the stove."

"Oh, thank you, but there's a lot of us," I said.

Nadia snickered. "I'm used to feeding a crew."

"We'd be delighted, then," Chief Roy said. "My ma learned to cook Russian borsch from a village elder who must have spent time in a Doukhobor colony. Never forgot the taste."

Ten minutes later, Nadia rang a bell and called everyone for lunch. I laughed and held my ears when dozens of children rushed into the backyard.

Wolf barked and twirled around, catching his tail.

"Let our company help themselves first," Nadia said. "The rest of you lot ate breakfast not two hours ago, anywho."

The thick, red vegetable soup soothed my stomach, and I helped myself to large chunks of Doukhobor bread slathered in real butter.

Pete grabbed a seat next to me on the enormous wooden picnic table and made puppy-dog eyes. I ignored him, but thank goodness he had put on some pants.

Benji sneaked a piece of bread to Wolf and crumbs to Gecki. "I ain't never tasted anything so good."

Nadia nodded at the three squat beehive ovens sitting in the corner of the yard. Smoke and yeasty flavors poured out of the middle one. "Still bake bread in the clay ovens my ancestors used, tastes better that way."

Benji tapped my shoulder. "Hali, can we play? Us kids are finished."

I waved them away, and they dashed for a big red barn.

Pete stretched and nodded at me. "You know, I'd be mighty pleased taking this one off your hands, chief. Been looking for another wife. Betcha she'd birth me a few strong sons." Pete cackled. "Could offer you some plump roasting hens in trade."

I bristled. "Why of all the—"

"She's mine."

Atian wrapped his arms around me. Good thing or I would have decked the old geezer.

"Halerine Ananda and I betrothed last month. When we reach our destination, I'll tame her."

"Chief!"

Chief Roy held his sore ribs with his good arm and tried not to laugh. He was unsuccessful. "Well, I guess we'll have to make do without those hens. Too bad though."

"Chief!"

I stomped away, too angry to do more than sputter and glare. The kids' shouts drew me to the barn.

Benji waved. "Hali! Come see the baby horse."

I cooed and petted the spindly colt on its black velvet nose. "He's beautiful."

Some day he would race across the valley, a lucky rider on his back. Honey. I swallowed the lump in my throat. "Let's jump in the hayloft."

"Yay!"

We threw each other into the soft yellow hay and scampered up stacks of bales, then tumbled down again. Shrieks of laughter filled the hayloft, the first laughs for joy since we lost Etta.

"Miss Halerine!"

I picked straw out of my hair and teeth and leaned over the trap door. "What is it?"

Pete spat on the barn floor. "Chief Roy wants the kiddies."

The boys dashed for the house, but Pete grabbed my arm with his greasy fingers. His dirty nails dug into my skin. "Mind if we talk a spell?" At my frown, he added, "Now look, girlie, I mean you no harm, but you should have a listen."

I groaned and followed Pete the creep farther into the barn. He kept a tight hold on my arm. The rank odor emanating from his unwashed body turned my stomach. If not for Nadia's kind hospitality, he would be drinking the dust on the barn floor by now. "I won't marry you, so don't waste your time."

Pete's thin lips curled into a sneer. "Oh, I think you might change your mind, girlie. See, my boys, the almost growed ones you haven't met, have rifles trained on your pack, and the kiddies don't even know it."

"But why?"

Pete hawked and spat. Spittle landed on his chin, but he seemed not to notice or care. "A little insurance you behave and all. Now, we're gonna walk back to my house, and you're gonna make yourself all pretty-like. When we're finished our business, you'll be my wife in the eyes of the lord. Else your kinfolk will be paying the price for your stubbornness."

A forced marriage? I was Halerine Ananda of the Siksiká Blackfoot First Nations. I couldn't be forced to marry, could I? And yet, the mean streak in Pete's eyes meant trouble. I'd play along and wait for my chance. "All right."

Peter grunted and licked his lips. "Let's go then, time's a-wasting."

The coarse exterior of Pete's house gave little hint to the luxurious Persian rugs and fancy teak furniture inside, including a massive bed piled high with silk comforters and pillows. "Not exactly the home of a frugal Doukhobor."

Pete shrugged. "A man needs his comforts. Anywho, this be the bridal suite, where I bring my new brides, if you take my meaning."

My stomach tightened, but a computer screen flickered against the far wall, and I headed for it. "You have electricity?"

"Diesel generator. Won't last long, running out of fuel."

"Do you ever receive transmissions?"

Pete shook his head. "Not much, an occasional weather update from somewhere in France, and gibberish from Africa."

He opened a closet full of sparkling gowns in every color. "Help yourself, and I'll be back right soon."

Flashes of Cardiff's love nest rose in my mind, and I shuddered. I stepped away from Pete's odorous breath and kept my face neutral while I pretended to examine the gowns.

Pete left and I ran to the back door, but it was locked. "Well, I'm out of here." I smashed the window with a cleaver and crawled out, then sprinted to the rear of Nadia's house.

Wolf was chained in the back yard. He wagged his tail and woofed.

"Hush Wolf."

I unchained him, then climbed on a tree stump and peered in the window. Chief Roy and the children sat on the wooden floor in a near-empty room. Leyla was asleep on the chief's lap, her thumb in her mouth. Samoset squatted in a corner, a smirk on his rat face. My predicament must be delighting him. Atian and Matwau prowled the length of the room, muttering, and getting in each other's way. A boy holding a rifle stood guard at the door, but his head lolled to the side.

I tapped on the window. "Psst, chief, can you hear me?"

Atian spotted me at the window and limped over. He opened the window a crack. "Hali, we thought Pete kidnapped you."

"He did. I'm supposed to be waiting for him in the bridal house. We're getting married."

He clenched his fists, and his square jaw set in a grim line.

"I broke a window and escaped."

"But not for long, girlie."

Rifles clicked behind me, and I jumped to the ground. Hands on my hips, I faced Pete and his sons. Enough was enough. "Look you creep, I won't marry you! You're a disgusting, revolting, naked pig."

Anger flashed in Pete's shifty eyes. "Well then, say goodbye to your friends here, cuz it's me or them."

Pete opened the back door and out charged Atian.

"Hold it, pup." Pete raised his rifle. "She ain't yours no more, she's mine."

"I'm not anybody's!"

The men ignored me.

"Now, if you fellas and the kiddies leave real easy-like, we'll have no trouble. And we'll take your bus, too. Fuel's mighty scarce in these parts. Have to rely on horses and buggies soon enough. So off you go."

Benji screamed. "No! She's my sister, we're not leaving her!"

"What's that young fella, you sassing me?" Pete sauntered over and stuck the tip of his rifle barrel in Benji's ear.

He paled and tears welled up in his terrified eyes.

Pete glanced sideways at me. "You wouldn't want anything bad happening to this sweet laddie, now would you, girlie?"

Chief Roy glanced at me, a worried frown creasing his forehead.

That did it. "Go chief. Take the kids and get out of here."

Warring emotions crossed Atian's face. "You can't leave Hali with that old coot."

Chief Roy threw up his hands. "We don't have much choice, lad."

Sensing he had won the upper hand, Pete dismissed my family in the direction of an overgrown road with a wave of his gun. "Be on your way, before I change my mind and do in the lot of you."

I wiped away tears as my family walked down the road. Leyla clung to Benji and sobbed, and Atian limped along, miserable and defeated. Matwau kept glancing back at me, his face a mirror of my sorrow. Only Samoset seemed unperturbed.

"Go Wolf," I said. "Go with Atian."

Wolf whimpered, but obeyed me.

They would be all right. Chief Roy would get them to Maniton.

At a sniff, I turned. Nadia stood behind me. "I'm sorry, missy. I couldn't warn you. Pete took us with much the same threats and abuse. Shot my pa in the leg when he tried to stop our marriage. Caught others stranded on the Sky Trail. Kilt their husbands." Nadia heaved a sigh. "You'll get used to him. He don't expect much, and us women, we're good company."

Get used to him? No woman should ever have to do that. "We were going to live a wonderful, safe life in Maniton."

"Ain't no such thing," Nadia said. "Not for the likes of us."

Chapter Seventeen

Leave No One Behind

I hid in a corner in the bridal suite and cried, partly because I was heartsick, and partly because my tears kept Pete away. Nadia had torn a strip off him and threatened to leave and take all the women and children with her if he assaulted me. "Let her be for a spell, and she'll come around," she'd said.

I would never come around.

Dirty, bare feet stopped in front of me. Against my better judgment, I looked up. Pete glared at me, naked and fuming. "Now look, girlie. You be my wife, and you got a duty to me."

I put my head back on my knees and let out a wail.

Pete grabbed one of my braids and pulled.

"Ow, let go of me, you creep!"

He pulled me to my feet and slapped me across the face. "Have some respect, wife!"

I swung my leg back and brought my knee up in his crotch. His eyes rolled back in his head, and he collapsed on the rough-hewn floor. Still not uttering a sound, he rolled into a fetal position.

Nadia walked in. "What's wrong with Pete?"

"I kneed him in the balls."

Nadia snort-gurgled. She nudged Pete with her broom, and he came out of his daze howling at the top of his lungs.

"Oh, stop that caterwauling and go soak your boys."

Pete struggled to his feet and stomped out of the house holding his private parts. Nadia followed close behind, but not before giving me a thumbs up.

Maybe he would stay away for a few hours and give me some peace. But then what? I couldn't keep him at bay forever. I had to make a plan.

"Psst. Hali? Are you in there?"

Atian's head peeked through the broken window Pete still hadn't fixed. Fear and worry were etched on his tired face.

"Atian! What are you doing here? Pete will kill you."

He reached through the window and stroked my cheek. "We've brought reinforcements. Seems old Pete isn't too popular among the other polygamist sects around here. Keeps stealing their women and cattle." He frowned. "Did Pete hurt you? He didn't ...?"

I shook my head. "Nadia kept him away. Maybe she hoped you guys would come back."

"We don't leave our people behind, remember?" Atian grinned. "Sides which, I haven't tamed you yet."

Warmth spread through my body at the promise on his face, and I returned his grin. "I suppose you could try."

"Where's the cretin now?"

"Nursing his privates. I kneed him."

Atian chuckled and his eyes brightened. "As soon as it gets a bit darker, we'll demand your release or come in firing. Be ready to duck."

I nodded. "I know a good hiding place, but what about the children and their mothers? They played no part in this."

"Pete's a coward. We're hoping he doesn't put up a fight." He kissed my hand and slipped back into the forest.

At dusk, Atian stepped out of the forest and whistled. "Hey Verigin, we want to talk to you!"

Pete strutted out of Nadia's house, naked again. "What in tarnation are you doing back here, boy?"

Chief Roy stepped out of the bushes. "We've brought some folks you might know."

A line of grim-faced men and women, a few carrying rifles, others rakes and hoes, stepped out of the trees and surrounded the village. They dragged Pete's sons, gagged and handcuffed, out of the trees.

"You've lost your back-up," one man said.

Pete's shoulders, scrawny from lack of exercise, hunched in, and he stamped his bare foot. "Leave my boys be!"

A shot hit the ground near Pete's feet, and he danced around like a circus clown.

"We've come for our women, Verigin!"

"They ain't your women no more, Chernoff! They're mine, done married me and birthed a parcel of young ones!"

"Not so fast, mister."

Nadia stuck a rifle barrel against Pete's skinny, naked butt. "I made allowances for you time and again, but no more. You're a lazy, shiftless bum, and you ain't no Doukhobor." Over her shoulder, she shouted, "Any of you women that wants to leave, go now. This old fool won't be stopping you."

Twelve women, their children in tow, rushed to join the men and women standing on the edge of the village. Some of the older boys reunited with their mothers.

Pete turned red, right down to his toes. "You women get back here, or I'll whip you raw!"

A young woman, not much older than me, turned around and flipped Pete the bird.

An elderly woman broke away from the group and approached Nadia. Tears shone in her blue eyes, and she tugged at her straggly gray hair. "Is that my girl, Nadia? It's been so long, I can't be certain."

"Mama." Nadia hugged her mother. "Oh mama, I missed you so much, where's papa?"

Nadia's mother shook her head. "Never did bounce back from the leg wound. Gone three years now."

Nadia burst into tears.

I wiped away my own tears. What these poor women had gone through at the hands of that miserable tyrant.

Greasy fingers wrapped around my neck. "You're the cause of all my troubles, girlie. You'll not get away so easy. I'll be paying you back for disrespecting my vitals."

I fought to breathe, but the more I struggled the tighter Pete gripped my throat. He pulled me toward the nearest house. I struggled against him, but my vision was blurring around the edges. I couldn't hold out much longer.

A shot rang out.

Pete howled and let go of me. He danced around the yard holding his butt. "My arse! My arse! They done kilt me!"

I collapsed on the ground and lay there gasping.

Nadia cuffed Pete behind the ears. "Quit your hollering, it's nothing but a little buckshot."

Pete dashed into Nadia's house, holding his red-speckled butt.

Chief Roy shook Mr. Chernoff's hand. "Thank you for your assistance, sir. Buckshot did the trick."

"No, it is I who should be thanking you. We didn't fight back until you and your young people came along." His face darkened. "We won't make that mistake again."

One of Chernoff's men interrupted. "A storm's coming, Mike. We'll be needing shelter mighty quick."

Black clouds swirled above the forest, and the trees bent from the force of the wind. I wiped a dirty wet spot off my cheek. Mud rain.

Nadia whistled. "Into the storm cellars everybody."

Pete dashed out of the house, pulling up red suspenders. Nadia poked him in the chest. "Not you, find your own place, these cellars are for decent folks."

I counted off twenty Siksiká children as they scrambled into one of the storm cellars, plus Atian, Matwau, Chief Roy, and one terrified wolf.

A funnel cloud dipped down in the stubble field. Blinding dust and debris swirled in the air and turned day into night.

Chief Roy paused in the entrance. "It's headed straight for us."

I hurried down the rickety stairs, and the chief latched the door. We huddled in the bunker, too afraid to move or speak. The racket above us intensified as machinery and tools flew through the air.

Nadia cursed behind me. "There goes my tractor."

A thunderous crash shook the cellar.

"Good lord, now the barn's gone."

I covered my ears and blocked out the frightened horses' shrieks. Wolf whimpered and burrowed his cold nose in my armpit.

Benji sobbed into his hands. "Hali, I loved them horses."

Atian patted his back. "Easy buddy, horses are smart, they'll be okay. I'm more worried about the bus. We can't reach Vancouver in time for the pick-up if the bus is wrecked."

"It's well hidden in the trees," Chief Roy said. "All we can do is hope."

Wind gusts rattled the cellar so much the door blew off its hinges and splintered into a thousand pieces. The wind tore through the small room and whipped away anything not bolted down.

Nadia cupped her hands. "Hold onto the kids! Else some might get sucked out! Seen it happen before!"

I gathered children into my arms. Atian, Matwau, and Chief Roy did the same. Wolf lay on top of two of the smallest ones. Hours went by and still the wind screamed.

Leyla tugged on my tunic. "Hali, I need a toilet."

"Me too. Hold on a little longer?"

She nodded.

I was digging through the shelves of junk for a chamber pot when the wind calmed down, and an eerie silence settled over the village. We crawled out of the cellar and surveyed the damage. A cottage roof hung from a grove of trees, and the four walls on Pete's bridal house had fallen in, like a turnover pie. Seemed apt to me. The barn lay in a jumbled heap of splintered wood, and loose straw floated in the air, turning the sky a golden sheen. The horses were gone, except for the newborn colt dying under a broken plow.

"What a mess," Nadia said.

Pete skulked out of the backyard. "That was a humdinger of a storm."

A red gash ran across his forehead, but otherwise he appeared unharmed.

"Did we lose anybody?"

"Not that you'd care," Nadia said. "When was the last time you checked the hinges on these cellar doors, you old coot? We lost three doors, and you're the one what's gonna fix them."

Pete nodded meekly.

I hid a snicker. Chernoff and his men were not so kind. They laughed as they led their womenfolk into the forest. None of the women looked back, except for Donya who waved to Leyla.

Nadia winked at me. Despite her anger, she would stay with her husband, but his days of collecting wives and slacking off were over. "Get the medi-kit, and I'll tend to your scratch."

"Quit bossing me, woman," Pete said, but he did her bidding.

"And my ma is visitin' whenever she wants to."

Chief Roy's sides heaved, and he surrendered to laughter. "Well, we'd best be leaving. Any suggestions?"

"Stick to the back roads, stay off the Sky Trail. Folks thought they had an easy way to the coast, though why they was heading to the coast, I'll never figure. Anywho, they got stuck up there when the belts shut down, running out of gas first, then food and water." She tucked strands of blond hair into her blue kerchief. "Some tried walking out, don't know what happened to them folks, likely died along the way. Others came down here, hell bent on raiding and stealing. Folks here shot a few." She grimaced. "Course old Pete collected a few of the younger ones for wives, but none lived long."

I shuddered. "We won't be going back on the Sky Trail."

"Then you'll be all right, I reckon, not much competition left. Looters used to hide in the mountains, but I'm thinking they're all dead by now."

Except for Claude. The mountains would be a perfect place for him to stage a hijack, but maybe he had lost interest since *Voyageur* died. And Cardiff, for a whole different set of reasons.

Chief Roy bowed and kissed Nadia's hand. "Thank you for your kindness, ma'am, and I wish you good fortune."

Nadia giggled and covered her mouth. "Oh, we'll make it. Won't have much, but I'm hoping my grandkids will be better off."

If Cardiff and his ilk never discovered Nadia and her Doukhobor village, they had a chance.

We picked our way over the debris and pushed into the forest where Atian had parked the school bus. Broken branches covered the back end, and a tractor tire sat in the middle of the roof.

"Looks in good enough shape," Chief Roy said.

Atian tossed the tire down and nearly hit Samoset slinking out of the trees. "Figures you'd survive."

"Samoset, good to see you," the chief said. "You can help clear the branches off the bus."

Samoset backed away. "Sorry chief, but my back's acting up again."

Chief Roy lip curled. "Well, that's too bad. I guess you'll have to stay here with the Doukhobors since a bouncing bus is too rough for a sore back."

Samoset scowled, and the evil look he sent the chief's way chilled me.

He picked up a few smaller branches. "Maybe I can lift a little."

Atian snickered and Samoset glared at him. "Getting on the wrong side of me ain't smart, gimp."

Atian hopped in the bus and pumped the pedal. The old bus sputtered, then shot black smoke out the backend as it started. "All aboard!"

"Yay!"

Two klicks down the trail, the headlights dimmed and the motor quit.

"Well, that's that." Atian switched off the key. "We're walking to the next town."

"Maybe not," Chief Roy said.

I followed his gaze.

Beep beep, wait me-ee. Beep beep

"Voyageur!"

The battered biopod lumbered up the trail, hooting and whistling, and dragging her mangled back end. She skidded to a stop beside Leyla.

Whoopee, ooh-ooh, whoopee. Leyee, here am me

Her dull gray skin flickered and changed to a glorious yellow. She rubbed against Leyla and purred. Leyla wrapped her arms around the pod's battered front screen and hugged her. "Oh Vogy, I'm so happy to see you."

Tears rolled down Leyla's thin cheeks and she beamed. "We gots part of our family back."

Chapter Eighteen

Day of the Lizard

We crowded around the screens, mesmerized by the lush rainforest paradise. Massive red cedars whispered in the still air, telling secrets not meant for human ears, and green vines as thick as a man's arm wound their way between the branches and around gnarled tree trunks. Green and gold suckers waved in the air, searching for food and light.

Leyla pressed her nose against the view screen. "The forest is kind a pretty, Hali, but it's kind a spooky, too."

Spooky.

"Another new word?"

Leyla grinned. "She copies everything I say."

I kissed the top of her head. "I'm glad you're feeling better, sweetie."

No fever for two days now, and she was slowly accepting Etta's death. The night before, she told me the Sky Beings had taken Etta to be with Santa Claus.

We'd had enough of the open croplands and the constant fear that Cardiff's drones would spot us in the battered biopod. We moved deep into the rainforest to elude anyone following us. But Leyla and *Voyageur* were right. The forest was spooky.

Benji gulped. "Maybe you shouldn't have read me *The Day of the Triffids*, Hali. Maybe those vine-thingies are searching for people blood."

The temps were cooler, but steam rose from the plants and seeped through the biopod's cracks and dents. The thick fog coated my lungs and wrapped around my body like a damp blanket. I wiped my face and neck with a bandana and piled my damp braids on top of my head. "Gawd, I'm sticky, somebody fix the a/c."

"Won't do any good," Chief Roy said. "Too many holes in the hull. The old girl needs to fix those before her innards."

Matwau cleared his throat, and I spun around. He was staring at me, a strange and disconcerting look on his face. I turned away, certain my cheeks had pinked up.

Voyageur groaned and grew another section of shielding, but she was still in bad shape. Our supplies for the replicator lay at the bottom of the landslide, not that it mattered. The synthor wasn't working either, and our recycling water supply had dropped to a dangerously low level.

"That's it troops, no more flushing," Chief Roy had announced that morning.

"Gonna get mighty stinky in here," Benji said.

Tomko cuffed Benji's head. "Yeah, thanks to you."

"Hey, you stink, too."

A scuffle had broken out, but we ignored them.

Voyageur inched her way along an old road. Her worn-out jets hissed as she glided over a washed-out spot. Moments later she skimmed over a dead tree blocking her way. Red-striped canna shrubs leaned into the biopod and caressed her membrane.

Bad-bad me no like

Chief Roy grunted. "I see Leyla's lessons are paying off. Could you teach her to call me sir?"

Leyla giggled. "I'll try."

The silence in the forest grew more oppressive the deeper we moved in.

"How long is this tree tunnel gonna last?" Benji said.

Matwau covered his face with a damp cloth and refused to look outside. "Not long, I hope, or I'm a goner. Gawd, I could use a drink."

Benji jumped back from the screen. "Aihee! Dinosaurs!"

"Not dinosaurs, Benjamin Kitchi, but the day of the lizard may have arrived, at least in these parts."

I peered through the skylight. Lizards of all shapes and sizes hung from the trees. *Voyageur's* comm picked up grunts and eerie blowing noises.

A three-foot lizard crawled up the side of the biopod.

Leyee help

"Easy Vogy, we'll mosey along, real slow, and they'll leave us alone."

Yessir

"They're everywhere, even on the road," Samoset said. "Now what have you gotten us into?"

Atian slowed *Voyageur*. "Maybe the reptiles will move on if you beep, Vogy."

She beeped and threw in an ear-piercing siren for good measure, but the lizards did not budge.

"So what do we do now, chief?"

Leyla squealed. "A st-stegosaurus!"

An elephant-sized lizard with black stripes and yellow spikes along its back pushed against a tree trunk next to the pod. Reptilian yellow eyes stared at us.

"That lizard must be five meters long!"

"Quiet lad," Chief Roy said. "I'm betting they've excellent hearing even through Vogy."

"Yepper, here they come," Tomko said.

Dozens of giant lizards slithered out of the shadows and crept closer to the pod until a sea of green and yellow scales surrounded us.

Me no like sir

A low growl rumbled in Wolf's throat, and the hair on his back stood up.

"Don't move Wolf."

Samoset threw up his hands. "Gimme a laser, I'll wipe them lizards out."

Atian scowled. "Yeah, really."

A loud thud shook the biopod.

"They're on the roof," Chief Roy said.

Get way get way

Atian patted *Voyageur's* membrane. "They can't hurt you, Vogy. Chief, what are those things?"

"Iguanas. Pets abandoned by their owners. They're thriving in this hot climate and breeding as fast as rabbits in Australia. All the vegetation they can eat, and no competition, they're growing larger with every generation."

Leyla's lip quivered. "Do they eat little kids?"

I hugged her. "No, sweetie, they're vegetarian." A little lie?

Tomko gasped and scurried back to zis cushion seat. "They're puffing up and batting their heads. We think that's a bad sign, chief."

A five meter alpha male with a tail at least that long again weaved from side to side and hissed at *Voyageur.*

"Attack mode. Let's move on," Chief Roy said.

Atian threw up his hands. "We can't. The whole trail is blocked, and they're too big for Vogy to skim over."

"Be ready to move this crate."

Chief Roy opened the escape hatch at the back of the storage pod and stomped through the reptiles, swinging his cane and cursing a blue streak. "Out of my way, vermin."

Thinking the chief might be food, they followed him to the edge of the road.

"Now stay there." He hobbled back to *Voyageur*.

A green iguana took a swipe at him with its whip-like tail, and he jumped out of the way in the nick of time. The iguanas turned *en masse* and charged the biopod.

"Okay, they're plenty pissed off," Matwau said.

He helped me open the mangled airlock, and the chief fell into the pod as a lizard the size of a truck lunged at him. Sharp teeth snapped empty air where his leg had been.

"Move Atian!"

The angry iguana smacked its tail against the side of the pod. *Voyageur* shuddered and slid across the mud-slick ground toward a sharp drop off.

"Whoa! I'm losing her!"

The pod's mangled back end hung over the precipice. Cracks popped up along her membrane and the floor tilted under us.

Help me Leyee help help

Leyla lost her balance and fell on the sloping floor. "No Vogy."

Matwau staggered over and picked her up. "I've got you." She sobbed into his shoulder.

Benji and Tomko held onto their consoles.

"Take it easy, kids." Atian punched in codes. "*Voyageur*, you can do this, come on girl, dig in those jets."

Her jets hissed and groaned. She inched her way back from the brink and waddled down the overgrown road.

I collapsed on my cushion, and Matwau deposited Leyla in my arms. "You're okay, sweetie."

She sniffed. "No, I'm not. I won't ever be okay."

Voyageur quivered.

"What's wrong, Vogy?"

She quivered again.

Back back.

"*Voyageur*, stop as fast as you can," Chief Roy said.

Yessir.

She skidded to a full stop. A mid-sized yellow iguana rolled off the roof and splattered on the road.

Benji and Tomko cheered. "Yay!"

But a dozen bloated iguanas were gaining on us.

"Get us out of here," Matwau said.

Voyageur leaped forward and she didn't stop until we cleared the thickest part of the rainforest.

I leaned back in my cushion and cuddled Leyla. Would this nightmare ever end? First, looters and Cardiff, then cannibals and a crazy Doukhobor, and now monster lizards. What was next?

I dozed off, but not before hearing Tomko whisper to Benji, "You squealed like a little goil."

We stopped beside a shallow lake for lunch. Atian and Matwau argued as they struggled to build a campfire.

"What kind of Firsts are you, if you can't build a simple campfire?" I said.

"The councilors always took care of it," Atian said.

We settled for canned Spam I'd scrounged from under a shelf in a looted grocery store.

Matwau licked his fingers. "Spam's been my lifesaver more than once, but I'm gonna fix that synthor and feed it leaves if I have to."

I cooled my feet in the gently rippling waves until snake-like vines dipped down and sucked at the water. I shuddered and pulled my feet up.

I stretched out on a patch of yellow grass below a hole in the vine jungle. Atian joined me and played a perky tune on his clarinet. The soft breeze calmed, and the trees stilled. How long since this forest heard music? "What's that song called?"

"*The Joy of Life.* My pa taught me, it's a Beforetimes song."

A rare patch of blue sky shone down on the lake, and I breathed a little easier. But for how long? We were so caught up in our struggle to reach the gathering site, we had forgotten what that meant. Did I want to spend the rest of my life in an underwater bubble? This claustrophobic rainforest reminded me of how much I loved open spaces. The thought of never again walking across dry land, feeling the wind on my face, or watching the sun rise, hurt my heart.

The air shimmered and I was standing on a wharf, but not a wharf open to the sky. Children, all looking slightly dazed and lost, stepped off dozens of submarines and swarmed the wharf. A mechanical voice floating in the air said, "Welcome Rainbow Warriors, please come this way."

We followed the voice and entered a gigantic room, its translucent ceiling hundreds of feet high. A large fish, perhaps a whale, swam along the ceiling. Maniton!

The image blurred, then disappeared, and I was back in the rainforest with Atian, far away from the safety in Maniton.

Atian chewed on a blade of dry grass. "What are you thinking about?"

"Maniton." More than thinking. I was there for a moment.

He raised a suspicious eyebrow. "Yeah, what about it?"

"Well, for starters, do you honestly want to live under water?"

He shrugged. "What choice do I have?"

Sometimes he could be so dense. "We all have choices. We're not prisoners. We can go anywhere."

"So you want to spend the rest of your life dodging one disaster after another or dealing with crazy old coots and monsters?"

That was the crux of my dilemma. If I turned my back on Maniton, I would struggle for the rest of my life without a guarantee of ever finding a safe haven, and even if I did, how long would it last? Could I condemn Benji and Leyla to that kind of life, or worse still, say good-bye to them if they chose Maniton?

Atian rolled over and ran his blade of grass across my stomach.

His eyes met mine and held them. My breath caught in my throat. And what about Atian? How could I say good-bye to him?

"I know you're worried, Hali, but I think we'll love living in Maniton. We'll be safe, and we'll have enough food to eat, a real home, and guardians to take care of us. I want to be a kid again for a little while longer."

"You're looking forward to it?"

His lips curled in a soft smile. "Sure. Maniton has a university and a database of every book ever written and every piece of music ever played. I want to explore science and music, and ..." He ran his hands through his long black hair. "... and I want some peace."

He was so close. I took a chance and caressed his cheek.

A crooked smile softened the frown lines marring his forehead. He kissed the tips of my fingers, and a wave of pleasure coursed through my body. "We deserve to live some kind of normal life."

His hands roamed over my body, and for a second I yielded to him. Then I came to my senses and stopped his hands. "I've always wanted to study anthropology, and medicine, and history. Maybe fashion, too."

He nibbled my ear. "We've got lots to look forward to, especially no more danger."

On cue, a blood-curdling scream pierced the air. Wolf barked and ran into the woods. We jumped to our feet, and I scanned the kids. "Who's missing?"

Benji scowled. "Leyla, that goil's screaming again."

Tomko tossed a pebble at Benji and danced away. "You're jealous cuz your baby sister's braver than you."

Benji balled his hands into fists. "I am too brave, you'll see."

We followed Leyla's screams.

"Leyla, where are you?"

"Over here."

Leyla and Wolf were staring at a pile of white rocks the size of melons. Only they weren't rocks, they were iguana eggs, about fifty of them nestled in a deep burrow. Some had already hatched and left the nest, others were working on it. While we watched, a stubborn little reptile picked through its shell and climbed out of the burrow.

Wolf quivered and his tail shook. I grabbed his collar. "Oh no, boy-o. You're not going near them."

Benji sidled up to me, a guilty look on his face.

"What are you up to, Benji?"

He blinked. "Me? Nothing, I followed you guys." He stroked Gecki's pointy head. "I'm not doing nothing, honest."

"No more pets, you got that?" No reply.

Atian swiveled around. "Where's the mother of these eggs?"

"Iguana females don't protect their offspring. She's long gone," Chief Roy said.

I stiffened at a guttural hiss behind me. Foul fire breath brushed my neck. "Please tell me that's not what I think it is."

"Halerine Ananda, no sudden moves."

An enormous gray iguana was looming over me. "You picked a bad time to be wrong, chief."

"All right kids, we'll walk away real slow-like. Keep your heads down and act submissive. Matwau, take hold of Leyla in case we have to make a run for it."

We plotted a wide circle around the lizard and almost made it, but then the iguana nodded its head up and down and hissed.

"Run!"

Chief Roy took off in a lumbering sprint. We dashed after him.

"It's gaining, we won't make it!"

Chief Roy stopped in his tracks and faced the angry iguana. He swung his cane like a baseball bat and hit the lizard on the nose, then Wolf jumped in front of the chief and barked.

The iguana weaved from side to side, but held back long enough for the chief and Wolf to roll into the pod.

Chief Roy climbed to his feet and rubbed his sore arm. "This is getting to be a bad habit." He patted Wolf on the head. "Sure glad your mistress convinced me to bring you along, fella."

"Get us out of this lizard land," Matwau said.

Chapter Nineteen

DEADLY MIX

The lizards had given up on us, but not the dense roof of vines and canopy trees. The dark green vines hissed and groaned and moved of their own accord, dipping and looping around the ruins of an abandoned village.

"Can't be more than five meters clearance above us," Atian said.

"Yeah, but Cardiff's drones won't spot us in here," I said.

"That's the only good thing," Matwau muttered.

Leyla peered through *Voyageur's* sunroof. "It's an upside down world."

Voyageur grumbled and twitched her back end.

No good Leyee no good

The sun should be shining and birds should be flying across the blue sky. Instead, a roof of vines hid the town from the outside world, and the moss-covered houses beneath the roof sat frozen in time. Spider webs swung from the windows, and weeds the size of small trees snarled gardens and lawns and cracked open the once-paved streets. The air hung still and lifeless, so unlike the angry, but alive wind gusts on the prairies.

"Where are we, anyway?" My words came out muffled, like I was speaking under water.

Chief Roy consulted his bio-comm. "Outside Hope, British Columbia. A mudslide buried half the town close to the end of Beforetimes, and most of the survivors left then."

"Archaeologists a thousand years from now will unearth these remains," Matwau said. "That's if any humans are still here."

I squinted in the dim light. "Are you sure those vines aren't snakes?"

With a sideways glance at Matwau, Atian wrapped his arm around my shoulders. "They're vines, Hali, big vines, that's all."

The tail of a rattler disappeared into a hole under the front step of a house. "Oh yeah, well that was definitely a snake."

"Come on, Hali, at least they're not iguanas. The snakes will move on if we tromp around a bit."

Leyla clutched my hand and hid her face in my shirt. "I don't want to stay here."

The upside-down world faded from my view and a pretty mountain village took its place, except something was wrong. A young man approached me, clutching his throat. His lips were black, and his eyes bugged out of his face. I backed away and nearly tripped over a child's prone body laying half in the street and half on the sidewalk. Sky Beings fluttered in front of my face and my dreamcatcher quivered.

I blinked and I was back in the upside-down world, but my dreamcatcher was still quivering. "Chief, we need to leave."

Chief Roy raised an eyebrow. "We need rest, Halerine Ananda."

"But not here."

"Why not?"

I'd never told anyone about my visions. "I have a bad feeling."

Voyageur's skin slowly changed from yellow to a dark green hue, and she sank to the ground.

Leyee me no like me sleep

Beads of sweat glistened on Matwau's forehead, and he hunched over. "I'm with you two. I need open sky."

Chief Roy considered Matwau, a pensive look on his weathered face. "*Aa*, that you do, lad."

Atian sighed and ran his hands through his hair. "Hali, I'm pooped. I can't guide *Voyageur* without rest. Sorry, but we need to stay put for a while."

His face was drawn and his eyes were two sunken holes. I pushed back my foreboding and nodded. "Come on, kids, let's see if we can find any food and a place for a bath."

Benji patted his matted hair in place and wiped dirt across his cheek with his grubby hands. Dirt and grime smudged his torn shirt and matched the holes in both his pant knees. "Ah Hali, I don't wanna bath."

I sighed. "I can't do anything about your clothes right now, but I can wash your hair and get you cleaned up."

Benji scrunched up his nose and crossed his arms. "I ain't taking no bath."

I knew that look. "Listen young man, you take a bath, and I'll feed you. No bath, no food, got it?"

Atian snickered. "Come on, Wolf, let's explore before she makes us take a bath."

"Thanks for the help."

Samoset dragged Matwau in the opposite direction. "Me and my boy's going for a look-see." He handed Matwau a small silver flask.

Chief Roy frowned and shook his head. "Well, I guess that leaves me fixing that blasted synthor, for better or worse."

"Fix the replicator first. We need new clothes."

The children followed me down the street, Pied Piper style. I stomped my feet when we climbed the steps to a handsome two-story house. Thorns from wild rose bushes curled and wrangled around the steps, and I pricked my finger opening the front door. "Hello, anybody home?"

No answer.

"Okay kids, we'll make camp in here."

Vines had crept under the window sills and door frames, and swept up the inner walls. They rippled through the flowery pink wallpaper and dug into the cracked ceiling. Where the vines hadn't made a foothold, fat spiders spun webs reaching from one corner of the front room to the next. We flailed our arms against the cobwebs hanging from the ceiling.

Tomko patted zis newly woven dreadlocks, streaked yellow and purple. "Them cobwebs better not get in our hair."

"Wow, wouldja look at this place," Benji said. "It's like a palace."

The front foyer was larger than our cabin back home. A crystal chandelier hung from the twenty foot ceiling, and a green marble staircase wound its way to the second floor. Heavy satin drapes, the color of sand, blocked out what little light peeked through the vines.

"Move in."

The vines on the ceiling hissed and shuddered when we passed. At least I hoped they were vines. I turned on a tap in a gold and gray bathroom off the entrance. Brown water sputtered and the taps jerked and shook, then pure mountain water gushed into the silver sink.

"Let's check out the kitchen, maybe they left some food," Benji said.

An odd smell lingered in the kitchen, beyond house mustiness, but when I opened the pantry door, a wonderland of canned goods and drinks greeted us.

Benji dived in. "Food!"

"Not so fast, young fella."

An elderly woman stood in the doorway pointing a shot gun at Benji. Her steely gray eyes meant business, despite her diminutive size.

"I-I'm sorry," I said. "We didn't know anyone lived here."

The old woman cackled. "That's what they all said, dearie."

"Excuse me?"

Her pale face darkened, and she jerked her head toward the backyard.

I peered through the grimy window and counted a dozen mounds of loose dirt in the overgrown garden. I frowned, certain I misunderstood her. "You don't mean ...?"

Her tangled mass of gray hair bobbed as she nodded. "Killed the looters where you're standing, good and swift."

Leyla whimpered and clutched my leg.

"But we're not looters, ma'am. We're a bunch of hungry kids, and we need a bath and a bed to sleep on, a-and we're so tired." I bit my lip to keep it from trembling.

The woman lowered her gun and her eyes softened, though they still seemed off. "I guess you be honest. You can stay the night, I got plenty of room." Gaps from missing teeth marred her weak smile. "And I'll cook for your young ones."

"Oh, but that isn't necessary."

"Nonsense, be right unneighborly of me not to offer up some grub. Now you take care of your kiddies, dearie, and I'll cook us a feast. The name's Marcie."

I hustled the children into half a dozen upstairs bathrooms and soon squeals and laughter reverberated through the house.

"Don't need my hair washed."

"Benji, you haven't washed your hair in over a week."

"So?"

I plopped a bar of soap on his spikes and lathered.

"Ow, that hurts! Hey, you're ruining my hair, and you're getting soap in my ears. Let me go!"

I pushed him under water.

Washed and smelling good for a change, we congregated in the dining room. Marcie had set an array of dusty crystal glasses and chipped fine china on a long mahogany table. Half a dozen cats skittered across the table hoping for a handout. Marcie bustled in and out of the dining room, humming a tuneless song under her breath and talking to an invisible audience. "So nice having decent company for a change, don't you think, Marvin?"

The juicy aroma of chicken wafted through the air and my stomach growled. "Can I help you with anything, Marcie?"

"Oh goodness, no, dearie. I've got everything well in hand, just one more ingredient to add."

She hurried into the kitchen and returned laden with a pot of chicken stew, followed by a mound of fluffy white rice, and fresh peas and carrots.

"Oh boy," Benji said and dug in.

My dreamcatcher shivered. *"No Hali."*

No what? I ate a spoonful of stew and smelled the strange odor again. I opened my mouth to warn the kids, then nothing.

"Oh, my head."

The words came out slurred, and when I tried swallowing, my thick tongue got in the way.

"She's coming around."

Dark shadows slowly took on blurry form. "W-what happened?" I tried sitting up, but the room spun, and I fell back on the bed.

Chief Roy placed his hand on my shoulder. "Easy, young woman, you gave us quite a fright."

Wolf whimpered and edged closer to my side. He licked my hand and tucked his cold nose into my armpit.

I opened my eyes a bit more. The chief and Atian looked as bad as I felt. "The kids?"

"Some doing better than you," Atian said. He avoided meeting my eyes.

"And?"

"Hali, a few of the kids are bad off. It's a wait-and-see game."

"And?"

Atian glanced at the chief.

I pushed Wolf away and struggled onto my elbows. The room swirled. "Come on, you're not telling me everything."

Chief Roy sighed and rubbed his bloodshot eyes. "Benji ate the most stew, and he's the sickest."

My head fell back on the pillow. "What did this?"

Atian shrugged. "Poison. We gave you syrup of ipecac, good thing you stocked up in St. Albert. You threw up pretty fast, don't you remember?"

"No."

Matwau came to stand by my bed. "Well, we were knee deep in barf for a time."

"Hali?"

Leyla clutched her Raggedy Ann doll and squeezed in between Chief Roy and Matwau.

I opened my arms. "Come here, baby girl."

She slipped into bed beside me and sucked her thumb. Wolf plopped his gigantic head on her legs and sighed.

"Leyla was playing with her doll and hadn't eaten anything," Chief Roy said. "Then the kids started passing out, and she hid under the table until Marcie left the room. She snuck out to find us and saved your lives."

"That mean old lady laughed when you gots sick."

"Marcie?'

Matwau scowled. "Escaped, but she'll limp for the rest of her miserable life."

Atian sat on the edge of my bed and took my hand in his. "She's a homicidal maniac, but we can't waste any more time searching for her."

I struggled out of the bed covers. "Help me up and find my clothes, I need to go to Benji."

"Hali, you're in no shape—"

A glare and Atian gave in.

I collapsed beside the kids' beds and sobbed at the sight of their swollen faces and black lips, just like my vision. "How could anyone do this to little kids?"

Five of the youngest children, including Benji, hovered near death for two days. Fever burned them during the day, and chills rattled their teeth all night. Coughing fits wracked their weak bodies, and they kept throwing up the water we gave them. But on the third day, when I had almost given up hope, they began coming around.

Tears rolled down Benji's no longer chubby cheeks. "Hali, I feel so bad."

"I know sweetie, but you're getting better. Have a sip of water."

He pushed the glass away. "No, I don't wanna barf again."

Chief Roy called me aside. "Halerine Ananda, we need to move on, or we won't make the pick-up."

"But the kids—"

"They'll be as comfortable in their sleeper pods as in this moldy old house."

The chief sent Atian and Matwau on a scavenging hunt. "We'll gather all the food, bedding, and supplies. We won't leave anything behind for that old crone, and maybe we'll find someone along the way who needs it."

We carried the sickest children and tucked them into their sleeper pods.

Leyla handed Benji her Raggedy Ann doll. "You're safe on Vogy."

Benji closed his eyes, a slight smile on his bluish lips, and went to sleep.

That afternoon we emerged from the tree jungle.

"Can't believe I'm thrilled to see green and pink sky," Matwau said. "But it's gloriously high, and sometimes it's even blue."

"Up we go Vogy, high into the mountains," I said.

Yippee

Leyla grunted. "Good, I'm sick of jungle."

Aa, me too Leyee

Chapter Twenty

THE NORTHERNERS

The stunning view across the valley filled me with hope. The tips of mountains peeked through low-lying green and pink clouds hanging far below us. Nothing bad could happen way up here, could it? No giant lizards or creepy, naked men. No psychopaths or bandits. Just cool air, even if it was tinged with brown guck.

We parked in an abandoned loggers' camp beside a waterfall that ebbed and flowed and sputtered at times. How long before it dried up?

"*Voyageur*, make camp."

Atian frowned. "So soon chief, we've barely made any klicks today."

"Can't be helped, lad, the climb up here was tough. The old girl's about done for."

Me pooped

A silver tower was perched on the next mountain. Yellow and blue lights flashed up and down the tripod, and the air hummed with energy. The fear bug coiled in the pit of my stomach. We were too close. I scrunched up my eyes at a black speck coming our way. A bird or one of Cardiff's drones?

Raven landed on *Voyageur's* dented hull and flapped his wings. He wasn't screeching for a change. I relaxed a bit.

Chief Roy handed Atian his binocs. "Check for any action around that colossal."

A rush of air swayed the dead spruce trees overhead.

"A glider just landed on the disk, and parts of the tower don't look finished," Atian said.

I pulled on Chief Roy's sleeve. "Let's go. Please chief, they'll catch us and make us slaves."

"Easy, Halerine Ananda, we're not in their line of sight."

The chief's words did little to calm me. He didn't know Cardiff like I did. Who knew how far out their soldiers patrolled? A squadron might be on our trail even now.

Benji frowned. "I got a funny feeling about this place. Monsters are hiding in them trees."

"*Voyageur* has her shields up."

He shook his head. "Nope. I feel their eyes on us."

"Tell you what, Benji, I'll take the glider up and check for monsters."

"I'll go with you," Matwau said.

I bristled. "I can manage a simple reconnaissance myself."

He held up his hands. "Hey, I know your strength, but this valley is getting to me."

Chief Roy grinned. "Go along, kiddies and try not to squabble."

I scowled at Matwau. "Well, I'm driving."

Matwau stepped on the glider behind me and wrapped his ape arms around my waist. Atian was watching us, a scowl on his face. "Do you have to do that?"

"Wouldn't want to fall off, now would I?"

His body molded against mine, and tingles ran up my spine. Maybe a little Matwau time wasn't such a bad idea. I smiled and waved to Atian. His frown lines deepened, and he turned away.

The glider dodged spindly fir trees and zoomed up the mountain. We perched on a basalt outcropping and searched for marauding patrols and red-eyed drones. Mount St. Helens, in all her magnificent glory, loomed in the distance. A plume of brown and gray smoke swirled into the sky from inside its caldera.

Matwau went quiet, like he always did. "I've known you for a year, Mat, but I hardly know you. Why are you so sad?"

He flushed and looked down at his worn boots. "I was married, and I lost her."

I gasped. "Oh Mat, I never knew."

"No one knows, and I prefer to keep it that way."

"Tell me about her."

His eyes brightened for a moment. "Her name was Kimowan, and she was my warrior woman."

He smiled at me, and for a moment that other Matwau slipped through. The one I wanted to get to know.

"You would have liked her. She was spunky and brave and funny ..." He trailed off, then pulled a colorful skirt out of the leather bag that never left his side. "This was her ribbon skirt. It helps keep me strong, like Kimowan."

I traced the soft folds of a pink ribbon. "How did Kimowan die?"

"Halfway here, we helped people escape an Arker slave gang. Kimowan got caught in the cross-fires." His jaw clenched. "Our chief called me a caretaker, for our People and for Mother Earth, but I vowed never to help another human being after losing Kimi."

"I'm so sorry you lost your wife, but not helping ..." I shook my head and swallowed the tears. "Mat, don't you realize you help us every day? You are a caretaker. A Rainbow Warrior caretaker."

He wrapped his arm around me. "Seems I can't help myself. But I'm working on it." He sighed. "Okay, let's stop the sad talk and enjoy the view."

His dark eyes pulled me in, and I lightly grazed his lips with mine.

He moaned. "Hali." And kissed me hard.

My body responded, but Atian's face flashed before me. I stepped out of his embrace. "Mat, I—"

A strong tremor shook the ground and pent-up gases hissed out of fissures in the cone.

He chuckled. "Talk about bad timing."

I craned my neck to see the infamous volcano. "Are we far enough away if that caldera blows?"

He shrugged. "Chief said we're two hundred klicks out. Last two eruptions, in 2047 and 2098, flattened a hundred klick radius, but who knows? First Peoples call St. Helens Smokey Mountain for good reason." He held up a recorder. "Might be a volcanologist or two in Maniton interested in this latest hissy-fit."

A deep rumble echoed across the valley, and a column of ash, steam, and super-heated gas spewed rock and debris thousands of meters into the sky.

I gasped and grabbed Matwau's arm. "Great Apistotoke, the mountain is coming apart."

"Relax Hali, it's far away."

Fissures in the side of the mountain bulged like an old man burping, and red hot magma spewed out of the cracks and flowed down the mountain at supersonic speed.

Matwau pulled me into a shallow crevasse and stretched over me. I pushed against his heavy chest. "Mat, what are you doing? Get off me!"

He touched his lips to mine. "Brace for the shock wave, and I don't mean me."

An air concussion, louder than a freight train, roared through the mountain range. The shock flipped us over and rolled us into a grove of swaying trees. Day turned to night, and a mushroom cloud larger than the mountain rose high into the sky.

He cocked his ear. "Do you hear that?"

"I can't hear anything with you on top of me."

"Just listen."

I did. A noise, like metal tearing, reverberated through the messed up air.

He jumped up and grabbed my hands. "Come on."

He called the glider, and I hopped on behind him. We rose above the mountain peak in time to see the tower bend, and in tortuous slow motion, fall over the side of the mountain. A roiling dust cloud rose into the air and joined the volcanic ash.

"That's two."

"Can't help but feel good," Matwau said. "I wish Etta was here to see that monster crash and burn."

A deep sadness that I kept hidden in the back of my mind, back where all the other sadness lurked, surfaced. Etta would have been tickled.

A deep growl startled us while we were getting ready for bed.

"What was that?" Tomko said, a toothbrush sticking out of zis mouth. "Wild animals? Cuz, we're afraid of wild animals even more than lizards."

"*Voyageur* will protect us." Brave words, but who knew what lurked up here?

Benji peeked out of the bathroom. "See, we should a listened to my funny feeling. I don't like these trees and mountains."

"Brush your teeth." I kept a tight rein on Wolf. "Not a sound, understand, Wolf?"

Wolf whimpered and covered his nose with his great paws. He flopped on the mat beside my sleeper.

Another roar.

"Sounds like bears," Chief Roy said.

Benji clung to me, and his weak body trembled. "We should a stayed in the rainforest, no bears live down there."

"Dinos do," Leyla said. "And poison ladies. I like it better up here."

I glanced from one child to the next. How much more could they take? How much more could any of us take? Chief Roy and Atian weaved on their feet, and Matwau hadn't spoken since we came down from the mountain. Even *Voyageur* was groaning.

I opened a view screen. Two fierce black eyes and a large brown snout stared back at me. "Oh!"

The grizzly rose on its hind legs and roared. Other bears joined in the chorus, and the valley reverberated. We were surrounded.

"It's gonna eat us," Tomko said.

Wolf barked and hopped from one side of the pod to the other.

"The bears can't hurt us if we stay inside *Voyageur*," Chief Roy said. "Quiet, Wolf. Atian, code the biopod for a tornado."

"Sorry chief. She lost her spikes in the landslide."

"Well, can we drive out?"

"Nope, her night lights are too weak. I can't risk driving off a cliff."

One of the bears, an alpha, stood up and pushed on *Voyageur* with paws the size of dinner plates. Its eyes glowered in the pod's exterior lights as it raised the biopod on her side.

Ow-ee ow-ee

"If we tip over, we'll roll down the canyon," Atian said.

"Drive boy, we'll take our chances with the lights."

A shot rang out, then another. The bears dropped to the ground. They growled and whined, and swayed from side to side. Another shot and they scurried into the dense bush.

We huddled in *Voyageur* until the sun crept over the horizon, then Chief Roy and Atian climbed out of the biopod, lasers ready. We followed close behind.

A sneeze.

"Okay, that wasn't one of us. Who's out there?" Atian said. "Show yourself."

Another sneeze.

"Please excuse the intrusion," a disembodied voice said. "I've a parcel of wee bairns, and we're in need of assistance."

The sun rose higher, and the dim light revealed a most unusual man dressed in brown and black furs. Bushy red hair covered his face.

Leyla yelped and dived into the pod. "A bear-man."

Wolf bared his teeth and a low growl built in his throat.

"Easy boy."

A bedraggled collection of weary children covered in leather and fur hides hovered close to the bear-man.

"Why, you're Inuit," Chief Roy said.

"Aye, they be Netsilik Inuit from the far North," the bear-man said. "We've been traveling for many a week now, and the wee bairns are about done in." He bowed. "The name's Jacques Cartier, intrepid Northerner, at your service."

"Pleased to meet you, Jacques," the chief said. "My name is Roy Danforth. Thank you for chasing the bears away, we appreciate the help." The chief squinted at the odd man. "But you're not Inuit."

"No sir, I be Scottish Métis. These bairns happened across my trapping lodge after wandering in the Arctic for many a day." Jacques shrugged. "I couldn't leave them stranded, so here we be."

"Poor little kids."

His pale green eyes held a spark of amusement. "Don't you be feeling sorry for these bairns, missy. They're a resilient lot, trained from birth to survive in the harshest of conditions."

"We hunted caribou," one boy said. He grinned, his white teeth a startling contrast to his dirty face. "We roasted meat and dried more to bring along." His face closed up. "It's all gone now."

"The Netsilik returned to their roots two generations ago," Jacques said. "They moved far north onto what's left of the Arctic. Elders taught the young ones ancient hunting and survival skills, otherwise these kiddies wouldn't have lasted a day."

One little girl weaved back and forth. I caught her as her knees buckled. "Here sweetie, come sit by the fire."

Without a word, Leyla handed the sleepy child her Raggedy Ann doll. The little girl cuddled the doll and rocked back and forth, humming an Inuit song.

I handed out raspberry energy bars we had scarfed from a gas station, and Atian programmed the synthor for elk stew. The Inuit children ate the bars in quiet desperation and reached for the stew with shaky hands.

Jacques waited until the children were eating, then he helped himself to a bowl. "Wildlife's in short supply. Haven't made a kill in three days."

"Lots of dino-lizards in the rainforest," Leyla said.

Jacques grunted. "Never had the pleasure, kept to the highlands, we did."

Wolf plopped down among the Inuit children and licked their faces clean. They played with him and offered scraps from their stew.

With a flick of his wrist, Chief Roy's bio-comm began recording. "Tell us."

Tulimak, the oldest boy, told their story in a voice devoid of any emotion. "The message came to us in the night. A great whale sang a song of invitation from *Sanna*, goddess of the sea. "You must leave this land," she told us, "and seek a city hidden beneath the sea." Our People knew not what to do, but disobeying the gods is a foolhardy path, so they sent us eight on the long journey."

"By yourself?"

"Shaman Aariak led us."

Tulimak glanced from one face to another, his brown-black eyes haunted. "It's easier travelling in the winter. The land's frozen in most places in the coldest months. Aariak decided to take sleds as far south as possible, then we would keep the dogs for hunting.

"We traveled across the barren grounds for many days. The cold wind blistered our lips and froze our eyelids. At night we huddled together in igloos we helped Aariak build." Tulimak sighed. "The wind kept howling, it never stopped. The dogs were old, and they grew weak. One by one they died until Aariak said we must leave the sleds if we lost another. But the air grew warmer, and we hoped the worst was over."

Tulimak hung his head, and one of the little kids hiccup-sobbed before being shushed. "We were wrong, the worst was yet to come. On the last day, as we traveled across a great expanse, the ice broke and one of our sleds sank into the sea. Aariak bravely fought to save the supplies from the sled."

"But he died," the little girl beside Leyla whispered. "And so did the dogs."

I took the child in my arms. "What's your name, sweetie?"

She gazed at me. "Sila."

I hugged her. "You're safe here, Sila."

Tulimak continued in a monotone. "We walked and walked through lands empty of life, no caribou or elk, not even birds. Nor did we meet any other people. We were alone in the North."

"How did you survive in the cold without food?"

"Oh, we had food," Sila said. "Agoolik, the good water spirit, saved the other sled and we took all we could carry."

"And we kilt a caribou," the little boy said.

"Hush, Nuvuk," Tulimak said. "At night we built an igloo out of ice snow and slept the night away."

"When you reached the snow line?" Chief Roy said.

"We slept in the open."

"The ground was squishy," Nuvuk said.

Tulimak nodded. "The tundra thawed many years ago. It's more muskeg than solid ground now."

"I slipped in the water, and got muddy and cold." Sila shivered at the memory and crept closer to the fire.

"The days stretched into weeks and our food pack dwindled," Tulimak said. "The younger children were beginning to weaken, especially Paj." He nodded at the smallest child huddled beside Jacques. She struggled for each breath, and her face was flushed with fever.

Chief Roy gazed at Paj, then me, and shook his head.

Tulimak's voice cracked. "It was hard."

Chief Roy snorted. "That's a bloody understatement."

The Siksiká children giggled, but not the Inuit.

At my look, Tulimak said, "Netsilik children are raised to hide their emotions, to do otherwise shows weakness." He took a deep breath and picked up the story. "As we made our way south, we began noticing signs of life. A caribou herd had passed our way a day or two earlier. We followed the herd, catching up on the third day."

"Yeah, Tulimak kilt one with his whale bone sling, hit them right in the eye," Nuvuk said.

Tulimak shrugged. "I was lucky, but the meat saved our lives and kept us going for many days. Our fathers would be proud. Still, we were trapped in the middle of nowhere, and a spring storm was brewing."

"A really bad storm," Sila said. "The sky god was angry."

"The freak snow storm blinded us, and we lost our way. We could not go on much longer, yet we did not find any shelter or hard-packed snow to build an igloo. At our lowest point, we stumbled across Jacques' cabin."

Tulimak glanced at the trapper. "We rode out the storm with him." He paused.

"I'll take over, lad," Jacques said. "The kids told me a strange enough tale." He squinted at us. "But I be thinking the tale might not seem so strange to you folks. These young'uns were sent on a perilous journey. They be searching for a secret underwater city built for First Peoples to wait out Turmoil. Any truth to this tale?"

Chief Roy grunted. "A great deal of truth, Mr. Jacques. First Peoples all over the world are heading to gathering sites. Boats are waiting to take the children to Maniton."

Jacques whistled. "Maniton. Such a city exists then?"

"Aa."

"And you be heading on the same journey?"

Chief Roy nodded. "I'm escorting these children to their destination."

Jacques shifted on the ground. "Any chance you might add a few more to your entourage?"

The Inuit children turned as one and gazed at Jacques. They wore their hearts on their sleeves.

I choked back a blistering retort. Emotional control or not, the children worshiped Jacques. He was their anchor and now he wanted to dump them? My face must have mirrored my scorn.

"What? Look, I had a life. I'm riding out Turmoil, too."

"Not much of a life, hiding in the tundra with nothing but a few wolves keeping you company," Chief Roy said.

"Good enough for me. I'm not one for crowds, and two's a crowd in my mind."

Chief Roy sighed. "If that's your meaning, then we welcome the children. Eight more will stretch us, but we won't abandon them."

Jacques wiped at his sheepish face. "I've never taken care of kids. They need mothering, more than I can offer."

"They'll be well in our care."

Samoset was skulking within hearing distance. "Chief, might I have a word."

Chief Roy sighed. "Say your piece here and now, Samoset."

"We can't take these kids with us. Where we gonna put them, the pod's crowded now?"

"We'll make beds on the loungers and the floor with the bedding we took from Marcia."

"What about food? We'll run out."

Chief Roy nodded at Samoset's paunch. "You don't seem to be suffering much."

Samoset's jaw jutted out. "Well, I ain't helping them eskimos."

"How would that be any different than before?" The chief nodded at Jacques. "The children are welcome, Mr. Jacques."

Jacques glanced from one child's face to the next. Sorrow and regret crossed his face. "Well, maybe I'll stick around for a night or two, and help you out."

The kids relaxed and Jacques grinned. "These four you've met," he said, nodding at Tulimak, Nuvuk, Sila, and Paj. He put his arm around a young girl with a broad, serious face. "Now this here's sweet Makkovik, she's about twelve. And this here is Qisuk, he's a strong young man already. Chu, soon he'll stretch as tall as Tulimak, and little Aama, why she's my special girl."

Aama smiled and hid her face. Even stoic Inuit children could not hold back around Jacques.

"Why are you living so far north?" Matwau said.

Jacques grinned. "Had me a little run-in with the local law a few years back. Needed to cool my heels for a spell."

The story slowly unfolded.

"So you see, I never had a chance to explain myself, the vigilantes assumed I'd taken the cache. That's why I left civilization. I'd had enough of suspicious people and their accusations."

For someone who preferred a solitary life in the boreal forest, he sure talked a lot. "Did you steal their cache?"

Jacques harrumphed and colored. "Well, I might have borrowed it some. There's a difference, you know."

The children laughed, even the Inuit.

That night we camped on the edge of a town reduced to rubble.

Leyla kicked at pieces of blue and white ceramics. "Wonder who lived here. Hope they're not lizard people."

I wrapped a newly replicated clip in my unruly hair. "Okay, time to get to work. *Voyageur* we need new clothes for the Inuit children."

The replicator produced a dozen canary yellow t-shirts. "Redo the colors Vogy, these shirts are ugly."

Yellow pretty. Like me.

"On you, yes, but the boys won't go for yellow." I threw the shirts into the tube. "I'll be back in ten minutes, and I'd better find some green, blue, and black shirts waiting for me."

Yessir, Hayee.

In the morning we buried Paj.

"She was too weak to continue on, poor young'un," Jacques said.

Leyla sobbed for the little girl she hardly knew, but the Inuit children stood solemn while Chief Roy said a few words, and Atian played a mourning song on his clarinet. They turned away, not a tear shed.

Raven's cry greeted us in camp.

Chief Roy looked to the trees. "Ah, our guide has returned."

A good or a bad sign?

That evening, the Inuit children huddled close to Jacques as they sat around the fire, one by one falling asleep, until even Tulimak gave in.

In the morning Jacques was gone.

The Inuit children took the news bravely, but they hardly touched their breakfast, and they stayed quiet for the rest of the day.

Chapter Twenty-One

THE SHADOW PEOPLE

Forty-five days after leaving the Siksiká Blackfoot refuge, Atian had parked *Voyageur* on a hill on the outskirts of the legendary city of Vancouver. Moss-covered skyscrapers stretched to the horizon, and I made out an eco-dome near the coast. At street level, blown-out windows littered the pavement, and weeds grew through cracks in the pavement.

I was leaning against *Voyageur*, nibbling on toasted bannock, when Matwau joined me. "Some view, huh?"

"More ruins, nothing new."

Matwau scoffed. "Not much of a romantic, are you?"

I wiped crumbs off my tunic. "I haven't the energy." We had five days to reach the gathering site, and from the looks of the jumbled ruins, we needed every moment.

A lone bird flew overhead. "No sign of Raven." No sign of the Sky Beings either.

Matwau nodded at the dense haze floating over the doomed city. "Raven's too smart to fly through that muck." He gazed at me, an odd expression on his face.

My body tensed. "What is it, Mat?"

"Have you made up your mind?"

"About what?"

He sighed and ran his hands through his dreadlocks. "Hali, I've made my feelings clear. I want you, don't you know that?"

I tossed crumbs to a cocky crow. "Sort of, but all I want at this point is to reach Maniton. I can't think about anything else."

He nodded. "I figured, but you can't blame a guy for trying. Those moments on the mountain. You felt it, same as me."

"Now's not the right time, Mat."

"We might not have any other time." He pulled me into his arms and kissed me. My body melted against his, and I returned the kiss.

"Promise me you won't make any rash decisions without giving me a fair shot," he whispered in my ear.

I stiffened. What was this, a contest?

Leyla and Tomko ran around the corner of *Voyageur*, and I stepped away from Matwau.

"Hey Hali, what are you doing?" Leyla said.

"Nothing."

Tomko batted at a puff of pink smog hovering in the air, and Leyla held her nose. "Sure smells bad here." She coughed, then coughed again. She crouched on the ground and whipped out her inhaler.

I knelt beside her. "Slowly Leyla, that's right, take deep breaths."

Chief Roy hobbled over, his arms full of breathers. "The city's a polluted cesspool. It'll take centuries for this air to clean up."

Wolf whimpered when I fit the canine breather over his snout. "You have to wear a mask Wolf or you'll die."

I handed out breathers and helped the children into biosuits they hadn't worn since we left the prairies.

The Inuit children had neither.

Chief Roy scratched his head. "Those leathers should protect their skin, but I'm perplexed about breathers. Pull out the glider, Atian."

Atian backed the glider out of *Voyageur* and powered it up. "Where are we going, chief?"

"We are not going anywhere. I'm heading into town for some breathers."

"Ah chief."

Chief Roy stepped on the glider and grasped the handholds. "This blasted contraption better not conk out." The glider lifted off the ground, and he zoomed away.

We ate a barbecue lunch inside *Voyageur* and waited for Chief Roy to return. The children cheered when he roared into camp.

Atian secured the glider. "Did you find anything?"

"Yes and no." He produced a gigantic roll of white gauze. "No breathers, but this cheesecloth should filter out most of the pollutants for the next few days, then they'll need respiratory rejuv."

He handed me the gauze. "Program the replicator to make 4-ply breathers in the kids' sizes."

"Can it do that?"

"We'll soon see."

Tomko pointed to a concrete ledge. "What's that?"

Ten meters thick, the ledge rose high into the air and cast a shadow over a goodly portion of the outlying city.

"It's a launch pad, for ships flying to the space stations, or maybe a liner searching for habitable planets."

"Oh wow!" Tomko said. "Spacers."

"Aa, they moved the launchers up north when riots threatened the venture in the South. More than one ship was pulled down."

"Why?"

"Mobs angry they couldn't go, no doubt." He raised his eyes skyward. "I wonder how people in the space stations are faring."

Spacers who abandoned us after wrecking Mother Earth. "I wonder if they're still alive."

"Oh, they'll be good for a couple centuries. After that, who knows? I'm pinning my hopes on the real spacers, those searching for new planets. Even if we don't survive, humankind might flourish on another planet."

Atian staggered out of the control pod, his hair disheveled and his eyes bleary. "Hey chief, can we cut through this mess?"

"Atian, you need to rest."

I'd guided *Voyageur* for a couple hours, but then he insisted on taking over: "You make me nervous. I can't sleep, so I'd rather drive."

He wiped his tired eyes. "I'll rest on the sub."

"Chief, I've flown a skimmer, don't you think it's time I took on *Voyageur*?" Matwau said.

Chief Roy glanced at Samoset and set his lips. "We'll see."

The chime on the replicator went off. I scooped out perfectly-shaped, if soft, breathers. "You did it, Vogy."

Aa, I goodie

I wrapped the breathers around each of the Inuit children.

Tulimak backed away when it was his turn. "I do not like my face trapped."

I sighed and frowned like my mother used to when I ticked her off. "Tulimak, you will wear a mask until we board the sub. That's an order."

The corners of Tulimak's eyes crinkled in the beginnings of a smile. "Yes ma'am."

Chief Roy checked his bio-comm. "We'll head northwest, the shortest route to English Bay.

"We have five days," I said.

"And we'll need them. Vancouver may not be the megalopolis of a hundred years ago, but I'm thinking we'll be in for more trouble."

"How come the city got smaller?" Tomko said.

"People moved away from the coast when the air got too bad, and the city withered."

"Why didn't they wear breathers?"

"More to it than that, lad. Coastal storms and tidal surges flooded low-lying areas, and folks had little choice but to leave. Those lucky enough fled the city for refugiums in mountain caverns."

"Wow, living in a cave, that'd be cool," Tomko said. "Maybe we can try it?"

I nodded at one of the larger mountains. A black tower squatted on a windswept summit. "Hope they're not anywhere near that thing."

Chief Roy followed my gaze. "A portal to evil."

A flying machine landed on the crown while we watched.

"Promise me you won't take any foolish chances, chief."

He lifted a bushy eyebrow. "Halerine Ananda, for the rest of my life, I'll be taking foolish chances. Nothing else but to do."

What could I say?

Matwau pointed up the street. "Not all the survivors live in caves, chief. Take a look at what's coming our way."

The raggedy men swooped out of nowhere and lined the street. We scrambled into *Voyageur* and moved out. They danced along, keeping pace with the biopod, and waved their makeshift weapons at us. Guttural sounds and high-pitched screams pierced *Voyageur's* membrane.

"Shadow people," Leyla said.

Most of the men appeared youngish, but their features were lost in layers of grime and shapeless clothing. Strings of greasy hair hung to their shoulders, and they hunched over as if their backs hurt. One man shook his club at us and made threatening gestures.

Benji backed away from the viewer. "Why do they act so weird? We didn't do nothing to them."

"Gone savage after three or four generations." Chief Roy squinted at the men. "And I'm thinking some genetic damage, likely from breathing this foul air." He sighed. "We're witnessing fast-tracked human devolution, I'm afraid." He opened the portal and shot his laser above the crowd. "Settle down!"

The Shadow People backed away, muttering among themselves.

Would this never end? "Don't stop, please chief."

We passed a collection of shabby huts crammed into a narrow space between two crumbling office buildings. Unkempt women stumbled around the dismal camp, showing little interest in our passage. Naked children, their bellies swollen from malnutrition, stared at us and pointed at *Voyageur*.

My heart broke for the children. We were heading to a wonderful new life, while those kids did not have future. "Let's leave them some food and bedding."

Samoset grabbed Chief Roy's tunic. "You're gonna give them our food?"

"We've got plenty and most of us won't need our stocks in a couple days."

Samoset snarled and stalked away, but not before throwing a malevolent glare in my direction. I kept the cretin fed and this was how he thanked me?

Matwau and Atian carried two boxes of canned goods and dried meat to the side of the street, and Atian handed out milk cartons to the children. I staggered out of the biopod with a large bag of quilts and blankets, even a couple pillows.

The men pounced on the boxes. One, maybe the leader, held up a leg of beef and nodded in our direction.

"Right, let's move on, we can't do any more for these folks."

We left the Shadow People behind, but their unhappy lot kept intruding on my thoughts. What would happen to them, what would happen to humanity in the coming decades? When our descendants returned to this land, what would they find?

Tomko waved zis arm and the view screen expanded to half the wall. The children crowded around and talked among themselves.

"Wouldja look at those shiny blue skyscrapers," Benji said. "They're taller than the sky."

Tomko smoothed zis rainbow hair. "No, they're not, you dope. The sky goes on forever."

"Well, they're taller than the clouds."

Tomko shook zis head. "Good grief."

Gecki slipped out of Benji's shirt and climbed on his head, squashing the black and yellow spikes. He scolded Tomko in a high pitched chirp and nodded his head up and down.

Tomko stuck out zis pierced tongue.

Gecki shrieked and ducked inside Benji's biosuit. "See, you even annoy Gecki."

Tulimak listened to the exchange, a bewildered expression on his face.

I grinned at his puzzlement. "Noisy, aren't they?"

"Southern children aren't afraid of expressing their feelings or thoughts, loudly if necessary," he said. "And they do not lose face for doing so?"

"No, they might even gain some if they get in the last word."

Tulimak shook his head. "I have much to learn. I wonder if Inuit children will fit in with other Manitons."

I snort-laughed. "None of us will fit in, not after what we've been through."

"I'm unsure if humans were meant to live under the water."

"We weren't, but what choice do we have, we destroyed topside."

He smiled. "If you are there, Miss Halerine, I will adjust with you."

I returned his smile. "My pleasure."

"Whoa, wouldja look at that?" Tomko said.

A city of glass skyscrapers, some narrowing to a needle point, others shaped like sailboats or black eggs, towered over us.

"Look, there's a giant golf ball on top of that building," Benji said.

"Aa, this be little Dubai. Near the end of Beforetimes, foreign investors had a pipe dream to re-create Dubai in Vancouver."

Leyla raised her arms. "They're messengers to the sky gods."

The kids snickered at her poetics, and she hid her face.

"Listen, you urchins, when young Leyla's a famous poet, you'll be begging for her autograph," Chief Roy said.

A jagged crack ran up the side of a golden egg-shaped building, but flickering candlelight shone from a few windows, most high in the skyscraper, as if height meant safety and distance from the disintegrating society on street level.

Makkovik sniffed. "I smell something strange, does anybody else?"

Chief Roy lifted his breather and sniffed. "Gas leak!"

The air exploded and shook the ground. A ball of fire blew into the sky, and the golden building slowly crumbled.

"Best we move on before that structure settles on top of us."

"Look at the fire up there!" Tomko said.

Office paper that lay in the streets was catching fire and floating up, toward the rooftops. Fanned by the powerful winds, firestorms danced from rooftop to rooftop, and the high rises around us caught fire.

I held onto Leyla. How could we make it through if the whole city burned?

"*Voyageur*, get us out of here!" Chief Roy said.

Aa, sir

Voyageur careened around the corner and pushed through a pile of garbage. Her crumbled back end swayed and threatened to take out a whole block of street lights, but she kept going and left the firestorm behind.

"We're heading for the harbor, chief. Should I keep going?" Atian said.

"*Aa*, might be interesting to see what's happening on the water."

Abandoned cargo ships, rusty barges, and heavy freighters choked the harbor. Smoke stacks from sunken ships and masts from sailing boats poked above the water line. Most of the floating ships were close to sinking, except for an enormous cruise ship called *Princess Ariel*.

Atian slowed *Voyageur*. "That ship looks ready to sail."

"*Aa*. Heard tell some rich folks bought a mega-cruiser in the hopes of sailing to a safe haven."

"What about the superstorm cells? Won't they sink the ship?" Matwau said.

Chief Roy shrugged. "Easier sailing around a storm than out-running it on land. Besides, some of the powerbrokers never did admit, even to themselves, that climate change would destroy their way of life. Climate deniers, they were called in Beforetimes." He nodded at the cruise ship.

"Betting a fair number of those on board that ship believe the weather will settle down in a few years."

Matwau gazed at the cruise ship, a thoughtful expression on his face. What was he thinking?

Thunder boomed overhead, and we slipped and slid down a steep hill in the poison rain.

Me hurtin

"Put your shields up, old girl. That'll save you from the acid."

At the bottom of the hill, a slow moving river of garbage floated in the greasy water. The putrid smell of rot slipped past our filters.

Too deep, too deep.

"Storm surge," Chief Roy said. "Back track, and we'll find a route on higher ground."

Atian punched codes into *Voyageur's* control panel. "I'm done with streets, let's ride the skyways."

The chief looked up. "I'm not sure the skyways are any better, lad, but we'll give it a go once the rain stops."

Skyways and monorails circled high above the city, but in some places chunks of concrete the size of *Voyageur* had broken away. We came across a monorail, five cars long, dangling from a collapsed tower. A mound of bodies slumped in the bottom car.

I shielded Leyla when *Voyageur* drove under the rail.

She pushed my hands away. "What did you do that for? I've ridden on a train full of dead people. Nothing tops that."

Two orange tabby cats stopped in the middle of the street to fight. Atian braked *Voyageur*. "Blasted vermin."

I hid a snicker. Atian hated cats.

"I want a kitty," Leyla said.

"Sorry sweetie, not going to happen."

"If Benji can have a gecko and an iguana egg, why can't I have a kitty?"

"Not—" I did a double-take. "Wait—what? Did you say iguana egg?"

We all turned on Benji.

He fidgeted and wouldn't look up.

I crossed my arms and glared at my little brother. "Come on kid, spill."

Benji shot Leyla a dirty look. "Last time I tell a goil a secret." He reached into his pack and pulled out a brown-speckled egg.

I gasped. "You took one of the iguana eggs? When? How?"

He scuffed his shoes against the worn floor. "Tomko called me chicken, so I snuck out when you was kissing Atian and picked one up."

Chief Roy pulled up his baggy pants. "No wonder the female iguana was angry."

"Wait, you were kissing Atian?" Matwau said. "Why?"

"We'll have an interesting specimen for Maniton," Chief Roy said.

Atian bristled. "We kiss lots."

Benji peeked at me from beneath his curly eyelashes. "There's more."

"What more?"

"It's wiggling."

Chief Roy's bushy eyebrows nearly touched, and his good eye glared at Benji. "Come again?"

"Gecki's been keeping the egg warm, and now it's moving around. I think it's gonna hatch."

I shook my finger at him. "Well, that iguana better wait until we're on board the sub, or you and Gecki are in big trouble, young man."

"Ah Hali."

Gecki peeked out and hissed at me. I thumbed his nose.

"So can I have a kitty?"

"They're feral," Chief Roy said. "Abandoned by their owners, those cats and dogs have taken over the streets."

"More than cats and dogs, chief," Atian said. "It's a full on zoo out there."

A black and white ostrich ran across the street, holding its scrawny neck high and squawking. Close behind, a Bengal tiger stalked the hapless bird.

Wolf whimpered and shook his tail.

"Sorry Wolf."

Unflappable Matwau gasped. "Z-zoo animals aren't our biggest concern, chief. L-look!"

A wall of water rushed toward us, tossing vehicles, trees, and splintered pieces of construction in front of it.

"Shields up, *Voyageur*!"

I dropped into my cushion seat. "Strap in, we're going for a ride!"

Atian waved at the console. "Hold on everybody!"

Me no like

The wave swamped *Voyageur*, and for a terrifying moment we rolled along underwater with the rest of the debris, but she struggled to the surface and rode the dirty water down the street. We twisted and turned, and if not for her deflectors, we would have crashed into buildings along the streets or detritus churning in the wave.

Tomko danced up and down. "Ride the wave, Vogy!"

I yanked him down on his seat. "Strap up!"

We passed the ostrich and tiger swimming for their lives, no longer the hunter and hunted. Lions, giraffes, and wildebeests struggled in the wave, and one by one disappeared.

"Look at that hippo," Benji said. "Bet this is a day in the park for him."

A street sign tossed high into the air and landed on the hippo's head. The hippo sank beneath the surface.

"Maybe he's swimming under water," Benji said. "Hippos do that, you know." Tears streamed down his cheeks.

Leyla buried her head in her arms and sobbed. "Them poor aminals."

"Oh my gawd." I blinked, but the horrifying image would not go away. Three adults and half a dozen children floated the wave on what looked like a wooden gate. One of the kids slid off the raft, but an adult male hauled him up as he went under. "We can't leave them to drown."

"*Aa*, but I'm not sure how to go about rescuing them."

"What if Vogy lowers her hull and we pull them onto our roof?" Atian said. "Chief, if you take over the console, Matwau and I can climb on the roof and pull them off."

"*Aa*, that be a worthy plan."

"Except I'm coming, too, and Atian you can't with your back."

"Hali, you aren't strong enough. My back's fine."

"I am too strong enough. You won't get them all in time without my help, and your back's too beat up."

"Tulimak, you take Atian's place alongside Matwau and Hali. Benji and Tomko, be ready to pull them inside," Chief Roy said.

The three of us crawled through the hatch and lay flat on the biopod's roof. Poison rain sizzled on our biosuits. How long before the acid ate holes in the nano-fiber?

Voyageur groaned and hissed but lowered her bulk to water level and sailed over to the raft teetering close to the edge of the wave.

"If that raft goes over the crest, they're dead," Matwau said.

I pushed away memories of my raft going over the waterfall. This was worse. The monstrous wave and all the junk it carried would pulverize them.

Matwau waved and whistled to the Shadow People. One of the men understood and used a pole to steer the raft closer to us

I stretched my five foot nine frame and reached for the hand of a small child the man held up. "Gotcha!" I swung her up and into Tomko's arms. Zie tucked her into *Voyageur*.

I hauled in two more little girls. Then the man passed me another child, a larger boy. "Come on, take my hand."

The raft hit a chunk of debris and dodged away. The little boy lost his balance and fell into the water. "No!" But he was gone.

The man howled over the roar of the wave and beat his chest. I lay there, unable to move. A child died on my watch. Again.

Too close, too close

"*Voyageur's* out of time!" Matwau said. He reached for the last adult, the one who had handed me the children. He half crawled and half ran up the side of the biopod and collapsed on the roof.

Voyageur zoomed away from the water's crest.

Chapter Twenty-Two

The Mighty Voyageur

Raven's shrill cry echoed over *Voyageur*'s open comm, and my stomach heaved. The last time I heard that call a mountain came down on top of us. What now?

We rounded a corner and ran up against hundreds of rusty vehicles stacked high in the streets. Some held skeletons, others were empty hulks.

"How'd they get piled up?" Benji said.

"The burst dam, most likely."

My heart ached, and I hugged my dreamcatcher against the stabbing pain coursing through me. The horror from the wall of water was too raw. We saved seven of eight people, but the little boy we couldn't save, no, I couldn't save, haunted me. The terror on his face merged with Etta's sweet face in my nightmares.

The monster wave had receded, and a dozen klicks up the street *Voyageur* found dry land. We dropped the Shadow

People off at a small settlement tucked between two high-rises. Their feeble attempts at thanking us tore at my heart. The father of the little boy I lost hugged me, and I sobbed on his shoulder.

We stopped for dinner beside a megamall built out of pink and blue glass and shaped like a flying saucer. A giant yellow bird, a red munchkin, and a blue fur ball with bulgy white eyes hung over the entrance to the mall.

Tomko gazed at the view screen and sighed. "All those lovely stores and nobody's shopping."

"*Aa*. No need for all the paraphernalia folks thought they couldn't live without."

My exuberant, rude, and curious Rainbow Warriors sat in small groups, hardly speaking. Not even Tomko showed any interest in exploring the mall. Survivor's guilt or journey exhaustion?

"Hey kids, how about pizza for supper? Pineapple and ham? Pepperoni and mushroom? Mediterranean?"

"What's pizza?" Makkovik said.

"This should be good." I programmed the synthor.

Ten minutes later we sat down for a quiet meal. Even Chief Roy did not complain about kid food.

The Inuit children sniffed their pizza and looked at each other.

"It smells good," Tulimak said. He took a small bite, and his eyes lit up. He took another bite, then another.

"Is it any good?" Sila said.

"Well, it's not caribou, but yes, it's good."

The Inuit children ate their pizza and asked for seconds.

"Some things about the South are worthy," Tulimak said, taking his third piece.

"Benji, don't stuff food in your mouth, you'll choke."

Gecki slid down Benji's arm, and he offered the gecko a green pepper. "Well, we haven't eaten all day."

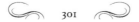

Tomko patted Benji's pudgy stomach. "You're a long way from starving, poopsie."

Benji scowled and popped Tomko in the nose. "You—"

Voyageur shuddered and shook her back end.

Get off get off Leyee help

Leyla pointed at the skylight. "Hali, bad people's on Vogy's roof."

A familiar scar face peered down on us, and a coldness like death pulsed through my body. Claude the bandit.

Chief Roy scowled. "Thought that vermin long dead. Appears he's a cat with nine lives."

"Or a skunk," Matwau said.

My heart raced. If they'd followed us all this way, they meant business, and they'd be out for revenge.

"They're gonna kill us," Leyla said. "Hali, I'm so scared."

Me too, Hayee, I scareded.

"Both of you, we'll get through this." Empty words. How could we fight them off?

"*Voyageur*, full shields!"

"Aihee!"

Bandits fell from the pod, some of them missing fingers and toes.

The children cheered.

"Don't get too excited, the shields won't keep them out for long."

Atian jumped into the driver's seat and prepped *Voyageur* for take-off, but her power source was low. "She's going to need a few minutes, chief."

Two men carrying a heavy black tube ran toward the biopod. The other bandits followed close behind, except for the men rolling on the ground holding their hands and feet.

"Now where in tarnation did they find a rocket launcher? Need to stall." The chief opened the comm. "Well, Claude the bandit, imagine meeting you again. Don't you have anything better to do than trail after us, hoping for a bone?"

Claude scowled, and his remaining hand curled into a fist. "You won't be mocking me and my boys for long, you no-good Indian."

Chief Roy cut the transmission. "Vogy, will the missile penetrate your armor?"

Nah but makin' hurts sir

Leyla patted *Voyageur's* membrane. "Don't worry Vogy, we'll fix you up."

Claude raised his hand. "Fire!"

A missile headed straight for *Voyageur*.

"Everybody down!"

The missile pierced Vogy's back end, and she rolled over. Brown smoke billowed, and the smell of scorched membrane choked the air.

"Vogy, Vogy, are you all right?"

Silence.

"Please Vogy, wake up."

Leyee, I hurt so bad.

Leyla sobbed into her Raggedy Ann doll. "But you can fix yourself, right?"

Don' know.

"Please, Vogy, you're my bestest friend, I can't lose you again."

Leyee...

The bandits swooped over the pod in search of the airlock.

"*Voyageur* switched her airlock to the underside. That'll keep them out for a time," Chief Roy whispered.

"Why don't you shoot the buzzards?" Samoset said.

Atian snorted. "Really? And open a portal to them?"

The bandits did not take long to figure out the location of the hidden entrance. A dozen of them began rocking the pod.

Ow-ee, ow-ee.

Chief Roy staggered to the storage pod and came back with a flamethrower in his hands. "I want everyone to listen carefully. When they break in, I'll use this contraption on them, and give you enough time to scoot out the rear exit. Smash the coder, Vogy can fix it later. Run as fast as you can to a hiding place. You got that?"

Solemn little faces nodded.

He handed lasers to Matwau, Atian, and me. "Use them when you have to."

I slipped the laser into my pocket. "But what about you?"

Chief Roy gazed at me. "You get these kids to the gathering site, understand?"

I gulped. "Yes chief."

The bandits rolled *Voyageur* onto her jets. Chief Roy stood ready. When the bandits opened the airlock and swept in, he stepped up and threw flames.

"Holy crap, get outta here, he's got a thrower," one of the bandits said.

They climbed over each other trying to get out, and clogged the airlock. The chief waved his flamer and scorched the bandits closest to him.

"Go now!"

I picked up Leyla, and we leaped out of the pod and ran for the mall entrance.

We zigzagged across the parking lot, dodging a volley of bullets splattering the weed-infested pavement, and dived behind derelict vehicles and piles of garbage. "Kids, stay down!"

Chief Roy jumped out the back end of *Voyageur* and took cover behind a burned-out transport, but his thrower was out of juice.

"Stay out of sight," I said to the children and hurried over to Atian. "What'll we do?"

He adjusted his laser. "Not looking good, we're pretty much trapped."

The bandits scurried from one cover to the next, and worked their way closer to our hiding places. Claude crouched and fired off a few shots. One ricocheted near Samoset and he howled.

"Get ready you two, they're making their move," Matwau said.

We aimed our lasers and fired. Two bandits went down, but more kept coming.

I shuddered. "Great Apistotoke, I beg you, protect the children from these angry men."

All seemed lost, and I was preparing for the worst when a band of straggly men leaped off the mall roof. They danced around and brandished their wooden clubs.

"Shadow People."

Matwau nodded. "Appears so. Question is, are they here to help us or join the attack."

The Shadows surrounded the bandits and chanted as they moved in, their clubs held high. The chanting grew louder. The bandits stopped advancing and looked to Claude.

Their distraction was our chance. "Come on."

Wolf led the way. I yanked the glass doors open, and a high-pitched voice greeted us. "Welcome to Shesamland." Lights came on and a wonderland of consumerism opened up.

"Whoa, wouldja look at that," Tomko said.

The abandoned mall was in good shape, considering. Storefront windows, dull from decades of dust, were full of clothing, electronics, even an art gallery.

"Nobody stole it," Leyla said.

Rats scurried away, and a sparrow flew into my face and scolded me for invading its territory. Gecki peeked out of Benji's biosuit and scolded back.

We hid behind a display case and watched the skirmish. Claude took aim and shot a man. The Shadows screamed and rushed the bandits.

Claude fired again. "Into the pod!"

The Shadows pelted the bandits with rocks as they pushed into *Voyageur*.

"I doubt they know the extent of *Voyageur's* injuries," Atian said. "They think they can drive her out of here."

Voyageur let out a high-pitched scream, and the Shadow People ran away.

Bye bye Leyee, I l-l-lova ya.

The explosion was almost soundless, but the result painfully effective. *Voyageur* blew herself to bits with the bandits inside. Smoke and pieces of membrane floated in the air and obscured our vision.

Leyla collapsed in tears. "No! Vogy, no!" She sobbed into her sleeve.

Matwau and Atian turned away. The Inuit children stood stoic, but flashes of sadness and pain crossed their tired faces. Tulimak kept glancing at me, a worry frown creasing his face.

I bit back my tears and comforted the distraught children. "She sacrificed herself to save us."

Chief Roy dashed into the mall and joined us. "That was one brave old machine."

"She wasn't a machine, she was a people," Leyla said between sobs.

Chapter Twenty-Three

ON THE BRINK

We found a dealership crammed with luxury sliders and sports utilities, but not a single van or bus. Atian and Matwau danced beside a couple heavy vehicles.

"We'll take the Hum-sliders then," Chief Roy said. "Halerine Ananda, you and Atian each pick one with a full tank, and I'll take that silver beauty over there."

"Chief, you can't manage a hum-slider with one arm," Matwau said. "Let me drive."

Chief Roy studied the young man. "Very well, let's see what you're made of young man." He wagged his finger. "But understand what that means."

Matwau's eyes clouded over for a moment, but he nodded. "I understand, sir."

Samoset snarled.

A convoy of military trucks passed us at mid-day. The soldiers carried automatic rifles and were dressed in full camouflage. They stared straight ahead, their haunted gazes fixed on the horizon.

"Where are they going, chief?"

"Nowhere."

Hours later we stood on a green suspension bridge spanning a wide harbor. The skeleton of a National guard slumped in the gatehouse at the edge of the bridge. Pieces of the bridge had fallen into the bay, but one lane seemed intact. "Do you think it will hold?"

Mischief danced in Atian's dark eyes. "Only one way to find out, to quote the chief. Tulimak keep the kids back, and I'll cross over this weak spot. If the road holds, follow behind me. Matwau, you're next, and Hali bring up the rear." Atian flashed me a lopsided grin. "If I fall in the drink, don't follow."

"That's not funny."

Atian sobered. "No, it's not, but I'm tired of being afraid, Hali. Sometimes I think we'll never reach the gathering site, so what's the point in worrying."

"Oh, we'll make it," I said. "But I want all of us climbing on that sub."

Atian lifted his breather and kissed me. "I'll be all right," he said, his lips close to my ear. "Besides, I wouldn't want to miss taming you."

He ducked my playful slap, and with a laugh jumped into his blue hummer. He eased the vehicle over the narrow roadway. Chunks of concrete broke off the edges and rusty steel girders creaked, but the road held.

"All right Tulimak, bring the kids across."

The children followed Tulimak in single file. Wolf took up the rear, his cold nose nudging along the smallest Inuit child.

Gusts of hot, damp wind rushed across the bridge. Sila staggered and nearly fell.

"Hold onto the railing!"

"Don't look down," Tulimak said as they edged around a gaping hole in the road.

Gecki took a peek, screeched, and dived inside Benji's biosuit.

I started breathing again when they reached the other side of the hole.

"Okay Mat, your turn," Atian said.

Matwau slowly crossed the bridge in his silver hummer. A look of pure terror crossed his face when small chunks of concrete peeled off the hole, but he made it.

"Okay, Halerine Ananda, your turn."

I took a deep breath and crept ahead. Thank goodness I picked a light expansion slider instead of a heavy hummer.

The groaning steel warned me, and right in front of my shiny red car the road broke off.

"Keep going, Hali!" Atian said. "It's a small piece. Keep moving, don't stop!"

I almost made it, but then the bottom fell out of my world, and the slider dropped like a stone. I was falling and falling. I squeezed my eyes shut. "Atian!"

The slider jerked to a stop, and I banged my forehead against the control panel. I couldn't move, couldn't breathe.

"Hali! Hali? Are you all right?"

I stared into the dirty gray water churning far below. My slider was swinging above Burrard Inlet. The flotsam from a crushed civilization floated in that water. A water spout danced across the water, swooping and looping around derelict ships clogging the seaway. Vertigo washed over me, and I closed my eyes again.

The slider slipped. I screamed.

"Well, at least we know she's alive," Chief Roy said.

"I heard that!"

"The car's hooked on a steel girder and looks pretty solid, unless the chassis gives way," Chief Roy said.

"So what do we do now, chief?"

"Halerine Ananda must climb high enough for you to reach her."

Atian whistled. "She's not gonna like that."

"Time to start taming her, lad." He laughed at his little joke, but I heard the strain in his voice.

Atian leaned over the bridge. "Hali, can you hear me?"

"I heard everything, you jerks."

"Okay, listen up. I want you to climb along the side of the slider."

"You want me to do what??"

"You have to climb, Hali, there's no other way."

"Don't you have a rope or something?"

"Nope, and there's no time to find one."

A gust of wind jostled the slider and grinding steel helped me make up my mind. I crawled out of the access window and inched along the side, using the window ledges for handholds. "My beautiful slider, you're all wrecked."

A Sky Being with silver skin and blue hair flittered in front of me. "Go away, I'm busy."

But the Sky Being stayed where she was, her wings beating in time to my heart.

The back of the slider presented a problem. No handholds. I half-crawled half-jumped onto the rear screen.

"Now hoist yourself onto the bumper."

"No, it's too slippery!"

"Move your butt, Halerine Ananda," Atian said.

"Nice pillow talk."

The car jerked and I started sliding. "Ooh noo!" At the last moment my hand caught the window frame.

"Hali, grab on with two hands."

"I'm trying!" I kicked and swung my arms over and held on. Now what?

"Can you swing your legs over and hook on the other window?"

"That's a lot of leg to swing, and this damn biosuit is too tight."

"Try."

I tried, again and again, until I no longer felt my fingers. The Sky Being whispered beside me, and a dozen more appeared. *Hali, hurry,* they hissed.

"Okay, okay, I'll try one more time."

Deep down, I summoned the strength. Something pushed me from behind, and this time my leg hooked into the window. I heaved my shaking body onto the view screen. "My nails, I broke three nails."

"Hali, for crying out loud, hoist yourself onto the bumper."

"No, I'll fall."

Chief Roy hauled Atian back from the brink. "Halerine Ananda, listen to me carefully, the chassis is separating, and the wind is picking up."

I gulped.

"Reach over the trunk and grab the bumper."

"I can't reach! This slider is seven meters long."

"Yes, you can. You're tall enough. Now spread your legs out and do as I say."

I pushed with my toes. My fingertips found a bridge of metal. Scarcely breathing, I pulled myself over the trunk lid and rested there, afraid to move.

"Hurry, Halerine Ananda."

The urgency in the chief's voice roused me from a terrified stupor. I crawled to my knees, then to my feet, and swayed in the blustery wind.

"I'll hold your feet, boy, you reach down and pull her up."

"Atian, your back! Get Matwau!"

"My back's fine."

Long arms reached for me. The strain on Atian's pale face and his bloodless lips terrified me. He grasped my hands. "Ready?"

I swallowed hard and nodded.

"Okay chief, pull us up."

"Not sure I can, boy. My arm's gone numb."

Terror flickered in Atian's eyes. "Hali, I love you."

I opened my mouth, but words did not come out.

Matwau's braids hung over the railing. He grabbed Atian's legs. "We'll take over, chief."

Atian inched backwards and pulled me over the railing. I collapsed in his arms and sobbed into his chest.

Tulimak and Matwau patted each other on the back. The children cheered, even the Inuit. Chief Roy stood nearby. His arms hung limp by his side, but he was grinning.

"Thanks boys, you saved us," Atian said.

We felt the snap of steel before we heard it, then a loud splash.

"And in the nick of time."

I didn't look.

Atian held me tighter. "Is a near-disaster what it takes to get you in my arms?" he whispered in my ear. His voice shook.

"Did you mean what you said?"

Atian grinned. "Refresh my memory, the moment was a bit tense."

I returned the grin and stepped away. My hands were covered in blood. I turned him around. "Atian, your back is bleeding again."

"I'll be fine."

"Okay troops, we've got thirty people for two vehicles. Kiddies under eight into the Hummers, bigger kids on the roof rack. The rest of us will walk alongside." Chief Roy glared at Samoset. "Got that?"

I dusted off my biosuit. "Hey kids, everyone okay?"

Benji and Leyla wrapped their arms around my legs and hugged me. Leyla sobbed. "Oh Hali, I was so scared."

"Me too, but I'm okay." I kissed the top of her head.

"Let's get off this nasty bridge and onto solid ground. The wind's getting worse, and I'm tired of all this nonsense." I led the way across the suspension bridge.

The Sky Beings fluttered away.

Chapter Twenty-Four

BEFORETIMES GLORY

Strong winds lifted the heavy smog and revealed the citi-bubble hovering over central Vancouver. For the first time, I dared hope we would make it, even without Vogy.

The dome resembled a giant cracked egg. During the dying days of the twenty-first century, the elite in wealthy cities commissioned transparent domes, partly to keep out destructive weather, and partly to keep out climate refugees escaping the weather. But Mother Earth was too strong. Domes, like ours, cracked against fierce winds, caught fire when the firestorms swept the land, or flooded in the rising waters. Papi told me abandoned carcasses were scattered all across Mother Earth. And we were heading into one.

We came across a dilapidated backpackers' inn on the edge of the dome.

"We'll stay here for the night, the city's too dangerous after dark," Chief Roy said. "Tomorrow, we'll slip through a crack in the dome."

In the middle of the night, I woke in a cold sweat.

"What is it?" Atian said. "What's wrong?"

"I was falling and falling, and I couldn't stop."

Atian pulled me onto his sleeping pad. "You're safe now, it's almost over, Hali."

I snuggled close and lay my head on his shoulder. He lifted my breather and kissed my forehead. His roaming hands slipped under my biosuit. His touch sent shivers up and down my back, and I ached for more. "Oh Atian."

He kissed me, but then reality rushed in. We were sleeping on the floor in a dormitory. All of us. My heart pounded in my chest, but no, not yet. Not until we were safe and alone. I slipped out of his arms. "Go back to sleep.

Atian groaned. "Hali."

"Not here, not now. I can't."

His breathing slowed, and he turned over. Bedding rustled nearby. Matwau.

The next morning we crammed into the hummers and an abandoned slider with enough fuel to get us to the gathering site.

Benji pushed Tomko's leg away. "Hali, Tomko's touching me."

"Yeah, well if you weren't so fat, we wouldn't have to."

"A few more klicks, kids, hold it together a while longer."

At noon we slipped between the broken gates at the entrance to the eco-dome and entered the once mighty city. The dome had collapsed inward leaving the city open to whatever bad weather came its way.

"Somebody's watching us over there."

Leyla pointed to a large man standing on a rooftop. His mess of shaggy blond hair, layers of furs, and scruffy facial hair gave him away.

Makkovik gasped. "Jacques!"

The Inuit children crowded around Jacques when he joined us. Even Tulimak smiled.

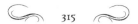

Jacques grinned. "I guess the wee bairns have gotten under my thick hide."

Leyla flopped on my lap. "I can't go any farther, Hali. I'm pooped."

"I know baby girl, we'll rest here for a while."

Dark blue and green clouds swirled above us, and the wind picked up speed. Chief Roy sighed. "Storm's a brewing, no surprise. Used to call this place Raincouver."

We parked the vehicles outside Hotel Vancouver. The ancient hotel sprawled across four city blocks. Some sections looked new, rebuilt after the 2060 quakes, other parts harkened back to the olden days of early twentieth century Antique.

"Look, gargoyles," Benji said.

"What's a gargoyle?" Makkovik said.

"Evil creatures that drop down on unsuspecting little girls and eat them," Tomko said, but zie couldn't keep a straight face, and bent over laughing.

Makkovik blinked. "Why is your hair green and pink?"

Tomko danced away. "I'm a Two Spirits. We favor bright."

"He's a girlie-boy," Samoset said.

Makkovik ignored Samoset. She was learning.

"I think you look nice."

Tomko preened. "What color should we use next? We were thinking red and yellow." Zis face fell. "But I'll have to wait until we get to Maniton."

Atian kicked at the front entrance to the hotel and scratched his head. "This place is shut up tight as a bank."

"Let the hooligan in you come forth, lad, and break us in."

The boys banged and chipped at the entrance, but it held fast.

The wind intensified and debris swirled in the air. I batted away a flattened box with the word Kleenex on it. "So much for the dome protecting us."

A dark cloud swooped down and pushed the old slider across the street and smack into a crooked light pole.

"Blasted, we just found that beast."

Atian patted the chief on the back. "We don't need transports anymore, remember?"

"Maybe you don't, but I could use a little help on my next venture."

"You can take my Hum-slider, chief. It's got enough gas to get you a couple hundred klicks," Atian said.

"Okay, I've had it." Matwau pulled out his laser and shot the bolt, and we scrambled inside moments before the storm struck.

Chief Roy switched on his gravi-lite, and we stepped into a silent Beforetimes shrine.

Bats clinging to the vaulted ceiling squealed at the light and flew deeper into the hotel. A thick layer of dust covered the chewed-up furniture and the long wooden counter with the word reception on it.

"Nobody's been in here for a while," Matwau muttered.

Leyla tiptoed across the black marble floor and headed for large wooden doors. I followed her. "Where are you going?"

"I hear voices."

She tugged on the doors, and we stepped into a high-ceilinged ballroom. Cobwebs hung from crystal chandeliers, and wide-sweeping velvet curtains covered a wall of windows.

"Oh!"

Leyla twirled in circles, her chin up and her eyes closed. "Do you hear it, Hali?"

"Hear what?"

"The music."

I listened, and softly at first, then with growing strength, the *Blue Danube* waltz hummed in my ears. Beautiful women dressed in shimmering silver gowns, their ears and necks dripping in diamonds, danced around the ballroom on the arms of tuxedo-clad men. Round and round they whirled until dizziness overwhelmed me. I sat on the floor and put my head between my knees.

Atian crouched beside me. "Hali, are you all right?"

"Yes, the dancing just made me dizzy."

"Dancing?"

"Didn't you hear the music and see the dancers?"

He shook his head.

"I did Hali," Leyla said. "They was beautiful."

So she did have visions.

Chief Roy smiled at me. "Appears I gave the dreamcatcher to the right person. Now, if you're feeling up to it, we'll move on."

We walked through a fancy restaurant set for a banquet. Creamy white tablecloths yellowed with age, blue Royal Doulton dinnerware, and once shiny crystal glasses graced every table.

"Never thought I'd stay in such a swanky place," Matwau said. "I can imagine what my grandfather would say."

"Too bloody fancy," Jacques growled. "Like my cabin better."

"That's about what he would say."

Glass display cabinets full of costume jewelry lined the corridor.

"So people took the real jewels?" Tomko said.

"Aa."

"Where? Why?"

"All good questions."

Benji skidded into the corridor. "There's a swimming pool, and it looks clean enough. Can we go swimming, Hali, can we?"

I laughed and followed him to the pool. "Benji, stop begging. Yes, you can go swimming."

The little boys tore off their clothes and jumped into the water in their skivvies.

Leyla pouted. "What about us? Girls need more than underwear."

"Let's explore, maybe we'll find some swimwear."

A children's clothing store hidden in the hotel's gallery had not been looted. "Help yourselves to the swim suits."

The Inuit children oohed and aahed, but dumped their leathers and climbed into bathing suits as fast as my kids. Leyla chose a two-piece with a pink bottom and a purple top. I kept my thoughts to myself, but my sister needed a lesson in color coordination. Maybe Tomko could help. Zie pranced by wearing sequined lime green dancer shorts. On second thought, maybe not.

"They gots swim toys here," Leyla said.

She picked up inflatable floaters and handed them out. The little girls ran back to the pool in spanking new swim suits, giggling and teasing each other.

"Aren't you coming?" Atian said. He'd found trunks, a bit too tight, but they would do.

"I don't have a suit."

Atian nodded at a rack of teen swim suits. "Pick one."

My cheeks warmed. I'd never worn a bathing suit.

"Come on Hali, don't be a sissy."

"I'll meet you there. Matwau and Tulimak shouldn't watch the kids by themselves, go help them."

I circled the rack. A few suits showed possibilities. Should I pick a demure one piece diving suit, or a skimpy two-piece? I picked up a white bikini with black tiger stripes. Could my body pull off a strapless top?

I twisted and turned in front of a full-length mirror, cracked and dusty. People called me pretty, but my nose and chin were too sharp, my eyes too wide apart, and I was too skinny, too tall, and too flat-chested. I picked up a silver hairbrush with golden horses etched into it, and with swift strokes loosened the tangles in my hair.

I smoothed the lines of the bikini with shaking hands and squared my shoulders.

The pool went quiet when I walked in. The click click of my beach heels was the only sound in the cavernous space.

"Wowsee," Benji said. "You look like them models in mama's magazines."

Gecki whistled.

Trust my little brother and a cheeky lizard to embarrass me. I peeked from under my eyelashes at Atian. He was staring at me, his mouth open. So was Matwau. "What? Do I look that bad?"

Atian swallowed. "N-no, you look nice." His voice cracked.

"Amazing," Matwau said.

Atian scowled at him, and the heat rose in my cheeks. Good grief.

Benji broke the awkward moment. "Come on in, Hali, the water's great."

I slid into the warm water. "Oh, this feels so good."

Atian swam over. His fingers danced against my skin under the water. "I had no idea."

"About what?"

He gulped. "N-nothing, just thinking out loud. Hey, do you know how to swim?"

I shook my head. "No pools or beaches in the North, remember?" I pushed down the memory of half-swimming, half-wading over to Leyla at the waterfall.

"Well, I learned in the creek."

Snakes from the South had swarmed the north creeks before I was born. Some of them liked the water. "Not a chance."

Atian laughed and dived under the water.

Leyla sailed by on a floatee Matwau blew up for her. "This is the bestest time." Her face clouded over. "Except ..."

Would she ever truly smile again? "I'm glad you're having fun, sweetie."

Benji grabbed my arms and pulled me away. "Come on, Hali, play with Tomi and me."

We dunked each other and played tag until my arms turned to rubber, and I couldn't lift them anymore.

Atian bounced on the diving board. "Hey Hali, watch this."

I sighed. Here we go again. Would they ever tire of showing off?

Atian performed a clumsy swan dive, then surfaced. "So who's the best diver? Me or Matwau?"

"Tulimak." Which was true.

Chief Roy woke from his snooze on a lounge chair. "Hey, you kids are gonna turn into fish."

"Ah chief, can't we stay a little longer? Hali says I'm finally clean."

"Nope, out you come. We've got an early start tomorrow morning."

"Besides, you need some new clothes," I said. "You don't want to be embarrassed when we're picked up, do you?'

Benji's lip stuck out. "Doesn't matter to me. I don't want to go shopping."

"We do," Tomko said.

I stamped my bare foot. "Move it, all of you, and don't come back without clean underwear and new shoes."

I found a pair of soft khaki pants and a white t-shirt to wear under my antelope dress, and a brown leather jacket.

Leyla showed up in a lime green and pink miniskirt, pink leggings, and a white and green polka dot blouse. She wore green sneakers with yellow laces, and she'd even found green sunglasses and pink hair ribbons.

She twirled around and giggled. "Yep, I'm cool."

Tomko's canary yellow t-shirt and purple short shorts rivaled Leyla for brightness. Zie patted zis spiky neon hair. "Couldn't find any shades worthy of our outfit."

Benji dropped a pile of mismatched clothing at my feet. "We got any food, I'm starving?"

Chief Roy growled and pushed the boys aside. "Never mind food, look for some real coffee."

Chrome appliances sat on the counters in the lavish kitchen, and the locked larder was stocked with food, including Starbuck's vanilla flavored coffee.

"Folks must have guarded this old hotel through the worst of the looting."

For a blissful hour we sat in the rooftop café and sipped coffee and munched on potato chips.

"Sure hope there's chips in Maniton," Benji said between crunches.

"Aye, there be benefits to civilization, I must admit," Jacques said. He smacked his lips. "Haven't enjoyed the taste of coffee for nigh onto three years."

"Stock up before you leave," Chief Roy said. "I'll be doing a bit of foraging before I head out."

His words jarred me out of a coffee daze. How would we manage without Chief Roy?

We dined by candlelight in the fabled Griffins Restaurant. Who knew what tomorrow or the rest of our lives would bring, but tonight we were living in style, drinking from crystal glasses, and eating on priceless chinaware.

Matwau found a bottle of Larose Le Grand Vin 2079. He poured each of us a glass. "I hear that was a grand year."

I didn't understand how someone became an alcoholic, but I knew they mustn't ever drink again. "Mat ..."

"I'm drinking water," he whispered in my ear.

Atian held up a fork of dark red beans. "Our last meal on dry land?"

"Our last meal of beans, I hope," Tomko said.

Benji shoved food in his mouth. "What is this?"

"Canned ham."

"Ain't never tasted anything so good."

"You say that about all the food," Tomko said.

"Yeah, but this time I really mean it."

Gecki sneaked down Benji's arm and perched on the rim of the plate. He daintily picked at the food.

"You should pick up some manners from your gecko," Tomko said.

Leyla hadn't touched her food. She clutched her Raggedy Ann doll and sniffed.

I felt her forehead. "Are you sick, Leyla?"

She sniffed again. "No, I'm just being sad."

I pulled her into my arms and rocked her back and forth. "We'll make it to Maniton, sweetheart, and then everything will be okay."

"No it won't, Hali. Nothing's ever gonna be okay. I lost Etta and Vogy, my two bestest friends. Nothing's ever gonna be okay, not ever again."

No one at the table said anything. What could they say?

Jacques cleared his throat and gazed at the Inuit children. "Well, I must admit, it's been a worthy adventure. Never thought I'd be any good with kiddies." His eyes shone unnaturally bright in the soft candlelight. "I'm glad you kids made it."

Jacques was leaving tonight, this time for good, and the Inuit knew it, but their unbreakable spirit kept them strong.

Atian and I tucked the children into bed in the old quarter's lavish penthouse suites, girls on one side, boys on the other. Tomorrow was our big day. No more struggling, no more disasters, but also no more sun and sky, and no more Chief Roy. Laughing for joy seemed wrong, but so did crying.

Atian walked me to my door and drew me close. He brushed his lips across my cheek. "Mind if I come in for a spell?"

I swallowed. Did he know how I felt, how hard it was for me to hold him off a little longer? "Now, what kind of example would that set for the children?"

"They're kids. They don't need an example."

He tilted my chin and kissed the tip of my nose, my eyes, and at last, my mouth. He tasted of cinnamon, and I wanted to wrap my arms around his neck and never let go. I disentangled myself. "Good night, Atian."

I closed the door in his surprised face, but not before blowing him a kiss.

Chapter Twenty-Five

Rats in the Cellar

"Why should I trust you?"

"Cuz I'm sick of that sappy girl and that old buck. They ain't the boss of me, and I got no plans on sticking with them. Learning you weren't kilt in the pod explosion, you seemed my best bet."

"Lost ten of my men in that blow up, six of us left, two not much use, burned crisp."

"You don't look so good yourself."

Besides missing half his right arm, Claude's left eye socket hung empty, and he limped.

Claude scowled. "Lucky I was behind a slider when that pod exploded." He hawked and spat. "Can't do any more about the pod, but I'm looking for revenge on them Indians."

My blood ran cold at his words.

"They're all yours, but you're gonna need more men."

Claude snorted. "I'll get them. You say they're headed for an underwater city that's got lots of food and stuff?"

"Lots of everything I hear tell and ripe for the picking. Place called Maniton."

"How do you plan on taking over this Maniton?"

"I'll stick with the kiddies and play along. We're staying at a fancy hotel until tomorrow morning. When the time's right, you come swooping in and take their place at the pick-up."

"But the sub's for kids, you told me yourself."

Samoset's nostrils flared and his nasty eyes shot sparks. "What choice will they have, a whole pack of guns pointed at them?" His mouth turned down in a sneer. "We take the sub, force the crew to sail to Maniton, and I figure it won't take but minutes to overthrow those old World Council coots. We'll be kings of the undersea."

Claude nodded at me. "What about her? She's hearing all this."

Samoset's voice dripped pure venom. "She won't get a chance to blab."

"Wait a spell, I'm taking a little comfort from the girlie-squaw before you snuff her."

I leaned back on the chair. What a nightmare. Samoset had slipped into my room after I went to bed and knocked me out. I'd woken up in an abandoned warehouse, at the mercy of pathological killers, with a tropical storm raging outside.

My head ached. I swallowed and coughed to ease my dry throat. I needed a breather. Flies buzzed around my head, attracted to the blood oozing into my right eye.

Samoset staggered by, a spiteful smirk on his face. I pretended to sleep.

"You'll get yours soon enough, girlie."

The smell of alcohol on his breath sickened me.

He shut the door and the room went dark.

I struggled to untie the bindings around my arms. I had to warn my family. "Come on Hali, think smart and get out of this mess before Claude ..." I swallowed, the bile rising in my throat. Before anything bad happened.

Squeaky things scurried across the floor. Rats. Lots of them, but at least they weren't slithering snakes. Shivers ran up and down my arms, but I would not cry and give these cretins, especially Samoset, the satisfaction.

I loosened the bindings on my left hand as howls and a strange yipping erupted in the next room. I ripped the bindings off my legs and other arm and rushed to the door. The Shadow People, some of whom I recognized, were swarming the hideout. A bandit sprawled on the floor, blood oozing from his open mouth, but Samoset and Claude were gone.

One of the Shadow men approached me. Was he going to kill me, too? He bowed and grimaced in a weak attempt at a smile, then backed away from the door. I stepped out of the warehouse and into the storm and the dark. Which way should I go?

The Shadow man joined me and pointed down the street. "Go, frens."

I took off at a slow jog, pushing against the gale force winds. The poison air sucked at my lungs, and my skin itched unbearably. How did the Shadow People survive in this guck? I staggered a block, maybe two. My throat and nose burned, and my eyes were so watery my vision blurred. I shook my head to clear it, but searing pains stabbed at my chest, and a coughing fit overtook me. I collapsed on the cracked pavement. My last thought was of Atian and how we would never get to be.

"Hali!"

Was a Sky Being calling me? "Go away. I'm done."

"Hali, hold on. We've got your suit."

Hands picked me up and shoved my feet into a biosuit. Someone fit a breather over my face, and I took a deep breath. My body convulsed, and I coughed out the poison.

"Aa, keep breathing Halerine Ananda, I've hooked a nebulizer to your filter."

Where did the chief find a nebulizer? Darkness swallowed me.

On our last morning on land, we assembled in the hotel lobby. I smoothed the folds on my antelope dress and wiggled my toes in my soft moccasins. Somehow wearing the dress over a slinky biosuit didn't seem the same.

"Hali, you looks beautiful," Leyla said.

I tied my dreamcatcher to the shoulder fringe. "Thank you, sweetheart."

I stifled a cough. My lungs would need major rejuv when we reached Maniton, but for now I was doing okay, and I'd warned the chief about Samoset and Claude.

Atian strutted into the room. Weasel, skunk, and possum furs hung from his split-horn headdress.

Benji sniffed. "Atian, you smell like a dead rat."

We all laughed, but a nervous laugh. What came next?

Samoset strode into the foyer. He sported a black eye and his right arm hung at an odd angle. Good on the Shadow People.

"Danforth, I wanna talk to you."

Chief Roy's bushy eyebrows nearly touched. "You dare show your face here, you scoundrel, after kidnapping Halerine Ananda? I ought to take you down right now." He aimed his laser. "Fact is, I think I will."

A beam scorched the marble floor between Samoset's feet, and he danced out of the way. Hate and defiance flashed across his face. "Maybe you ought to hear what I got to say, else you might be sorry."

Chief Roy re-aimed his laser. "Nothing you say interests me. Boys, tie this monster up."

Samoset held up his hand and backed away. "I want a spot on that sub."

"What? I told you before, Maniton is for children."

"Nonsense," Samoset said. "Adults are waiting for the kids, you said so yourself."

"All chosen for their skills and training."

"Well, I can raise these brats as good as anybody. I know full well how to deal with kids."

Atian juggled the laser in his hand. "Yeah, like you ever helped us."

Samoset scowled. "I ain't putting up with your sarcasm, gimp. I'm getting on the sub."

Chief Roy's mouth set in a grim line. "Not if I have anything to say about it. Tie him up, boys."

Samoset slapped Atian away and smirked. "Maybe you should re-think what I'm worth to you."

Chief Roy raised his eyebrow.

"Remember the stuff that useless twit lost?"

Atian moved in on Samoset but the chief held him back. "Your point?"

"Well, I got them. Found the canisters floating near shore, held onto them in case they came in handy. They're mine now."

The samples! If only we could get them back.

The chief motioned for the boys to move in. "And where might these samples be?"

"I want your word you won't put me off the sub once you get your grubby paws on the tubes."

Chief Roy glanced at me. "Well?"

I shrugged. We needed the DNA but Samoset in Maniton? Never.

"Very well, I won't put you off the sub. You have my word. Now where is the cache?"

Samoset opened his coat. The tubes were stuck to his undercoat. "Where I go, they go."

"Samoset, you can't do this, it isn't right."

"Shut up, boy. Why should these whelps live and I gotta die?"

"Chief Roy isn't going."

Samoset glowered. "Oh yes, the mighty Chief Roy, Chief Roy, the brave, Chief Roy the good. Well, I'm sick of Chief Roy. He can rot in this purgatory for all I care, but I'm getting out."

"Enough!" Atian decked Samoset, and he sprawled on the floor.

Atian nursed his fist and grinned. "Been waiting to do that for a long time."

Matwau helped me remove the canisters from Samoset's vest. "I'm sorry, Hali." His brow was furrowed, and a red flush crept up his neck.

I kissed his cheek. "None of this is your fault, Mat. He's a grown man and should know right from wrong."

He nodded. "I'm glad he's not going with you." His voice caught.

"Okay, everyone, shows over," Chief Roy said. "You've got a boat to catch."

We left Samoset lying in the lobby, and some of us never saw him again.

Chapter Twenty-Six

THE GATHERING SITE

Strong winds whipped the waves into frenzied whitecaps and smashed rusty fishing boats against the ancient wharves. Wave after wave rode up the shore, reaching the sidewalks lining the crumbling apartment buildings. A waterspout danced across the bay, higher than the highest buildings.

I sniffed the air for poisons, but only caught the foul smell of dead fish mixed with salty damp.

"Chief, you sure this is the right place?" Atian said.

Chief Roy checked his bio-comm. "*Aa*, these be the coordinates the messenger sent us."

But doubt and worry rang in his voice.

"Should you send a signal or something?" Matwau said.

Chief Roy shrugged. "I thought they would be waiting once I set the beacon."

Dense fog swooped over the water and enveloped us in a mysterious shroud. I wrapped my arms around my body to stop the tremors. None of us, except the Inuit, owned warm clothing. Stores hadn't stocked winter clothes for decades, and our biosuits protected us from poisons, not damp cold.

Even my antelope dress did little to block the ferocious wind covering us in sea spray.

Leyla huddled against me. "Hali, I'm so cold."

Tomko scurried over and squeezed into my arms. "Me too, Hali."

I kissed the top of Leyla's head and rubbed their arms. My two prima donnas in their miniskirts and short shorts. "Hold on a little longer, you two."

Wolf leaped up and licked Leyla's face.

"Ugh, Wolf, you stink."

Her laughter took the sting out of the words, and she wrapped her arms around his huge neck. Wolf snuggled close and warmed her legs.

Benji fidgeted in his biosuit. "Uh."

"What's wrong?"

"Nothing. These new clothes are itchy is all."

He avoided looking at me. That was never a good sign. "No, none of your stories, what's going on?"

Benji sighed. "The iguana's hatching."

I peeked inside his suit. A little green head popped out of the cracked egg and chirped at me. Gecki fussed like an old woman, and helped the baby break the egg away. "I bet you're hungry little guy, well you'll have to wait a while longer."

"What should I do?"

"Keep him in your suit, and we'll figure out something on board the sub."

I glanced at Atian. He was gazing at the gray water. A frown creased his brow. I shared his worry. What if no one came? What would we do then? Underwater bubble or not, I'd had enough of this forsaken land.

The Inuit children stood apart, unsure of anything except Jacques had left them, and they would never see him again. I sighed. That darn bear-man. I'd wring his neck if he wasn't so charming. He was standing on a rooftop watching over us, but I didn't let on.

"Hali?"

"What is it, Makkovik?"

"I'm scared."

I squeezed her hand. "We all are, but Maniton is our last, best chance."

She sniffed and gazed at me. "My weakness would embarrass Grandfather, but I miss the North. I miss snow, and seals, and sledding."

Oh boy. "Let's see what Maniton offers us. Maybe they've built a winter wonderland for northern First Peoples."

I turned inland, away from the harsh wind and Makkovik's sad eyes. Waves crashed over the pavement. We stayed well back, waiting on the sidewalk running along yellow and pink buildings. How would the sub pick us up in such vile weather?

"Rich people lived here once, but they're all gone," Leyla said.

"Where did they go?" Makkovik said.

Leyla shrugged. "Maybe they bought a spot on one of them space stations or a space ship." Her thick eyebrows frowned. "Or maybe they're dead."

A lonely cry pierced the morning air. Raven was beating his wings against the wind, and the Sky Beings danced above me, their dark faces smiling for the first time. Did that mean we were finally safe?

"Whoa, what's that?" Tomko said.

A black neo-glider swept over the gathering site. The Sky Beings shrieked and flittered away.

"Scatter!" Chief Roy said.

We darted behind the crumbling buildings. The glider circled back and dropped balls along the shoreline. Explosions tore up the sidewalk and one of the apartment buildings groaned and leaned over.

Chief Roy cursed. "Sat-bombs. Cardiff's hell-bent on stopping you youngsters." He stepped out of his hiding place. "Stay where you are, this isn't over."

The chief was right. Two gliders swooped in and dropped a series of sat-bombs. The air reverberated with concussions. I grasped Leyla and held her tight. "Hold on to something, I think that high-rise is coming down!"

The walls bulged and bursting pipes shot out of the side of the building. The whole structure groaned and in slow motion leaned to the left and toppled over. Dust and debris danced in the fierce winds.

Leyla coughed inside her breather. "Can't breathe."

"Yes, you can, your breather is sealed."

She shook her head and wheezed. "No can't."

I slipped the inhaler under her breather. "Your inhaler, Leyla, use your inhaler."

She stared at me with frightened eyes and took a deep breath.

"That's it, another deep breath. Hold on a few more minutes, then we'll get you help." Would we ever get help?

A powerful explosion detonated out of our sight, and a fireball rose above the shuddering buildings.

Chief Roy raised his hands. "Something got at least one of the gliders. Not sure who did that, but I'm hoping they took out both of them."

The air settled, and we stepped out of the shadows.

"Look, more people," Benji said.

Small groups of children, some with guardians, others alone, trickled out of the apartment buildings. Fear and weariness marred their little faces.

"Let's meet your new neighbors," Chief Roy said.

An older man separated from a group of children. He bowed low. "We are of the Bella Coola."

The chief returned the bow. "Good greetings. We are of the Siksiká Blackfoot."

One by one the leaders announced their heritage: Assiniboine, Cheyenne, Crow, Kwak'kwak'waku, Shoshone, and Dakota Sioux. Some were ancient enemies of the Siksiká, but that no longer mattered.

"The journey proved long and difficult. Many turned back," one man said. "Their people may be no more."

A bedraggled group approached along the shore line. A squat man carrying a harpoon and a sturdy woman both nodded to Chief Roy.

"The Caribou Inuit are honored to meet our cousins," the man said.

"And we be French Métis," the middle-aged woman said.

"Cool hair," Tomko said.

The woman patted her purple bun. "My name is Bentli the senior. Our journey was long and grievous. *Les enfants* are plumb tuckered." She wrapped her arm around a younger version of herself. "This is my daughter, Bentli the younger." A shadow of pain crossed her features, but she kept smiling.

I waved at Jacques and pointed to Bentli the senior. Jacques waved in return. Who knew? Maybe his cabin would no longer be so lonely.

Chief Roy bowed. "We are of the Siksiká Blackfoot."

Tulimak stepped forward. "And the Netsilik Inuit."

A Caribou Inuit woman with shiny black hair smiled at Tulimak. He glanced at me, a question in his eyes. I nodded. Tulimak reddened but returned the girl's smile.

I hid my grin. Netsilik stoicism might have met its match.

One leader held back. At Chief Roy's questioning glance, he approached. "We, too, are of the Blackfoot First Nations, the Kainah from the Cypress Hills refuge. I am called Apisi."

Chief Roy nodded his head. "Welcome, brave coyote."

At least two dozen Blackfoot children stood behind him. I choked back tears. We would have many of our People in Maniton.

A soft rain sprinkled the ground, then became a muddy downpour. So much for wearing my antelope dress to impress.

Chief Roy raised his voice above the roar of the rain. "The Rainbow Warriors have arrived. In a short time, they will board a water boat and journey to their new home in Maniton. May they grow and prosper in the name of Gitche Manitou and someday reclaim the lands of their ancestors."

The guardians raised their hands to the faint sun. "As long as the sun shines, the rivers flow, and the grass grows, the First Peoples shall live."

A shot ran out. Apisi stumbled and fell.

"Take cover!"

We crouched behind old boats and dead tree trunks.

Men armed with semi-automatic rifles fanned out along the shore. Cardiff? But no, Claude swaggered down the beach and snarled at Chief Roy. "Too bad I missed you." He leered at me. "Be nice to me, sweetheart, and I might take you with me."

"I'd rather die."

"That can be arranged." He waved his AK-40. "Come on Indians, gather round. We need a tidy bunch."

"What do you want?" Chief Roy said.

"Why, a berth on that boat, a course. Samoset told me everything." He looked around. "Where is he, anyway?"

"Taken care of."

Claude snickered and signaled his men. They herded us together. The smaller children stood wide-eyed and dazed, but us older ones knew what was happening. Some sobbed. Atian and Matwau stood ready to fight.

Claude pressed the tip of his gun to Atian's head. "Try anything, young buck, and I'll shoot every last kid, starting with your girlfriend."

Atian glowered, but stayed put.

"Now, where is this magical boat?"

No one said a word.

Claude strode over to Chief Roy. "I'm waiting for an answer, old buck. The longer I wait, the less I be inclined to let your pups go."

"The sub hasn't arrived yet."

"Oh, it hasn't arrived yet. Well, ain't that news." He grabbed the chief by the hair and yanked hard. "Tell me something I don't know, old buck, and tell me fast, or I'll start cherry-picking the kids."

Chief Roy blanched. "The boat's scheduled to arrive in half an hour."

Claude let go of the chief. "That's better. Well men, we'll wait with these delightful children." He reached out and touched my hair.

I jumped back.

He laughed. "Still spooky, eh, girlie-squaw. Well, that'll change soon enough. You got your choice, me or General Cardiff, the man who kindly agreed to arm us if we did his dirty work."

Atian balled his fists.

I shook my head slightly, but Claude noticed and frowned. "I'm thinking there's trouble brewing here."

He snapped his fingers and his men surrounded us. "Pick one and take them down on my command. Go for the gimp first, then the old ones. Finish with the kiddies."

A thug pointed his gun at Leyla and my heart stopped.

"No!" I said. "You can't kill the children!"

"Wanna bet?" Claude raised his hand. "Ready! Aim!"

A shot rang out, and my heart sank. Please don't let it be Leyla. But one of Claude's men lay in a pool of blood.

A dozen military men jogged up the street.

"Corporal Haskins," Chief Roy said. "I'm mighty glad to see you."

The corporal tipped his helmet and signaled his soldiers to surround Claude's men. "We came as soon as we received word."

At my questioning look, Chief Roy said, "I sent a message with Raven telling the good corporal about Cardiff."

"Sorry, we were delayed." Corporal Haskins grinned. "Had to take care of some Cardiff riffraff first." He pushed back his combat helmet and surveyed Claude's thugs. "So what's it gonna be? Leave or join your buddy feeding the ground."

The fight had gone out of the bandits, and they hunched against the heavy rain. They lay down their arms without a whimper. All except Claude. He snarled and tightened his grip on a machine gun. "Whoever you guys are, this is none of your business. Be gone."

Corporal Haskins studied Claude, a steely glint in his eyes that reminded me of the spaghetti westerner. "These good people are acquaintances of mine. I've got a vested interest in seeing they make their destination."

Claude's face grew sly. "Why don't you join us, then? We'll all go to Maniton. Our combined firepower will make short shrift of the Manitons."

I held my breath.

Corporal Haskins shook his head. "Low-lives like you and the self-righteous General Cardiff's of the world destroyed this planet for decent folks. We owe these kids a chance."

"Get real, they're Indians."

"Who better than the First Peoples to inherit the earth?"

Claude hawked and spat. "Indians."

Corporal Haskins raised his gun and aimed at Claude's chest. "I'm giving you the count of five to disappear, or my men will start shooting."

Claude wavered.

"One."

Claude's men took off at a sprint.

"Two."

Claude cursed and walked up the shore.

"Three."

He walked faster, and when Corporal Haskins shouted, "Four," he broke into a run that took him far down the street.

The children laughed and Tomko whistled.

Chief Roy shook Corporal Haskins' hand. "We owe you our lives once again, corporal."

"Just doing my duty, sir, but I took special pleasure in bringing down Cardiff's gliders."

"I don't suppose Cardiff was in one of them."

"Nah, he headed overseas some days ago."

I had to know. "Corporal, Cardiff threatened to destroy our village if I didn't stay with him. He had a drone hovering over the dome." I swallowed to ease my dry throat. "He didn't ...?"

Corporal Haskins shook his head. "No worries. We took out that drone soon after you kids left." He grinned. "If you'd waited a few more minutes, you would have had an escort to get you back to your pod."

Matwau snorted. "If we'd waited even a minute longer, Cardiff's thugs would have eviscerated us."

The good corporal eyed Matwau. "I could use someone like you on my squad. I don't suppose you'd be interested?"

Matwau grinned. "You never know, sir."

What did that mean?

Atian checked on the Kainah elder, and shook his head. "I'm sorry, Apisi is gone."

Apisi's charges dropped to the ground and wailed.

Leyla hugged one of the youngest girls. "We lost people we love, too, but it's gonna be all right." She handed the little girl her Pooh bear. "Want to be my friend?"

The little girl sniffed and cuddled Pooh. "I am called Mimiteh.

The corporal signaled two of his soldiers. They covered Apisi's body with a tarp. "We'll give the elder an honorable burial."

"Have you heard from the Manitons?" someone said. "Where are they?"

On cue, Atian shouted, "Look!"

A blue submarine with dolphins and stingrays painted on its sides rose from the water like a phoenix rising from the ashes of Mother Earth.

Benji clapped his hands and jumped up and down. "It's here! Our boat's here."

The sun burned through the haze of green clouds, and an arc of soft reds, blues, and yellows lit up the sky.

"Look! A rainbow! And it's just for us, the Rainbow Warriors," Leyla said.

The sun was shining on the First Peoples one last time. I lifted my face to the warm rays and soaked in a lifetime.

Two humpback whales broke the surface and sailed high into the air before falling back and sending a wave washing over the sub. The children cheered.

The Sky Beings fluttered in front of me then flew away.

I stole a glance at Chief Roy. He stood apart from the rest of us, a resigned expression on his weather-worn face. He had been our rock on the long journey. And his reward? For the rest of his life, he would fight to stay alive in a land ravaged by fires and floods, and populated with half-crazed savages and shysters. Could he survive in these terrible times? I hoped so, but in my heart I wondered.

"Hali."

I turned. His face told me before I asked. "What is it, Mat?"

He took my hand and kissed it. "I'm not going with you."

An ache grew in the pit of my stomach, where the fear bug used to live. "Why Mat, you're one of us. We need you in Maniton."

He shook his head and clutched his Morning Star. "I can't stand small spaces, I'd go insane in a week."

I swallowed a lump in my throat. "Where will you go then?"

Matwau grinned. "Remember that spiffy cruise ship we passed in the port? The *Princess Ariel*? I'm hoping to hitch a ride overseas. I'll check out some of those archaeological sites I never got to dig—the pyramids of Giza, Stonehenge, the Acropolis—whatever's still standing." He shrugged. "Maybe even find other Rainbow Warriors, see if they need help."

I smiled through my tears. "Our caretaker. May you serve them well."

He ducked his head, and a small smile played at the corners of his generous mouth. "Seems that's my destiny."

"What about your father?"

"He wasn't my real father, Hali. He latched onto me when a tornado killed my parents, hoping he'd find sanctuary because of me. I'm glad to be done with him."

I reached up and stroked his cheek. "I'll miss you, Mat."

He brushed a strand of hair off my face. "I'm not partial to watching Atian court you, it's for the best."

"You could have courted me, too."

He kissed me on the cheek, but I turned my face and our lips touched. I whispered in his ear. "It might have been you."

He shook his head. "Not in Maniton, Hali, that's your destiny." He sighed. "This is meant to be, sweetheart. You and Atian live a good life." He backed away and melted into the crowd.

A young sailor popped out of the sub's hatch and waved. "Ahoy there, Manitons!"

Manitons. The word sent waves of happiness coursing through my body. The bad weather, the constant danger, and the soul-draining fear were all behind me. I should be thrilled and I was, but a deep sadness pulled at me. I would never watch the sun rise or feel the wind on my face. Never again.

I turned back to Matwau, but he was gone, and out of my life forever.

Raven cried a final farewell and disappeared into the swirling fog. "Good-bye, old trickster."

Wolf nudged my hand, and I buried my face in his fur. "Oh Wolf." Wolf's ears stood straight, and he woofed. "I love you, Wolf. Don't ever forget me." He buried his cold nose in my armpit and whimpered.

"So what do we do now, chief?" Atian said with a catch in his voice.

"Grow and prosper, and teach your children the ways of the Siksiká," Chief Roy said.

"Chief, how can we ever thank you," I said. "Please, won't you come with us?"

The chief shook his head. "My journey has come to an end, and I must bid you farewell."

I wiped away tears. "But chief."

He smiled. "Do not grieve, Halerine Ananda. I have lived a long and eventful life. Sending you youngsters into the future is my greatest achievement."

"What will you do? Where will you go?"

"I'll be spending the rest of my days recounting the story of our adventures. Perhaps my musings will in some small way keep humanity from making the same mistakes again."

"The cells on your bio-comm won't last much longer."

"Oh, I plan on using old-fashioned paper, there's enough floating around. I'll leave stories in caches throughout this great land and perhaps a few others."

The children clustered around Chief Roy, and he raised his voice. "Your fathers and mothers and all the elders of the many lands are proud of you today, as am I. I wish you a long and happy life. You are the First Peoples' future. You are the Rainbow Warriors. Someday Mother Earth will heal, and your descendants will venture forth. They need to know about us, and what we did wrong. Teach your children well."

I bowed. "We promise to keep our history alive."

Chief Roy grinned. "And I have a little adventure of my own planned. Going to find out what those towers are all about."

"Will you take Wolf?"

"Aa, he'll be my trusty companion on my final journey."

I knelt. "Wolf, I'm sorry you can't come with me. They won't allow domesticated pets in Maniton. Go with Chief Roy, okay? Do you understand?"

Wolf whimpered a question and licked the tears off my face.

"Oh Wolf, I'll miss you so much." I stroked his great head. "Take care of the chief for me."

Chief Roy hugged each of us. "May Gitche Manitou guide you on your journey and keep you safe." His eye twinkled. "And may you be blessed with many healthy children."

He turned and walked away, a lone figure with a faithful wolf by his side. I watched them until they disappeared in the smog.

Atian took my hand. "It's time to go, Hali."

The Rainbow Warriors moved aside and let Atian and I lead the way onto the submarine. In unison, they formed an honor guard and followed us into our future.

AUTHOR NOTE

Thank you for reading *Rainbow Warriors*, book 1 in the *Rainbow Warriors* series. If you enjoyed this book, please leave an honest review or rating on Amazon.

Matwau, the caretaker's adventures continue in book 2, *The Golden Mast* as he joins the Malikun Rainbow Warriors on their dangerous journey across the Arabian Sea to the underwater city of Maniton.

To learn more about this series and upcoming series and spin-offs, or to ask me questions and make comments, check out my author website, https://www.shirleybearfedorak.com and join my twice-monthly newsletter.

All the best to you, my wonderful readers.

Shirley Bear Fedorak
2022

ACKNOWLEDGEMENTS

I owe a special thanks to the beta readers who read various drafts of this book. Their generous input helped make this story what it is today.

Several members of my family assisted with publishing *Rainbow Warriors*. My husband, Robert, served as webmaster for my new webpage where we placed *The Caretaker's Quest*, the prequel to the *Rainbow Warriors* series, and our son, Cory, provided technical support along the way. Our daughter, Lisa, and her husband, Simon, helped with the promotion of this book through social media, and our son Kris and his wife Rachel have always been there to encourage me.

Thank you to Miblart.com. I am so grateful to have found you. Your cover art and formatting have turned my books into works of art.

A final thank you to the many First Nations students I have met and taught. Your spirit and wisdom filled me with wonder and challenged me to write a story worthy of you.

ABOUT THE AUTHOR

Shirley Bear Fedorak has always been passionate about storytelling. She grew up on a farm in southern Saskatchewan, Canada. She taught anthropology and archaeology at the University of Saskatchewan for many years, and is the author of numerous academic books. She is now focusing on a career in genre fiction, beginning with a climate fiction series, *Rainbow Warriors*. She has three grown children and two granddaughters, and lives in Penang, Malaysia with her husband, Robert.

Excerpt from

THE GOLDEN MAST
Book 2
Rainbow Warriors

Maliku Island (Minicoy)
2129

The lazy waves rode up the narrow shore and dropped Beforetimes debris on my island. When I was a boy, I chased the waves and collected the washed-up relics, but the Elders refused to tell me where the strange objects came from, or what they were used for. I gave up collecting, though the desire to learn more about the mysterious Outside world still burned within me.

But the world beyond Maliku would have to wait. My simple, if boring, life was about to become way more complicated, and one of the reasons was climbing my ladder now.

"Good day, my son. I have come to help you prepare for your betrothal." Amina held up a ceremonial sarong the color of sea water. "I have finished your wedding lungi."

The last of our yellow sea hibiscus had drowned months ago, but the soothing scent of hibiscus drifted from Amina and settled in my hut. I breathed in her scent, and it gave me the courage to speak from my heart. "I beg your forgiveness, my mother, but I cannot marry Belani."

She blinked and set down my new sarong. "Don't be silly, Maumoon. Of course, you'll marry Belani."

I flopped down on my sleeping mat and gazed through cracks in the floorboards. A yellow butterfly fish the size of my hand swam in the blue-green water below my hut. Fish sure had it good. If I was a fish, the rising sea would not bother me, I would have enough to eat, and I would not be living in a hut perched on rickety stilts. If I was a fish, I could swim away from the doomed island of Maliku, and I would not have to marry the Island Chief's daughter.

"No, I can't marry Belani or anyone else right now."

My mother sank to her knees beside my mat. "But you must, it is our way. The Island Chief will not tolerate such an insult. If you refuse to marry Belani, Fatima will banish you."

I tried not to hear her words nor look into her beautiful, but troubled, brown eyes. I hated upsetting her when our lives were so hard. "I have other plans for my life," I said in a gentler voice.

Amina ignored my words as she straightened my ragged coverings and brushed away the baby gecko crawling down the wall. She picked up my spare sarong and t-shirt and hung them on a hook in the wall. "Belani is the perfect choice for a bride. She's your cousin, and she is the daughter of the most powerful woman on the island."

I gazed out the window. "Former island, you mean."

"Don't be smart, it isn't becoming."

I rescued my fishing pole from her cleaning spree and leaned it against a wall. "I love Belani, but I cannot marry her because I'm leaving Maliku." Even as I said the words, they became true.

My mother stopped straightening my hut and wrinkled her brow. "Leaving Maliku? But why? Where would you go?"

I had not worked out that part of my plan yet. I said the first thing that popped into my head. "India, to start."

"What? They won't take you."

"I'll find a way."

How could I explain my longings to a woman who had never left our isolated little island and had no desire to do so? "I feel blind here. What's happening Outside? The traders stopped coming three seasons ago. That must mean something."

"It means they don't make enough profit from us."

I tried again. "A mysterious and wonderful world is waiting out there, and I want to explore it."

She snorted. "From what I've heard of this world, it's no longer such a wonderful place. Famines, fires, and floods. Everyone is dying, and you will, too, if you venture off Maliku."

Her words might hold truth, but I had to find out for myself. "Our People used to be sailors. They left Maliku, and some of them travelled all over the world. Why did they stop?"

"That was Before."

She straightened her white headscarf and smoothed her long red robe. The conversation was over in her mind. "Enough of this foolishness, the betrothal celebration is tonight. Then we will begin planning your wedding ceremony."

She thrust a handwoven basket into my hands. "For now, make yourself useful. Get some greens from Auntie before the tide sweeps in, or we shall have no supper tonight."

I bit back a groan. Greens. I hated greens, and I didn't much like Auntie, either. But the fish did not always come, and I was hungry. I was always hungry. Steamed water cucumbers tasted better than nothing. "Perhaps father will catch a fish today."

A faint hope and we both knew it.

When the Indian government refused to recognize Malikuns as legal climate refugees, my father lost his will to live, my mother lost her devoted husband, and I lost my strong and fun-loving father.

"Oh, and for the betrothal, wear your red sarong and white shirt."

No one would care what I was wearing once I refused Belani.

I waded through the warm, waist-high water to Auntie's hut, pushing aside green seaweed, and skirting yellowing plants and prickly bushes peeking out of the water. The plants were drowning, and the sharp odor of rotting vegetation drifted in the air.

Pieces of flotsam, what Auntie called plastic bags, brushed against my legs as I pushed through the gentle waves. Belani's grandmother told stories of the early days when the beach was wide and sandy, and fish swam along the shoreline in large schools. But those days were long gone. Now the waves brought in debris from the Outside world. The best we could do was gather the trash and throw it in our dump.

A puff of dirty air floated in front of my face. I batted it away. The clouds in our sky had changed from fluffy white to pink and green strips of poison that would soon sink to the ground Even now, the air no longer smelled clean, and on bad days we struggled to breathe.

The sea bottom quivered, and the water rippled. Sand shifted under my feet, and I spread my legs to keep my balance until the shaking stopped. The sleepy little island of Maliku was growing restless, more so every day.

A sharp cry pierced the hot morning air, and a tiny bird swooped down from the sky. "Loki! Where have you been, boy?"

The little hoopoe landed on my shoulder and began cleaning his black and gold feathers.

I stroked his speckled crown. "Nice to see you, but you smell like an over-ripe fish."

Loki squawked at the insult and nibbled my ear. Oop-oop-oop. He flew away in search of insects hiding in the coconut fronds. What would happen to Loki when the coconut palms died?

I turned at laughter behind me.

Belani paddled her dugout canoe across my path. Her brown eyes twinkled. "You've spoiled that bird of yours, you know."

Her black hair hung loose down her back, and a white flower was tucked behind her ear. Belani had forsaken the white head scarf older women on Maliku wore, and she favored a short, red sari instead of long, flowing robes. All of which scandalized her elderly grandmother. "It's too hot," she said whenever they argued, and she stuck to it.

Her full red lips smiled invitingly, and she arched a perfect eyebrow at me. "Well, Maumoon, are you not speaking today?"

A hot flush crept up my neck. I wanted to dive under the water to cool my face, but that was cowardly. Besides, she would know. "Good morning, Belani."

She flicked water at me with her paddle. "Just because we'll soon be betrothed does not mean I like you any more than when we were kids."

A cheeky grin took the sting out of her words.

She drew closer, and the heady smell of jasmine brought back memories of our childhood, when we were still allowed to play together. She smelled of jasmine even when we were covered in mud.

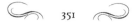

She wrinkled her pert nose at my ragged shorts. "I hope you're planning on dressing a bit better for the ceremony, or I might be tempted to toss you into the sea with all the other flotsam."

My stiff shoulders relaxed. Belani might be sixteen, but she was still the little brat who dropped coconuts on my head when we were seven and told my mother I pulled her hair. I got a switching for that one. And I fell in love with her on that day.

"Belani ..."

She fluttered her eyelashes and paddled her canoe up against me. "Yes, Maumoon?"

I gulped. She was too close. "No matter what happens tonight, I want you to know I care about you more than any other, and I will for the rest of my days."

A frown wrinkled her perfect brow at my strange words, and she touched my cheek with her soft hand. "And I for you."

The call to prayer rolled over the island, and the moment was lost. "I-I have to go."

Belani waved and paddled away. "I'll see you tonight." Her eyes and her smile held a secret promise.

I swallowed and willed my heart to stop hammering against my chest like a lovesick puppy. In a few hours, Belani would never speak to me again, but she was so fine, and I loved her.

Endnotes

1 Taken from https://allpoetry.com/poem/4277671-Rain-bow-Warriors-by-superkurd13.

Printed in Great Britain
by Amazon

10422731R00203